LOOSE LIPS

A Gay Sea Odyssey

THIS PAPERBACK EDITION 2023

2

FIRST PUBLISHED BY HARD CROSSING PRESS 2022

ISBN: 978-0-6455553-2-5

Hardback ISBN: 978-0-6455553-0-1
eISBN: 978-0-6455553-1-8

THIS NOVEL IS JUST THE START OF THE STORIES JOSEPH BRENNAN HAS PLANNED.
DISCOVER MORE AT **JOSEPHBRENNAN.COM**

Ahoy there, Sailor!

For Sophie

2023

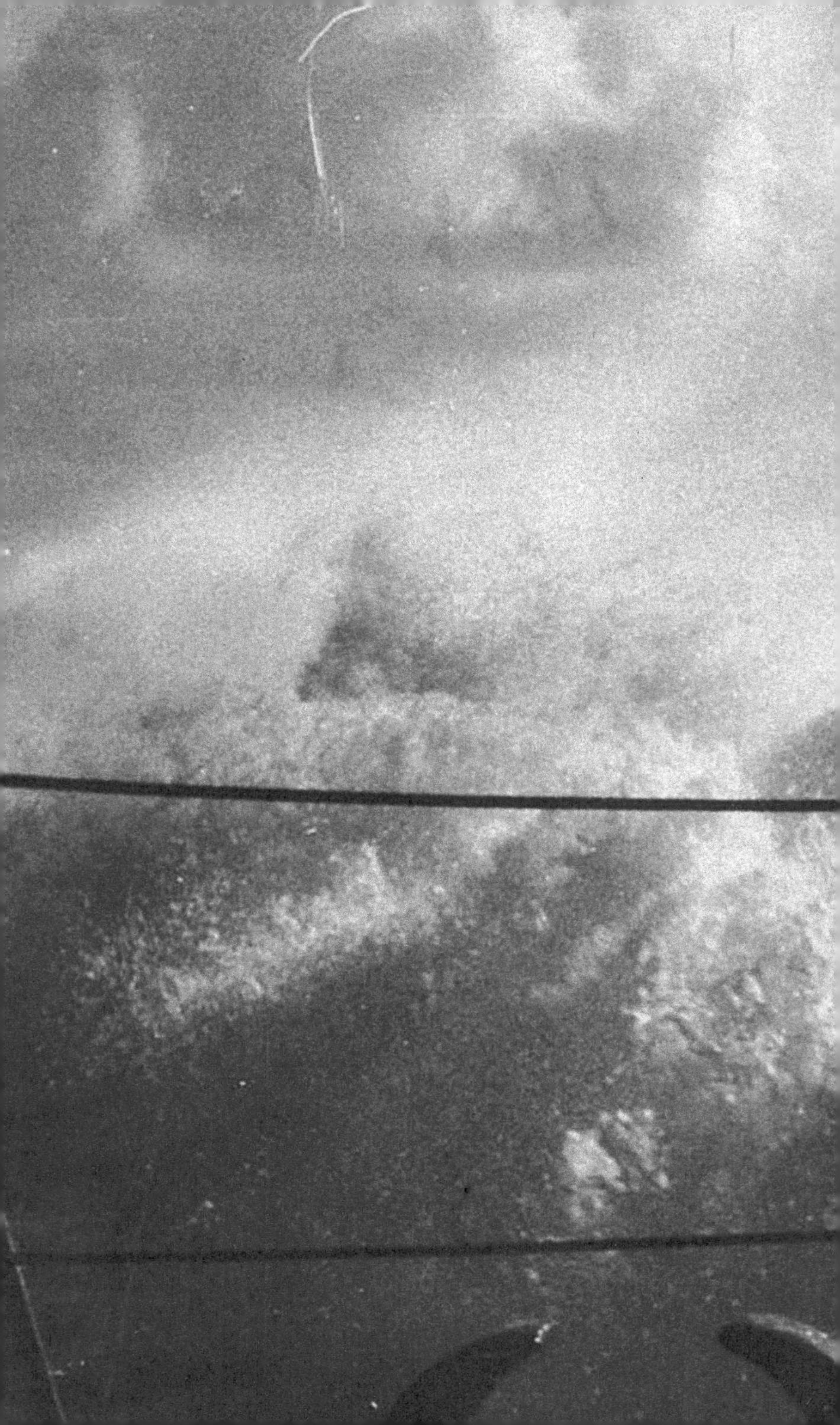

I

QUEEN ELIZABETH

She waited for him in the Clyde, her hull a heavy mass of metal born from the sweat of the labour of men. Her tender, *Romsey*, steamed her way in the early hours of a misty February 1940 morning. On board this tug was a Clydebank boy, bent on his mission to stow away within her, all the way to Southampton. She had a sister come before her who had long towered above the tenements of the workers that built her. But it was around the time of the building-up on *this one*, in slipway four, that men who riveted her together had started working on him, too. He was young. Young enough to take in the conflict-clouded Glasgow air with excitement rather than dread. He was drawn to her, *his* Queen. She who had brought hard men to him.

-

Elizabeth lay in wait in the Tail o' the Bank – the part of the Clyde where the draught was large enough to take her. She wore a drab military grey that made her features uncertain from a distance, keeping her mystery. They were called the monsters, and he could understand why as they approached her. She was the leviathan, drawing curious men from the shallows into the deep where she could snag them. The tender took them to her stern, and, once in swimming distance, her vastness was revealed, stretching into the mist, no sign of her end in sight. The Clyde was motionless that morning. Seeing her in the water was alien to him still. Even though she had a hull in Clydebank, in a fitting-out station since her launch in September of the previous year, the image conjured of her was still land-based. Even now, in water, she sat high, not *in* the water, not yet. Yet still, the point where her belly dipped below the surface, dropped deep and disappeared into the darkness of the Clyde channel drew him in like a deadly siren. She had propellers, he remembered. The size of workhouses with room for a pub underneath. Submerged and laying dormant down there, somewhere; ready to spin into life at command, ready to take him away, if he could successfully, stow away.

"Ready, sir," a flat-faced, young-but-aged-by-fat member of the tender staff said to his father, who nodded.

A rope ladder draped down from her side, but on account of its disappearing into the white above-mist, was more a fable set-piece than any rational man's stable entry into a modern Atlantic liner. He searched his father's face. It had bloated and become blood-blotched since the death. After losing his mother, he had come of age, found experience in the docks – while his father had found the bottle and neglect of his son and his own sanity. This latter part, though, his father had managed to keep from the attentions of employers.

"Stay," his father said. A stern-yet-low volume that did not carry above the engines of the tender. The fatherly ascent up the ladder, when it did come, came with some difficulty and clumsy-clutching of an attaché case.

His father was a representative of John Brown & Co., her builders. He was followed up and into her by the final contingent of her crew, who numbered less than a dozen and made their ascent with competency and a knowledge of ship ropes, and in apparent rank: the men of the tug averaging a younger and more boisterous bunch as the numbers thinned out.

In accord with his plan, he folded himself among the more youthful among them. The fibres of the rope-rungs prickled against his palms as he climbed.

Slower than the rest, dangling between the threshold of the tug and her side – the churning channel between the two boat-ly bodies promising to pull him under should he show the slightest sign of a slip. Cheeks and nose red, a slip that would be into the cold blue of the Clyde, all the way to the silty bottom.

He fortified when he burst through the mist canopy toward the cargo portal in her side. He was helped into her by two sailors. They were clean and in-white, with crisp Cunard White Star caps. The space into which they pulled him was stacked high with materials for her fitting out, jettisoned there, abandoned after war cry. He joined the clamber of the crew assembled – his father gone, set about his business; if all went to plan, he would not see him again.

"Stewards aft, seamen front," one of the sailors from her opening said, closing in behind the last of those from the tug.

Him, who spoke, as with his friend, was tall and tight in his service whites – a titillation, totally, of the treats in store for the journey. Stewards did not need to travel far, the tug having delivered them into a space already among their station. Seamen, however, had a trek to their beds – a path to follow that would meander them through her service corridors toward her front. Those were the men he followed when the group assembled divided in two.

His rationale was real simple: *they* the seamen were the fitter breed of his two choices. Stowaway-ing was like that. It swayed on impulse mostly.

In following the seamen, the incompleteness of her corridors became clear. There were bundles of wire where light fittings and switches should have been; portable lighting guiding the way. Following the young and athletic lads through her dimly-lit passages was akin to moving through a mineral mine shaft. The exposed wires of makeshift illumination were sufficient, glinting with deposits, but also: had a temporariness and otherworldliness to them. There was adventure lighted through them. Conspicuous without a rucksack of his own and knowing how vital it was to disappear within her belly soon for the plan to succeed, he actively looked for a chance to slip away. It came near signage for the first-class restaurant when the lads took a stairway up to the A deck promenade – to walk her length in open air.

Any chance for a smoke, lads, he thought.

He wanted to join them. Puff among their tight-buttocks-ness. But this was his opportunity to slip away into a first-class cabin.

Like the corridors outside, it was unfinished. Furniture and fabrics stacked at the points where its walls met in anticipation of a fitting that may not now come.

What now?

He felt his back pocket; sewn over his own plump buttock. From it, he retrieved a folded deck-plan that he had smuggled from his father's stacked-papers-study the night before. It helped un-jumble the maze of her. He traced a path to the seamen's quarters in her front. Knowing working men had tended to her for at least a day by this point, he would dip into the laundry rooms to retrieve a disguise for the journey. Finger on plan, the path brought him below where his father was meeting, in the Tourist dining salon, as he had sleuthed out earlier and marked on his map.

In the washing room, crew uniforms awaited cleaning in lumps according to a man's role on the ship: officer, seaman, engineer and steward, among others. Seeing the garments awaiting washing made him imagine the naked bodies of the men themselves, queuing up for the showers. He found himself picturing their musculature according to the state of their spent dress: the engineers and seamen piles were especially soiled from the degree of labour and oil of grease their duties demanded. Drawing up one of the engineers' overalls, still damp with sweat and turbine grease, he pulled the crotch seam to his face, covering his nostrils and absorbing in its ripeness like a breathing apparatus. He took in the scent like it were a Sunday dinner of the finest beast, envisioning the sweat-laced muscular contours of the man who had worn and worked it, grasping his arse as he did... then going in for a serving of a different species of fragrant meat.

After the third, temptation to grab for a fourth coverall, or even bury himself in the whole spent workwear mess and wallow a while, came as a test of the faith. But sensitivity to time pulled him away; it was barely enough, a short reprieve, a tease of his resolve in the decision to stow away on *Elizabeth* for her short journey to Southampton.

Equipped with fragrant seamen dress as his disguise, he left the laundry rooms and got back *en route* to the quarters of those whose uniform he now wore.

But a familiar voice stopped him.

His first decision-point of the journey; he decided to follow the voice he knew, taking it as an opportunity to learn how well he was tracking with regard to his plan of escape. He navigated the corridors with caution, up a service stairwell that led him close, yet also far enough. To hear, but remain hidden.

"A maist unorthodox doo," he heard his father say when in range, "tae haun ower a vessel afore her sea trials, or even afore she haes bin properly assembled."

"Most assuredly," said a second voice, deep and steady and English-ful.

"In fact, ne'er afore haes this happened in the history of the Line. For even a modest vessel, let alone one of this class; the largest and maist complex ever undertaken. Maist remarkable."

"Ah yes, but these are remarkable times."

"Bit surely Southampton was the steid for the handover, once John Brown haes actually completed her fur ye. And perhaps it would have been wise to allow members o' mah company to join *Queen Elizabeth* for the transit, given she is yit untested, to ensure–"

"–perhaps," deep-steady said, "that would have been prudent... had your company not already proved its reliability beyond question with the success of the *Mary*, the finest vessel in His Majesty's merchant fleet. Until now, that–"

"–pardon, Captain," came a new voice in the mix; still deep, assured, but less assertive, with something luring about it.

"Yes, Chief Officer."

"The ship's company is assembled on the promenade deck."

"Very good. You'll have to excuse me," the Captain, he now knew, said, "please pass on my gratitude to your company for the delivery of this fine ship. Our Chief Steward will show you back to the *Romsey*."

"Bit–," his father said.

"If you'll follow me, sir," came yet another voice, higher.

"Ta, Captain," his father said, followed by a collection of footsteps upon iron.

"Right, see you on deck, Bell."

"Aye, Captain," the something-of-a-more-than-slight-allure voice said, followed by further footsteps.

The ship's company is on deck, he thought. *This will be easy.*

Waiting until all sound of soles-on-iron had faded, he rounded the corridor corner to continue on his path to the seamen's quarters and, it seemed, an easier than expected settle-in. *However*, it had been a move too soon, and instead of an empty corridor leading off the dining salon, he came face-to-face with a uniformed officer.

A the-jigs-up panic of discovery flooded through him – at first. A jolt through the body like a wet live-wire shock. But the fear fizzled out upon acquainting himself with his opponent. A single officer before him. Late-thirties, he would guess, who cut a sex-fine shape in his officer-class suit with two gold-striped epaulettes.

His success with securing the roughest of men meant he had honed a skill for *knowing* – to draw from his shipyard wanderings –, which of the men rendered hard through the toughest of ship-building tasks would want to rivet his hole soft. That, and those who would complete the task without reprisals following the deed. Further, men not to hold any inclination to follow-up for anything more than an among-the-iron-sheets boy-hole offloading. It was a skilled form of masculine detective work, which saw him sort through and discount trade like a sleuth does with suspects. In this process, the obviously same-company-appreciative are set to one side and dismissed as too high-risk. He is after those with interest in men, yet not singularly or necessarily so. With this methodology, he had perfected the sourcing of man-sex with impunity.

But back to it.

The man before him – outwardly athletic and stern and young-fatherly enough to court the favour of women and move unquestioned and respected among the world of men –, was also as sure a conquest as he had ever before encountered. The unexpected run-in in the underlit corridor, in the unmanned lower decks of the *Queen*, with a boy, he knew, had rendered for the officer also: a shock, and one that this officer was slower to recover from.

In his discovery of a young seaman below deck, the officer took in *his* Clydebank body with a salivating appetite, one that would be better concealed in ordinary – non-abrupt-shock – circumstances. Before words were spoken, the youthful, muscular-yet-supple lines of his boyish body were observed. The *discovery* doubled as a moment of uncontrollable voyeurism. Officer eyes followed the lines of legs – not long, but meaty from working class company and teamly sports – and that rose to rest on a plump arse, round in brilliant white slacks that were a size smaller than was the fashion, but that he had selected, scented with arse sweat, for sublimely this purpose.

As the recovery from the shock of the run-in went on, officer eyes averted from arse. From the fat-and-full-at-the-back, balanced with packed front pocket, officer gaze moved up the V of his chest to arrive at his face. There, officer found cheeks youthfully colour-flushed, but, too, a squared jaw with the promise of a man on the way.

"All hands on deck, sailor," officer said.

A voice that was trying to be stern, authoritative, but that belied an embarrassment of desire. Officer lips, full and pink, quivered as they awaited a response. These lips – they were flanked by pronounced cheekbones. Bones that led to a pointed chin and a proud, slightly bony nose. A nose with a similar, artistically pleasing rank – as on *Elizabeth*'s bow. Officer had Grecian features, the kind that would be sacrificed in an arena, and as awaiting response, the quiver in officer lips grew until he needed to touch this surface with his tongue and the tip of his teeth just to keep them two still.

Sure about how to proceed, he, the boy, dropped eyes to the officer's crotch, which protruded with promise.

"Aye, sur," he said, in obedience to manhood above man, or any rank of the Royal Navy; the former sure and plump, the latter uncertain.

Finally. Feebly. Voice betraying further evidence of his eagerness for him. Officer said:

"Let's go."

"Aye, sur," he said again.

After a further pause of respect for the bulge of an officer of the *Queen*'s company, Clydebank boy led the way topside, tracing the plan of *Elizabeth* in his head to show them there. All the way, he was conscious of the eyes of a handsome officer upon his stern, which confirmed his new plan:

He would obey his officer but titillate with youthful defiance as well.

Aboveboard. The day had come of age. The mist had risen, and *Elizabeth*, woken – her foredeck at least partly whole with her company of men. His officer straightened up, too, in the sun, ascending to the promenade deck to join other uniformed men overlooking the assembled crew.

His intention to stow away for the short coastal voyage to Southampton, to remain unseen and deal with the consequences of his flee from Clydebank only once he had arrived, now needed a rethink. The tender's engines could be heard in the distance, on which his absence would have now been discovered.

Should I surrender?

Not yet.

He joined the other men dressed like him, who slung themselves on and around the three most visible markers of the *Queen*'s machinery: her three anchor chains, each second link of which was large enough to encase the arse of a sailor. There were many ropes bundled around the chains. They reminded him of the most pungent of those engineers' overalls he had inhaled below deck, and so, naturally, atop one of these piles was where he came down.

His officer must have been expected because no sooner than he was in a position overlooking the workers did a man, much his senior, step forward.

"Welcome to *Queen Elizabeth*," said the voice of the Captain. "It is my great privilege to command the latest and largest ship in the proud Cunard line as she embarks on her maiden voyage."

He scanned the crew assembled as the Captain spoke.

"In these extraordinary times, the triumphs of British ingenuity and pride must be protected from enemy forces, who would seek to tear them away from us at any cost. The maiden voyage of the *Elizabeth* will carry no passengers, it will have no fanfare, yet it will be perhaps the most important voyage of any merchant ship in history. And so, you all have been hand-picked to ensure this ship's survival.

"Many of you have come from the great *Aquitania*, which I have also had the privilege to command. As we stand at the dawn of another Great War, my orders come from the Admiralty directly, and they are simple: this ship must clear the British Isles and the range of the Luftwaffe, and she must do so as a matter of urgency and high secrecy. *Elizabeth*'s safety and the nation's pride depend on this. Where exactly we will go is a secret known not even to I, as yet, but it will be foreign shores."

Able seamen being as they are: *un*able to sit still when accustomed to tending to the ropes and wrenches of mariner work, were chatty when the captain started but fell silent as the address went on and details of the dangers of the voyage ahead of them came to the surface, like the air bubbles through blown bolts in an airtight compartment of a stricken ship on an uncharted seabed shelf.

"When you signed on, you were instructed by the Line to pack for the eventuality of several months at sea. Many of you, I know, concluded from this directive that duty might call upon more from you than a familiar coastal journey. I do not know myself the particulars of where this great liner is headed. Still, I can confirm that my first order is to, at approximately 0700 hours to-morrow, navigate this vessel down the Firth of Clyde to chart a course north through the Irish Sea, past Rathlin Island, and out into the Atlantic.

"We are a skeleton crew," switching now to a slower, more metronome beat that betrayed careful choice in the penning of words, "on an untested vessel, sailing into hostile waters. I want there to be no illusion about that. Most of you were chosen personally by this ship's incumbent department superiors for being up to the task. The rest have come highly recommended from other liners, and I implore you to do your duty. Arriving today will be a Board of Trade official, who will change each article on board from coastal to foreign. Any of you who do not feel *fit*," scanning those facing him more slowly, "to make this historic voyage, will be allowed to leave–"

Now he turned on the faces of his executive, like a watchman searching shores for any sign of enemy insurgency. He looked like a man set about seeking out uncertainty or any signal of insubordination and revolt. He took his time, too. All sound dropped on the Clyde as he searched, *Romsey*'s engines included; on the horizon, came a convoy of lifeboats headed for the *Queen*, like a wagon train crossing the plains of the New World in a dangerous, yet necessary, supply line. Floated up to *Elizabeth*, as had happened with *Mary* before her, as a measure to make the ship lighter in the water.

"–for those that do withdraw, and I expect you will be few, know this: you will be interned on the ship's tender until such a time as the remaining ship's company is safely at sea. This is–"

A late arrival on the speech deck interrupted the address. It was a gangly, upright sort, and with a moustache, who approached and spoke into the captain's ear. The report seemed to further layer concern into his face and bring the address to a shorter-than-intended conclusion.

"There is much to be done to prepare for to-morrow's journey," he said as a stop, then withdrew into her superstructure.

Men and voices rose on the foredeck even before the captain was gone from view. The remaining executive descended from the promenade podium and on to the workmen's area to confront the concerns of their men.

There were some sixty-odd seamen on *Elizabeth*. Some were on deck along her sides, helping with the securement of the lifeboats. Others were fore and aft, tending to the ropes, getting her sea-ready, while a more technical sort oversaw the wrapping of wire about her hull – degaussing her against attraction with magnetic mines. But the rest, in shifts throughout the day, were assembled in the seamen's mess, below the crew quarters of her bow – awaiting summons for change in their articles. He was with them. Natter about all goings-on throughout the ship thrived in the seamen's mess, making it the perfect place for a stowaway in sailor-dress to hide and learn. The mess had the atmosphere of some of the workers' pubs along the docks where he had sourced shipbuilders for sex. Basic decoration of photos of ships being built and at-sea adorned the walls and were bolted, along with tables, to room surfaces. He read it as expectation in the rowdiness of seamen. Smoke from sailors' cigarettes hung in the air like the mist had that morning, screening him from suspicion, keeping his mystery – cross-legged in the corner, inhaling his own infamy: news that the son of one of the John Brown and Co. pen-pushers had stowed away on board.

"The lad's likely tucked away aft in one of the baggage rooms, plenty of places to hide down there," one speculated.

"Unlikely to find him before we set sail," said another.

"Aye, but poor lad'll get a shock at sea, a mate on the *Mary* says this class has a mean storm roll. None stabilisers on a ship of her size."

Beyond-him issues of discussion included possible call-of-port destinations.

"I say we're headed for Halifax," one said – a widespread opinion.

"Bit far, I think," came one counter to this, "and not one with a port that'd take her."

Several hours had now passed since following the sailors into the mess, and the natter had changed course, too. The first hour or two were absorbed by the issue of foreign articles. All would sign up again, of course, these being men of adventure with the longing for lasting assignments in their blood. He enjoyed that certainty of outward journeying about seamen immediately. But they were also lads-awares, he observed – awares of the way things *worked* and their playing position in the system. This had rallied the men of the mess into a movement for more pay. 'Danger money', as was banded around the chains of the foredeck following the captain's address. The phrase, put forward by just one sly seaman, was then volleyed among the others; first by his peers, who passed it to the engine room greasers – men who had the brute to back it; lastly, it was picked up in earnest by the stewards with their sharper tongues. Soon enough, the National Union of Seamen had been called and delivered via *Romsey*, and an extra £30 per pocket was secured for the seamen's troubles. That the unionist sent for would be made to stay on *Romsey* in exile along with those without the stomach for a sea-bound adventure, was a fate that met much appreciation among the men of the mess.

He enjoyed observing it play out through his smokescreen. How these working men manoeuvred to make more monies from company men. Fully aware that their manpower was needed – their crew list already to the bone of the monster liner's demands –, yet able to conceal by their class the reality that they would have done it for nothing extra. It was crude to scrape a little off the top, just because. But he enjoyed them for it. Their antics – boasted about in the privacy of their own domain – had in fact been what made his mind up with how he would proceed. He would bend his own body – and the ways in which it was *needed for and by* other men on *Elizabeth* – to serve his own ambitions. The needs *by and for* one member-seaman of the executive class in particular.

The officers' quarters were in her superstructure, in the levels at her fore above main deck. This section, from its wheelhouse and three levels down, to the observation lounge, would usually be off-limits to working seamen; stowaways-posing-as-working-seamen especially. But the changing of articles had a fortuitous side effect: it necessitated freedom of movement into official quarters of her upper decks and *in*to the chambers of the men who commanded her. The opening up of these areas to the seamen from below gave him a reason to be there. A means of slipping up and onto those upper decks. Yet, like the rocks of a break wall, other obstacles were keeping his officer and his currents from combining. Most pressing for the present being that he did not even know by what name his officer went.

Any hopes of sleuthing out the name of his officer from his listening position in the mess were soon squashed. Not only were the various ranks and duties of her officers a mysterious foreign land and vernacular to him, but the familiarity of *this* crew with each other – almost all having come from another Cunarder, *Aquitania* – together with the jovial informality of the mess, meant that names that *were* thrown out were mostly crude nicknames for the officers in command. What he *had* gleaned from mess matters was that since around 1400 hours, once the sticking point of monies had been settled on with the union, turnaround in each individual seaman's change of articles had hit its stride. The junior officer – a pudgy, pompous type by the name of Rogers with an aversion to smoke – that summoned men by name from the mess was arriving with greater frequency and taking with him an increased number each time. This summoning – together with the knowledge that the Board of Trade official responsible for creating articles was also on hand, but only for a short while – spurred him into action.

He headed up in the direction of his officer's chambers tagged-on with a batch of six seamen that had been summoned. The corridors around the officers' chambers were equally unfinished, as with the rest of her accommodations, yet were marked by a distinction in the quality of their design. There was no exposed piping along these corridor ceilings, and adorning these walls, even, were suggestions of where panelling would be installed to bring these areas into line with the quality of the passenger quarters. Wood, in other words, would plush up these halls into passages for the enjoyment of senior seamen and their guests.

Two officers were engaged in re-signing the seamen, a procedure performed out of adjacent cabins. Men that had been summoned were ferried into their sign-over officer by Rogers. Given that all called-from-the-mess seamen were accounted for, he was not able to wait with the men. Officer lavatories separated these cabins from additional, unmanned executive accommodations around a corridor bend, which was where he waited. But this, around from the main waiting area of concealment, also prevented him from *seeing in*: to the officers' cabins and finding out which of these his officer was in. He was in the right place, however – as he realised when one of the "comes" that called through the open cabins for seamen to enter connected, unmistakably, with his below-deck run-in officer. The chance for an encounter, eventually, was signalled with out-of-his-cabin clarity.

"Won't be long, men," the voice said, approaching his concealed position.

These corridors will likely take carpet when *Elizabeth* is complete, but they were just iron now. His officer's soles alerted him to the approach, just in time for him to pull back and out of view. But his vantage-view was preserved – allowing him to watch as his officer came around the bend and into the lavatory. Into which, after the length of two long drags of air, he followed.

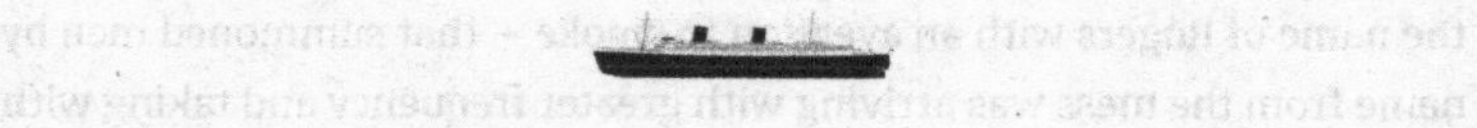

He entered upon his officer at ease at the urinal. His manhood in hand, his military training clear: feet apart, back straight, his narrow waist and broad shoulders in an officer's suit, casting a magnetic silhouette against the brilliant white of the walls. His officer's strong stream struck the porcelain bowl with a sound that was the only one in the space; at first. More careful listening found another audio line below it; an exhalation. Deep and chesty, in the rhythm of his officer's thought-private relief. The two sounds – urine stream above breathing line – grew in the space as he watched, his officer easing his stance into advancement of an offloading, a slight recline of the head. He advanced to add his own sounds to the space, steps that served as announcement of their second introduction. But he stopped short of joining his at-ease officer, whose stream, sturdy and continuing, he was not willing to disrupt – just yet. His officer tilted the angle of his recline. It met his company – at just enough of an inclination to glimpse the all-white of his companion.

"Officers only, seaman," he said.

It pleased him to hear. His officer sounding sure of himself, authoritative about his place in the chain of command, even as he held himself, exposed. It was a welcome addition of attraction toward a man who had appeared less-assured on first bumping into. But the sternness of his officer's tone also disrupted the formulation of his plan. Hesitation crept in, threatening to plant him firm; or, worse, force a retreat. He could feel the tops of his cheekbones flush with colour as he considered lines of entry into his officer's current or means of swimming sidewards. He adapted his plan to meet the stage of his officers' own lavatory and the directive he had received upon intrusion into it.

He stayed the course, further adding himself to the sound in the space with additional steps, striding closer, touching the extreme edge of the territory of his superior, and aligning himself alongside him, locking eyes with him. The move brought colour to his officer's cheeks – and betrayed recollection of their earlier encounter. To his satisfaction, and much credit owed to his officer's constitution, the urine stream suffered no interruption. It carried on striking porcelain without dissipation of determination, fighting on alone as now the only presence audible – the breath of them both out of the mix, below the register of sound. The temptation to *look*, to take it in, was too much. Like a free diver spotting something sparkling about to slip over a seabed shelf and out of reach into an undersea ravine, his eyes took the plunge toward the source of the sound below. And treasure was found.

His officer's member extended heavy and low from regulation Cunard liner trousers. His meat was full, laden, even at rest – with a sharp bend at the crest. Its lines were smooth, elegant, like the bow of the *Queen* currently being prepared by men for a maiden voyage slip-away. Pristine, milky, un-sun-touched and with a hint of pink at the tip, tucked under a hood of skin. His officer's manhood was fully matured, unlike his own. Plump and purposeful, like the decades between them had built in a bounty. Even upon looking, the stream was strong. Crystal with refractions of gold – pooling in the maybe-not-yet-used bowl below, sent with a force that gathered more than it drained. It would not have been right to draw away from the sight; in fact, he feared for the flecks of diamonds coming to an end before their time – the source of their sound, too, he worried that would enact a retreat. And so he maintained his gaze as encouragement, and the flowing from his officer responded with purpose and control, staying strong. Though the performance required something from him, too, he thought. Not a sound but a sight: his own below-there for viewing.

He would not use the facilities before him; he could not compete, even had he wanted. But he could be presented, exposed. And once he was, with this state, he turned to face his officer and brought himself to military attention – the click of his bootheels bouncing through the lavatory. It was an abrupt manoeuvre, a bold choice, to which his own meat bobbed in reaction to his legs coming together. Through this deed, he was coercing rank-and-file protocol. It served as a statement of intent for their conduct to come – smacking still of youthful insubordination, flagrant misuse of a proud military tradition. It was the equivalent of a soldier taking himself mid-climb to the door of a drop plane, thrusting it open and teasing the threshold with thoroughfare without a parachute. And the impact of its boldness was immediate. His officer collapsed himself upon him, any support out from under him, choosing to tumble through that threshold to the vast unknown of the patchwork countryside below – consequences be damned. His officer free-fell to the floor, his stream now a trickle down the front of his slacks. He landed as a breath-heavy heap before him, face upon younger meat. As if his legs had given up on carrying him after a long resistance of fever, it was with the same uncontrollable intensity that he took him in his mouth. He had succumbed finally to an ailment whose tending-to he had long been denied, his officer saw what hung before him as his only chance at treatment – provided he got it into him soon.

"I'm the stowaway," he said as fattening within his officer's mouth. "But if you let me stay," gripping his meat at its base – entire, but still malleable –, pulling it from his officer's mouth to trace the angle of his stumble with it, across his jaw and then back to his lips, wet and eager, "you could make *use* of me."

He had taken many a man's manhood into him before, along the banks of the Clyde, but this encounter was novel: a man at *his* service, taking him in. As he reached firmness, and the mouth within which he was held served as sufficient support, he dropped his hands from his own meat to the breadth of his officer's shoulders. They were sound in build but with tremors now.

"Name's Turner, Oliver Turner, aged sixteen, o' Clydebank."

His officer steadied somewhat with the sound of his speech, which was calm and clear and unconcerned about the potential for discovery.

"A'm able, sur," he said, bending into the depths of his officer's lips that sucked on him. "If ye arrange mah articles, ah wid be able tae serve as yer seaman."

He eased his officer into a rhythm from the back of his head, bringing his Scottishness to the fore; he led his officer into the encounter and edged him toward the riding of his mast, as a skilled look-out would at the crest of a succession of rolling waves. Now it was his time to recline, as his officer had with his stream, and add his own outpouring of chesty exhalation to the acoustics of the room. The leap of faith in the power of their chemistry had proved fruitful so far. Now he turned his mind to the to-follow stages of his plan. His officer, too, and to his credit, seemed to be formulating a goal of his own. Having come of age already, his plan appeared plain, centred: he seized the essentialism of treatment of his recruit but also steadied himself with rising awareness of the situation. From a bundle of limbs on the floor, he took up a more confident, kneed stance, which aided him to take Turner deeper into him; but also, it seemed, revived him to the need to protect his station. Awareness rose of the foolishness of this indulgence. His officer apparently decided on his plan; with hands wet but only slightly shaking, he took hold of the backs of Turner's thighs, pulling in the direction of the cubicles behind them and the measure of screening they promised.

He, of course, understood the plan and resisted, stood firm – had a contrary position of his own. Taking the cold porcelain of the urinal in one hand and the cusp of his officer's neck in the other, he kept them there. Full view of the entrance and potential for others to witness them amid the indecent, illegal act. When his officer persisted in tugging toward a more middle ground of semi-concealment offered by a cubicle door, he took hold of his face. A hand at each side of his jaw, he reclined his officer's head for him, urging him to a state of reprieve, and submission, once more. Back, and further back, until his own manhood was fully withdrawn. Then, returning his officer to face his front squarely, his meat, firm and wet, he rubbed himself up alongside his officer's face, pressing himself against the pronouncements of officer-nose, full and flaring from the deep taking-in of him. He extended his manhood all the way up to touch his officer's hairline, matted and damp with sweat.

"What's yer name, sur," he said, holding his officer's face firm against the private portions of himself.

"Row-bert," he said, his speech muffled by salty man-sack. "Robert Bell."

Bell-end, he thought, piecing Bell together with the nicknames that had been nattered throughout the mess.

Officer Bell – *his* officer – was well-liked among the men of the mess. He had a reputation for treating men fairly in the assignment and disciplining of their duties. He had even gone in to bat to secure a pay raise for their troubles in taking on this particular challenge.

"Let me bade 'n' serve ye," he said, dragging his meat back down the opposite flank of Bell's nose, returning it to its place between his lips in time with the speaking of his name, "Officer Bell."

Bell still held his thighs with a tug, but his arms had lost their tautness, were less intent on bringing them away from the urinals and the threat of uncovering. Bell resisted still, but feebly, was slack in his grasp: *inviting* his refusal to take cover from certain ruin were they disrupted. He allowed his own grip to loosen and his hands to come to rest on Bell's shoulders instead. Pulling at his epaulettes, the popping of stitches sounded out through the lavatory as his officer worked his newest crew member against the recesses of his mouth with increasing vigour. He moaned as Bell's motions took him deeper inside him, Bell's own moans a bass below his, muffled by the meat obstruction. He finished first with an outpouring that came without warning. Bell's eyes widened as he received the first ribbons released from his new seaman, who had been so well-embedded within him that the seed was planted without even the need to swallow. He then withdrew into the foyer of Bell's mouth, where his officer could then savour the saltiness of the deposit with subsequent bursts that came just behind his lips. Bell finished with the first taste of semen, and without having even touched himself, shooting his own seed with a life-withheld intensity that sent it travelling from his place near the lavatory floor to strike the wall of the urinal. They both shuddered with the collective release, folding in on each other. Bracing, as if their actions had spurred a movement of the *Queen* from her moorings. In fact, she *had* moved, her engines alive.

"It's started," Bell said, breathless, still firing with his final pumps of relief.

"Aye, sur," he said, running a thumb over the spent lips of his officer, full and pink, gaining tread and pull with each trace. "See ye on deck."

He secured himself and left Bell there, panting and pants-open, on his knees, on the floor of the officers-only lavatory.

He took to the seaman's life as if he had already lived it. Sailors were well-versed in taking new recruits through the ropes, and no one questioned him. He was Turner, Bell's boy. They had set off the following morning, down the Clyde on their way to the open ocean and a destination unknown. It was a still misty morning when they shipped off, like the one the day before, when his only ambition had been to stow away. Getting the *Queen* down the snake bends of the Clyde and to her setting-off point had been a challenge, as he heard from the men in the mess, and getting her out to sea would test her skeleton crew, too. He enjoyed tugging on ropes among the chaos of up-anchor chains on the foredeck. A novice but able, he welcomed the burn of the high-performance fibres across his unhardened hands. They would welt and weather with time and give him the hands of a man. Two tugs were along her hull to help turn her into position, but not *Romsey*, of course, she had sleeked off during the night into Gareloch with visitors and those unfit for the journey, as a measure to keep her secret.

Elizabeth – whose engines shuddering into life had marked the end of his interview-of-ableness with his officer – had moved about a little during the night. Her night-motions prepared her for the voyage; tested her engines, her compass, her wireless – downriver from the Tail o' the Bank. It was not enough to stretch her legs and nothing near what was customarily needed to test a liner of her size. But it was enough to ensure that all were at least, in theory, a go for the voyage – and the most of a trial she could hope for given the world and its state. Word in the mess was that the captain received special permission for the trails from Admiralty headquarters and the Commander-in-Chief on HMS *Warspite* – and that the Commander had been ferried on board to oversee her preparedness in person. It was a prequel for the challenges that navigating her out of the Clyde would pose that day. Her body too big by far; moving her was akin to turning an animal that had outgrown its cage. The trials of the night previous had given him the chance to be among seamen, to observe the setting sail procedures. It gave him the confidence to get in among them that morning, to haul rope and chain for himself.

"Turner," came a call from the entrance hatch nearest the foredeck.

It was pompous-pudgy Rogers. "Report to Senior First Officer Bell on the gallery deck," he said with no attempt at concealing his distaste for Turner's newfound favour.

He knew the area well, it being outside of the officers' quarters. Bell stood alone on the deck at the railing, the *Queen* getting into stride in anticipation of open sea.

"Morning, Turner," Bell said as he reached his side, but without turning his attentions from *Elizabeth*'s progress. "I have your articles."

"Ta, sur."

"How are you settling in?"

"Guid, sur."

He had not seen his officer since their time at the urinal. Bell looked more handsome that day, proud and strong against the Scottish landscape that rose behind him from the Clyde like a monumental black iceberg from some ancient Scottish myth. He was more rugged in that setting, craggier in a dirty-dapper sense. The brisk, salty air had brought out a rash of red specks across his cheeks and added glitter of the sea to his full brown hair, slicked back, neatly parted, but with the slight disarray of vitality that came from a man at the dawn of leadership duty.

"Good," Bell said with a small smile.

He watched him with interest. Had he been surprised by how easy it all was, he wondered. A stranger interrupting his stream as supposition that sex would follow, with nothing more expected in return other than the chance to stay and to serve.

"What do you know of ships, Turner?"

"Nae much, sur. Bit I'm eager tae learn."

"Good man. I hear that you have taken to the labour on deck."

"Aye, sur. It's guid tae be useful."

"Indeed, but I'd like to make use of you elsewhere. We have a trying voyage ahead, and I could use an extra man in my navigation and charts department. I need a man I can trust, you see. Many obstacles lay ahead, which are not helped with a captain," and he looked at him then like he might be speaking out of turn, "who does not yet know where we are headed. Having you; by my side; will be of special service to me professionally; and personally," he said. "Are you up to it?"

"Aye, sur."

And so commenced his tutorage in ship navigation. Bell had him stay by his side the whole first leg of her journey, pointing out aspects of navigational seamanship as they went. Bell explained that her first hurdle had come even before they met, along a particularly narrow point in the Clyde, where her sister had been caught broadside only some few years before. *There are only two tides on which a vessel of this class can carry the journey out, you see*, Bell had said, *so our opportunity was a narrow window.* That section of the river had been further dredged for the coming of the second *Queen*, but not enough; she had caught herself, briefly. And so anxieties were high now that the open ocean called her. Part of him was glad he would not be by Bell's side for the passing of Clydebank shipyards. The experience was a foreign enough one already and much had happened in the short time since he had left: lending the place already to the past of father and his ledger. The tenements there, seen from *Romsey*, slanted on the outward journey of the day before from an entirely new angle.

How queer they look, he had thought.

Stacked up behind the cranes of the yard like discarded milk crates of a forgotten run, beyond their usefulness now. There was no logic to them. Unlike the *Queens* that had risen before him throughout childhood – the second of which was now setting out on her own. The second, unyielding;

by comparison, these slanting structures were stuck, land-locked, cobbled together with less purpose. How satisfying it was for him to steam past that place of smog and, without the *Queens*, now-emptiness. The initial stages of the *Queen*'s passage were a complex engagement, brought forth by defences put in place to protect her during her stay so far.

"He came on board by tender this morning," Bell said of the pilot they could glimpse in the wheelhouse. "Especial-versed, he is, to guide us through Clyde's anti-submarine boom and on our way...wherever that may be."

He spoke in a round-vowed, educated way. A worldly way. But embellished by the add at the end of confidante suggestion. Once they had cleared the mouth of the Clyde and curved around the headland for a course north of the isles, the waters of the Irish Sea added sway to her. But she was Clydebank built, and as she stretched her legs and gathered speed, the sea was soon tamed and sliced through with purpose. Bell stayed with him up the entire strait between Ireland and Wales, until sight of her convoy at the tip of the Northern Ireland mainland.

"I am needed now," Bell said, passing over his binoculars so Turner could see too. "Keep them," he said after Turner had taken a look. "And come by my cabin after supper... For your articles."

He had never been at sea before. Did not know, even, whether he would have the stomach for it or how long it would take for his 'sea legs' to come in, as those in the mess had said to him sensing his greenery. Standing there, binoculars-in-hand, alone on the gallery deck, the drama spread out ahead of him against a choppy backdrop of the vast Atlantic, the cold, wet salt striking his face like a warning shot.

"That was the most dangerous part of her dash from home," Bell told him later in his cabin.

To give her the best chance, she had merged with an Irish-tip convoy for her push out to sea. Four destroyers encased her as protection for her flanks, while from above, seaplanes and military aircraft offered aerial cover. She did not slow, steaming into the middle of the convoy at 26 knots and setting a zigzag course to evade U-boats, already known to stalk these waters. She had been built for direct-course steaming, not for sharp manoeuvring. This meant she tilted frightfully with each turn – terror at the prospect of her not righting herself being a sensation, he suspected, that never would leave him. For the first time on his adventure so far, he felt the shadow of the war over him, bearing down upon him. Sounds of convoy-engines and the magnified sight of gunners at the ready served as empirical proof of his cause for alarm. But the true terror came later that day, when at 200 miles west of Rathlin Island, the destroyers adopted a course contrary to the *Queen*, allowing her and her crew of 399 – less than one-third of her complement – to carry on alone and unarmed. Unaided into the deep uncertainty of the North Atlantic, destination still unknown.

Tension on the *Queen* tightened as they lost light, and the isolation of her full-blackout instructions and strict wireless silence rules set in. But she steamed forth still, without trials, confidently charting her jagged route across the North Atlantic. She resisted the changing pressures of waves upon her broadside as the night sky, pricked with a billion beacons of tiny light, lit her way. He *should* have been terrified, questioning his decision, seeing it for the foolish folly that it was. But instead, he felt his fibres anneal to it, forged by *her* confidence. He settled into her rhythm, felt unflinching faith in her ability to deliver the men inside her safely to a foreign port. As instructed, he felt his way to Bell's door after supper, the experience much different from his stealthy journey up there only the day before. Up and away from the men of the mess. Away from the seamen sleeping areas; disappointingly not used on account of the space on board for each man, every one to his own suite. The *Queen* felt like a ghost ship that night. Bell's door was ajar on arrival, a faint light the only sign of life in that part of the *Queen*: beckoning him to enter. In front of the door-ajar, he chose not to knock or otherwise make himself known, pushing Bell's door in and exposing his quarters to the full view of the officers' corridor.

"Close the door," Bell said, shaky, from the bed directly in front, naked, his legs flat and spread in full view of the corridor.

Although he had followed instructions during the day and in getting there, he ignored this order. He was on board to serve, yes, but his service in the bedroom was *of a different kind* – one freed from the bounds of seagoing convention, strike that, British law. Door left gaping, he climbed on palms and knees atop his officer's bed and into a position between his legs as far up as his knees, resting back so his posterior perched on the soles of his feet. Bell's vantage was of Turner before him, framed by the cabin's door, wide and dangerously inviting discovery by others. Bell's body glistened wet. He could smell that this was part from soap from having recently showered and part from sweat – the latter formed in beads across his brow and in his in-between chest hairs. Beads multiplied as he sat there, watching his officer presented on the bed, in full view of other officers that might be passing. A desire to break their formation and head for the door that would seal them away from the prying eyes of his peers was palpable in Bell's pose. The rises of his chest – peppered with golden, sweat-tipped hairs – grew more frequent toward what Turner suspected was an inevitable cave in the pressure of the situation. He watched unaffected as the tension built in his officer, whose temples began to pulse as he teetered on the brink of calling it off. Then, just as Bell seemed set to spring into action, to seize control and put a stop to the recklessness, he took the opportunity to act himself. With one swift swipe of his arms, he poked his own limbs through the loops of his officer's legs so that the bend in his arms touched with the wet hook of his officer's under-joints, locking in gaze with him as he folded him up, over and onto himself.

Bell bent in and to the next stage of his coming-of-age narrative. At first, an expression of alarm at the sudden manoeuvre rippled across his features. That then morphed into surprise, to then rest on incomprehension, once his knees had themselves come to rest, flanking his head. He took in what his commanding officer had to offer, like a pirate appraising his latest loot. Bell's knot, pink and plump, spread before him like a Sunday roast – the twitch of sweaty angst switching from his temples to his taint as Turner eyed up his opening: tight and untested, like the cogs of the *Queen*. Taking his time, taking it in, sensing, as he did, Bell's slip, again, into abandon... The threat of being seen presented itself like Bell had on his cabin bed. Being sized up for sodomy by a fully-clothed new recruit was so alien, so *arousing* to him, that allowing himself to be used at the will of his new crew member stood as his only wish in a wartime world; Turner could see and sense for himself – as a snapping of a switch. It manifested in how Bell returned his look and through the release of tension in the body he had folded. He widened his arm-span, over which his officer's legs were draped. This had the effect of opening his officer up to him further, spreading his cheeks and easing the grip of his officer seal, peeling it open for him. He took it as a permit to enter, though he was tentative, planting of his month first, itself pink and plump, onto the arse of his officer: bringing their lips to touch for the first time. Bell was one whole-bodied receiver who pulsed at the sensation of a tongue inside and reaching into him. As he worked loose the knot of his officer, their bodies a heaving heap with the sway of the *Queen*, Bell abandoned all concern for their discovery.

"Oliver, Oliver, Oliver," he cried in a chesty chant using his Christian name.

Bell's call was as insistent as a sergeant's drill but without any of the power of authority behind it. His senior officer had succumbed utterly to his takeover. When Bell was at his most open, filled with the encompassed length of Turner-tongue, tightness returned suddenly; Bell's body seized, and he was pushed out in jolts as Bell spilt over. Arched back, Bell flooded forth, coating his chest in bursts – his finish, once again, coming without need to touch himself. A jolt from Bell, push out of Turner. Jolt, push. Jolt, push. Their bodies acted in rhythm, each ribbon release from his officer leading to a slight Turner withdrawal until his tongue slipped free with the final pulse from Bell's spent shaft. He sat back, looking at the opened hole before him. After all the work in readying it, it seemed a shame not to use it. But he resisted the requirement for Bell to be run in...for now. His spent officer shipmate eased back onto the bed. He had served him by forcing this officer himself to obey and to have their affair in the face of potential ruin. But now that his officer had finished, he granted a reprieve, closing the cabin door and easing his officer into his afterglow. Wet all over, Bell exhaled heavy, audible relief from potential peril. He lit a cigarette.

"I have your articles," he said.

"Ta, sur."

Bell paused, as if waiting for Turner to add more – a request for proof of Bell's promise, perhaps, or even to use his point of advantage after the second occasion of climaxing his officer, this time without himself finishing, to get something further from him. Perhaps. A small, self-loathing part of himself half-expected his new recruit to take a swipe at his manhood for having succumbed to anal stimulation. But he said nothing, *had* had all he needed in getting to work with his tongue.

"We're headed for New York," Bell said, dragging deeply.

He had known this already from murmurs in the mess.

"We are averaging 26 knots," Bell added, "but our progress is impeded by this erratic course the *captain* has seen fit to order."

The confessional, insubordinate quip showed Bell's comfort with his company, while the sway of the cabin as the *Queen* performed another hairpin turn punctuated his point. But still, resisting complete abandon of confidence in him, Bell studied his new mate's face, letting seconds slip past before continuing – admiring his youth, Turner suspected, too.

"She's fast," he said, "but she's also *alone*," another drag, "and word on the bridge is that the *Deutschland* stalks these waters."

None of this information was news to him; the *Queen* was an echo chamber of intel; as soon as information was received on the bridge, it made its way through the crew, right down to the men deep in her hull. The seamen, being on deck and close to the officers, were often the first to receive it. Though relaying it, in increasing drips, did demonstrate a growing surety in their confidence. He said nothing still, emoted nothing, allowing the process to play out within his officer. He could sense that for Bell, he was gaining the guaranteed status of confidante and comfort: a rare thing in the churning cold of the vast Atlantic. Bell thrived through his silent witness. He grew at ease in the closed cabin, a master of his domain. He took his time finishing his cigarette without further word, seeming to relish both the smoke and the company. And in turn he watched his officer from his place by the door, attentive but removed. The roar of the engines and the waves against the *Queen*'s side filled the silence as he took in Bell's decor. His cabin was unfinished, like the rest of the *Queen*, but already he had personalised it with the ornaments an officer no doubt carried with him from posting to posting. On his desk was a picture of a sandy-haired boy, no more than ten. And beside it was another picture, recently taken, it seemed. It was of Bell with a woman. Stern, strict and angular, and more advanced in age. She stood with him on docks, New York, by the looks of the backdrop. Two ships behind them, one Cunard's *Aquitania*, the other, *Rex* of the Italian line, inscribed on their sides. The one on the left, *Aquitania*, a four-fuelled Great War veteran, the right, newer and two-funnelled, a symbol of the rising of the Italians, as he had learnt from the natter of mess-men. Bell watched him watching, un-objecting to his peering into the artefacts of his off-board life, un-ashamed by their dirty secret, their illegal tryst.

This, he thought, *is new*.

In a post-relief state, curiosity and comfort emerged for them both.

"When we reach New York," Bell said, playing with the gold-matrimonial ornamentation on his left hand, "I will be returning to the *Aquitania*." He stubbed out his cigarette. "And I want–" his face told that this experience was surprising him, too. Abandoning the ring on his finger, turning his attentions to tracing his ring below, his tongue-opened hole – still wet and ready. His finger looked coarse, hardened, and seemed to grate against the softness of his lower lips, pouted and prepared for the first time. "And I *need*," he corrected, venturing beyond the surface, probing into himself, "for you to come–," all the way to the knuckle, just beyond where Turner's tongue had been, "–too."

He did not respond. Rather, he stripped on the spot, folding his whites with crisp corners of newly-acquired seamanship. He then took up his previous position between his officer's knee bends. Bell was still open, but this time, instead of draping his legs over his shoulders, he took this officer's feet and pressed them together, so they were sole-to-sole, in a position of meditative opening. Then he lifted, and lifted, and lifted; until Bell was spread much wider than he had been before. Once his officer's joined soles were over his head, he took two feet in one hand and threaded Bell's head through the gap so that his feet came to rest behind his head as a cushion, and so that his chin was to his chest, giving him a full view of the boarding-into-him about to commence. Shock and satisfaction spread across Bell's face as he witnessed – from a contortionist's vantage – a young recruit getting him ready. How naturally his body had yielded into a wide-open position, how *right* this was for him, Turner thought. Once his officer's ring had reached its optimal wideness, with his free hand, he scooped up what wet remained on Bell's chest and used it as a lather for himself and his officer's lower lips. And slid in. Pain flooded in with him as Bell tightened again with apprehension. But he had anticipated this. He kept control. He held himself inside, allowing his officer's ring time to relax, to expand, to take him. And once he felt the clamp loosen and saw his officer's grimace subside, he started to move around, to reach in, to acquaint himself. Further and fuller than he had before when he had only a tongue as an explorer. And as he felt his officer once again near the point of spilling over, he spoke softly in response to Bell's beckoning.

"Aye, sur," he said. "I'll come with ye."

The words came as they both did. He floated inside his officer like a breach in the bulkhead. Filling him with the salt from himself. In the shine-light of the Atlantic moon, across the knot of a novice seaman inside a novice-at-receiving officer.

Sea-life breeds a life of routine, and he settled into this with his officer. He would visit each evening, enter him, leave him alone with a filling and the still-novel discovery of an erotic entrance into himself after. The days' work portions passed without incident as if the journey had been a peacetime one – an occasion for leisure, even. Watch-outs were worked ceaselessly, of course. And able seamen, many much harder, often spent their idle time searching the skies and swell as well: for any sign of enemy ambush. But none came, and the days rolled into nights with the sureness of the sea herself.

No disruptions to the sea suggestive of U-boats or streaks across the sky pointing to hostile planes were found. Not even other merchant ships were sighted. There was a nothingness to the passage. Abyss is frightening, and for many men on board the *Queen*, nothingness was a source of high anxiety – his officer included. And so his nightly calls became a *turning* of a valve in his lover, a release of his fears. But he did not fear the nothing. For him, the *Queen*, steaming at her average of 27½ knots – and with potential to much exceed this if the situation called for it – proceeded with invincibility-of-purpose toward New York. The jaggedness of her zigzag journeying, in his view, just the nervousness of men charting her way, and an annoyance to the promptness of an inevitable arrival. His faith in her was absolute.

Slowly the more nervous among her journeymen came around to his view, allowing jovial-ness and surety to seep into their spirits as the voyage wore on. It was a sentiment that had spread through most of the crew by the night before her arrival, as New York neared. There was much merriment in the mess, even though the continued need for darkness kept this spirit from bubbling up and onto the open decks. He preferred it that way, having found a space atop the *Queen* that was secluded at night – even from her watchmen. On the first-class games deck, it was; in a tucked-away nook among a bundle of life jackets; this was where he would often lie and did again on the eve of their New York arrival. Above him, the *Queen*'s two funnels towered; monuments of industry; gently reclining, like the resting cigars of giants. Smoke plumed from their ghostly grey ends to blend with the black beyond, blocking out starlight and keeping *her* hidden, screening her like the ink of a defensive creature from the deep. He had taken to going there as an after-activity of being inside his officer, to smoke, to relax. He even stowed blankets from one of the cabin class cabins there, stored in a nearby hatch throughout the day – to warm him for the nights, in case he might choose to stay until duty called, just ahead of dawn. The view was oddly assuring for him, like the black-out paint across her portholes potted along her hull. The plumes of black-on-black were becoming familiar to him.

"You're the stowaway," came a voice in the shadow of one of her funnels, dragging him back to Clydebank and the life he had almost escaped.

He bolted upright, searching his surrounds. From the mode of approach, he was expecting to find an arrest party. But instead stepped one man from her aft funnel. Upright, thin and with-moustache – he recognised him as the late arrival to the captain's foredeck briefing on his first day onboard.

"Sur?"

"I've known for some time now," he said, approaching, in a voice that was thin and high and in contrast with the depth of the *Queen*'s tones. "I've been...*observing* you."

He's the queer sort, he thought, relaxing into the knowledge of his opponent and how to handle him.

The stranger approached with a gait of awkward shame. Unmasculine and unable to conceal his leanings. He was a steward, probably Chief Steward, he wagered, judging by his positioning alongside the Captain. And he approached with an appetite that was plain.

"I'm Turner," he said sharply. "Bell's laddie."

"I noticed," he smiled, searching Turner's eyes.

The steward, on his scan, was easing into confidence he did not expect. Typically, men like him, the ones unable to move unmarked by suspension among men, were...less-assured. But some, and this must have been the case here too, also felt they could take advantage of younger men, especially when they had something to hold over them.

"You've no need to worry," he went on. "I won't *expose* you. I know what it's like to run away from something. I just wanted to let you know that I knew because we will reach port soon. And you may need assistance getting on to another ship."

Was there evidence of a double meaning, he thought as he searched his opponent, some flicker of eyelid or curl of the lips to suggest that payment was required for his silence, or more likely, in this case, some exchange of sexual service? But there was none proffered, just a gaunt paleness.

"I'll leave you to your night," he said, receding back into the *Queen*.

He chose to spend his last night on her deck, after all, retrieving extra blankets for the stay and pushing the encounter with the crocked steward from his mind.

It was an early rise for all who were not already on duty. The excitement for arrival ran through the *Queen* with a glow like the filament of an incandescent bulb. He joined Bell at the same spot where they had stood as she navigated the Clyde. Land was in sight. Dotted across space between the terrain and the *Queen* was a bounty of working boats.

It was a distinct peacetime sight that confirmed in Turner the protection of this port. There would not be a rapturous welcome for *this Queen* like her sister had received, yet still, the harbour and its activity embraced her as she entered.

"Turner's not your real name, is it?" Bell said as they steamed past Fire Island.

He let it hang there.

It was not, of course.

As they approached the Ambrose Channel, the *Queen* passed by her first vessel since leaving the convoy days before.

CONEY ISLAND was spelt out along her side.

She was a sludge vessel and sounded her greeting with three lasting blasts of her whistle. This was met with cheers from the crew, cheers soon overcome by the bellow of the *Queen*'s horn deeper and louder.

It was enough to move Bell to take his hand, just for a few seconds, until the *Queen* had finished her call.

There was a romance of a maiden voyage in the air, against the odds.

"She will need a skeleton crew in port," Bell said, back in his tone of confession as they approached Ambrose Light, the final milestone before safety. "I will be in command until the *Aquitania* is ready, I expect."

An order came for Bell to assemble on the bridge.

"Stay with me if you still wish to," Bell said.

"Aye, sur."

He did not see Bell again during the final leg of her maiden voyage. She passed Ambrose Light at seventeen past nine on 7 March. Her arrival had created much commotion among the city's authorities, and her officers were kept busy with the transition. He was put to work on the deck, readying her ropes and chains for porting. A pilot from Long Island navigated her through the Ambrose Channel. City officials were also on board for the occasion, though requests from the press to board were denied. Cunard had said it was because she was unfinished. As he toiled among other seamen on the foredeck for her berthing, he felt fortunate for the success of his stowaway and the fruits his adopted name had borne him so far.

Men grow hard quick in the Clydebank shipyards, he thought.

He had initially wanted to grow hard with them, which had inspired him to persuade his father to take him out on the tender, just to *see* her up close one last time. He had thought he would follow her to Southampton, where the men who finished her could continue their work on him, too. But this journey had carried him to a whole different city of men with a crew unfamiliar and presented him with the opportunity to bend the destiny of his adopted name to his own needs and the vocation forming firm inside him: to tend to the turning of the wood of men further afield.

II

NORMANDIE

He walked the New York docks awaiting his officer. The planks were wet and awash with white-dressed, hard-buttock-ed military men in variations of uniform: French, British and American soldiers standing guard over the world's largest liners, who were seeking shelter there. It turned out, *Aquitania* was not in and *Elizabeth*'s future was still uncertain, so Bell would be reposted to another vessel in the interim. His officer had promised him onward passage with him, but now that he was there, in the New World, away from the war winds and bleakness of the Clydebank dockyards, he felt fine should his officer change his mind. *She* had delivered on hope for that *some place entirely new* and populated by another world of hard men. Should his officer go and he need to stay, the adventure of New York would be welcome. Uncertainty was the condition that the majority of the Cunard crew arrived in to – their futures unknowable. They left *Elizabeth* with their belongings and some urgency in the direction of the company offices. Turner, un-baggage-d down, took the time to walk the docks in his new whites instead, weaving between men-on-patrol. Yet as fine as the men were, it were the iron-marvels-of-men that rose from the water that took his focus. France's SS *Normandie* next to RMS *Queen Mary*, next to his own *Elizabeth.* His *Queen* had come to rest in the company of her own class, waiting, like him, to hear a fate as yet unknown, but somehow, still steely in facing an unset future.

He was not to know this, but by now, her dash across the Atlantic had been covered in all the American papers. The genius of deception of her enemy, being relayed across the world, too. So well-executed, in fact, had been her plan that the day she had left the Clyde and headed north then west for New York, German bombers were already in action. Using the intelligence of their Clydebank spies, they had commenced a campaign of assault on Southampton and its approaches. It had started the day of the *Queen*'s earliest possible arrival and then returned for three days that followed, acting out an assault that she had cleverly set up for them: a cover story that had allowed her to quietly slip away.

Two *Queens* rose before him. It was their first meeting, the first time they had berthed together and already they dared defiance. As two sides of a weekly transatlantic service, they were never intended to meet like this. But this was the dawn of an unordinary decade. He stood between them, looking for difference like a print-maker comparing proofs. More British, he thought about *Mary*, more the ocean liner. His admiration for *Elizabeth* grew as his comparison of their superstructures advanced. Difference was obvious: three to two. The newer *Queen* excelled beyond the familiarity of the three funnel-design in a megaship, he felt, to proffer a more slender, forties proposition. There was an engine-less potential of the two in *Elizabeth*, he thought. Two funnels at the recline (between which he too had reclined). She was the more refined, the more elegant of the two. This elegance was written into her in more subtle regards and in ways that he may not have noticed had they not been docked before him side-by-side. Her bow, he compared, had a greater rake. Her shape was more of an ornate figurehead than a superliner. Even beyond the two-to-three, between them, there was space. Taking cues from *Normandie*, *Elizabeth* sported wide-open, uncluttered sports decks – would he have even been able to recline on *Mary*? *Mary* was a companion, not a twin, a sister, at best, and a clunkier conception, too, an older design, though he may be biased.

His *Queen*, mainly, was cleared of her crew by now. He wandered further along her new docks, his eye moving to its men more, their appetites newly available to him. But the allure of the iron-hulled giants that these men guarded kept drawing him back. His own *Queen* particularly, last seen from this angle at the start of their adventure together – from a Clyde tender. They had endured much, coupled, already, including an Atlantic swell and the after-entry-glow-confessionals of a new lover. One evening in particular returned to him as he walked the docks. Bell – freshly opened up and filled after a tense day in command capacity – had described a communiqué the bridge received from London forbidding press boarding on arrival in New York, and a request of the officers, in all their dealings with the press, to discourage any use of the *Queens*-as-"monsters" moniker in their reporting. But that was what they were, he thought from their base, vastly overwhelmed by their combined and competing sizes. Even the buildings, through which they were boarded and that stood like break walls between them seemed small and un-swell-worthy compared to the crispness of the rivets bolting these ships together. They were fantastical beasts like those of fiction, fabled as being raised from the valleys of the ocean floors. Unfathomable creatures, even when caught and displayed for disbelievers to witness. And yet here they were, three of them, giants of the sea, side-by-side; as if they were the tallest buildings of this city: plucked from the New York skyline and made to lie flat, and most fantastical of all, to float. They were skyscrapers of the sea.

"Turner," came his officer from behind, "follow me."

And away from his *Queen* he was led. Along the dock to Pier 86 and up and into his next appointment in service of Bell. Not into *Aquitania*, as he had expected, but a newer Cunarder – *Mauretania.* A handsome ship, assuredly, though markedly smaller than the three great liners she had berthed beside. Smaller so in fact that he had not noticed her until led in her side. In design, she resembled his *Queen*, more so even than *Mary*. She had two funnels and a streamlined shape: she was a young *Elizabeth*, and though unseen until entering, there was something warming to him about her. No sooner was he in her did Bell start *selling* her to him. 'She was the first Cunard White Star ship, you know,' he said on his tour, 'and the replacement of her namesake – that legend who snatched and retained the Blue Riband for 19 years, held from 1909 to 1929, the longest on record. She is the largest ship ever built in England and was built for the London to New York service. Especially, to fill in for the Queens whenever they were being maintained.' Bell's history came through as a justification, a gilded brochure, even, for the drafting of him into joining him on a lesser vessel – a Cunard mediumship. Inside, she was finely furnished, finished to the highest standard. But he actually preferred the harder edge of *Elizabeth*, which still showed the graft of men.

She was already painted in her war greys, which was a start, and he noticed guns affixed to her deck as well, but while a sweet thing, his attractions remained – elsewhere. Regarding *Elizabeth*, she was to remain laid up in New York, unfinished. In the press coverage of her arrival, one masthead read: "*Queen Elizabeth* arrives! Her safe harbor for the duration of the war." What truth there was in this, he could not know. But while she awaited reassignment in port, she continued her hold over him, like a magnetic mine, tease-repulsed degaussing about her hull. He felt her pull, tempting him to her under hull, to bunk down in her and wait it out, for a resolution to her future and a chance to join her in it. Yet such impulses were madness, he reasoned with himself. Bell had thrown him a lifeline by developing a compulsion for Turner-intrusion into him, and with the assignment to *Mauretania*, had extended his prospects for adventure – however smaller a vessel she might be.

"You'll stay beside me...," Bell panted during sex on their first night back at sea, their bodies rolling, entwined again in the open Atlantic. "You'll stay...*in*side me."

He edged deeper *in* on the second plead from his officer, holding and building there. The move was met with a grimace and a gasp, then a grin, legs wrapping around his waist to ease even further onto him. He grabbed his officer by the scruff of his neck and aligned him until they were eye-to-eye. Then, *turning* himself inside him, he replied:

"Aye, sur."

His *Mauretania* duties had commenced with immediate effect – ferrying the Chief Officer messages, along with his Member. It was a step up in articles that Bell had arranged and one that necessitated him being kept close at hand, by his side for most of the day, and into the nights, too. The arrangement fed the appetite for him within his officer and was an agreeable arrangement to him, too, for the most part. With his officer's hunger also grew complications borne out of newfound dependences. His unusual rise through the ranks had not gone unquestioned in the smoke room gatherings of his now-on-par-with shipmates. Sharp-tongued sentiments were relayed to him by the low rank seamen of his former stowaway-station, who had few qualms themselves with his ascent, as it had little direct impact on them. Working seamen had a seasoned nonchalance about the inequalities of promotion at sea. They were well-accustomed to officer-class appointments coming without a clear raison d'être or deserve. But the other officers had been less accepting, feeling passed over by the new boy in the realm of proper protocols for progression through the ranks. He found such annoyances of the officer classes amusing, having little interest in climbing the seafarer ladder himself. One consequence of his companionship with Bell he did mind, however, was the limits it placed on his pursuit of other prospects – as an incident from his two weeks of in-port *Mauretania* service had shown him.

Normandie, of the French line *Compagnie Générale Transatlantique*, had been berthed left of the two *Queens*. Streamlined like *Elizabeth* but achieved through a three-funnelled design – in fact, Cunard spies, it was said, drew from *Normandie*'s sleek triumphs for a chic British design. All her funnels reclined and fuller than any others in her company and boasting a bulbous bow. She had the formation of the French about her that made *Mary*, her chief competition, appear stiff-upper-lipped by comparison. She was aesthetically alluring, and he felt an attraction to her during his time in the New York docks, as he did toward the men who served her. Since the commencement of his officer duties, whenever sent off-ship – to relay a message or retrieve an item from *Elizabeth* – he took time to watch them, the men guarding *Normandie*. Like the other liners docked alongside her, she was a refugee in the New World. But in the bodies of her men, he observed something further: signs of a sublime symbol of liberty and beauty, like the statue she had passed in reaching this safe harbour and her countrymen had bestowed. She was French, and as yet, he had not experienced the sensation of Frenchmen. But from the first days in port watching them, he wanted to. Like the smooth lines of hull they stood to watch over, need for the sensation of Frenchmen-on-him seemed sowed into the softness of the trousers of those standing guard.

Working above the dock guards, on her deck, were her crew, also with delicate lines...and peachy behinds – ripe in tight Continental clothing. The crème of these boys revealed their feminine form in the dock bar, named 'Liner Lane'. In peacetime, Liner Lane served alcoholic alchemy to its privileged patronage, which consisted, particularly, of feather-hatted and tweed-tied passengers, sipping to the sight of ships, comparing their choice of transport ahead of their *bon voyage*. But the onset of war put a stop to transatlantic pleasure travel. Cocktail menus were shelved as Liner Line turned its talents to a new trade: the crews of Cunard White Star, *Compagnie Générale Transatlantique*, *Italia Flotta Riunite* and others with ships currently in port, who debated just as hard the virtues of their lines and flagship vessels – bolstered by beer instead of brandy, and with seamen slurs in place of pleasantries. Though the bar's location in the French-line corridor did help stem the rough somewhat, and ensured a steady Frenchmen flow. Occasions for him to slip into Liner Lane – or 'Porthole', as she became known by the rougher docker trade – were slim. Bell kept him and his Member on tight-tender. And having his chambers alongside Bell's on the officers' deck of *Mauretania*, well, it did not help. Through the nights it was not uncommon for Bell to call by and require further services of him; trial and error over the two weeks of their docking taught him that his best mode of giving his officer the slip was to delay his evening seeding until Bell was first full of drink. The pressures of high office took their toll, particularly in wartime toiling, and the later he visited, the more likely he was to encounter a liquored-up first officer.

The later into the evening that he delivered his rapidly-into-him repetitions, the more his officer tended to talk to him, too. Talk was about his home life, about his wife, about the boy of his own blood, and the pressures these placed on the role he found himself in servitude to. And the more Bell talked, the more he tended to stress and sip at drink drawn out of a crystal decanter into a cut crystal glass from his private bar. When he sat quietly, listening, then took his officer later into lament, he found Bell looser for the taking – a *Lus-i-tania* to torpedo. And the louder in his unloading into him. But also, this schedule of later-into-the-candle-burning seduction of his officer offered advantages for a slip-off-ship – as Bell was more likely to stay bedded after. He still enjoyed the taking of his officer, assuredly. And was willing to remain *in* service, for sure. But he also enjoyed the freedom to leave afterwards and to seek out pleasures, among others. By the twilight of their second week in port, he felt he had mastered the art of the stealthy fill and slip-away. Each time, for the occasion, he would leave his officer to sleep, freshly seeded. Then, he would head down *Mauretania*'s gangway and into Porthole. By the time of his arrival, new-day merriment had invariably set in among the men. As the time 'til dawn drew closer, and they brimmed themselves with drink, debates over which line was superior became more impassioned. The Frenchmen of *Compagnie Générale Transatlantique* built a case for *Normandie* that was based around her capturing the Blue Riband for the fastest Atlantic crossing on her maiden voyage. The Brits countered with *Mary*'s record, the current Riband holder, and likely to remain so for some time.

As was his way, he did not weigh, went in with a longer want-game. Instead, he joined the bar late, with a fresh beer intake against an average of at least tenfold more among the others assembled. Men were easier to move around to man-sex in this state, he knew. He was also seasoned enough to never target the beautiful or dainty ones – those that would likely have pursued sex with him even without drinks down. Each of the nights he had managed to slip into Porthole, he had found one or two, or in one particularly officious occasion, three – volleyed between them along the docks like a lad's mag passed among randy chums – from the assembled for a drunken dalliance down by the mooring ties. But the *incident-in-question* – the inward *encounter* that drew now his reflection from a present Atlantic position on *Mauretania* – occurred on the night before their outward heading. He, flushed with the fruitful achievements of the preceding evenings, turned talents to commandeering the head of the French crew's bar-flies, the roughest and manliest of the lot. The other Frenchmen called him *Taureau*, French for 'bull', and it was true, he was bullish. Square-jawed and ugly, with a broken nose, a boxer's nose, and built big in each direction. 'Taureau' was a beast of a man. What rank he held in the hierarchy of *Normandie*, he did not know, and frankly, this was of little consequence. He lusted only after the bulk of the beast standing among the sweat and smoke of seamen in Porthole, where the bull was King.

Determined to get a taste of the beast and feeling time as against him, he arrived late following the filling of his officer and took up a place at the corner of the bar – to wait. As candles on the tables along the glass front of Porthole reached their end and snuffed out one by one, so too did the patrons, filing from the bar and back to ships stuck in port. One by one until Taureau was all who remained. Already, sky was starting to warm with the embers of the encroaching dawn. The beast bore down on him over the beers of his fallen *amis* – and that he now finished for them. Some of his fallen *ami* remained hunched and out in the bar. Struck down, softly snoring, enjoying their spoils.

"What you stareng at, boy?"

There was genuine interest from the beast, to whom he would have appeared as no threat.

"Nothing, sur," he said, no break in his stare.

The bar curved out over the docks, bringing all in port into view, *Normandie*, as jewel of the French line, in best vantage. Like watchmen posted at opposite wings of an observation deck, they searched each other, lit by the few candles that remained ablaze at their stub, and with a growing glow from outside, the Porthole offering a salt-stained view of the world of New York dock life. Scars on the bull's face were illuminated, being explored by light, like valley crags gaining definition-cum-dawn. When Taureau downed the final glasses before him and left the bar, he followed. Down onto the docks, past *Mary* to Pier 88 and up into *Normandie*. She was guarded, of course, by Americans mostly, but the beast was not questioned. And nor was he; he was so close in tow that beast odour was all he could smell, no trace of even the smog of the city at their feet. He stuck close like a pilot fish, ready to feed off the body of the shark he straddled. Inside *Normandie* was alive with Frenchmen and apparently untouched by war-purpose conversion, but the path the beast chose...it took them both deep into *Normandie*'s bowels, away from the French stewards. Deck upon deck upon deck, the beast descended, like a predator big fish into the crevices of a shipwreck, searching for – or *luring* – prey. All the way to her turbines, and through a bulkhead and into a cramped office. Taureau struck suddenly, spinning and grasping him by the neck, tugging him off the floor and against the iron wall of her hull, riveting him there.

"What you went, boy?"

Gripped at the neck, he lowered his eyes to the V formation below his beast's waist:

"La bite, monsieur."

He had no great competency for French but was well-versed in the currency of cock.

The beast bore into him with sharp, narrow, untiring eyes – his breath, beer-full and putrid sweet. With as swift a motion as the first strike, Taureau had him spun around, his pants and briefs torn aside, beast cock-tip coated with spit, and then bored into him. His vision blurred with the violence of the beast's entry, which came without preparation or eased-in penetration. Breathing was broken, too. Difficult. With the beast still holding him – by the neck, off the floor, against the inside of the hull. The office in which he was taken by the beast was cramped and cluttered. It would have been easily forgotten in a ship of her proportions. As Taureau bore on, the grip on his neck tightened, his cheek clamped against the cold iron. The crushing of bone seemed only a slight degree of pressure away. But, by now, in the proceedings, the pain of the abrupt entry began to subside. His vision began to clear as his body came out of the shock and into agreement – with the beast's tide rhythm. When he could see again, the sex spectacle was shown to him through a grubby mirror opposite.

He was beautiful, he saw. Brunette, young, cheeks flushed red and growing redder. Blood in the water. In this presentation, he could see his own allure: the way he thrashed with the thrusts of the beast into him, his tight body breaking through the tears in his clothing, and involuntary tears from his eyes. The beast's beating made him more beautiful, more purposeful. The sex was brutal, his neck already pooling purple beneath the hand that gripped him. But by bringing him close to breaking, the beast performed the role he had laid out for it, like a mythical, too-large-below centaur bending to a path laid out by the fates. *His* beast was big and brilliant, like all the drunken men of the Clyde dockyards stitched together: a scarred, angry, monster amalgamation of a man.

And then the tide went out.

The beast withdrew, both his *bite* and his binding, leaving him to land as a lump of bones and bruised flesh at the predator's scraps-heap. At first, Taureau rose his boot, apparently for a kick, but stopped short – with a look himself through the mirror.

Does he see what I see?

Taureau decided to spit on him instead, then retreated back into his ship's corridors, leaving him to find his own way back to his Cunard liner, Frenchman hate-spit on his split lip, just as her engines were being warmed and work was getting underway for her voyage from New York that evening. His new maiden, his smaller Queen, was bound for Australia, where her finery would be overlaid with functionality, and she would get outfitted as a troop carrier – or so he had heard. Much promise was knotted to this prospect: of a destination of southern men, though an increase over the power of the *Normandie* penetration would be impossible for him to endure.

He limped to *Mauretania* with relieved self-loathing for the danger-fuck he had courted.

Having promised to stay beside him, *in*side him, he remained on the bed with Bell – he on his back, him on his stomach. Heavy rain had helped her slip out of New York unobserved, and these same conditions now battered her in an Atlantic storm. He watched with a feeling of aroused accomplishment, the wet downy fluff along the curve of Bell's arse mounds, a trail of his seed disappearing into the fold toward a well run-in hole, fragrant with the musk of a new-to-this man being fucked. If they stayed on together much longer that evening, he could see himself going in for a top-up. That was until Bell started tracing *his* body, with a light touch, across the long purples and blacks about his neck, hovering on the blood-split of his bottom lip, down to the bruises dotted across his thighs, where the beast had pried him open – movements that ended his wish to reseed.

"Will you tell me what happened?" Bell said, back at his neck again, his hand-span far short of the beast's.

He was not comfortable or accustomed to talking with his officer this way. They would often speak *beforehand*, as a lead up to a filling, but scarcely would utterances come in the afterglow. This time was reserved for cigarettes, sometimes sleep, or more often a return to respective rooms, as the itch had been scratched and reality set in. Never was this time for him to explain himself.

"Na, sur," he said.

It was his first time denying his officer; the line of questioning was out of character. And when Bell continued to trace him, in an apparent search for some rhyme to the reason for rough treatment, the interaction became out of line as well. He left the bed and started to dress. *Mauretania* was smaller than *Elizabeth*, smaller by far; it gave her a greater roll in the Atlantic swell and made dressing more difficult. Bell watched intently as he struggled to re-attire, his eyes tracing buttocks especially, with bruise spots that disappeared into the crevasse in which his still-ruinous arsehole resided, again from where the beast had opened him up. He could not make sense of the looks he was being given. Not judgement, nor jealousy, even. *A longing?* Whatever its intention, it made him uncomfortable, turned his attention to elsewhere in the cabin while he finished redressing.

Bell had little in the way of decoration. *Mauretania* was a complete, functioning liner, and so, the officer accommodations were already decorated with Cunard apparel complete with end-finery that, for *Elizabeth*, was in storage some where. All the comforts of the executive officer class, such as a bar and solid wood furniture, were present and accounted for. And Bell had unpacked his own keepsakes, his compass, and journal, and books. He was an ordered man, neat. Clean. Each item had its place and its purpose. And were laid out precisely as they had been on the *Queen* as if having his *keepsakes being just-so* was a means of keeping a home at sea. There was a scent of boot polish and brandy to his cabin. It spoke too to this clean and ordered nature. And all of his *Elizabeth* items were there, save some photographs. Of his wife, he just realised, of his own boy, of them together. These were missing. He searched the room for them as he finished buttoning up, just to be sure, and as an excuse to avoid forensic eyes on him and his intimate bruises.

They *were* gone.

"Goodnight, sur," he said once he was done, making for the door.

Bell stopped him with an urgent call from the bed.

"I would do anything for you," he blurted.

He stopped, the door open, halfway out.

"I love you, Olli."

He felt suddenly sick.

Unable to return to his room aside Bell, he fled into the recesses of the smaller-than-familiar ship instead. Though he had been aboard her for two weeks by this point, he had not yet had the opportunity to explore her nightlife – the dockside boys having proved too enticing a pull prior ship-off. This night, her first at sea, in a strong swell, he found the sway of her course hard to sync with. He bumped along her corridors like a ball sent at a queer angle down an alleyway; ill-co-ordination of which was not helped by his own lack of sleep and general throbbing soreness from the beast – the brutality of his embrace that would take some time to heal. A meander through *Mauretania*'s corridors led him to a first-class bar on A deck. Though *Mauretania*'s mission still involved risk, there was not the urgency of direction that had clouded the *Queen*'s transatlantic dash, and *Mauretania*'s completed state came with certain advantages, such as stocked bars and fully outfitted recreation areas. She still ran on a skeleton crew, though, which kept the stewards below deck in the kitchens, unavailable to man the passenger bars. This confined the rest-of-crew to their own bars, none of which he was keen on frequenting that night, fearing a run-in with Bell. It was late, well into the early hours of a new day, and the promise of helping himself to a quiet drink in an unmanned bar on the first night at sea held particular appeal for him. Lights were on low, in line with the wartime blackout rules. The bar appeared empty, even as he touched the surface where drinks were served, until a voice out of vision told him otherwise.

"Hullo again."

It was the queer steward, smart enough in appearance, probably handsome back in the day, but more a dried-up fruit now, with skin too soft and oily and being someone he would always avoid.

"Awright," turning to leave.

"Fancy a drink?"

This *man* had known, somehow, that he was *Elizabeth*'s stowaway, and while that still could harm him, he did now enjoy some protection, on a new ship, in a more senior role...a tonic right there to the Bell debacle. In alternate logic, after the confusion of his departing conversation with Bell, having a drink with the one man who could test the level of protection he had attained since their first encounter, well, it actually intrigued him and might help with the unease of it all.

"Lik' what?"

"Martinis," he said, pulling down two slim and tall Y glasses from above the bar.

He nodded. He had never had a martini before but had enough knowledge to know it was a stiffener. Swinging a bar towel over his shoulder, the steward set to work assembling utensils. The bar workspace was lit with a row of candles. Their flames tilted with the swaying of the ship like lanterns on a deep-sea trawler.

"Vodka or gin?" steward asked.

He shrugged, sitting up at the bar, grimacing slightly when pressure hit his bruised arse and healing hole-lips. There was a mirror behind; it picked up the colouring along his neck in the candlelight, and beyond that were hints of the void of the vast Atlantic, swaying – the night sky picking out the whites of its swell.

"I prefer vodka," steward said.

Steward scooped ice into the glasses to chill them and retrieved vermouth and spirit from the wall behind him, stealing glimpses of his guest and his bruises as he did.

"Turner, isn't it?"

"Aye."

He considered whether to add a 'sir', but decided against it. This meeting was an opportunity for him to test the parameters of his new role on a different ship, to make him feel better.

"Who urr ye?"

The steward seemed amused by his directness.

"White," he said. "Edward White."

Steward seemed to be assessing the situation too and how to tread ahead with his new acquaintance.

"I'm Chief Steward," he said as liquids were poured into the cocktail shaker.

"Aye."

"And you are?"

"Olli."

"Olli, I take my martini dirty," he said, "is that agreeable to you?"

"Aye, ah suppose."

White finished their drinks, serving them up with a flourish, stacked olives in each as a garnish. He slid one in front of his guest and took the other for himself.

"So," White said, holding his glass forward, "you're Robert's boy."

He brought their glasses to meet, the clink carrying through the otherwise empty bar. It was in contrast to the crashing of the sea outside and tasted sharp, dry, sour. Heavy.

"Aye, ah suppose."

"He's a good man, Robert," White said as if the statement served as a toast. "A family man."

"Is he?"

He took back more; it was easier on subsequent sips.

"Oh yes," White said, leaning across the bar.

White pulled an olive off his cocktail stick with his teeth, then returned the spike with olives, still stacked, to his drink for a swirl, all while reclined across the bar. Actions like this marked the bar-serve as unmanly, unable to pass among men, he thought.

"I've known Robert since he was a boy," White said, playing with his drink, settling in for the story. "He came to *Aquitania* twenty years ago for her return to passenger travel after the Great War. He would have been about your age then, though perhaps somewhat less...," picking another olive, "worldly. His father was high up in the Admiralty. Even higher up now. There was especial expectation placed on his performance in the fleet. *Aquitania*, the Cunard flagship, with a valiant war record to boot, was fertile ground for Robert to prove himself. And he did...for the most part."

There was gloat to his story style. Like White viewed him as a schoolboy in for tutorage. Carrying this same downward address, White recalled Bell's early years as a junior officer on *Aquitania*, with anecdotes of how he had proved his worth. White savoured his martini as he told the tale, eating an olive for points of note within the story, such as when he explained that *Aquitania* bore the future of the Cunard line on her shoulders, being, in the opening years of the '20s, Cunard's only large liner.

"*Mauretania*, you see, not this one," White said, swinging his arms in a gesture to their current vessel as he chewed his last olive, "the *first*

Mauretania, she was laid up after a fire," downing his drink. "Another?"

"Aye," he said, emptying his glass too.

The story of his officer's service and rise through the ranks on *Aquitania* continued for three more martinis each, much more than both their limits.

"He'a married young-en," White said, on the last of their cocktails, "this were a duty, too. But he a good man. He is loyal, this man."

White held his glass to his lips, missing a little, spirit-wetting his suit.

"Don't hurt him," White said in first clarity this drink, downing the final third of his fourth martini.

White's eyes came to rest on the marks pressed into his neck. Where the charging bull had failed to pierce skin. White succeeded with his stare: seeing the marks for what they were. Regardless of his youth, of the violence marked upon him, White, it unnerved him to think, could – even in his cloud of olive-flavoured martinis – *see* him and his situation exactly as it was. He left what remained of his own drink there and the bar, White not breaking his gaze upon him. On his way back to his cabin, he noticed that Bell's door was ajar. He left it that way, left him – though after a pause –, returning to his own room instead, and to sleep.

His bruising lightened briskly in the Atlantic sea air in the days that followed. And as it did. As the traces of foreign fingers faded from his neck, the routine returned with his officer. Yet, the drink with White had struck somewhere within him, too. It solidified a sense of duty beyond the sexual needs of his officer. He found himself, quite to his surprise, wanting to serve Bell's career as well, to protect his good name. His promotion to Bell's boy had been unfair, yes. A pure carnal appointment of face value only. He had felt fine with that, liked it, in fact. But it was also an appointment made at particular personal risk to Bell, for whose fortunes he had started to care. Surely, at the least, his duty now extended to the safeguarding of his officer. Safe from any negative consequence of having supported him and their extravagance in the first place, he reasoned. And, propelled as he had been that first week into what life was like for an officer – including the workings of a ship-at-sea-during-wartime – along with the pressures this entailed, he now realised that Bell's sex with him was a necessary outlet.

Don't hurt him.

White's words returned to him in waves over the first seven days of their southward journey, en route to Bermuda. They were dogged each day by packs of U-boats. Stalked, and without the speed nor singular-course-bearing of the *Queen*. In ferrying the Admiralty-warning messages to Bell, where he charted new courses, then forwarding these in turn to their captain, who was not of the calibre of the *Queen*'s, he came to appreciate the ramifications of Bell's role; and his own, in keeping him sane. During the day, it was down to Bell to evade German wolf pack submariners. Standing on deck with the lookouts and guns manned, the horizon bobbing in and out of view, with the Atlantic swell and spray across him, Bell was unsure how long their new course would hold before word would come of the enemy being back on tow and he would need to recourse, or worse, face a hit if word was not received in time. Against this backdrop, he saw his officer as a stronghold of duty, a lion at sea. But at night, when Bell finally retired and turned over duties to his second officer, there was softness again.

It was his '*real*' role, because it was only when unloading into First Officer Bell, opened up on his bed – or among the changing, pencilled-over ordinances of the charts room, door bolted; or behind chains on a hidden corner of the deck; or wherever it might be – that Bell was able to recover. As if taking in of a part and essence of his lover was the elixir releasing stresses of the sea. As if it were the only wartime tonic that, once inside him, brought on a release of breath. The taking down of family photos from his private space was, he now realised, his officer's way of showing the importance of this real role for him. Mixed into the resumption of their routine was the pouring of an occasional White cocktail, which was where he heard of Bell's past and rise through the peacetime ranks.

"Prohibition brought the Americans to Cunard," White recalled one night out of port from Bermuda after Turner had put his officer to bed, full and fulfilled. "And they brought with them jazz and the martini. I worked the bar in those days, so the need for me to learn how to mix *these*," he said, with a swish of drink, "was paramount. And a taste for them has stuck with me since."

White's story of those days stretched over the next two drinks as well and segued into more serious territory.

"Prohibition saves Cunard," he said matter-of-factly, though in-fog, amid their third cocktail, "and *Aquitania*, he saves too. Wartime austerity followed by immigration quotas, these had decimated the transatlantic trade, you see. So we could offer our passengers a stiff drink! At a time when their own liners were unable! – believe me, it saved us, was what got us through."

White would often end their drinks with a cautionary tale, a proclamation of protectionism for 'Robert' the man, and that night was no different.

"Even so," White continued, "the loss of that immigrant trade by quotas shrunk our crew numbers by a third, putting many of us out of a livelihood, and out of these conditions emerged many *desperate men*."

White paused on this last point, raising his glass and waiting. For emphasis or response, he was unsure. There was a knowingness about the way he had said it, though. In fact, knowingness had crept into White's cocktail talks increasingly. The passing of each drink naturally freed White to make plain his view. This growing knowingness of tone told Turner that the nature of his arrangement with Bell was well known to his martini maker. It was implied in the way White spoke and became less cloaked as the cocktails rolled out. It never quite reached the surface, however, or the arena of becoming outrightly spoken about. It bobbed just below the break of open air, like a rock shelf on the edge of an island at high water. White's cautionary manner made him recall the first night they met, when the steward confessed to knowing what it is like to run away from something. White, he was beginning to realise, did not mean running in a literal capacity. He meant an action more understated than that, a symbolic stowaway, a need to be hidden, to run away from the truth of himself, to hold himself back. He thought that was it, anyway.

Because, he thought, swirling his hypothesis along with his drink, letting some flamboyance flow into his hand, *it was only by hiding that the likes of him would be get by.*

White would never be elusive to others in the way he, and now Bell, had managed to be.

It was necessary for men like him, he thought, for those with something *queer about them*, to keep running.

White would never pass in the company of men, he believed; White's only hope was that men would tolerate him, and this only applied to certain stations: as a bartender, as a steward, as a womanly man.

He can't conceal the way I can, he concluded as he neared the end of their drinks. Questioning whether, perhaps, he should stop calling by, he weighed up, too, with a booze-full belly, whether he would pop in on his officer for a manly, fully passable refill before retiring.

"Beware desperate men!" White broke through, bringing his glass to the bar with stem-testing force.

It intruded upon his thoughts, White speaking loudly, clear and commanding. As if intuition was there for something of the substance of his thinking. *Was it a warning about a particular something to come or an urge to just be seen for once*? He did not know.

"I was on *Aquitania* for the Great War," White said, clarity continued.

Sobered up? Or, maybe, were earlier slurs a deception? His own fog made sense of it difficult.

"Robert was not," White went on. "He was there for the challenges of migration quotas as a too-young officer class boy. Still, damaging effects of these challenges were curbed by prohibition and our American clientele. Plus, the sway of his father satisfied by his recent marriage to an eligible woman helped him. But now, in another war, something is brewing, and Robert is changing. You've joined us, but look around you and ask yourself: who else is here from the *Elizabeth*? Count them. How many failed to re-sign with Cunard? Which fortunate few on the new *Mauretania* – you and I and Robert included among them – managed to make this voyage, to get articles while the *Elizabeth* remains in limbo? And who was passed over for your articles? Know that they will, count on it, be remembering this. Most aboard this ship are strangers to me; they joined us two days before we set sail, they came from *Aquitania*. And all these men will, you can be sure, be having minds that are directed already beyond this voyage. Minds on to Sydney and where they might sign next. For fresh in them too will be the men from their previous assignment who did not re-sign. And already, trust me, they will be looking to the crew they now find themselves among for weaknesses within. And while you might feel protected as 'Bell's-boy', that could mean destruction for you both."

White's last drinks' ideas lingered with him as if a soliloquy from his own quivering lips. He did not know what to make of it. It was a truly remarkable delivery, given the level of alcohol they had each consumed. A triumphant tirade of clarity. *Jealousy*? Yes. That was obvious. That was comfortable. But there was more to it than that, he thought. He downed his drink on "both" and left without a further word. And decided, yes, he would call in on Bell tonight, who had left his door ajar for him...again. And once he had filled the first officer, with another topping upon topping, he decided, quite despite himself, to bolt Bell's cabin door and to stay the night in his bed. Was it because, perhaps, and he felt weakened in thinking it, that there was a warning in White's words?

The North Atlantic proved relentlessly risky. Even the brief Bermuda refuel offered little relief. But change was on the horizon – as the packs of U-boat squadrons thinned and the waters warmed. With the Caribbean came calm, reprieve even. And in Panama, a feeling of getting away from the worst of it settled in. *Mauretania* passed through the Panama Canal on 27 March 1940, being only a man's breadth on either side small enough to achieve it. Bell had him on the gun deck with him for the thread through. It was the first time in daylight that Bell was away from his charts and the blacked-out portholes of his cabin. The canal, like *Mauretania* herself, was a marvel of man – though a sliver snug for the modern liners. It rose on each of her sides, encasing them like the miraculous passage of Moses through the Red Sea that flows through the other great canal, the Suez – only this time it was the land that was tamed. She was so large through there that the canal walls were close to fingertip distance away at some points. The air was warm, the sky blue, and for the first time since New York, the ship was sheltered, its grey not necessary. More importantly, from his view, Bell seemed relaxed, sheltered, too. Bell even moved his hand to touch the side of Turner's thigh. And as much as White's words remained with him, he too took the chance to touch, running his hand down the small of Bell's back, to rest on the peachy crest of his behind.

Feeling his arse there, the canal walls stretching above them, casting shadows as they passed through a part the sun could not reach, he took the chance to take their on-deck intimacy further: tracing his way to and then beneath the band of Bell's pants. With his central finger, like an arrow, he slid down through the fold of Bell's cheeks to his target, still moist from that morning's filling, then circled the entrance, telling him and his hole that it would be needed again. There. Now. In the shade of the first reprieve they had had since New York, he would take advantage of the distraction of the rest of the crew under the command of the captain, and help loosen up his officer, help his rest, by venturing into him, boldly, with fresh ammo from their position on the gun deck. Decided on his course of action, he knew they would need to be swift. He withdrew his middle finger – already to where it branched off from the hand by this point, and cream-coated, like Bell's bottom, was a sweet custard pie. He put his finger to and into his mouth, tasting salt of himself there – warm and musky from its place inside Bell. Then, he gestured for Bell to get down. He had expected resistance to the suggestion, but Bell obeyed – without even a look around to check they were clear. Lying on his back, his knees at 45 degrees without needing to be instructed, Bell was unflinching in his obedience, awaiting further direction. This was their boldest manoeuvre yet. Their brassiest bucking of gross indecency yet. Bell's trust in him was absolute, leaving him to question himself. He had tested his officer, and this was a self-test: was penetration in the Panama passage worth risking exposure?

Worth the gamble, he decided, dropping between Bell's legs, sliding both hands beneath his officer, and taking tight hold of the band of his pants.

"Ready, sur," he said, their noses touching, his officer's whole body trembling atop his grip.

Bell nodded, intense eye-contact, like a recruit to a trainer before a daring leap of military danger.

And with his go-ahead, he pulled. Pants and underwear came down, over Bell's arse, around the bend of his knees. The garment ended in a bunch at the tongues of black Bell boots.

"'ere we go, sur," he said with a smile.

With Bell's underwear, pants and boots bound by a one-fisted bunch, he rose his officer up by the ankles, up and over in one eighty-degree motion, so that Bell's feet came to rest back on the iron deck over his head. Bell folded open out like an accordion; a sweet sight it was: his face flushed as it had been on the first occasion of their sex, when contorted into positions the married father had never before imagined. But on this occasion of succumbing to another man's will, awe replaced surprise as *his* Bell came along for the ride, marvelling at Turner, too: pilot of his arse rise; up into the Panama sky, higher and higher, and holding at 90 degrees; just for a moment, at the tipping point, like that famous of all tragic Atlantic liners before the end. Then, movement again, brought Bell all the way to the floor once more, completing the rotation up and over himself. Bell's folded body blocked out the northern blue of the Caribbean sky as once again he had him pulled into position. Bell's neck was at its acutest, his face completely covered. White and black, shirt and jacket, was all that could be seen of his head space. Bell's weight on the crown of his head, against the wet iron of the gun deck. Especially vulnerable, poised to break.

He had not intended to bend Bell all the way over...but he opened out with such ease, and with Bell's body taking his direction as well as it did, he could not help himself by feeding his own fascination for a man who seemed devoted to him. And so he continued to fold, even now: to see whether Bell would come to a limit, reach a point where he would take his trust away. But that point did not come, and Bell's bundle arched a full half-circle. Holding Bell by his feet to the iron, seeing the strain it was taking on his officer's neck, but without complaint, he realised there were no limits. From here, he could have continued to push, flattened Bell's body curve until his neck gave way utterly. He had his trust, true trust, and he held it by the bunched trousers of ankles.

Don't hurt him.

He released Bell-limbs, holding onto only his bundle of pants and briefs. Bell's legs splayed out, releasing the pressure on his neck, helping him breathe again. He pinned Bell's pant bundle to the iron with his foot, allowing the material to flex. Bell sprung back some degrees. Still tied to his moorings, but his body now permitted to bob. Bell's shoulders taking more of the weight. He slid his hands from Bell's hips and down to armpits, collecting upper clothing as he went and curling it for cushioning around Bell's neck and chin, bringing Bell comfort and returned sight-line of the spectacle.

"That better, sur?" he said having finished his adjustments.

Bell smiled and nodded, as much as he now could, bobbing on his anchor like a joyous puppet on rubber strings. He stood to admire his work. He grazed a thumb over Bell's lips, first those near the ground, then those up in the air – then he licked his thumb as if in a gesture of checking the wind or turning a page. Both Bell-ends responded to his touch, like a fishing float, quaking with the nibble but anticipating the bite – more. Sailor shouts further along the ship brought him back to his surrounds, and ahead he could see an end in sight for the canal. At his feet, Bell remained unfazed. Trusting. Satisfied with his handiwork. He stepped over Bell, keeping one foot on his moorings, the other coming to rest behind his head, mindful of his servicing stance. It was a unique angle, Bell side-on between his legs. Bell's own legs and manhood jiggled with the wind and rumble of the ship. He opened the front of his own pants to release his tool of entry; it pleased him to see traces of himself inside his passive spread of a superior officer, dribbling there, which had the benefit of rendering him a ready source to slick up himself for reentry. The angle of reentry required considerable downward bending on his behalf. To steady Bell's bouncing, he took hold of his officer's meat from its root, sack included, tugging it up in such a way that the eye of Bell's manhood looked skyward. Once lined up with his officer's port, he slid in: a sensation of coming home.

Bell's gripped meat, grasped like a labour front worker would a bunch of wheat, continued in its service as a stick he used to keep the action in line, and was an expanding force in his hand as the frequency of his own meat insertions increased. With them, frictions lessened, like the well-greased piston of an internal combustion engine reaching speed. Bell grew to a size that his palm – with fingers at full extension – could barely hold. Bell hardened in his hand, his engorged steering stick straining in its current configuration. Bell's mouth widened, too, in unison with his hole as the hammering went on, layered in such a way that, from Turner's vantage, and with metronomic pumps into his officer, it seemed like he was reaching all the way to his mouth as well. In their sessions, Bell often finished fast, sometimes with even further finishes before he was ready to fill him even once. But this time, it did not take long. The need to fill *his* Bell was everything, with the chance of exposure-disgrace coupled there, too. Well, it meant nothing but a quick finish would do.

"Finish, with, me," he said in breathless bursts, withdrawing to stop himself from spilling over before Bell.

The sight of his tool, slick and pulsing, nearing the point of shooting forth, was enough to bring Bell to his finishing point as well, with a forget-himself cry as he did. Ready for it, he directed Bell's aim so that each wad was targeted toward the curves of his own arse, where it trailed to pool atop his opening, worked enough into recession to allow some of the seed to seep straight in. He allowed himself to tip over, too, adding his own seed to the mix, binding them together in a lovers' pact. Bell needed no encouragement; with each pump of seed onto his lips, he widened then sealed, yawning open, drinking in them both in grateful, glutinous gulps.

"I love you, too," he said, as Bell took in the last trace of their pact.

III

MAURETANIA

Mauretania left the Balboa district of Panama at 1 am on 27 March 1940. She sailed under a full tropical moon into the Pacific, with only her riding lights showing. It would be nine days until she would next reach port. He found peace with his love partner in the Pacific. Bell had time to take in training him, and he took well to the mathematics of navigation; he also, in turn, upped his officer-opening-up tutorage, Bell's bending benefiting from the balmy nights. They took full advantage of the various no-passenger provisions that a half-empty luxury liner could offer two officer lovers. Below her decks, deep-in-her-hull, hideaway options were bountiful, too, giving him the proper scope to put Bell through his sea trials. *Mauretania* matured their bond; he still visited White for martinis, but Bell gave him his Robert history. And over those glorious Pacific days, they sketched out a future for themselves. *Mauretania* would bunker in Honolulu before her onward passage to Sydney for refitting. There, he would continue his service of his officer in the Cunard line but join a different ship – Bell had made the arrangement in advance via telegram, he was told. As lovers, it was decided that they would settle on *Aquitania*, Bell's belle, who had been saved by war from the scrapyard to once again carry troops. War, it seemed, had brought them together, and how potently poetic that *Aquitania* would see they stayed that way.

Honolulu, however, had other plans.

"You should be with me, by my side," Bell said as he had his bow tie finished by his junior-lover officer's hand. "Perhaps if you came along, father wou–"

"Na, Robert. Have yer meal wi' yer faither, 'n' tell me about it efter. Ah can amuse myself. And," pressing his palms to Bell's chest, kissing him, "ye'r done."

"You're still a mystery to me," Bell said, sizing up the sharpness of the bow in the mirror. "For someone so young..."

He touched Bell's arse, still warm where he had planted seed, less than an hour before. It was a gesture to keep the tone light.

"Aff ye go," he said with a squeeze of Bell cheek.

They parted ways on A deck. He tracked his officer's descent of the gangway, pleased when Bell glanced back toward him for the turn onto the Hawaii harbour dock. The tropical red over a mountain-scape Honolulu at sundown made him miss Robert as he blacked into silhouette, to be stopped partway along the pier by two other shapes.

"Spectacular isn't it," White said, joining him at the railing.

"Aye."

"Come on," White said, "I'll buy you a drink."

White was not someone he would publicly drink with, be seen with, socially. It was against the fabric of his faith. It was unfair of him, but that was the reality of getting man-sex without arrest, and White was not someone he would deem worth disrepute by being seen with. But staying on a docked *Mauretania* without Robert on the first night on an island in the Pacific was a lower ebb. It frightened him, though this truth he would conceal from himself. *Mauretania* had changed things. He had embraced New York dock life and snuck away from his officer for other men...but now, a new dock held no appeal – his officer was taken from him, and he felt no draw into the night, not for men, only to push time along until Robert would return to him.

"Aye."

"Sorry, by the by," White said, two martinis in, "and," back in his usual sissy-speak swirl of a glass, "not *nearly* as dirty as I would like."

"What're ye sorry fur?"

"Robert not taking you to dinner," playing with his olive spike. "But you mustn't take it personally, you need to–"

"He asked, ah said na."

"Oh," removing an olive with his teeth, White eyes elsewhere.

He took the opportunity in the White distraction way to take in the surroundings himself. The bar White had chosen was particular, historical, with stained glass and brass bar accents. Absorbing in the bar space was a welcome distraction from the awkwardness of their exchange. Again, he gleaned jealousy off him, White's performed pity betrayed by the underlining flaws of an overall flamboyant demeanour.

"I'm happy for you," White said at last, taking his attentions back. "Why didn't you go then?"

He deep out-breathed. It was precisely the type of conversation he had wanted to avoid, White-avoid especially.

"Forget it," White said, "of course, I know."

"Tell me aboot Robert's faither."

White smiled, seeing into him again.

"That's a third-martini-topic, Turner," he said with a finishing swig.

While White busied himself at the bar, offering pointers for the cocktail-shaker, he took in the environs further. American men, soldiers and sailors, served up for him, all young and combat-ready. Why was he only now noticing? Men *only*; was it a man-sex bar, or just a military one? He wondered. And if it was a sex venue, why had he not noticed – before the bottom of his second martini – all the tight man-meat in sailor slacks and slight tops, alongside khaki-clad, made-for-command men.

"Think I helped him perfect it with this one," White said, sliding the cocktails in front of them. "And we'll need them for the story of Robert-hood I have for you," White said, taking a generous first sip, followed by a nod in the direction of the young barman who had made it for them. "Now stop me if I tell you anything that you already know," White said, tracing the base of his glass.

White began his cocktail story by his first introduction to Turner's officer in 1920 when Bell came to *Aquitania* fresh from the Royal Naval College in Greenwich. It was soon transparent that George Bell, Robert's father, had a hand in almost everything that went into the making of the man he loved, or so White's salacious storytelling suggested.

"George was just an Admiralty underling then," White said, lighting a cigarette, "with none of the clout that he has today. But still, he had influence enough to see that Robert received an appropriate, career-track appointment in the merchant service when he got him on to *Aquitania.* Though I've now known the man twenty years, I expect he has told *you* more about himself than he has me, or anyone else for that matter–"

"We ain't *blether* much, aye," he interrupted, the vodka speaking for him.

It was a jab, a sly, womanly aside. Retribution for the steward's accumulation of snide remarks. White projected an air of pomp and surety of himself amidst his haze of smoke and martinis. And his interruption had been an attack on the charade of confidence he hid behind. White raised an eyebrow in concert with his glass.

"Indeed," he said, matching Turner's tone. Taking it as a win, it seemed. "But as I was saying, dear boy...*I* have had the luxury of observing *him* and being in his, let's say, *professional*," he took a smoke drag after emphasising the word, so there could be no doubt of its meaning, "company for long enough to feel that I have insights to share."

"Fur example."

"*For* example: Robert is a man of few words, even fewer in certain company, I'm sure–"

He regretted the jab. The bar-speak had moved into drunk-queer terrain.

"–but of what he has told me, together with what I have observed, I deduce that it was never his father's intention for him to become a naval man. Robert might tell you, as is his nature, that this was because he was George's only son – his mother having died in childbirth–"

He did not know this, and the parallels with parts of his own horrid upbringing, tied to the bit of knowledge of his lover that he had, made him question whether they had the substance of a relationship that would last another ship.

"–and therefore, Robert believed the push into *Aquitania* was a fatherly measure to keep his son seaworthy yet safe. But if he has told you that, I wouldn't buy that for a dime. George is a *bastard.* He wants the Admiralty to himself. He blames Robert for the death of his wife, and sending him to sea was a way to be rid of him."

"Why dae ye say that?"

"The man was always a climber," White said, leaning abreast the table and lowering his tone – as if there was the risk of an overhearing. "Always keen for any enterprise that would claw him further up the Admiralty ladder. But when Winifred – his wife – died, he became bitter, too: of Robert. *I* think that old Georgie wanted the Admiralty path for himself." White brought down his glass with clumsy force. "Another?"

"'n' th' wife?" he asked when White had returned with another round, "whit's her story?"

"Why that, my friend, was Georgie's greatest claw of all, and–"

"Robert!"

"Oh. Robert, my boy," White said, swinging to his side with a slap on his lover's back and a slop of cocktail across White lap – and part of Bell's pants. "You're just in time, my good man. Your *boy* here, your *much younger boy*. He has been bending my ear all evening for every drop of scandal there is to be had of you."

The alcohol-altered address was relayed without decorum or awareness for the protocols. The awkwardness of Robert at the performance was pronounced, yet lost, on White. As White's innuendo interlude rang on, he realised that stood, out of sight of White, was another man in Bell's company. He was not alone, his companion capturing every entendre-ing remark.

"But I've revealed nothing," White said, with a nudge, "nothing at all. But–"

"Bit," he interjected, "ye hae company."

Robert stood silent a moment, stunned by the whole unruly welcome. He wanted to efface the entire encounter. Smiling at Robert's guest, wishing to be swallowed up and to sleek away, all the way, back to *Mauretania*.

"Yes," Robert said, clearing his throat, "allow me to introduce Kenneth Arnold."

Arnold stepped out from behind Robert to take his place at Bell's side and into White's eyeline. White, visibly embarrassed, was sufficiently watered to not let his own salacious slips tighten his tongue, too much.

"Oh, didn't see you there. Good to meet you. Edward White," extending his hand, "and this is Master Oliver Turner," gesturing vaguely.

"A pleasure, I'm sure," Arnold said, shaking his hand with a steely stare, Arnold's voice deep and formidable.

"Kenneth will be accompanying us on *Mauretania* for the Australia leg."

"How marvellous," White said, pulling out a barstool. "Do join us, dear boy."

The reluctance felt for Arnold to attend was written on his officer's face; though Arnold, actually, also seemed all-too-pleased to accept. Arnold was early-twenties, he would guess, taller than them all, and broad-shouldered, square-jawed. Attractive. But in a hard-edged sort of way. Aqua-Atlantic eyes, bright and blue and boundless. But there was a bleakness beneath those eyes, made more menacing in the bar-light.

"And in what capacity do we have the honour of you joining us on the second *Mauretania*," White waxed on.

Robert looked set to answer himself, although Arnold was faster.

"As an assistant to First Officer Bell," Arnold said, matter-of-factly. Flatly. With eyes fixed on Turner, Arnold as taker of his post.

Arnold had a look that was both difficult and definite. Intimidating, definitely. But difficult, too. To discern in terms of its true intention; alluring, but with an overwhelming sensation of it-couldn't-be-good about it. Robert's eyes were fixed on Turner also as Arnold gave his answer. And the contrast could not be starker. Apologetic; sheepish, even.

"I *see*," White said, sipping his cocktail, observing the scene with no attempt to hide his sating for scandalous waters ahead.

Had White not had as much spirit inside him, the steward would have been thoroughly jealous, Turner thought. Shown by the lack of regard for White, even in answers given to the steward's own questioning. But with the drink and the looseness of mood it brought through, White could enjoy the tension of the table, the tribulations of sea-going trysts.

"Well welcome, I am Chief Steward, so I suspect you will have little need for *dealings* with me," the innuendo still laced in his speech, "this one, however," White raising glass to him, "you will find *need for*, no doubt."

Robert's eyes widened, his cheeks reddened, with all the properness Turner loved him for.

Loved. Yes.

"What is your role, Oliver?" Arnold asked, malice cloaked by innocent interest.

"He's my apprentice," Robert said, followed by a clearing of the throat, getting in first for a change.

The shutdown tone of his officer made him smile.

"How wis tea wi' yer faither," he asked, encouraging his officer to take command as the more senior person around their circular bar table.

"Insightful," Robert said, relaxing after the awkwardness of the initial introduction.

"I'm gonna need another drink for this," White said. "What will it be, boys?" Turning to the other two, "martinis all around?"

White headed for the bar without waiting for a response, leaving awkwardness in his wake.

Arnold stared silently at him, searching him.

"Kenneth comes highly recommended," his officer said, eyeing White chatting up the bartender, clearly eager for chattiness to be brought back to their table. "Finished top of his class last year at the Royal in Greenwich."

He could tell that Bell was speaking more for Arnold than for himself.

"He'll make a real contribution to *Mauritania*'s crew-list."

He was not the sort to respond to such prompts for conversation filler; and would not indulge his officer, love or not. Bell should be less concerned about the appearance of their affair, he thought, Bell having the rank to ignore appearances.

"Where in Scotland are you from?" Arnold asked, ignoring also Robert's polite-talk attempts.

"Glasgow."

"Thought so, and–" Arnold's gaze still stern and probing, "where did you complete your *studies*?"

"Aroond thare."

"Here we go," White said, sliding out their drinks. "So, tell us, what did *el Capitan* have to say?"

White's tone was one of familiarity.

But he disliked the stranger, did not trust him, right from the outset.

"A fair amount, actually," Robert said, again to Turner. Bell would have preferred conveying this information afterwards, in private, but was now compelled to present it to the assembled crew, remaining sheepishly sorry for this. "*Aquitania* may not be where I end up, after all."

By "I" he meant "we", and his look at him confirmed this.

"Best laid plans go awry even in the smoothest of sea conditions, of course, and so really it is little surprise that many of Cunard's ships are struggling to keep on schedule – especially as they now find themselves at the service of the Royal Navy."

"So what's happened to the old girl, then?" White said.

"She was held up initially for repairs, but now the decision has been made that she will come here to Honolulu instead."

Robert explained that this was due to her unusually deep draft, her near-Edwardian below-water proportions, making anchorage at Sydney hazardous.

Though, he thought, surely this was known to her owners already. It made him wonder whether there might have been another reason for her redirection, plus Sydney is well known for having a particularly deep draught.

Where he had heard that he could not finger – from his father, probably.

“What does this all mean for us,” he asked back on *Mauretania*, fondling Robert’s in-need-of-refill after a stressed evening behind.

They had staggered back to Robert’s cabin after several more martini rounds. He had his officer naked and parallel on the bed, his back to him. He peeled open the cheeks of his officer, closing one eye as he lined himself up, then, poking clumsily, until he managed to make his way in.

“It changes noth-*ing*,” Robert said, his final syllable punctuated by a short intake of breath in beat with being entered.

He pulled out, watching with fascination as Robert, Bell, closed up in the absence of him, like an inverse *sea anemone*, opening for entry but sealing when not in use. After their martini marathon, solving the enigma of his officer-class seaman’s private porthole engrossed him. An acquired taste, of course, the arseholes of seamen – but like the dirty martini, flavoursome and full, with a depth of clarity that was wholly pleasing to the palette once properly prepared and acquainted with. *What was it*, he thought as he poked, prodded, as one would with an olive-skewed stick, bobbing into Bell as one might at the outset of some refined alcoholic concoction. *Sea anemone* was not quite it. Though a salty creature, it was for sure. No, this was a hole that had been sea-beaten since their introduction, he thought, withdrawing and moving in to watch it close up tight before him. Its lips had grown tough from pushed-in treatment, yet still remained supple to press against, having the resilience of those sea creatures that get battered by the tides and the whitewash, yet that are still squishy to touch.

As he thought of a possible species for the sucky point before him, he kept probing, his officer writhing on the bed, wanting more of him, though a little unsure of him, too – also loosened by spirits, Robert was protective of his offering point as well; open to violence as long as it preserved future passages. When in, he deprived Bell of deep-ward thrusts. *Was it retribution*, he wondered, *and if so, what for?* The drink in him meant that his cock-head-only entry was not always precise, skirting around the subject – nor as firm as his ego would like. Oddly, the stillness of ship-in-sheltered-harbour put him off. All his usual counterbalances were to the *Mauritania*-sway – as she had come to be named. This led to an off-course overcompensating in an already off-ward command of officer orifice, which he felt some ownership over now. *Ownership, was that it?* The occasions of Bell bum-hole teasing where he failed to get the line of sight just right would lead to pushing-against-cheek, or, when closer but still missing the mark, a run-in with the soft, smooth, web-like skin just around the lips. These points were the most precious of Bell's entrance, so yielding that it were inclined to tear. Pushing there, but with gentleness for the integrity of its skin, served to prompt Bell, himself slighted by drink – *as he had noted already* in his own slur – to make a slight adjustment, a mere stretch of the spine, that helped guide him home once more. But not to stay, just to play, or to tease.

"Take me," Bell breathed, a plead of desire and tiredness.

But he would not. Actually, it felt like he was betraying himself more at this stage by withdrawing. But he would not, still; the night felt broken by the bar, and besides, he was now besotted by the species hunt at hand: *what was this creature*, he thought, that sucked shut again on slide-out, and that caused its host to tremble so terribly with the tension of touch, that thrived at sea? *I should be happy for free reign*, he thought and folded down further for even closer a look, widening cheeks again for inspection of lips left wanting. The solution came to him when close enough to absorb the creature's scent: sea squirt! Or the *Cunjevoi*, in the Aboriginal tongue. How he knew that was unclear, a proxy of the Australia-leg he now knew them to be on, perhaps, a strange remanent of some absorbed knowledge of his father-before-ruin. His Bell-probing had been, after all – continued to be – during journeying to land at the bottom of their maps. This journey through which it would make sense that in service to his officer's mouth, between the in-depth cheeks between his legs, the naming of this species would find its etymological root in an organism native to that *down under*-land.

Where he had read it – no, never. Where he had heard it, and could now recall it – yes, father probably – he could not know for sure. Divine that it should come to him, here, face to lower mouth, from some marine biological archive of sea life in his mind. Living on rocky intertidal shores, *Cunjevoi* retains water, nutrients, sea spray for its sustenance. But then, it squirts it out when touched, or when spent, to make room for more and more sea to be sucked in. It needs to take the sea, constantly, to keep it from drying out. And makes a spectacle of its thirst: squirting spent sea in ginormous jets into the air. From these thirsty sea creatures, there is a tough tunic exterior that shows. Hardened on the outside, with a goo interior. But Bell was better, just as supple on his lips as within. Without, however, any depreciation in dexterity-of-desire to take sea in, and in and in. That explained Bell's reticence to take not too much of a rough entering, even full of vodka-not-gin martinis.

"I've solved you," he whispered to Bell's lips below, kissing them gently, but only half-ly with the drink.

As expected, Bell's sea squirt tasted salty but hungry, sucking him in, pulling him toward the interior with a desperate search for a restock.

"I can't deny you," he said, kissing him deeply, then sliding in again to pump him full.

Once spent, he returned to his cabin to sleep, vowing to swim in with the next tide to keep his officer's urchin hydrated – though still, un-pinpoint-ably new-lovers cross with him.

When *Mauritania* set off from Hawaii for Australia after her few days' layover, Bell's new crew member Arnold was on board. He sought out his officer's side for the voyage out. Plus, too, on any occasion presented after that. He felt himself changing, solidifying into his role – like ice shelves in the arctic, gaining soundness for the winter. He did not like it. He felt solid with his officer. Sure. But being drawn to stay at his side also left him less secure, more rigid, like escape was now the harsher winter. Arnold was, he had learned, Bell's wife's cousin. Though the temptation to freeze out White completely after the farce of their night in port in Hawaii had been high, that

White would have information to bring to bear on the situation kept the man in with him.

"Whit shuid ah know aboot Robert's wife," he asked White, their first night back at sea.

White stared and smiled, as was his way. The steward harboured a perverse, pathetic pleasure, he thought. To White, the question would be read as evidence that he, youthful and attractive as he was, only had sex with Robert – and that White, in fact, held the keys to Robert's history. He did not mind that White thought this way, however. He could have, quite quickly, asked Robert himself about *her*. And would have received a candid response. But he chose not to, as a matter of strategy. He knew, having been with many married men before, that such lines of inquiry were dangerous. It would also turn power over to his officer, loosen the grip and cloud of mystery that already he felt to be fading away with each day, each day that a need to be near Robert grew in stature within him. He loved him. Yes, loved, though now uncomfortably. In un-comfort, he remembered that what had snared his officer was what he had netted all men with. The same snare that had been the genesis of their bond was based on his talent for bending men. And that is why White was of use to him. White had *had* men, but he had never had *real* men; certainly, clearly, White had never taken a *taken* man and bent him to his will. What he *did* have was information.

"It's a sad story," White said. "Edith Arnold, of the Arnold line – lowercase 'l' in 'line' but still formidable. The only child of the most successful member of an already successful family. Her father, Archibald Arnold, owned practically all of Central London, and any parts not in his ownership were in debt to him in one way or another. The man made his fortune manufacturing machines and munitions during the Great War, tanks mostly. He bankrupted his competition through contracts without morality, selling to both sides – or so I've heard. Edith stands to inherit it all. And were she not the only child, she would have been just the type to have strangled a brother or sister, just to have it all to herself, anyhow. She's ruthless. A nasty, nasty woman. And our timid, lovable Robert never stood a chance."

White set out the story of Mrs Arnold with all the intrigue – and no doubt embellishment – of a Gothic ghost story, with an hysterical madwoman in the attic back home of our dashing hero: her villain portrait grew only darker over the serving of subsequent drinks. The tale began with her introduction to Robert on the eve of the twenties, which came through Admiralty contracts with her father's firm. These were for amphibious tank testing, or so, again, *so I've had heard.* She echoed Robert's father's insistence that he get seaworthy, and like his father, White claimed, did not think of him as having the fibre for the Royal Navy, a combined weight behind a merchant posting instead. Their courting had been brief, punctuated by transatlantic voyages on *Aquitania*, where Edith would occasionally travel. These passages, the martini-maker claimed, were more about furthering her father's and her own interests than they were romantic overtones toward and with a handsome young officer – to make representations to the American military spending authorities. She was a formidable, modern woman, by White's compliments. Made up mostly of unkind and unattractive characteristics, with a vast dislike for Robert from the outset – men too, it seemed. Though what truth from conjecture and evidence of experience White had to inform his gossip was impossible to know.

"Their marriage is a farce," White said. "A cruel chess match played by herself and his father, in which Robert is but a pawn."

White was smugly. Self-congratulatory, of the analogy, it seemed; like it were borne of the stuff of riddle-solving.

Robert's father was the one to secure the union, White went on to explain, and probably thought he stood to gain the most by it.

"But what was the Archibald view, would be the will of Edith, too," White said, still in cryptography. "Them both, arriving, and at union, at the matter of mutual agreeability.

"Archibald secured further Admiralty contracts through the marriage, and a wider pool of high-rank military introductions," White said, "while Edith's satisfaction came through the procurement of a puppet husband; absent most of the year and unassertive overall, but sufficient enough in purpose to secure her an heir. And, in the ultimate act of humiliation, she refused Robert's name. Something most irregular, even in the jazz age, you understand. *And*," White ran on, devouring his final olive of their last cocktail for the night at the height of his top-shelf Robert story, "as a punishment for the perceived weakness in her husband: Edith has kept their son, Alfred Archibald Arnold, from him. He would never say such things, of course, even to you. But she did this not out of hatred for him, worse than that, it was out of ill-respect; Edith not believing Robert to be fatherly-fit to exert influence and in-fearing that he might infect the boy with his own failures. She chose a weak husband, we can deduce – even if present company connotes him as tender, instead –, for her own ends and conscious not to let him derail the development of the Arnold line through the nurturing of her heir."

White's narrative reeked of hyperbole. The stuff of Victorian women's fiction. And thoughts of *he's one to talk* poked through Turner's listening, most pricking whenever Robert was described as weak, unmanly – *tender*, even. Like a spotlight searches the shore on the night of a shipwreck. He, too, scoured the story on his way through the ship from the bar to Robert's cabin. Sifting as he went, through the scenes and debris of his own experiences with Bell – looking for evidence of cause and whether what he had been told offered clues to where it all went wrong. Even in reruns, White's history of Edith – the formidable Mrs Arnold – was relayed with all the melodrama of the before-his-time, turn-of-the-century theatre. He had come to expect this from White. Use of statements like: "to the best of my knowledge" and "so I've heard" thrown in. And, too, as dilution to some of the wilder turns. In his afternoon high-teatime tale, these tales all worked to up the drama.

Large swathes of White's story were stitched-up speculation, must be. White was just the sort to sip-up idle gossip like it was one of his heavy-handed vodka cocktails. What of the history he was being told was truth? And what was fancy? He could not tell for sure. But if there was even a nugget of the genuine to White's account, then his officer's hole-bodied embrace of takeover took on a different tone; had a portion of the psychological about it. Was how he had taken Bell on since *Elizabeth* and then continued to take him and bend him more and more on *Mauritania* contributing to Bell's misuse? Or had it freed him? And would he ever raise this with Bell himself? Ask for his officer's own take on the tale, to get at the truth beneath the White-wash?

Or was that a step beyond their class of relation-fuckship?

These were uncomfortable questions, for, beneath the melodrama of White's tale-spin, he knew there was an ill-erasable truth: the story slotted in with aspects of Robert's character that he had himself observed. And so he would call and fill Bell extra surely this eve before turning in, he resolved. Bell's door was ajar, as he was now accustomed to seeing it, light emanating from its gape. Maybe one night soon he would ask those questions of his officer, but that night, the overwhelming instinct was for no words, to just be inside the man he loved, to hold him, to spill him over. He slipped silently into the room, hand at the waist of his pants, ready to undo and to take—

—but was stopped by what awaited him inside.

Bell had company.

Kenneth Arnold was there. Near-wholly clothed, yet his privates entirely exposed; his manhood out and atop of the elastic of his white slacks. There he stood, bold, door still ajar and, *cruelly*, he thought, Bell still inviting him in by keeping the entrance that way. It was like a honey trap. Arnold had his meat in hand, boyhood, actually, small and thin, emphasising his youth. His positioning placed him to the side of Arnold and the door; if Bell had seen or heard him enter, he did not let on. Bell was seated, naked, it seemed, all of himself on offer to his new boy. He felt frozen, red hot, fixed – how contradictory it all was. It felt that he had stood there an age, when in fact, it had only been seconds. What stung most was that there was no reaction at all, like what he had stumbled upon was not worth mention. In fact, that he was the one intruding, with no right to be there. Bell cleared his throat awkwardly; Bell must have captured a glimpse of the intrusion through the reflection of the blacked-out cabin portholes and was now making his position on the situation clear. He chose to flee, stopping by his cabin to fetch just a blanket and pillow. He would not sleep in a cabin adjacent that night. That night, he would sleep on deck.

He spent the next day as a stowaway once more. *Mauritania* may have been smaller than the *Queen*, but she was still vast enough and housed a crew small enough that there were ample places within her for him to hide, and more comfortably, he discovered, with her furnished suites and still-full swimming pools. It was restorative, brought him back to his roots, to his original drive as a stowaway on the *Queen* at the start of her Clyde flee to American freedom. He even dipped into the laundry to snatch up a linen bag of engineers' jocks, taking their fragrance to a forgotten fold of *Mauritania*'s service corridors – the crew in the suites, as on *Elizabeth* – and, when he was done, slipping southward into the sweat and manly odour of the engine room. Though stopped short of selecting one of the men-of-sweat to have a crack at, content just to observe.

Maybe I'm spent from the underpants, he told himself, to seal off the real reason in a watertight compartment within…though those only went as high as tourist class.

He promised that he would return to-morrow – as they still had two sailing days before reaching Sydney. *Plus*, he thought, erecting a ramshackle bulkhead up to cabin class inside himself, *the engineer-scent-release really was enough after the brutal engine of* Normandie, *and his arse beating, from which he was still recovering.* It was a half-truth and a thought process that aligned him with a narrative for Bell's actions that was storyboarding the partitions of his mind. Though like Edwardian-dated panelling on a four funneller, it was a fixture-fading, if any were left in existence at all.

He had made jealous inquiry, into me, about my obvious fuck the night before we shipped off, he thought, *and this now – Arnold – was his feminine way of getting angry, getting back.*

This inside-his-hull narrative sobered him, and served the reverse of its initial intention. Guided him, to his own hypocrisy; and seeded a resolve to return to his officer, to apologise as well, given his whole-day neglect of duties. It was only natural that Bell was branching out, enjoying other male options – and Kenneth, in every regard save personality, was an appetising prospect. Pretty, yet sharp-edged: someone to pursue. And why should Bell not pursue? He reasoned. After all, Robert had not had the opportunities for men that he had, and if anything of White's story held water, Bell desired these prospects, too. Robert's door was closed off to him when he returned to it. Light from inside ran along the base of the door, though, telling him he was in.

Maybe he was with Kenneth, he thought, *and what if he is? Fair play to him*. He knocked.

"Who is it?"

"Olli."

The door swung in with the force of a breeched watertight. Robert met him with a smile – forced. He surprised himself with how much he missed that face, those lips, that pronounced-with-hump nose. Robert took him by the hand and pulled him in, sealing the door.

"You had me worried."

"Ah wantit some time...efter last nicht."

Smiled pretence gave way to furrowed brow.

"Ye 'n' Kenneth, ah wantit some time...efter walking in oan ye."

The effect was immediate. Robert dropped to his knees like his feet had been knocked back clean from under him. Face at his waist.

"Olli, so you did walk in. I thought it was just me being irrational."

"It's fine."

"No, it's not," Robert said, weeping. "I should have run after you, but I wasn't sure you were even here. I didn't see you, I just *sensed* you, and I thought it was my mind playing tricks. After all, it was just a second. And now that you have said it first. I, I, I should have told you right away just now."

"It's fine."

"No, it's not," Robert said, sinking, to rest at bottom on his feet. "You will never believe me now, but I need you to. Please, Olli."

"Whit?"

"I was waiting for you, the door ajar, just like I leave it for you," he said, wiping the back of his hand against his nose, "and *he* came in. I thought it was you. When I realised, I got a towel and asked him to leave, but he said he was sorry for intruding, but had something urgent to seek counsel about. I sat down to hear him out, but he just stood there. Then, out of nowhere, he pulled *it* out. And I just stared, shocked. I heard something behind me, but I didn't respond. Then, I asked him to leave, and he did. That was all there was to it. Please, Olli. I *need* you to believe me."

Robert sunk further, he would not have thought it possible, compressed into a sobbing ball at his feet. He took Robert's face into his hands, wet and messy, shaking. He loved him most at that moment. Not because he believed him, but because of the intensity with which his officer had needed him to believe, to believe *in* him – truth, as was the way with men who sleep with men, was secondary to intention, for Olli at least. But he hesitated in his response, thinking of his own conduct. Then he thought of aspects of White-given-to-him backstory. His Robert was a romantic, wronged. And he loved him for it and would, he resolved at that moment, solemnly, do what he could to make up for how the man before him had been wronged – including through the continued concealment of his own conduct with the beast of *Normandie*.

"O' coorse, mah love," he said, "ah believe ye."

He took Robert into his arms and then to bed it was for him, for a filling. Robert was still trembling and sobbing, right until release, when tears stopped, and sleep came. He stayed with him, holding him for the night, protecting him, keeping him safe. And when he woke, his officer was facing him in the bed, his eyes puffy and red.

"Mornin', sur," he said. "How did ye sleep?"

Robert did not answer, just wriggled forward through the sheets until their chests pressed.

He wrapped him in his arms, and his Robert buried his face into the space beneath his chin, hiding from the world. He kissed the crown of his head.

"Aboot lest nicht. Aboot Kenneth."

Robert rustled in his arms, like a fern in a wind. He held tighter and slid a hand down to his cheek, one then the other, then the between-cheeks, slipping a finger in where there was filling. It pacified him.

"Ye needn't tremble, sur," he said in his ear. "Ah treasure ye."

It tapped into his Robert. By *treasure*, he had meant: I trust you, I believe you, I take you, as you are. Robert would do anything for him; he had shown that to be true. But the revelation here was not the actions of Robert, it were his own. He would protect his officer, work to undo the damage that had been done to him. Undo damage and fulfil him. He slipped three fingers and a thumb inside him to his gooey centre. His fingertips expanded and contracted, spreading open his sea squirt. Some of Robert's filling started to spill out as he did, and he could see his officer showing the early signs of distress at the loss. To pacify again, he used his own filling as a batter, to lather, make adjustments and slide in – hooking Robert's leg around his arm and elevating him for easier access. Suction on him was suckier than usual, with the drain of recent distress taking its toll, heightening the hunger. The covers were soon off, their bodies entwined with the effort of him gearing up to deliver Robert his morning feed. Robert rode him astride for much of their session this time, more eager to work out and into him the offering.

Flashes of morning light shuttered through the cabin, the bed clicking at certain intervals of Robert's bouncing on the bed. As he neared release, he turned his Robert over, easing his hips to an incline to ensure the feeding reached in deep. The *flashes and clicks*, in sync, grew in frequency. From the finishing vantage, he could see, at the non-returnable escalation to the end, that it was not from pricks in the blackout porthole paint that the light was escaping, nor from the bed springs that clicking came in an off-beat with his into-Robert strides.

It was a camera.

Their photographer...the pornographer...emerged from his hiding place in the cabin closet, coming close in clicks and flashes to catch the end.

It was Kenneth.

I should stop him, take the camera from him, destroy the record, he thought as he convulsed at the edge.

"Don't stop," Robert pleaded, seeing in him, his eyes welling up once more. "I need it."

Did Robert see the intruder? Did the severity of the situation register with him? It would mean the wreck of them. He reached for the lens while maintaining his Robert-reach-in-rhythm, incredulously, inching back from a state of spent. His finger grazing the metal of the machine. Kenneth stepped casually out of reach, continuing to document the feeding like an insatiable ethnographer without ethics. Robert had not broken eye contact with his lover and generous penetrator, all the while the perpetrator was in sight.

"Please, Olli," Robert said as the rhythm started breaking and his approaching climax convulsing stabilised. "Stay with me."

"Aye, sur," he said, spiting logic.

Setting his intention true. Focusing on what was important, getting himself to the path to climax again, and thrusting through the threshold stopping return this time.

Kenneth, in turn, took full advantage of the situation, moving in for close-ups, then back for wide-angles, then in again for clearer Kodak incrimination.

But he blurred out the intrusion, got the feeding back on track, seeing it through to completion. Robert spilt over with the feeling of the first mouthful being delivered inside his low lips, an intensity high for him, collapsed onto Robert's chest as he deposited at length, each jolt of release more intense than the last.

Kenneth waited until they were both blind-sighted spent. Even taking one final shot of their sweat-laced, entwined lump of bodies on the bed – capturing the glistening afterglow of *Mauritania*'s First Officer after being sodomised and seeded to a plane of sublime satisfaction by a boy under his command.

Kenneth then fled wordlessly from the cabin, camera tucked underarm like the Crown jewels from the Tower of London.

"Whatever he wants," Robert said calmly, with a smile, reaching for his silver, initialled cigarette case, "it was worth it to see that through. You made me proud."

He had understood the *stay with me* for what it was: a veiled order to stay the course, the only test Robert had ever put to him. He had passed it. They had now proven themselves to each other: a love, be damned the consequences.

"Ah need tae halt him," he said. "Permission tae tak' mah lea, sur."

It was more formally than he would normally speak. Yet the formality seemed fitting given the sacrifice of ruin that they had both just embarked on, Robert most profoundly.

"Granted," Robert said, a fag already retrieved, and an overall manner that was more carefree than his nature.

He was dressed and out the door within just a few officer-drags of post-feeding cigarette. In pursuit, with all the liveliness of a life preserver. The stupidity of not stopping Kenneth when he had the chance spread through him as he chased the halls of the small monster ship – his role as protector should have come over penetrator, surely. It was panic. Red running before his eyes with all the terror of a submariner's dive alarm.

Go! Go! Go! he shouted inside himself. *Find him.*

"Sorry, First Officer," he said, queerly with rank, when he arrived back to the chart room around 1100 hours.

"What for?"

"Ah coudnae fin' him. Ah let him git awa'."

"You both did," came a third voice from behind.

"Ah, Arnold. Good of you to join us," Robert said. "Won't you come in? Olli, close the door, will you?"

He wanted to grab hold and shake Arnold down until the camera tumbled forth, and he ceased breathing. Robert was seated at his desk, covered in charts. There were two chairs across from him; he took one of them and moved it to Robert's side of the desk so he would not need to sit beside Kenneth.

"What is it you want from us, Mr Arnold?"

"So direct, Officer Bell," Arnold said, rubbing his crotch. "I thought we might get *better acquainted* first."

He bolted from his chair and grabbed Arnold's shirtfront, "give us the film, Arnold".

How he had changed. How sacred sex had suddenly become.

"Pity," Arnold sighed, touching himself still, even as he was tugged across charts, "I thought this assignment might be an occasion for mixing business with pleasure. But as for the *business* part of our new partnership, I can assure you that the film is safe."

He pulled Arnold to his feet and patted him down, feeling for the film, even venturing to his inner thigh, but there was only angry-small firming flesh to be found there.

"It's not on me, obviously," Arnold said, gripping Turner's hand to his crotch, "but feel free to give me the thorough going over."

He pulled his hand away and slouched back into the chair, "so blackmail then, is it?"

"Oh no," indignant but with the same stern stare that he had hated about him on their first introduction, "how little you must think of me. We are the same, gents. Blackmail is such a nasty business, and we are better than that."

"Then why have you hidden the film?"

"Let's call it...insurance."

"Against what?"

"*For*...job security, Olli."

He hated hearing him use his informal Christian name like that – so familiar, so personal, so as-Robert-would.

"We all have our little jobs to do, Olli. Granted, some of us have a better lot in life with the jobs we've been assigned," with a glance and prick-ish grin at his officer, his Robert.

He was up again, Arnold's shirtfront in one fist, the other raised.

"I wouldn't do that if I were you, Olli boy. Unless you want those photographs getting out."

Reluctantly, he released him and returned to his chair.

"What do you know," Arnold said. "I *am* blackmailing you. Nasty business, that."

"We have one more day at sea before we reach Sydney, Mr Arnold," Robert said. "From there, I can wire you funds to the amount of your choosing."

Arnold had smirked with the blackmail comment, but now slid back into a stare. Cold and stern.

"Don't insult me, sir. I am a patriot, a soldier. We are friends, comrades now...but much more talk like that and, well...our *friendship* is tested with statements like that."

"My apologies, Mr Arnold." Robert was composed, professional, respectful even. "It was not my intention to insult you."

"Thank you."

"But I confess that I am at a loss. If it is not money that you want from us, then what?"

And just like that, the cartoon curve of Arnold's mouth was back: bigger than his face seemed intended to take, twisting it out of shape, like a freak carnival clown.

"Why, Robert, don't you see? I want *you*."

"Noo you're mah mystery."

Robert had gone from wholly hysterical the night before – at the prospect of a chink in their romantic armour – to now – when they faced real peril and complete and utter social, and court martial, ruination – a calm. Robert just smiled, on the gun deck they had made their own in Panama, taking in the haze of their desert destination continent on the horizon.

"You have filled me," Robert said. "Given me everything that I could want, more than I could have hoped for from what was a wretched life. Every minute. Every moment. Every beat of my heart with you from now on is superfluous to this. More than I deserve."

He understood. Putting his hand on Robert's below cheek – boldly, without even a glance about to check for one of the markedly more people about, compared with Panama.

Perhaps Arnold has given us a gift, freed us from ourselves. But he only permitted *that* thought for an instant.

"Bit we need to *keep* this, mah love. That Kenneth lad git one thing richt. *This*," tracing the crest of Robert's cheek, "is ma job, tae protect ye, tae *provide* fur ye," pressing to the doughy centre of his entrance, "tae keep us."

"I know," Robert said, eyes tracing the land instead, "but for me, you have already done that. And more. Please know that."

Soon enough, Sydney spread out before them like a wild southern frontier land. Its sandstone cliffs topped with dense, uninhabitable bushland, greeting but guarding from them too as they entered the heads and into the harbour to anchor alongside other Cunard liners. *Mauritania* was out of place there, with her clean lines and orderly Englishness. How would she fare among the men of convict country? He wondered. There was a metaphor in there, he thought, as he anchored a hand to the top of Robert's under-leg and as they lined up the heads for entry, a sight that made him insist that they take time to mark it. Taking his officer there, again, as he had in Panama. This time, Robert bent all of his own accord. Opened up like the sail of a bygone ship.

Then, his Robert topped up once more, *Mauritania* moored at Cockatoo Island, an Australian naval base not far from the harbour's coat-hanger bridge of the same decade as their boat. They disembarked together into the humid heat of a young and foreign land. Compared with New York, Sydney was parochial, primitive, safe. Arnold was an afterthought as soon as they trod foot on Circular Quay – his Robert, satisfied and full, the only matter of the southern day. For them as a couple, for their unit, they had security. But for him personally, as the gatekeeper of their forbidden happiness, Arnold had taken up positions in his mind. He was a hindrance, and one he wished desperately to shake.

What did he want?

"We have money, Olli," Robert said, with the playfulness of a love-struck sweetheart. "Where will we stay?"

His Robert bubbled with the forgetfulness of the fool in love. No regard for Arnold or the promise of ruin around the bend. The quay at the basin of the city centre was thronged with men. Rough, military, bronzed and broad – the smell of them! And so he could see how this spirit of forgetfulness could grip a man in such surrounds. Though for him, it was still too fresh to be entertained.

"Awa' from 'ere," he said.

"Well, we have two nights until we are required back. She," and by she he meant *Aquitania*, "will be busy with her outfitting."

He led the way away, not knowing where to, just away, from the harbourfront, packed with men awaiting departure, and to the streets of the city's centre. It reminded him of Glasgow, the way it sloped to the wet chop. But the buildings were brighter here, a yellow-gold from the local sandstone. The people, too, were rather Glasgowian, he thought. Lacking the fine clothes and refinement of an English city but still smartly dressed in the vein of a British outpost.

"Whaur wid ye lik' tae go, mah love," he said as they stood outside a tour office along George Street, working at the whole forgetfulness routine himself.

"You choose."

He chose the image that was the furthermost-looking from the oceans over which they had been. Outbreak of war had swept austerity across the seas, even as far afield as Australia, making it an affordable time to travel. He booked tickets and accommodation with the money he had received on the articles Robert had arranged for him, and they set off by steam train from Central Station, bound for the 'Blue Mountains'. The journey took several hours. The first hour was spent in the dining carriage, though they did not eat. His Robert took an old fashioned and a cigar; he had a martini, but with gin and, for their landward exploration, flavoured with a twist of lemon peel. Because, precisely, he was distancing himself from White. This sensation, to do so, well...it was a growing impulse, entertained. Once Robert was on to his second old fashioned, he relished watching him uncoil like the lemon of his own tipple; the slight creases at the corner of his eyes – that he felt added distinction to him – softening...un-deepen-ing with each sip.

"Shall we finish our drinks...privately?" Robert suggested.

The bulk of travel time was for the steep inclines and bends up the Great Dividing Range that twisted them, through the occasional cloud of steam, into dense, boundary-less bushland. He had booked them into a First Class compartment and bolted them in after retiring. It included a seating area and separate sleeping compartment, where the bed opened onto a picture window of the vast Australian landscape – hot and horrid, but beautiful. The shortish journey helped him in securing a room with just one double bed for two travelling gentlemen. They would only be using the seating area, he had said on making the cheaper booking – when in train-ing, the reverse was true. He continued the uncoiling of Robert as through steam they climbed the great mountain range – feeding him, filling him. The only interludes in their lovemaking were to return to the bar for refreshments. Arrival at Katoomba coincided with the completion of Robert's second serving; it tempted him to pay for a return to Sydney there, so his in-officer activities could be continued without interruption. Though the call of the thick bush, high mountain setting was enough of a draw to pull them from the privacy of their compartment and into the highland town.

Their first night was spent in the Carrington Hotel, a short walk from Katoomba Train Station – on the main street, sat back high after landscaped lawns, like a grand house in a lumber town. A two-bedroom, upper-floored, corner suite gave them the cover they needed to share a bed, without clothes or speech. Nothing was discussed. Arnold, well, he was not brought up. Not even a breath about what their next steps would be once they returned to Sydney after just one more day was uttered. It was a respite, he understood that: it was a reprieve for them both. And he would not let anything distract from his function of nourishing Robert and, the higher order, ensuring the rested return of a Cunard First Officer. Feeding-up Robert was necessary initially. For the next day – their only full day away from ships and sea – he packed for exertion, r.e.: a ramble of the ranges. For the ramble, he piled their sacks with clothes and supplies. They set off at first light for trails that took them along cascades and to the sight displayed in the window of the travel office in Sydney. 'Three Sisters' – jagged rock formations that towered over a wasteland of a brutal, inhabitable bush. Bush that stretched into the horizon with all the vastness and deep trenches of a savage sea, with other, smaller mountains weaving through the view as signs of a storm in the distance.

Robert appeared well-absorbed by the vista. Was its endlessness exactly the escape he needed? As his beloved Robert took in the view, he readied him from behind, lowering his slacks and unfolding Robert too, like a swagman would a rucksack to retrieve refreshments. Robert's *Cunjevoi*, like the fourth sister of myth, opened to his touch. Twitching for story time, the spiritual place that was Robert's lower mouth spurring his tending-to of the sea squirt, which he did by native remedies; and inspired improvisation. A hand between his officer's shoulder blades, Robert still transfixed by the vista, he eased him forward to allow more room for his anal-work alchemy. He took limbs from the surrounding bush to tend to his officer's orifice, folding the branches down and crisscrossing them over Robert's lower back, holding them there, pinning him down into position. Robert stayed transfixed as he worked at his back, as if under a trace from an ancient always-was act. He did not want to *hurt* him, never the way he had been hurt himself on *Normandie*, never with such brutality and guilt and shame after. But, that said, his officer needed some next-level feeding; it is what he had been training him for, *turning* him toward. He needed to break him a little to help him heal right.

Robert pinned and in position, he looked about them for that added ingredient, some essence out of the land they were in, some essential oils to mix with his own, to weave with his Clydebank filling. Eucalyptus leaves! There they were, on the limbs pinning his officer into position. He did not even need to remove them from the tree. He had simply to gather them in a bunch. Then, place them one atop another and over the sucky point.

"Perfect," he said, inserting himself in through the flat top of the stack, taking the leaves with him inside his officer-in-training.

As oiled leaves creased and crumpled into a British merchant officer, they cracked open, releasing Eucalyptus oil, lining him. He felt it instantly as heat on himself, but Robert, for whom this was now inside, would have felt it far, far more intensely. Robert reeled back as if a stud threatened, bringing forward a deep, primal roar that rang forth, over the cliff of their view and down into the valley. It was grand, an outpouring that reverberated through the ravine and out into the distance. He ensured his seed flowed swiftly after, arching deep and shooting from the back, flooding his stallion's interior, covering the dry leaf shards and softening them there – taking the sting out of the oil. The effect was instantaneous, like a divine antidote administered just in time. Robert shuddered out an exhale of sweet relief as the balm spread through him. As he neared the end of his unloading, he felt himself being pushed out, his officer's orifice overflowing. Once out, he detached the leaves lodged inside Robert from their branches, allowing his officer's opening to close up. Just the stems protruded, the essence of himself inside his Robert, neutralising the oil and the leaf-tips, binding these inside like a witch doctor concoction padded into an open wound: sealing it from exposure to the elements, allowing the potion to brew within. Robert's treatment complete he unbranched him from his placement.

"Mah scent pot," he said, breathing it in, then packing Robert's arse back into pants – ready for the rest of their walk. "Noo we allow ye time tae diffuse."

Their second Blue Mountains stay was not far away; only one township over in Medlow Bath, where he would complete his rejuvenation-of-Robert project. Hydro Majestic Hotel was built in the reign of Edward VII; it boasted just the right pedigree of restorative mineral water properties through which he could remove his remedy and allow Robert to soak. He took the ritual seriously-as-a-spa and, despite insistent pleads, resisted refeeding during their stay. Robert needed to rest and restore.

"Why," Robert asked that night, with the indignation of a deprived infant.

"Fur we return tae sea th'morra," he said, tracing the seaweed he had wrapped Robert's arse in. "'n' a'm going tae need regular uise of ye," teasing the corners of the wrap, resisting the impulse to inch it open and peek at progress, probably to be followed by a delve inside for a top-up, "if we are going tae see aff Arnold 'n' this war."

"The war," Robert said, distant, in fact, a rare voice this trip, slipping off towards sleep, "that seems so far away here."

In the caretaker role, the war was everywhere. It hung over their stay like a brewing storm, doubly. There seemed to be reminders of it all over. That evening even, as he went to fetch a towel for Robert after emptying his entrance and allowing it to soak in a salt bath for an hour, he had come across soldiers in the lobby. They were in discussion with the Manager about preparations to receive damaged men of their own. Speak was of the particulars of repurposing the hotel as an army hospital.

Even here, war had found them.

They arrived back to Sydney-town the next day. Restoration of Robert complete as shore leave would allow, officer orifice put through its semen trials on the steam-train return trip. Robert, still tasting of Eucalyptus, had a renewed softness-yet-dexterity. It told him he was ready to face whatever lay ahead. Waiting for them in the harbour were thousands of Australian troops assembled for assignment to a carrier. He felt boastful of his transformation of his returning officer's wellbeing and preparedness to provide passage for phallus. Perhaps, he thought, it was time to extend his officer and the offering. Among the men assembled, musky in the quay, he entertained the idea of 'hole-istic benefits', of Robert's arsehole's elasticity, which he could test through the ferrying of men from the docks to officer quarters. All this was in their future. But before he could present the idea to his officer. In fact, even while he still weighed up within himself whether he truly wanted others to have access to the hole he had meticulously renovated. Or whether, even, the sight of all these tanned and hardy men had stirred in him a recitation of his original sea-going memorandum. Before this, a voice broke through, brought him and them both back to the world their train journey and Carrington–Hydro Hotel stay had steamed them away from.

"Gentlemen."

Arnold's voice corroded through the noise of the Australian men assembled – acid against firm meat.

"My associate said that you had fled, that I had failed by letting you slip away. But I knew better. That you are men of duty, one of you at least, and that you would be back for the convoy. If you'll follow me."

The fine, fine, *fine* men of the harbour were sidelined as he came over with fear for the future of Robert, and a feeling of undoing, unravelling of control over his officer and the reparative work he had undertaken. Arnold did not wait for a response, slicing them and snaking a trail in the crowd of men toward the waiting ships.

"It will be okay, my love," Robert said.

Robert exhibited that calm certainty he had before. Leading the way in the wake of Arnold, brushing his hand as he went, as a gesture that said it would work out in the end. Sydney harbour, as large and as deep as was her draft. She could not accommodate both of the Cunard Queens. And so, *Mary* was in port while *Elizabeth* waited further out – to have men ferried to her. He missed the sight of her and the simplicity of his time on her before New York. But having *his Queen* not there did allow him time to take in the elegance of Robert's favourite liner, *Aquitania*, proud and grey and ready to serve – tall against the backdrop of the much younger bridge behind her, a noble liner of the past. She was as Robert had described her. The 'ship beautiful' was what he had called her. And as they passed beneath her, he could see why. 'The last of an era,' Robert had said to him the night before, a little loose from drink, smelling strongly of Eucalyptus, and more subtly of home – of cigars and that indescribable, *him*. That below feeding was off the menu while he was wrapped and healing made for a memorable last night. A homosocial escape together. It meant they spent the night with fine food – of the upper mouth kind –, of spirits and *speak*. Learning about each other.

You don't see four-funnelled liners like her anymore, Robert had said, while he traced the curves of officer sea-weeded behind. *It has been a pleasure to serve in her for as long as I have. I wish you could have known me then, Olli.*

I know you now, he had said, a gentle squeeze of his left cheek, tips teasing the Eucalyptus pot. *And I wouldn't change a thing.*

Arnold led them into an office right where *Aquitania* docked, near under the bridge. She disappeared from their view as they followed Arnold in, leaving them like a curtain call, come too soon. Inside was strangely cold and stale;

like Arnold had split into silent ushers in a concert hall, and by entering, they had been transported somewhere entirely new. Shushing them. It was a formal setting, with views of the harbour but not of any of the ships anchored there. That they had happened upon a room with a vantage of the harbour removed from all signs of the outward heading ships did not make sense to him. Even if it had been purpose-built to screen out the liners and the troops. Such a task, with the fullness of fore-planning, seemed like an impossible undertaking.

"Well gentlemen," Arnold said, "you've had time to think it over."

"Yes, Mr Arnold," Robert-the-calm said. "But before we talk business, perhaps a drink is in order."

I've done it, he thought, *it's worked, I've restored him to the Chief Officer I knew he could be, the one I had seen on* Elizabeth, *the one that I have heard so much from White about.*

"Why not," Arnold said, with his snake smirk.

And so his officer fixed them each a drink. He watched the harbour as his officer worked. There was no sight of grey liners or any war-coloured craft, in fact. Just white sails, like the white horses of the wash onto a beach. And he felt certain there, safe. They would sort this out as long as he had his Robert officer by his side. They could survive anything.

"Here you go, my love," his Robert said, handing him a drink.

And they drank. Robert's calmness was a rash. They had nothing to worry about *as long as they were together.* It was his last thought, the look of love and gratitude from Robert, his last sight before darkness descended.

IV

QUEEN MARY

Light peeled in, unwelcome.

"You're okay," said a familiar voice.

As clarity came to the room, White took form before him.

"You're safe."

"Whit?"

Confusion turned to panic as he realised Robert was gone.

"Whaur is he?"

"I'm sorry, Olli. I didn't know, I swear, not until minutes ago."

"Whaur is he?"

"He's gone, Olli," White said with a glance to the window, which was now filled with the grey shape of Robert's ship. "It was his condition."

"Ah dinnae understand," he said, hand to throbbing head.

"That you be kept out of it. That was his condition of compliance."

Panic spread through him as recollection of their conversation the night before played over inside his head. *What if we didn't go back*, he had said in the drift towards sleep. *What if we get on a train and continue west away from the sea until we reach somewhere that the war could not reach*?

Chills paralysed him with the recall of Robert's response. *But I have to go, my love, it is the only way. Forgive me.*

"Haes th' convoy left," he said, clamping hold of White's wrist.

"All but the *Mauretania.* But she'll shove off at any moment now, too...

You're too late."

Whether intended or not, there was cruelty in his final phrase.

"Ye kin git us oan her," he said, struggling to steady himself onto his feet.

"No, Olli, we're to stay in Sydney, at least for the time being. That's the deal Robert has struck."

"Damn th' deal, ye coward. You'll git us oan that ship," hand on White's throat, "by God, or I'll murdurr ye, ye hear," pulling White to the door, "get us oan *Mauretania.*"

White did.

Mauretania's troopship refit meant she could now carry thousands in her and was full-up with an Australian contingent, the vast majority that crammed on her open-air deck to bid farewell to Sydney – their chorus as loud as a liner's horn.

"I've arranged my articles, and yours, too," White said at his side as they steamed around the bends of Sydney's Port Jackson, "but an appointment to the officer classes was one step beyond my deceptive talents, I'm afraid."

He spoke with a sharpness to his tongue; retribution, probably, for the rough treatment.

"I'm sorry, Edward," he said, watching the crowds that filled the beaches and headland paths of Sydney's pretty inlets swell as *Mauretania* passed. "Ah couldn't let him lea wi'oot me. Why did he think that ah wid?"

White ignored the question, rubbing his neck where he had been gripped into action.

"Fortunately for you," he continued, "Cunard is in desperate need of stewards. As long as you stay with the Cunard liners, you should always be able to gain passage...with these articles."

He stowed the papers in his back pocket, "ta."

"They are expecting you in the kitchens; report to Rodney Ward." White turned to leave but then stopped and came in close. "I'm sorry he left you,

Olli," then left himself.

He waited on deck with the high-spirited Australians until *Mauretania* was out of the heads and on her way to join the largest convoy of troops ever assembled. With close to a dozen liners, his attentions remained fixed on *Aquitania.* She distinguished herself with her four-funnels – the last of her kind. The two *Queens* took centre stage as most important in the formation and were flanked by *Mauretania* and *Aquitania.* Two even lesser liners ran alongside *Aquitania*, one of which he recognised from New York as *Île de France.*

How am I going to get to you? He thought.

He skipped across the sea between the liners in convoy, counting the space between them, the distance between *Mauretania* and *Aquitania.* But the solution to the math of subtracting their distance eluded him. In frustration, he descended to the kitchens to report for duty under his new articles.

His own officer's departure and the subsequent downgrade to steward service in the kitchens seemed to delight *Mauritania*'s officer class. In Bell's absence, they spoke freely about his entirely inappropriate rise through the ranks. As he served them from the kitchen, they used gossip as a high-pitched garnish atop the meals they were served – salted with speak of Chief Officer Bell 'jumping ship' to take up with another young boy, they had heard.

"It will catch up with him soon enough," one said.

"Here here," another agreed as he left the room.

He started to wonder whether White's securing him this particular post was payback for how he was treated – his shifts shaping up that way. One advantage of his kitchen posting, however, was that it made him privy to some core pieces of intelligence, namely which ship Bell had found himself on. *Île de France.* Bell's father had been right; Robert would not, in fact, join his beloved *Aquitania* in Sydney as planned.

He proved himself hard-working in the kitchens, and at the root of it, did not mind the work itself. He found Ward heavy-handed and prone to pedantic bouts. But after two days in his role, understood the manner of Ward's working of the kitchen and its staff – and he showed himself to invite grit 'n' graft, which helped. Ward agreed to let him change duties from the serving of crew to help out with the meal service for the troops instead. These were the gruffer sort, for sure, and he showed himself to be the true giver in their service. Truth was, it was the easy decision for 'the ward', as he was known: troops needed the extra hands, and in the eyes of the stewards, tending to those above their station was the more aspirational assignment. Troops are rough and unruly, Australians more than many, and stewards worked with soft hands, accustomed to the service of the leisure classes rather than the rowdy crowds of men on their way to war. Ward was not unkind in the reassigning, it was in fact beneficial for his own labour scheduling.

Reassignment kept future run-ins with the officers and White to a minimum, allowing him to focus on the graft of hard work. To focus, too, on feeding the prime male masses. Where the convoy was headed was privileged information, and he was no longer in circles that allowed access to such intel. But this did not concern him too much, as they all steamed together in the Pacific-pact convoy. That was until, three days into sailing, in the middle of breakfast service, *Mauritania*'s engines came to a dead stop, and uncertainty spread through crew and troops combined like a fire of unknown origin.

"Ain't only us, mates," one trooper eating breakfast shouted, "the entire bleedin' convoy's stopped."

"We're sitting ducks," shouted another, stirring panic in the Grand Dining Hall where breakfast was being served.

Those assembled started abandoning the breakfast line and hightailing toward the stairwells. These steps led to the upper decks, packed as panic took hold. Before he had time to determine for himself what his own course of action would be – whether he would abandon his station to follow the Australians up onto deck – his next move was determined for him.

"Turner," Ward bellowed, as only a burly working-class cook could, from a table over, across the commotion of down under troops. "Chief Steward

White wants you in the First Class Cocktail Lounge. Now!"

Urgency was clear, and he knew the way. Of course, he did, having made it plenty of times on his previous *Mauritania* passages. Though this time, the journey there did feel different. Not only was it made difficult by the need to push through the mass of men: rambunctious and riled up by their first excitement at sea. But the route was also made foreign by the troop conversion itself. The ship had already been partially prepared in New York. But her stay in Sydney had completed the covering of her fittings. Covered over her fine veneers. Christ, her very character was gone – a loss that was made to feel final by the absence of Robert. Though he expected that White had chosen the cocktail lounge because it was a familiar location to them both. On seeing it 'completed' in a war sense – without alcohol, without even its furniture – drove home the sensation of *Mauritania* being closed off to him, as this choice of meeting as a stab in his heart.

"Olli," White said, alien in a space now filled with bunks and the smell of soldiers. "We don't have much time. Something, I, I don't know how to tell you this–"

White in part did not need to, emoting it plainly: the loss.

"Whit?"

"The entire convoy has stopped because, because, because something awful has happened."

He repeated his question, though whether it actually registered at a level of audible sound, he was not sure. He ran red hot through, knowing, in some impossible, intuitive way, what he was about to have confirmed.

"It's Robert. He's dead, Olli."

His legs went out from under him as if the hull herself had grabbed hold of him and dragged him down deep off a shelf in the seafloor. The unfamiliar bar blurred around him. As a hundred questions spun inside him. *How?* was most dominant of these, shouting to the surface.

But: "ah don't believe ye," is what he blurted out instead.

"Please, Olli, there's no time."

In an out-of-character display of strength, White took hold of him and pulled him to his feet. White tore a path through the soldiers and onto the deck.

"Robert trusted me–" White said.

The salt air hit him like an evacuation drill.

"–and now I need you to, too. You need to leave this ship. Otherwise, his death will have been in utter vain."

"Ah don't believe ye," he said again, his surroundings starting to steady out of the stuffiness of downstairs.

What the soldiers had said was true. The convoy, the entire convoy, was at a standstill in the middle of the open sea. They *were* sitting ducks in hostile waters.

"He killed himself, Olli," White spat, grabbing hold of his shoulders, shaking him. "Here, this is for you if you don't believe me. It came with today's post. He must have mailed it after learning what you'd done. That you'd come after him."

White pressed a piece of paper to his chest. A handwritten note. It was Robert's hand. There was no doubt.

"He did it for you, Olli. When he found out that you had followed him into danger, this was his way out, for you both."

As much as he did not want to acknowledge it, it seemed sure – like the Robert he knew. Struggling, broken, unable to cope, not yet healed.

"He's left *us*, Olli. And now *you* have to leave, too."

White pushed him to the edge of the bridge wing, where he had been led. Cruel irony that he should be shoved-to-depart there. The start of a rope ladder hung off the edge, at his feet, leading to a convoy tender.

"Go now, join the *Queen Mary*; you'll be safe there."

He did as he was told, believed White, grasped the cracked sea-braid. It was a shocking descent of the ladder. The winds of the open sea swept at his broadside. These twisted him, attempted to thread him with the ladder as the rungs of the roped descent teased apart. Tested his grip. He paused for a moment, at midway, the feel of Robert's folded note felt throughout him. He looked to the crushing point, thought about letting go, just allowing the sea and the wind and the tight embrace to take him. The thought of how the fall between the ship and tender might mangle his body was actually welcome to him, an extreme warm of an end, a distraction from the single idea that overwhelmed:

I failed him.

"I've got you, lad," said a coarse voice with hands to match, taking hold of him and wrenching him into the vessel.

He did not remember even continuing his descent to the waiting tender. The shock rendered him *out* of himself. It was like a boat separate from the main body of a ship. *Robert was dead.* It was too...unreal.

"What's happened," he said, dazed, as the tender's pilot steamed away from *Mauritania.*

"There's been a suicide," coarse said. "Sad, sad affair."

"Who?"

The question came absently, though driven by the last haze of hope that it might not be true.

"A Chief Officer Bell."

"Ye certain?"

Clarity-in-questioning, the last that he could muster.

"Yes, lad. I know the name because he was on my roster, you hear. In fact, was due to be transferred to *Aquitania* today. She joined the convoy off Sydney Heads from New Zealand, you know. But, I guess, when faced with it, he decided to...depart early."

It was a second verification, a second opinion. A corroborated account. Now his denials were without foundation. He took the letter from his pocket.

Forgive me, my love.

That was the first line.

He could not bring himself to read below that line. It was all Robert's raw hand. The page otherwise unmarked; Robert painfully alone, even on paper.

"Guess we're not all up to serving," coarse-r said to the horizon.

"Whaur is he?" His eyes were wet and red already. "Tak' me tae him."

"Can't lad, he was buried at sea this morning. These ships are fill-up. They need all the space they have for the living. But I can take you to his ship, if you want. I be headed there anyway, for another transfer."

"Who?"

"Bell's deputy, an Officer Arnold. I'm headed there now to collect him for transfer to *Mauritania*. Though my orders are to deliver you to *Queen Mary* before."

"Who gave that order?"

"Queer that part, you see. *You*, my friend, were never on the roster at all. First, a stop-all order is issued as news breaks of a high-ranking suicide. Then I deliver a message to *Mauritania*, all this ahead of a transfer already scheduled. You, my friend, are added to the schedule for priority transfer to *Queen Mary* after I deliver that sorry message to *Mauretania*."

"Whit wis th' original transfer order?"

"Sadder that, lad. It was of the victim, Bell, with an Arnold to *Aquitania*. But, then, Bell departs...early, and Arnold decides that, instead of going to *Aquitania*, he will go to *Mauritania* instead. So not stopping at *Mary* first will actually save some time, if that is your wish. What's it to be?"

As the pieces presented themselves, confirmation set in and White's words rung, *His death will have been in vain. He's left us.* And the realisation of impending danger came:

Arnold, he's coming for you now.

"Tak' me tae th' *Maìri*."

I hate ye.

He repeated it within, with every second rung of the rope ladder onto the *other* Queen. For the rungs that ran in between, he could not help but think of the Clyde. Taking him back to his climb to become a stowaway. How different he was now, how hurt he felt, more unfinished than *her* initially. Promising himself, at these points, as he neared inevitable entering of *Mary*: *Never again, I will never never forgive you.* She was a ghost ship, troop-shipped out, but without any troops. This served as a symbol of the emptiness he felt and was a curious comfort to him. They were alone together. Empty together. Once the convoy was underway once more, that she then parted ways with the rest and carried on with only *Elizabeth* as company was a comfort, too. She had branched off in an entirely new direction, away from Arnold, away from R–. He couldn't bring himself to even think it, but he needed now to branch away too. She would give him the scope to disappear again. To be that sole traveller he was at the start of his journey, a sea of men for company.

The main convoy, with their ANZAC troops, were bound for Suez and service. But the two *Queens*, together for the first time, sailed as a duo and at speed. They were bound for San Francisco, where they would collect Americans. He did not engage the crew on boarding – in fact, the sisters were similar enough that he could disappear into *Mary*'s crevices, and properly so: to set himself up for the stowaway life that he should have had. The sister-skeleton-Queen gave him ample space to be alone, and he slept most of the steam while also using her hollow hull as an echo chamber of grief. And only when their destination was a sight, when the birds of shore made themselves heard, did he feel ready to reach for the letter Robert had left him.

Forgive me, my love.

For drugging you. For stopping you from joining me on this final journey. I thought I was strong enough to take it on by myself, but I was wrong. What has been asked of me is too much for me to bear. I know that I risk your hatred for this decision. Please, know that, for me, it was more than I could manage.

No words, I'm sure, will ease the pain and hurt you feel at this time. But for me, all I feel is gratitude. And my only regret is that I was not strong enough to see a way forward that did not involve pushing you away. You have always kept me safe, and perhaps, as one final, grand gesture, I can do the same for you.

Please forgive me, and know that the idea of saying goodbye to you was more than I can bear.

No signature, no sign-off. He had asked for forgiveness, but not once in his ridiculous letter did he even say sorry.

I don't forgive ye, he said in his mind and aloud, "I never will."

He took the two sides of the letter, one in each hand, urging himself to tear it up. But not being able to bring himself to do it, to destroy the last piece of fragile, flawed, weak Robert that he now had. And so he folded it up again neatly, though now-crumpled, and returned it to his back pocket, vowing to resume his original ways and not get hurt this way again. The sharp cold change in climate weighed on his grief as they approached port like the very air was heavier here, was crushing him. He knew nothing of the men on board *Mary* and seemed to get by unnoticed enough, even on deck. Probably because he sourced his own meals and accommodation while on board. When he did emerge, he apparently appeared as someone confident in their articles. When, actually, this was more a matter of moving with the nonchalance of a shadow-man – with little left to lose. Would he even continue on in the Cunard line's service once they docked? He was not sure.

Often times, on deck – the fresh, cold, sombre air in his lungs –, Robert rolled in. He arrived without warning, without regard for how he would be received or whether Olli was ready for him. Like the way a sea mist might take even the most experienced of deep-sea anglers by surprise. Grief was like that; it haunted the lungs, making breath difficult with the panic of a person's place in the world turning evermore translucent with time; someone shifting to memory, their traces twisting in unpredictable ways when they visit. Instead of retreating back to the nest he had built below, as had been his strategy so far, on this particular roll-in, the knowledge that he would soon need to forfeit that warm place of blankets and stuffy silence when troops flooded in propelled him into work instead. Folding into the scattering of men in the arrow of the foredeck, returning to the first skill of shipman-ship he had acquired when last in a cold waters port: managing the ropes.

It helped. Being part of the workings of a ship once more, not just service within her but toward more instrumental regards as well: finessing her riggings, wrangling her ropes, feeling part of her fabric. Through work, he also gained exposure to other persons, those living, who helped pull him into a possible future through their discussions of what would come next. War had picked up the turnover pace; he learnt through work on the foredeck. The *Queens* were on an urgent troop supply run to Canada and would only dock one night on arrival, which was barely enough time for her to be loaded with manpower and supplies. While time was dragging for him after Robert's departure, in the world around him, the heartbeat of the days of 1940 was gaining speed.

Elizabeth was already in dock. As they piloted toward her, he felt her pull. As if the tender had taken hold of him, too, nudging him into a preordained position. He would stay at sea, he thought, and he would stay with *Mary* – in the hope that she might guide him back to the spirit of his original intention. Though *Elizabeth* was where he desired to be more, *Mary* promised a new beginning on which he might find solace in the hard hands of men off to war.

7 December 1941

America enters the war.

A major power is brought to arms, but not by her own choosing – she has had her hand forced into action. The atrocities of the Hawaii harbour hit were played for much dramatic effect over the American wireless. As, among the already engaged and overextended Allied forces, a silent sigh of hope was triggered. Hope for what the Imperial Japanese move might actually mean: an at-last and vast reprieve. By the declaration, merchant fleet service held a renewed appeal, had settled into him, in fact. He was still on *Mary*, one of Cunard's troop-carrying flagships, when it happened. He had been for a year by that time. But America's entrance would signal a vast swing eastward: to scoop up the men desperately needed for the Africa campaign, and would be a welcome change of scenery from the Australia route that had become routine. Already – and before even the announcement was made – it seemed to some that preparations were being made for *her*. For example, she was fortunately en route to an American port at the time, along with her sister, *Elizabeth*. Therefore, she would not waste much time in mobilising herself, drilling deep into the new wellspring of men: fresh flesh to transport into action.

He had remained on *Mary* for all that time. Constantly, since the shock of Robert up until the attack on Pearl Harbor. He had served and overseen more than a ferry or three of men to the fronts. His time on *Mary* had become fruitful. She had yielded her below decks – and his too – to the accommodation of many. Easing, in what small combined-effort way they could, the passage of fine men to the theatres of war. Like an opera house green room, he had come to adore the masculine talent that passed through him. And there was a small measure of selfish excitement after the Hawaii affair announcement: it would provide him access to previously untrappable men. It may have been guilt at his gluttony, but a sea mist of sadness for the Americans now drawn into this conflict swept in hours after the announcement. And he found himself questioning his choice of vessel once again. This questioning was felt especially during the final stage of their steam into New York when he paused from rope-work on deck to soak up the thread-through of the heads and passage past the Statue of Liberty. That is where he heard *her* call loudest.

Over more than a year of solid service, he had carved out a sea role for himself that suited his unique Cunard talents. Like a kind of sea-going, for-military-men-in-waiting gofer. He did odd jobs about the ship that few others wanted to do, attending to the cleaning and maintenance of *Mary*'s makeshift communal showers and urinal blocks, which allowed for free passage throughout the ship at all times of strict blackout curfew nights. This was a cover for his *true* onboard purpose: pleasure in a ship built for speedy pleasure, but on an otherwise pleasureless voyage. There was nervous electricity onboard to complete the New York gambit to collect their first American batch. By this time, the *Queens*, like him, were well-versed in their service roles. Now, each of them, able to carry an entire division in a single go. The two *Queens* had traversed the seas, carrying men. *Grey ghosts* they were being called, expert at evading the enemy, with speeds no German U-boat or cruiser could hope to match, protecting their precious cargo. All while he, on a smaller scale, serviced the precious cargo being carried by floating iron on a more individual basis – keeping their libidos ship-shape, giving their loins a reason to continue. The two *Queens* would often pass each other as they ferried men, as sisters in the night. But not since New York, at the dawn of the war, had they been together in such a way. Winds of change were airborne. As *Mary* docked alongside her sister once more, bringing memories back.

America, he thought, *she just might change everything.*

It's a man-grab, he thought, arousal a cocktail of desire and indignation stirring within him.

The thought came from the foredeck, as *Mary* got her moorings, while *Elizabeth* was already receiving men.

Men of war jellyfish.

These thoughts came in reaction to the ordered, purposeful, layered-but-also-mindless and driven-by-forces-beyond-their-own-control, herding of men into carriers. The tides, the shifting, unforgiving seas, had brought with them metaphors for men. Metaphors that were fished from the oceans and shorelines – as he had done once before, for Robert. *Elizabeth* would shove off first, perhaps even be out of the gates before *Mary* had been refuelled.

Jump ship!

It came so suddenly as a thought that it was as if someone else had said it. It was the first time he had seen her, up close, within reach, in many months. It was all eerily, gut-wrenchingly familiar. Even *Normandie* was here, now orphaned, her homeland fallen completely. The trio of them, though only two of them ready: *Normandie* had hurried conversions and stripping of finery underway, so she, too, could ferry the troops into the service of war theatrics.

Now, Ollie. Go now!

This time he did not question it. Did not try to rationalise it or even allow himself to reflect on its source – he just ran. Along the promenade deck, down the pilot's rope ladder, and the wharf's length. As if everything depended on it. As if he was already too late. As if *his Queen* was calling him, yet had already left. He watched *her* as he ran, leaving all his possessions behind as if that would keep her there; his watching, ensuring that she stayed until he could rejoin her. He stumbled on the occasional uneven plank of the deck but did not let this break his gaze. Running, toward the mass assembled to enter her, men moving with much more trepidation than he, much less certainty about–

Collision

He crashed into an American, a man. So immovable a man that he did not budge on impact, yet so agile also, so adept to any attack of the rushing onslaught kind, that he caught him with ease, wrapping sweet muscle around him. Like he was a ball, a misguided oval object skilfully swept into the trough of his glove.

He's caught me, and he's wrapped me tight.

It was a chain reaction: an entry and a wrap. He felt firm-chest against his cheek. A heartbeat. And lingered there, longer than he should. Taking the catch as a hold and leaning into it.

"Ahem," his catcher said by way of a clearing of the throat.

He had forgot himself, on the dock, surrounded by thousands of boarding Yanks. But still...lingered a moment longer.

"Ahem."

Fuller this time. The second throat clear – complemented by an arm hug withdrawn and lightly clenched fist – tore him back, to his purpose, to rejoining *his Queen*.

Though, leaning back to take in his catcher... *His other arm still holds me and is at my lower back.*

He is Adonis, America's Adonis. Young and round-muscled and cornfed: like a Hollywood film fantasy of Kansas.

"Sorry," Olli said, looking at him – *into* him.

Normally, he would say 'soldier', but "Sur" came out instead...after a long pause.

He is heaven.

Time lost meaning. How long it was – a second, a sequence of seconds – he did not know, but his catcher's response seemed equal as it was evasive.

"Slow down, buddy," deep, long, his throat a well into an undiscovered cavern.

Voices around them broke through, drawing the meeting of two out to an assembly of thousands. And then his American let go. He felt like he was falling. Like at last, he had found a steadying force, only to lose it. Turns out, he had reactionary physical points of his own, gripping his American's upper arms but unable to gain traction, tenuously holding just the front. He, who had serviced hundreds, if not thousands, by now, had nothing to say – *what have I to offer?* Reluctantly, remorsefully, the first tragedy of his self-transfer, he removed himself, running from his American, past the slow-moving crew of Yankee soldiers and up the gangway leading into his *Queen.* Sole white against a sea of men in khaki, he was able to pass the men unobstructed. His eagerness to get on board, to return to her, contrasted with a more solemn march of men to war, who had already seen through their war bulletin cinema screenings and post-enlisting training to glimpse the grim conditions that awaited them across the sea.

He would have stood out in the crowd like a pearl among black beads, but *his American* stood out too, even from the distance he had run out between them. Taller, broader, handsome-r than all the rest. He could not help himself in back-pocketing a glimpse before he disappeared through her hatch – even allowing himself to believe that the stare was reciprocated. His steward-articles would only get him so far, just into the door. While his time with *Mary* had allowed him to fashion a role suited to his own talents, he had never attempted a revision of the war-duration, base-level Cunard steward articles White had issued him. Not speaking up was partly as protection against a haunting of his stowaway past and his father – no doubt still searching for him; but more to the point, he had avoided all Cunard office officials in chronic pursuit of forgetting that time when all was good.

Since leaving him in New York, *his Queen* had transformed herself, like every other morsel of himself since his last visit to the city. Both completed in wartime conversion, but also undone. Her lighting fixtures and other essential mechanisms were all in place and already aged with use. And, any finery that had been in place when he joined her initially, in her state of partial fitting out, was now entirely removed, replaced with brutal functionalism of mass accommodation and extreme space economy, with whatever parts of her that were finished and immovable, now time-capsuled behind wooden boards. This condition had become familiar on *Mary*, and he felt it befitted his *Queen* more, the functionalism, giving her greater elegance even greater purpose. It was a homecoming, of sorts, but also a first meeting of *Elizabeth* in her military come of age state.

Once inside on his steward articles, his own suggestions – of tending to troop ablutions as his primary duties, and helping out on the foredeck when required – washed well with the rest.

It was the vocation *Mary* had given him.

In addition to vantages presented by young military men in their prime – showering in unison – and his own skills in lingering in such spaces. And; as a means of securing later visits from those men; it was a vocation that vested in him what he had to offer: his general demeanour and ability to 'pass' among the men. As one of the lads, proving vital in procuring plentiful penis processionals. But as his procurement had progressed from a passion into a profession, his *true* purpose in transporting troops manifested: pleasure in an otherwise pleasureless pursuit. Having washing facilities on hand served an essential, professional drive, too.

Mansex without preparations was a messy, unpalatable affair. Part of his duty to his troops was ensuring the penetrations were always about them and their pleasure, with clean entry and, often, cleaner lines of retreat. Penetration-as-baptism; thorough cleaning of cocks that perhaps were not washed as vigorously in communal, on-ship, makeshift ablutions. Invariably, he offered men release into an abyss absent from bodily functions. But the reality, for him, in a life at sea, meant success struck, like all good trades, on the chord of perfection through practice. Devotion; to procedures of efficiency and improvement that were informed by constant refinement and fine-tuning. The temporal, out-of-wall plumbing of troopship conversion on *Mary* had been intended to protect the ship's double shell, on *Elizabeth* now too. To allow for anticipated return to pleasure passenger service after conflict, and the strip-out of all her communal washing, pissing and shitting stations. But outward plumbing also added benefit to his practice. Its exposed water tubing, of which, in private – with drainage nooks in her design, flowing to the troubled seas – he could turn: to the flushing out of himself. His duties, carefully refined through experience, permitted the ducking in and out of such crevices: to ensure he was always freshly flushed out and an always-ripe receptacle for the reception of those that relied upon his pleasuring-troopers service.

His success laid, and always had, in a relishing of relinquishing a right to self-pleasure. Also, in a no-conditions, entirely charitable ethos to his operation: military men, he had come to learn through trial, were in this age, mostly, willing to meet sexual needs in other men, as these inserts and off-loads lowered the risk – of infection, child-burden and sacrifice of income – that came through more traditional, on-shore securement of sexual services via the female sex. While his edge over other males who sought to exploit soldiers' desires lay, principally, in a lack of financial incentive, and thus, purity of his pursuit of pleasuring others as a receptive, clean, non-suspicious orifice.

His second edge was adeptness at *passing* – something he held, bitterly, as one over on White.

But back to the homecoming: transfer to his men-maximised, though still home, *Queen* was made smoother by a near mirror with *Mary* troopship configuration. This enabled him to up his penetration-services-*practice* – in the formal rather than practising sense – with ease.

And so, in the chaos of first Yank boarding, he constructed his pure-profitless-business bathing station.

Setting up on the ground of a fresh campaign allowed ample time for him to turn himself inside out, ready for that night's intake, even in advance of sailing. These preparations, not pleasant, were in their initial set-up, not convenient, either, given troopship conditions. But they were necessary, an essential puzzle of the service, keeping the mystery of cleanliness and the frequenters of his use keen.

In peacetime, the two super-liners were like floating villages. But the need to cram the men in during war swelled them to towns. With their own districts, in each, for every crossing across the seas. This capacity was built up over time, from 5,000 to 8,000 to 10,000, and above, to a complete division of men. The Americans spearheaded this growth in storing-of-bodies capability, in an informal capacity, before their entrance into the war. This increase worked to his advantage. Essential to managing the transports' swell included limiting men to remain in distinct colour-coded districts and sleeping and eating in shifts. This regime of men management allowed him to spread his services throughout her hull, sharing the provision evenly and swiftly in keeping with his one proviso: one penetration per soldier. When he had first set up the service on *Mary*, he did not think it would work. The men were two numerous, he thought, and therefore his previous, tried-and-tested turning of the meat of hard dockyard men – namely: to have himself available to them on anonymous, darkened, behind-iron-panelling terms – would not work here. But he was wrong. Surprised and delighted to discover that, with the waves of war stretched out before them, the hulls of the *Queens* were also mystical *between*-spaces where men gave other men a pass, in light of the circumstances they found themselves in.

There was a communal civility code among the men. It was like what went on in the trenches of the Great War. Yet also, with a larger echo chamber of it's-okay-we're-in-this-togetherness about it. All in keeping with the global contours of the current conflict. The *Queens* were known to be 'lively' in seas, even when empty – something exaggerated when their capacities were maxed out by the bulk of men. Some found this soothing and slept with the sway of a super-liner in deep ocean, while others were put off at the gut or the brains by the behaviour, the latter his audience: generally too pent-up to entertain slumber. They would strike up conversations with other pent-up bunkmates, so close that they could smell every part of each other, and pass the nights, sating their fears, by turning to manly pleasures. Talking about the nurses on board was a popular early topic, but these maidens were well guarded and out of reach, except, perhaps, for the odd handsome officer. Some would then turn to their girl-back-home, only touchable through a photograph but still passing her among new mates, with permission to take pleasure in her petite physique.

The forward-planners among them had brought along Tijuana bibles that they pulled out at the advanced stage of these nocturnal manly distraction-of-distress discussions. Many had succumbed to sleep by this stage, but those who remained came over in relish of the palm-fitting pages. Like they were parchments of the ancients, these comics, sacred-sexual hieroglyphics. Initially, words and crude drawings were enough as these publications made the rounds, but soon touching of selves occurred – as a natural progression, from raunch bibles in palms to balmy rubs of brief-released bulges. Individually each man removed himself to commence a stroke and might have reasoned that the refashioned dining or entertaining hall was dark enough and their canvas bunk curved enough around their person to shield the self-gratification from view.

But he preferred a different position: That all knew when the first man took it upon himself to remove his manhood and were thankful to him for it, for it gave permission for them to do the same, and soon the space was pulsing with in-synch with ship sway strokes.

It was at this point that his services came into play. When the camaraderie of men coming to terms with perils that were to follow could find comfort with each other, comforting themselves together, that he would complete his evening attendance of that quadrant of the hull's showers and urinals. There he would pass men who had taken their touching beyond their beds. They had not set out in search of an act in particular; they were open to persuasion, something had taken them from their bunk to seek something more. The comfort of communal touching, the understanding from others of the *need* for it, had spurred them to action. And he provided an outlet for that. Clean and safe and without consequence. That would send them back to their bunk with an unexpected satisfaction, helped by the disappearance of him and his services the next night, as he turned himself to the needs of others on board, from a different quadrant, not to return to their part of the ship again that voyage.

As he had learnt on *Mary*, his service was met with genuine appreciation from the men of the majority who used it, which was in stark contrast with his Clydebank, rough service days. Of course, roughness, even hatred, was expected from some who partook – his ugly giant from *Normandie*. These hatred-fucks, he accepted, as part of his service. But many felt genuine relief in the unloading and, he suspected, gained additional comfort from the warmth they felt of other men who had come before, others' release encouraging their own, warming its flow. Those who *got it*, he had come to suspect, would even go so far as to encourage others to use the service, too. Not as a replacement for the girl back home, simply as a stopgap, a bridge between the bibles and their brides. Encouragement to others would come by a gentle tap on the shoulder as they returned to the bunk, as they passed by someone they did not yet know, an average, red-blooded lad, who looked like he could benefit from releasing into someone there simply to receive. Even pointing the way in certain satisfied-cloud cases.

Olli was a well-oiled machine. But that night, the maiden voyage of the Yankee Elizabeth *Queen*, he would change all his rules of engagement.

Having completed the set up of his facilities deep in the hull, he was on the foredeck helping prepare the ropes and chains, as was customary in the hours before a departure. Only the crew were permitted on the foredeck, making it one of the few places on the *Queen*'s deck with room to swing a rope. Everywhere else, the deck was so moulded with men that it was standing room only for whole stretches of the day – even their standings done in shifts, two men sharing a bunk and space on deck or in-dining at different times of the day. Their sailing schedule was stricter than usual, which lent the *Queen* a humming of activity, next level from what he had known on her sister. To make sharing work, sleeping, eating, bathing and fresh air arrangements for the troops were carefully coordinated in advance of their arrival.

For many of the men crammed onboard her, this would serve as their first introduction to on-the-move sleeping formation formality. The success of super-liner troopship-ing was simple sub-division. One division of 10,000 men, subbed into brigades of 2,000 – one per deck. This was further subbed into regiments and then into battalions of between 500 and 1,000. *Elizabeth*'s grander dining and ballrooms carried entire regiments, with men stacked in multiples of three – generally, on folding 'standee' bunks – an American innovation. In her smoking and reception rooms, still grand, there slept battalions of up to 500. Companies of 100 or more were squeezed into her bars, and platoons of 50 crowded into her recreation rooms. This subbing was rounded off by squadrons of 20 in the first-class cabins, with sections of 10 in the smaller, tourist-class rooms. Troop-town planning was everything, the key to the Queens' ferrying conquests. It meant that each man could be accounted for, and made his own planning precision-essential, too.

Order was achieved through rank and file protocol. Each section of her that housed sleeping (and restless) soldiers was under that respective unit's commander, with the division's major general overseeing the entire able-men-haul from the wheelhouse, alongside the captain. This was the divisive difference of the wartime-commandeered liner. She was under the direction of two generals, one for her safe seaward passage, the other for the security and discipline of her manly cargo. On the military side, it was a concentrated system of hierarchical accountability, adherence to which proved essential in maintaining order in such close quarters across hostile and sometimes unforgiving seas.

He respected the sea-trooping system, had come to understand it, navigate it, work its peculiarities to his particular inclines, even. He had become well-versed in the hierarchy of the troopship configuration, strategising as if on the battlefield, moving his preparation and penetration stations in line with near-impossible to find gaps in the same side's front line. Experience, and a few near-misses, had taught him his limits, too. He'd learnt to keep his pool big. Stay with the brigades and the regiments, for their commanders, typically brigadiers and colonels, oversaw the bulk of bunks that made his offering easier to operate under the radar of discovery, like how a single scout into enemy camp had a better chance of intel and evading discovery than a group. But also, he had learned that regal responsibility came with a greater sense of self-importance and, therefore, a real likelihood of absence of supervisors – off to dine, cigar-with, and generally brown-nose the ranks of generals instead.

Smaller units came with razor risks and piercers to his entire business. Therefore, a code of practice was developed. He never ventured beyond battalions, as the numbers below them came with commanders of less access to high-ranking social engagements; and, therefore, a greater incentive to prove themselves through order enacted at a local level. But! *His* American – his collided-with Yank – forced rethink of his entire battleplan and, above this, a crisis of course of action. What was his business ethos? What was his design? What did he wish – no, mean – no, *need* – to achieve through his service? And... If achievement was satisfied through safety, was it triumph at all for these men on the precipice of almost certain, absolute sacrifice? It was a dangerous business proposition that went against his own codes of professional conduct and self-preservation.

His strategy had been to commence his services at the stern. Beginning in the larger sleeping units, far away from where the commanders were often dining. Also, where the 'someones' resided – at the fore, with the rest of the officers and authorities on board. But, dangerously, he had honed in on one individual who had snared his attention, *his* American, who happened to find himself in a company in the seaman's bar at the fore of the ship – so in-the-walls stalk had told him. That the fates had seemingly seen fit to position *his* American there, where he, a boy running away from his father, had spent much of his initial time as a stowaway on his *Queen*...

It fuelled propulsion toward the risk-taking decision:

Tackle him first.

The seaman's bar would peacetime hold up to fifty thirsty sailors. But in her wartime configuration, her salty bar's breachers bellowed to hold 200 men. He had observed his American's movements through *Elizabeth* since boarding. His ability to do this was most unusual. So many men spread throughout so many corners of her hull. It meant that the vast majority of those he sighted on board were never seen again. Only a barely-perceptible percentage of men did he see more than once, and never, so far, were any that he had *seen to* seen again. His *serviced men*, these disappeared into the depths of the *Queen*. They moved about within her until disembarking at the destination-end, without coming into contact again.

Men-of-war.

This was the metaphor he had devised to make sense of troopship men. They moved through the sea in a layered pack. In all conditions, and facing all manner of threat. There were big ones, little ones, broad ones; skinny ones, too; yet, they were all the same. Young and brave and unrelenting in their movement, to him. Just when he thought he had locked eyes on one, found one that seemed somewhat unique, unicorn-ic, that he might like to follow through the sea; just as fast his focus had shifted, the pack had moved on, and a whole fresh batch of jellyfish flooded in to work on.

Not this time. Not this one.

Whether by his own determination for an extraordinary homecoming or the sheer uniqueness of new-to-him American mettle: this one was different. That evening – once total blackout was in effect and the upper deck off-limits –, having completed his showers and urinals cleaning-run, inclusive of his own flush out, he made his way into the bar.

The hour was advanced. Calculations meant it should have aligned with most men asleep, allowing him to file the bunk lines, court the custom of any self-pleasuring or at-the-precipice. This file was to give them the incentive needed to follow him back to the hidden space he had 'specially furnished for a trooper's sexual fulfilment. But it was not as expected inside. There was life in the bar, jovial-ness among the men. Being the first time he had returned to the seaman's bar since his first sea voyage, it reminded him of that atmosphere, though now it had the aroma of a military mess about the space. He caught sight of his American immediately, reclined in his bunk, his arms folded behind his head in the manner of support, his biceps ballooned in relaxed tension in the style of duck-feather pillows. He locked on to Olli, too, still reclined, unfazed, just a glint of curiosity in his look. It was all too familiar, all too similar to the sequence with Robert.

Was being back here causing this?

He left. Fled.

It was a mistake, he thought.

Too small of a talent pool, *too personal* a pursuit. Out of the service quarters and into a dining hall on the same deck brought him to more familiar prospects, a battalion of at least 500, mostly sleeping, some still restless, the familiar sounds of ruffled pages and flapping flesh.

And from here, cowardly, he commenced his secondary choice servicing of his first Americans.

His sex spaces amounted to a series of storage chambers running the length of her hull and dotted along each deck. They housed pipes and wires that came together in an almighty jumble at the base of the chamber, resembling the trunk of an ancient tree. During the day, when the *Queen*'s systems were in full swing, these were loud, unliveable, electricity-generating spaces – something that had ruled them out as troop housing options. But on the night run, in the infant hours of morning, in full blackout conditions, came only the distant rumble of her engines as breathing up through the iron from below, making for serviceable *service* quarters. His usual scouting process proved successful. Soon the Yanks were coming by to avail themselves of the British pipe on offer. The service boy they happened upon once they had clambered over the tubes and wires to the tucked-away corner of the chamber was always the same:

He was away from them, face down, unseeing; arse up, accepting. He never turned to peek, never took a look at who was making use of him. It was about them, that was the service. For some, the trust in the sincerity of his offering was not forthcoming; they would sneak up on him, unsure; enter him, unsure; and then secure his face to the iron with a force that would *make sure*: that the encounter was just a fuck.

The men who came were rough. Preferable to the Australians, certainly. The Aussies, he had found, of all the Allied troops to take transport inside him, the most hateful of having had him. In the aftermath of their release, Aussies would sometimes make a point of their distaste, punching out their hate on the mouth of his entrance, in the in-between of his shoulder blades, and sometimes, into the back of his head, too. Yet, alarmingly, he found the experience harder to bear being back on *his Queen*. Something of a trial, something to endure. He felt it more intensely, the servicing, the skin around his entry point, more tender.

It hurts.

The Yanks that used him that night were not unusually violent, beyond the stage where he wanted them to roughly enter. It was more their tone. He was used to dirty talk, but the freshness of the Pearl Harbor incident seemed to take priority to such an extent that unleash into him became a mere secondary objective. It was unsettling. "Jap" was substituted for "Fag."

"Take *that*, you *filthy* Jap," one especially vocal patron proclaimed as he deposited.

These were the stealth bombers, he thought, consistently in unloadings into him that night, bombing his gut as retribution for Pearl Harbor. It confused him, this upset. On *Mary*, such vitriol from his troops – even the Australians with their violence – would have invigorated him; that he had given them a soft, safe outlet for their aggression on the eve of their own service in what was shaping up to be humanity's most inhumane hour. But instead, this time, it exposed something about the whole experience. It *was* just fucking, and he was *just* a fuck thing.

Hawaii destroyed everything, he thought, as another Yank yielded seed inside him and spat on his back as he withdrew.

He was ready to call it a night. The service had taken a toll it never had before. It had become what he had promised himself, *after Robert*, it would not: *personal*. He reached back to trace his entrance; it was at-the-brim and throbbing. That night's use was nothing compared to his average, and yet he felt like he had passed his limit several Yanks ago.

It hurts.

"Get up," he urged, out and in, *leave*.

But he couldn't. He stuck frozen to her iron floor; dry iced, like the only moisture in him had seeped from his eyes and bonded against him in a pact with the floor, sticking him to the metal, forcing him to carry on as receptacle. And when footsteps started ringing from somewhere behind the mangled mess of tubes and wires, he felt cold terror rise within him. He elevated his arse, pressed his face further into the frigid floor – in the hope that his easing of access might make for a faster finish.

As the steps toward him grew closer, heavier, he felt the terror rise, riling his body to a tremor. When his next depositor was close enough for Olli to hear him breathe... Suddenly, the unease started to subside. His visitor undressed slowly, carefully – so much so that he found himself envisioning the folding of garments into neat piles by his upturned feet. Security returned when the stranger placed a hand; hard, large – but warm –, on his thigh, guiding him from an upright-arse position to lie on his side. Under him was fabric, clothes recently removed which, by comparison with the chill of uncovered iron, felt like a duck-feather bed.

His visitor then pulled him into himself, and warmth washed over him. The hard hand slid from his waist to his entrance. He was gaping and gooey-full but also sore and spent and unwitting for more. Yet, to *this* touch, he reared up again, yawning open in a primal, unthinking way, beckoning *this American* in.

But his reviving visitor was in no rush. He traced Olli's lips, turning them from sore to soft again with a teasing touch. Other soldiers' seed made for ample lubricant, and skilfully, carefully, *his* visitor kept tracing the curvature of his lips while lathering himself. Olli felt him growing at his mouth, getting fuller and fuller. His visitor's lather hand was back at his waist now, and kissed his neck tenderly as he fed himself to Olli's mouth – impossibly, surely, how-could-it-be? –, now hungry again.

Connection came with an arched neck and a curt outtake of breath. As the visitor loomed large. Though his entrance had been well basted by this stage, his visitor filled it all; stretched it, too. Kissing Adam's apple in the arch of Olli's neck, knowing about his own size but also possessing the skill to soften it. His visitor was fully in control of the threading of himself down below, tracing his way from Olli's waist... Along the ripples of his ribs, over the point of his nipple, to rest at his neck. But not to grip, not to grab, not to choke. Not to be sentimental, either. Knowingly, his visitor traced the bruises that were growing there. Not enough to add to them, just to tell him that he knew they were there. That, and, with him, there would be no more.

When Olli's breathing started syncing with the movement of his visitor inside him, his visitor's hand moved to his cheek, and his cheek; lower then upper, both flushed red; and turned him, gently, so their uttering lips met. Olli kept his eyes closed, initially, as he took his visitor from both ends, feeling himself healing. The passion of their kiss spurred his visitor's lower attention points into action, scooping into him in a massaging manner borne of experience in pleasuring – selfless, knowing scoops-into.

He's servicing me, Olli thought, gratitude filling him.

He opened his eyes, yet by this stage did not even need to. Only *his* American could do this to him. He lost himself in New World sea blues as the rhythm picked up. He was himself, broken as service had made him, more beautiful here, sweet-smelling. Perfect. And with that, throwing his head back again, released as a first, himself – his American kissing his neck as he did.

"Can I finish inside you?"

It was the first time anyone had asked him that; what a gent, to extend that level of respect to a loose Brit already full of several Yankees' seed. He kissed his gent deep. Gripped hold from the small of his back, holding him inside him as he whispered:

"Aye."

And not a moment too soon. His Yank shuddering and splashing inside him in the same second of consent, Olli kissing his neck as he did.

And now he leaves, he thought, panicked once more, more pathetic than before.

But when the shuddering had stopped, leaving him so full, he spilt out over them both – the gent Yank did not leave him, did not even withdraw. The hardness subsided with time, leaving a soft swell as he remained inside him. Bringing one limb under Olli's neck, allowing his head to rest on the pillow of the bulging cushion of his upper arm. With his other arm, his visitor wrapped his waist. Getting them comfortable, settled it seemed, for the night.

"What's ya name?" His visitor asked.

His was a voice that ran full and low, like the bubbling of a brook at the base of a deep ravine. Even at a whisper pitch, its bassy tones made it feel like it must have carried through the entire hull. But in practice, it was spoken so close that his visitor's lips grazed his ear, sending the question into Olli only, bouncing through one chamber all the way through to his plugged-by-meat passage at the base of his own ravine.

Even soft, he stretched Olli out, keeping him sated.

The question was another first.

No one's asked that before, he thought.

"Olli," he said.

So complete with his visitor, he felt like the word had hardly made it out.

"Olli," he repeated, still a distant echo in the company of his visitor's speech.

"A pleasure to meet ya, Olli."

He could feel a smile in the rolls and rhythms of his American's deep, dulcet diction.

"Harris here. Good night, Olli."

Harris pulled him into a whole-bodied embrace. He was a hard man, the epitome of all-American, home-grown, corn-fed man-beef. But there, on the floor of Olli's sex room, his bulk rounded and softened to comfort him. From the wide-bulge of bicep that Olli rested his head on, to the broad chest that filled the gap between his shoulder blades, then on: to the other arm, which wrapped around Olli's slender waist – in a complete circumnavigation that was resolved with the resting a hand in Olli's lower back –, to his legs, the crests atop which Olli's own legs reclined.

The consequence of this configuration was the most secure and comfortable sleeping arrangement. *Harris* held him into himself, keeping any of Olli's naked body from touching the chill of the floor; with his arms and chest and legs, Harris safeguarded the chance for sleep. But the sweetest comfort of all came from Harris's *cock*, at ease but still scandalously, expansionist-ly Germanic, occupying space, even as it found rest inside him.

After Robert, Olli had turned his arse to receiving, vowing to never feed another again. He was to be fed instead. He was to take for his officer all the nutrients that Robert could no longer take. But it had not played out that way for all his time on *Mary* – and not on *Elizabeth* so far. The troop-men semen had become insincere, a mere formality to the act of allowing men an outlet. Until this moment, this man. And for the first time, the semen received was genuine.

Genuine.

But, ironically, selfishly, like the Holy Grail when finally grasped by the for-King crusading knight; once found; this life-sacrificing treasure...

He hoarded it, savoured it, just for himself.

This is what safe feels like.

And tears burst forth like a breach in the hull. Shuddering through him, his body reeling from the surprise attack, the gravity of his failure with Robert taking root inside him like a grave.

Hawaii ruined everything, thinking of Robert. *I'm sorry I couldn't keep you safe.*

It was a messy display, unman- and even boy-ly, never how he had behaved with a man before. As he sobbed on Harris, burying his face into the fold in his arm, Harris did not react – except to flex his support points slightly, pulling Olli further into the comfort of his hold, until sleep came for them both.

V

ELIZABETH

Olli woke alone, wrapped in another's clothing.

Warm and well-slept. Comfortable. He would have continued to sleep had it not been for the clammer of water through tubes and current through wires. He was thankful for this commotion, too, as, in his windowless chamber, this was all he had to tell him that the day was underway, and duties waited. But today, these could wait a few minutes more. He was wrapped in an army overcoat, smelling of Harris and their night spent together. He pulled Harris's scent into him and traced his entrance, still flexed and warm from where *he* had been.

Olli returned the coat-by-stealth before going about his morning rounds, folded neatly and tucked into the bunk on which he had seen Harris reclined the night before. It was fortunate, for the bar was clear; all were up on deck, where the excitement was. The Pacific was transformed since the Japanese attack, far more treacherous now for the two *Queens*, who sailed together but without convoy, for none could keep with them, and it was safer that way. But still, it was a risk-filled gambit, with a crossing-feel of the last-ditch affair.

The great speeds on the Pacific were a spectacle that got the blood pumping for the troops, for whom the front seemed still foreign. It was a thrilling journey: aboard the world's largest moving object, alongside her sister, steaming at record speeds, evading fire from air, sea's surface and below it.

For the first half of their first full day at sea with the Yanks, he occupied himself with troop service below deck. And enjoyed it more this time, after the night spent with Harris.

The once-secondary tending to clogged troop showers and fragrant urinal trays… Once secondary to his *true* service role, seemed more meaningful this day. No doubt because his hole still gaped and brushed on the cotton fibres of his briefs, from where Harris – his wholesome, and it pained him, *perfect*, visitor – had spent the night stretching it into remission.

Focusing on the stern shower rows, replenishing the soap and restocking the towels amid the roster of troop-washing. His relaxed, open entrance twitched as he laboured and with the recollection of its stuffing, especially in these spaces where, in again-stealth, he took in the sights as a removed remembrance. Line after line of youthful, lean men. Lathering their chests, their arse cheeks, their cocks – in-shift. The lads lingered on that last one, the *cocks*, lathering up their loins as they jousted with their shower-sparring partners, fattening to self- and rough house-touch.

This was the longer-linger of the troopship carrier and he had come to know it well, to study its movements. It was a unique breed of military intimacy, completely innocent yet sublimely indecent, too. Water glistening off their shimmering, shiny, soaped-up physiques in the company of comrades, arse-bare brothers-at-arms talking trash about women while they washed their manhoods hard and eyed up the assets of their G.I. kin.

As he watched them himself, as he took in the farce of their water-based, communal pleasuring, Harris was who he thought of.

He had not seen 'the front'. Did not know what these men might actually face when they disembarked from the *Queen*. Admittedly, while telling himself he was offering his own brand of reprieve from horrors to come, he had never, truly, confronted what those horrors might be… But he had imagined and hoped that similar wash stations would be fashioned on the frontlines. For the men to wash away their day, and to be used for talk of absent women as a buffer to enjoy each other in a woman's absence.

He thought on his thesis as he finished his shower run. Then he scrubbed up – including a freshen-up of his own plumbing, the seal now tight again, before heading above board in the direction of the foredeck… Choppy but sunny that day.

That's the case with Harris, he thought, his hole kept loose as that name reverberated inside him and the wish for frontline washing stations gained a vividly experienced-by-him future patron.

The decks were sandwiched with out-of-sleeping-shift soldiers, slowing any movement along the promenades. The crunch gave him time to reflect on the experience he had gained in the realm of men…

The men he had procured, the ones that his *practice* has yielded for him – dating back to his shipyard start –, they were typically men who took women as a primary provision but, in choice circumstances, could be inclined to puncture the right boy, often when his penis prescribed, and for any kind of pleasure: yes, the 'any port in a storm' idiom.

But Harris's special, he thought as he squeezed his way through the mass of men at the half-point of his *Queen*.

The way he had *worked him* – though that was not how, he knew, Harris would see it – was different: had something of the war about it.

Last night was Harris's first time with a man.

Because he made love to me, he thought. *He fucked me like I was a woman, and then held me after.*

His men never did that.

Women are soft, men are hard; another idiom, granted, but one born of his own empiricism.

Accurate, he thought, *in the realm of man-sex.*

The men he cruised were, deliberately, not those who sought out other men as a matter of course, but instead those that would turn their attentions to a man in certain conditions.

Harris was a narrower-conditions sort of man, he agreed with his own reasoning.

There was a resilience-against-Harris's-charms that came with the light of day and seaspray – and a tightening up anus, he thought. Though all that pretence slipped away, leaving him loose again, when he heard his name called again in the same deep register that it had been whispered it to him while that perfect Yank stretched him out the night before.

"Olli," Harris called again, as if he didn't hear it. "Come join us."

Here was yet another point of departure compared with the men who had had him in the past, none of whom sought a follow-up so publicly, just hours after disengaging.

"Awright again," Olli said, in attempt at keeping it casual.

His cheeks flushed with colour at the sight of Harris in day.

Harris was leaned casually against the railing of the *Queen*'s starboard side, his posture slightly slouched, yet still disciplined – his build one of muscle and height and handsomeness. He looked like a Greek god against the wild white-tipped deep-navy of the Pacific – *Mary* in the distance. Like Poseidon, Harris was confident, even in the face of a considerable roll and a blistering wind, that brought the occasional spray of sea across his features.

He licked his lips, tasting salt, longing for the taste of Harris *in* him again.

Harris carried on as if oblivious, or simply unaffected, by his lust:

"Fellas, this is Olli."

Such was his tunnel vision that he had not noticed the entourage of Harris mates. Each young and fit, supremely handsome, but still nothing on *him*. The mates showed knowingness, too, flanked at Harris peripheries, like the side set-dressings of an ancient amphitheatre: beauty, poetry, and tragedy at the centre.

When they had clashed paths, at boarding, the day previous on the docks, he would have said that Harris was of capital B biblical beauty, the kind that a father would lead into (hope-not) slaughter by a lion as the ultimate sacrifice and test of faith. Today, against the drama of the sun-blue Pacific, he realised that Harris was much more.

The height of Classical Romanticism.

Harris was the one for whom other men were sacrificed.

There were close to ten in the Harris posse.

He went through each in turn... There was a name and state of origin for all.

Introducing Johnny from Nantucket, Charlie from West Virginia, Willie from New York state, Georgie from Tennessee, Tommy from Nebraska... He put it down to an American style of getting to know each other – each a familiar take on their proper names. He did not try to remember any of them, just nodded and shook a hand with each, finding the exercise especially curious.

By the end of the introductions, he now had twice the information on each other assembled than he did on Harris. Double on strangers compared with the first man he had spent the night with for more than a year. The only new information gleaned being that Harris went by 'Harry' among friends, though he still preferred Harris.

"Where're ya from, Olli," one asked.

Freddy from Colorado? Or was it Carolina?

"Glasgow."

Harris gave a grin telling him that the irony of how little they knew about each other after getting to *know* each other so intimately was not lost on him, either.

"Swell, never been m'self," the fresh faces of all assembled telling him that none of them had, "enjoyed a few whiskeys, though. Do you have a bird waiting for you back home? Harry here hasn't let up about his."

He could not resist a glance Harris's way before answering. But his American's relaxed confidence went unchallenged.

There were no telltale signs of nervousness or needing to compensate or subtle gestures to keep the exploits of 'last night' between them. Harris was not only unflinching. But, actually, seemed genuinely interested in hearing his response.

He did not know what to make of it. But, he gave an answer he thought most men put in a similar position might:

"Aye, a lass or two, if ye catch m' meaning."

The assembled laughed and nudged each other, suggesting they did.

"Nae serious though," he added, more sincerely, and to Harris directly – a display of his own boldness in the matter.

Part of this performance was a joust, and at its crux was the proving of a point to Harris: that he could pass as one of the *fellas*, that he could fly below the radar of suspicion, and flirt, even as he flew low. That he could *stay*.

This, the fly low, was the quality he had always prided himself on; it had been the mantra by which he lived his life. The *need* he felt to *pass*, never more so than on this particular occasion – driven by a desperate desire for Harris to permit him to remain near.

Was this a test? He thought.

Studying Harris's face, without a definitive answer.

A ball came between them, hurled from players from the deck. Harris caught it with one hand above his shoulder, stopping it from hurtling into the sea.

"Sorry, Harry," said the one who had missed the catch.

It was tossed casually back to the player – casually, though stronger and more skilled than it had come.

"Shall we join them, Harry?" One of his group asked, eager to go but wanting to stay with their alpha more.

"Y'all go ahead. I'm gonna hang with Olli for a bit. I'll catch y'all later."

The moment his group had left to play ball, Harris said:

"Sorry I weren't there when you woke."

Harris said it matter-of-factly, tenderly, kindly. And quickly. As if it was important that this be known to him, fresh off the bat – that letting him know this was chief among the reasons Harris had for summoning him over.

He felt like the eyes of one thousand men were on them. Closer to ten, perhaps. Like it was a risky move with a genealogy that he could not reason.

I don't understand you, he thought.

"Nae problem, ye understand."

Harris gave him the same confident, calm grin that he did not know what to make of. As if it were a joke he was not in on.

Harris turned toward him, paused a moment, then continued a rotation to face out to sea and toward *Mary*, resting forearms on the railing, letting legs swing and hang too, breathing in deep, bringing air between them.

He took it as an invite to join, though more clumsily and with an apprehension for the drop to the churning Pacific.

Turned to the sea. With the ocean stretching out before them. Away from the noise and heat of the mess of deckmen. In the fresh face of the wind...

Alone again. There was illusion of intimacy there, facing each other. The sea to their front and the chaos of troopship toiling and sardine-ing seafaring G.I.s at their backs.

After much air, Harris finally spoke:

"You do, huh?"

Harris leant in and into the small slices of seclusion that they had carved out for themselves.

"Heck, that's a relief. You can explain it to me then?"

Harris said it in such a way that left meaning open.

Did he expect me to actually explain why we had sex? He thought.

No.

The cheek of his American's general demeanour suggested that it was a question-hypothetical, where no explanation was really necessary.

Was it perhaps because their *whole affair* was just that, a fling, a one-off, a hypothetical not intended to be dwelt upon?

The Yank's comfort in bringing him into the lad-fold at least supported this latter position, in principle... A rough-house among pent-up mates.

I don't know which I prefer, he thought.

Actually, *I did.*

That sex with this man was in any way irrelevant was just about the worst possible outcome. Bring on sublime scandal. Especially now, after Robert, after letting loss back in, and opening up to anoth–

"I didn't want to wake you," Harris said when he did not answer. "I slept soundly, best I have in months. But you slept even better. You didn't even stir when I, *ahem*, slipped out–"

He felt himself redden and his arsehole slacken at verbal confirmation of their night.

It was real, it happened.

In the light of day, it was welcome to have confirmation that a night like he remembered having, had *really* happened with the likes of this man.

Otherwise it had started to seem more plausible as a false memory. A vivid damp-pants dream.

"–so I wrapped you in my coat to keep you warm. It seemed like ya needed it."

Needing it had double meaning. What he had *needed* was both a good night's sleep and Harris's penis inside him for the duration of it; in fact, the former was dependant on a provision of the latter.

He did not reply, however.

Harris looked at his face as if it were a puzzle, whereby one piece of the original thought had slipped out.

Harris studied him, searching for meaning.

I now know more about your friends than I do about you, he thought.

No, I can't say that.

He searched for an appropriate response, but everything that came to him was hysterical-sounding... Possessive.

Come on, Olli, this is what you do.

"Whaur ur ye from?" He settled upon.

Harris seemed relieved with the standard enquiry and launched into charting a Yank's story, with *Mary* steaming as scenery.

Told to him was how a ranch boy from Arkansas had come to enrol at West Point military academy fresh out of high school. And how a senior year sweetheart, Alice, had supported a heading toward New York to take up the offer to train there. Also recalled in the story was how worried she was when, Harris, still a cadet, was present in the academy as war broke out, and, then, being witness to the instinct of this Yank to want to be the first to enrol.

He makes it sound like it were every man's first instinct.

Harris told of the return home before enlisting. To spend time with *her*, the sweetheart, before shipping out... And how Harris had almost missed the boat. Arrived just in time, too, to join the end of boarding on *Queen Elizabeth*, the biggest of all and, rumour had it, outbound on a haste journey, a special charter, to the most exciting front other than the East.

The *underbelly*, up through Egypt and into the heart of the beast.

The mystery of Harris grew mistier in the setting out of this story. How openly his perfect Yank spoke of an Alice. How much respect and gratitude and genuine love Harris had for her.

Proposal for marriage was made during this before-enlisting visit, just before joining *Elizabeth*. Harris even spoke of how they had set out their plans for the future, for after-war returning to the family ranch to raise children.

It made no sense. Certainly, it couldn't, in light of *this* – now-confirmed post-fuck on the Pacific – audience.

Harris, he was realising legs dangling on *Elizabeth*'s edge, possessed a power that no other man had – to see *into* him and others too.

Or perhaps, was it that Harris was the first man to make him turn transparent.

Harris ended the story by answering the question he had not even posed.

"There were something about ya, Olli."

The wind whip brought drama to his Yank's interpretation.

"At the academy," Harris went on, "once the basic training were done, and the importance of chains of command and following orders were drilled in, they teach ya that, above all, in battle, ya should trust your instincts. And from the moment you collided with me until I saw you in the door of our dorm, every instinct in me told me I should follow ya. So I did."

It was simple, sincere. Unsexual.

None of the usual erotic realisation rhetoric.

Nothing about some switch being flicked.

Nothing of the need to offload in someone or anything of that nature.

And it made sense. Of course, it did. *Instincts*. Olli had acted on these, too.

"Cap," came a shout from back on deck that tore Harry's attentions away, "you gonna join us?"

"I'm the captain of the rugby team at West Point," Harris said to a cocked eyebrow.

Of course you are.

"Better get in there, teach those boys how da throw."

"Aye," he said, "got duties to attend to meself."

He thought it the brush off, the gentlemanly letdown.

The instinct had been acted upon, the *itch* scratched.

But then, before he headed to join mates, Harris added:

"Care to meet me later here, say sunset?"

"Na," he said.

This time it was Harris with a look of taken back.

"Aye, I do," he said and smiled, "but somewhere, more *private.*"

Inspired to see how far Harris would follow those instincts of his, he leaned in close; boldly, as the men whose ball-play had ceased watched on, pending the entry of their captain.

Harris's composure returned. Confident and calm, leaning in to match his angle, with little outward regard for their onlookers.

"A'm needin' tae wirk late. Bit if ye care tae jyne me, privately, continue fore, doon th' corridor that led ye tae th' room ye fun me in lest nicht. At th' extreme end o' this corridor ye wull come tae a set o' stairs, atop they ye wull fin' a ladder leadin' tae a hatch. If ye fancy it, ye will be at that hatch at midnight. Bit be canny, thare kin be some patrols aboot."

Harris grinned. "No problem, I can be *canny.* Enjoy ya afternoon, Olli," and Harris joined his mates.

He stayed a while, watching *his captain* share some knowledge. The way fit men crowded around him, hanging on his every instruction, him taller and broader and handsome-r than them all – it turned him on, his down-under twitching with anticipation for their hatch-rendezvous.

"Richt oan schedule," he said, having opened the hatch on the stroke of midnight to find his captain climbing its ladder.

"We're on deck," Harris said in the husky voice he had missed.

His captain thrust through the threshold, filling it as he did all openings he entered. He forgave the obviousness of his statement, recalling his own astonishment at first sight of stars from a lightless hull in the middle of the ocean.

"It's deid calm," Olli said, "juist as th' forecast said it wid be."

He sealed the hatch once his captain was through.

"Follow me, bit keep doon, we ainlie hae a few minutes' grace while th' chaynge in watchmen."

He led a path that hugged the start of the foredeck. If one travelled, hunched and close to the wall, he remained hidden from all watchmen's view. The path took them to the *Queen*'s side. The most hidden portion of her deck: on the foredeck, where crew did not go at night, and this part shielded from the view from the bridge and the watchmen posts, by virtue of the foredeck drop – the *working* portion of the deck – sitting lower down. He had sourced blankets and pillows from the crew storeroom for their sleep-out. Harris lay on his back on the blankets Olli had laid out. His hands behind his head, the round muscle of his arms pillowing again, inviting Olli back in. He went stiff. Not in an aroused way – though arousal was there – at the sight of his captain reclined. Harris bulged. Even when flaccid. Harris projecting down in front like another round muscle from the cotton of his track pants with "West Point" down the side.

Was this courting? He thought at the sight of the man before him, bulging but not sex-advancing. Such a question being the origin of his stiffening.

He stood there a good while pondering this. How did he *play* this? He did not know. His meetings with men were always sex-first. With Robert, conversation and caring for each other had followed afterwards. But only after a time, and only after sex, for the first throes at least. He wanted Harris, certainly. Daresay more than he had ever wanted another man. But he also wanted their night to *last.* He wanted his captain to stay.

I don't want to sleep alone.

It was a desperate, reckless, unhelpful thought. Not at all what he needed when their time together was so unconscionably limited. Cruelly short. He lay beside Harris, resting a hand on his unbending chest as he lowered his head into the cushion of his arm. Its size continued to astound him, being fuller and – when in repose – more supple than any of the Cunard-supplied pillows he had sourced for their sleep. Duck-feathered. Harris remained unchanged by Olli's actions. When he had been standing – watching his reclining Poseidon – as when he had brought his head to rest upon his sea-shelf-sponge arm, Harris's face had remained the same. Skyward, in awe of the stars.

"Ya haven't told me ya story, Olli," he said.

"Ah don't hae ony lasses back hame," he confessed, watching his captain watching the stars.

Why he had led with that, he was not sure. He should not have. It just blurted out; what he was *thinking* instead of what he meant to start with. But it came out with urgency.

This time it was Harris who went quiet.

"In fact," and this went against all his rules, "ah have only, *ah* only, am with men."

Panic swept through him. He had ruined it. This was never something he said, supremely not something to lead with. Harris continued to look at the stars for another minute. Waiting, perhaps for him to continue. But he *refused* to, would not make it worse. When no response came after a sequence of minutes, Harris broke focus with the starscape and turned to him, searching his face again. Something in his eyes made Olli feel that he could see into his thoughts as well.

Sounds lonely, his captain's eyes said.

It cut through him. Stupidly. As nothing had been spoken with breath. But it made him feel weak, dependent. *Less*, in his eyes. But kindness and calm returned in his captain, frighteningly, perhaps because Olli's fears were showing symptoms. Slowly, teasingly, the captain locked eyes and moved in – inching closer. Beautiful, Greek-god-like in the moonlight, but too-good-to-be-true – toward him. He could not trust it, as if the captain would pull away at the last minute and his mates would appear around them, and it would have all been a dorm-room joke. A haze, whereby his infantile attractions had been exposed for laughs. But even if he did this, he would have forgiven him it, for the fantasy of his interest intoxicated him. All the way through, he feared this until... their lips linked, soft and both wanting, and his Harris kissed him. Passionately.

They made out.

He had never done that before, never thought it possible with a man. Never thought it was something he even *wanted*. It was the American dream. The college football captain, heavy petting him, but in an over-the-clothes, bible-belt acceptable way, in his Buick in the drive-in pictures.

He was treating him like a lady.

And it was perfect, under the stars.

Although Olli had already *had* him, *all* of him, *inside* him. The night before was, as cherished as he held it, fogged by the messiness of many other men, having already finished inside him, followed by the mess of his own tears over Robert. But this night was now purely them; it *was* a courting. In court, with a handsome, military cadet American en route to a war. He was with a suitor, freshly flushed out, his back passage an empty receptacle, and his companion, a stud of the highest order. He was eager for it, lived each passing second without having *it* in fear that some catastrophic cosmic event would intercede, keeping them, cruelly, from consummating. He allowed the need to have him to take over, sliding a hand to Harris's cushion below – the biggest of his muscle bulges. But Harris knew better. Being well-versed in the protocol for a heavy petty first outing, he drew Olli's hand away from his crotch each time and returned it to his chest. Solid, sacred soil. He had never understood it until now – amidst it. He had seen the American culture transfer across the Atlantic to the Glasgow post-game antics of the lead soccer lads and their up-standing pretty girls. But before now, he had seen it just as an annoying foreplaying, an antiquated, god-fearing, no-sex-before-marriage nonsense, and a way of women withholding sex from men. Until now, until the present. The engorging gift of his jock's manhood, *just there*, ready, throbbing, but still with the focus on the upper mouth and the tasting of each other.

This is what I have always wanted.

Again, the dependence, the reckless wanting, worried him. But he decided to surrender himself to a higher power. Resolving – in the presence of a specimen with, clearly, the anatomy and experience to know how this *should* be done – that he would let Harris take control. A sobering concession, just briefly, and that swiftly passed, as the pleasure of letting the man take course washed over him. Relinquishing control, he came to realise in the heat of their session, this extended beyond *presenting* to a man or *letting* him fuck you as coarse or dirty as he liked. That was the way to get riveters, rough men, to take your bait. And, it still stood – was enjoyable. But with Harris, there was more nuanced sex at play. Instinct had led him to Olli, and he had taken what Olli had offered, but not in the manner that all men before him had. Harris worked to a different beat. Was it because, perhaps, Olli was an instinct-only pursuit?

Meaning?

Harris saw Olli as no different. Before, he would have hated the notion, rejected it as stripping him of the one thing he offered that their wives and withholding girls could not: boundless intimacy.

But was what I had before this intimacy?

Harris had made him question as they kissed, and he dissolved into the arms of his hero. *This* lasted longer; it hurt less. It was comforting. Olli stood by his advantage of always being up for it, always willing to take it, however rough. But should these qualities preclude the pleasure of a more platonic, over-the-clothes intimacy?

Not necessarily.

And so he went with it, cascading into Harris's lead as if the slice of foredeck they made theirs on *Queen Elizabeth* was the semi-private backseat of his Buick at an all-American drive-in. He would surrender control conscientiously, like the cheerleader after-match with the game champion, but without curfew or a stern daddy waiting at home. And letting go, *playing the part* of the woman, came with power advantages. Once they had got into their roles, once Olli had stopped his petulant pursuit of Harris's loins and embraced subservience in a more modest sense, they found their behind-bleachers. His hands on-chest and pure focus on the teasing of lips and tongue of the footballer instead. He gained reward with the feeling of Harris *growing* into his own. Occupying space. But Olli pulled his leg away this time, instead of massaging its development, as would be his instinct. Adverse to his nature, he permitted Harris to grow on his own accord.

I'll let him get hungry.

It was a lesson to him, for someone who had honed the practice of *putting out*, Harris was teaching him how to make a man, a *real*, *red-blooded* man, want for it. *Work* for it. Like he would have on the sports field, employing strategy, but with romancing added. Working himself up to a point of no return.

And they got there. Only when Harris succumbed. Grateful, Olli thought, for trying it his way, for building the sex to come up to a necessary outcome. And at the precipice, when Olli felt damp against his leg, telling him that if this did not move *indoors*, then there was the risk of either pre-mature explosion or ultimate letdown. And he would never allow this, either outcome – being himself, too invested. And it was at this crosspoint where confidence flooded in, where Olli's talents came into their own. Where, at last, his perpetual willingness to take dick came into play. And where he felt that he could serve. Seizing the opportunity, he arched away from the kiss with his captain – by this point, heavy in breathing and wanting for it. And he gave the go-ahead, gripping hold of Harris's biggest muscle, rigid and full. By this time, tearing at its semen-soaked, splitting-stitches-seams. So large that – like their first clash on the docks only two days before – he could not grip in all in hand. And, louder than he should have given they were hideaways, said directly:

"Fuck me, captain."

Relief rushed across Harris's features. And gratitude. How gentlemanly, waiting for Olli's consent. Before he had hated the very notion of a woman holding this over a man, having the right – often exercised – of depriving a potential penetrator at the post with an opt-out. And the thankfulness across his captain's face – as Olli freed his manhood from its damp, cotton restraints and guided it into his, as part of the planning, pre-lubricated passage – was plain.

"There's something about ya, Olli," Harris panted in his breath-broken voice as Olli's Vaseline-slicked hole swallowed his captain-pole in a single greedy gulp, like a hungry, story-spun sperm whale.

Though well-greased, taking his captain's rod did come as a shock, did *hurt*; he was, after all, exceedingly and singularly large; and he slid in with a force of purpose, like the launching of the *Queen* into the Clyde, and without the benefit of previous users and their seeds, this time. Part of Olli feared he would not be able to take him. That his swelling and stretching to accommodate Harris would exceed still his hole's limits. And, he was sure, it almost did. Like the *Queen* had for her launch, stopping just short of breaching the banks: the largest liner the Clydebank boy's passage had ever berthed, teetering close to destruction to finally come to rest safely within him. An expression of genuine fair-play-to-ya-fella flashed across his caption's features as his V-cuts – the deepest sex lines of any man Olli could conjure – wedged between his well-widened arse cheeks. The sensation of Harris's wiry hair at the base of his shaft against his taint came as a welcome relief. And to his satisfaction, his captain stayed there, somehow, continuing to grow and stretch across to his far, bent banks.

"You're the first person I've ever given all of myself to," Harris said.

He had taken plenty of big dicks in his time and had heard variations of this claim from other men – most of those only a fraction of his size. Yet, in all other cases, the phrasing used had been along the lines of: "You're the first to be able to handle all of my dick"; or: "No-one's got all the way to the base before, not even a woman." And he had enjoyed hearing it, sure. But the way Harris said it was different. Better. Like he was privy to *more* of Harris as a whole... and not only his sex meat. With others, such comments had been met with one of two thought-processes from Olli: the first a sense of accomplishment at his own achievement, the second, and most common by far, a perception of his penetrator as 'cocky', with an inflated sense of filling power.

I would give anything–everything–all-of-myself for you, he thought – a new thought-process.

He ran over all the possible phrases he could himself use to match the weight of meaning he felt in that moment. But nothing rendered right. So he kissed Harris instead, passionately, with his hands on his waist, holding him in, at depth.

"Aye, it's an honour to 'ave ye."

Harris's publicly hidden hair then pulled away from his skin. His super-liner retreating from the river and back up to its breaches and the start of his lubricated slipway. To begin the whole process again, into the night, beneath the Pacific moon.

He waited facedown in the same place the night following, as they had agreed.

That morning they had both woken before dawn. Again, his captain had kept himself inside as his very own expansion tool. This time Olli slept on top, his captain on his back with them belly to belly. He kept his knees bent and up toward his armpits for most of the night. On the face of it, a configuration uncomfortable, but it was the best means of securing Harris inside him – something that, he had discovered, was the ideal circumstances for sleep. As the night rolled on and they shifted together as one, Harris – though soft – still managed to stay inside. In him, even in deep sleep, without any effort at all... such was his size. It was his captain who had stirred him in the early hours-cum-pre-morning, when the sky was still dark, though starting to warm, and therefore, the foredeck still free from crew and their love-making nest of blankets and each other's naked flesh, still safe from the sight-lines of the bridge officers and their watchmen. Harris woke him by hardening, putting forth the prospect of a before-flee for the day re-feeding. Once he was replenished and detachment became essential with the reddening of the sky, they parted ways. He to go about his duties, and him to hang on deck with his West Point friends, playing ball. He kept his caption's two large deposits inside him for the day, feeling that their nutrients were sustaining him. But when he reluctantly needed to refresh himself for another night together, this left him feeling empty, with withdrawals.

Hence his presentation on the foredeck, entrance up and ready: resolved that an into-him-first midnight rendezvous procedure was absolutely essential to his sanity.

Plus, he thought as he waited, arse up, full moon reflecting off full moon, *it will show him the advantages of man-sex, the pleasures of the pansy-bottom, always up for it, always ready, always willing to be had.*

Harris was apt at the surprise assault module of his training, as it was only when his lips pressed against Olli's opening that the presence became known. And his rhythm of love-making lived up to a captain's station. Harris had a stroke to working a hole that spoke of a man who had refined the act of selfless pleasure-giving. A rarity in Olli's experience.

"Your arse–" Harris began, with an out-of-character hesitation.

Olli rolled in closer over the expanse of the cushion of his arm after filling.

"–it *tasted* incredible," he completed at last.

"Glad ye liked it," he said. "I stole some cinnamon oil fae th' kitchens," kissing Harris's mouth, tasting traces of it there.

"You're full of surprises, Olli."

"Tonight's gonna be a cold one, aye, and cinnamon scrolls used to always warm me through the Scots winters. I thought: if I'm gonnae drag ye a' th' wey oot 'ere, ye micht fin' it warming tae."

"I appreciate the effort. But–" again, hesitating, turning from the stars to Olli's eyes instead, "–we–don't always have to have sex, Olli."

Fuck, he thought.

Sinking, wanting to crawl away.

"Don't get me wrong," Harris said as if he too had heard how it sounded. "I enjoy having sex with ya, Olli. I mean, *really* enjoy it. But that's not why I'm here tonight. You mean more to me than sex, Olli. In fact, after Alice, you're the only other person I've slept with. What I'm trying to say is that sex means a lot to me. You, Olli, mean a lot more."

For all the flicking of switches in the minds of married men that man-sex had made him privy to, what Harris said flicked something in *him* in exchange. He had intuited that Harris was not like most men, but this statement rung with the crispness of perfect intonation for just how different he was. For example, he had assumed that at West Point, in the dormitories, certain intimacies must have unfolded – based purely on how he had seen his bunkmates look at him, *idolise* him. This switched off such assumptions.

"Ye mean everything tae me, Harris. Everything. Na yin haes ever opened me up th' wey ye hae."

And to demonstrate this to his American, he opened up further about their first night together: why he had broken down, about *Robert*, and how guilty he felt for keeping him a secret – how this silence was yet another way in which he had failed him. And he spread himself open further about his past, how he came to join *Elizabeth* in the first place, what he was running away from, and why she had become *his Queen.* Harris heard without interruption, listened without flinching, without judgement. And at the end of it, kissed him tenderly, and *made love* to him again, and stayed with him through the night.

Foredeck sleep-outs became their routine. And during the day, he would visit Harris on deck when he could. Where Harris would teach him the basics of American football. He started to see *Elizabeth* in a different light, with a glimpse of her original intention, as a pleasure liner, as *his Queen* once more. And as with any pleasure dash, any more than A to B, any *holiday*, soon enough the fear of it ending, of it being over, would cloud in – as did Robert, now that his memory was shared between them. And as if the world at war sympathised with this... on their last night at sea before reaching port, the sky souped over, the wind blistered. Compounding the impending end and sense of dread, that morning, as Harris delivered him a meaty bottom breakfast, their heaving bodies running ruby red, this was reflected in the pre-dawn sky.

Red in the morning, sailor's warning, he remembered.

Something Robert had told him – a sign the ancient mariners had taken to mean rough seas were on the way.

"Aye oan fur th' nicht?" He asked, accent thicker with nerves and the setting sun.

"I'll be there," Harris said in his usual deep-assurance tone. "Hell or high water."

As the voice of Robert had predicted... that night, the seas were rough, giving her a heavy roll. But the skies were strikingly calm and clear like the ocean swell had been stirred up by forces from far buried. True to his word, Harris was there, on time. There was a sad finality to seeing him emerge from the hatch for the final filling, to follow him over to their bed-for-the-night... for the last night.

"Don't lea th'morra."

Olli blurted it out.

The plea came as soon as they were safely on their blankets, out of view. Before even they had kissed hullo. During the day, he had thought of all the manners in which he could make it work, all the places on board that they could stow away, all the way back to New York and to safety. He would even let him go back to Alice, and start that family ranch, just as long as he was safe.

I couldn't bear to lose you too, he thought.

But instead of all this, he put forward a simple, more selfish plea.

"Stay wi' me."

Harris just smiled; that calm, caring, in-control smile of his, and cupped Olli's face in his hands and kissed him.

"I have to go, Olli."

Sex, suddenly, did not matter to him – a profound upset of the order of things. All Olli wanted was to spend the night with his captain, whatever shape that took. As if, again, he could see into Olli, Harris slid his hands beneath his shirt and slid it up and over his head. Conditions on the foredeck were not ideal, but he would not trade being there for anything. Harris steadied them both. He was an immovable bulk that Olli, now chest-bare, clung to like a ship-wrecked sailor a solitary beam of debris. He held on tight, for stability, for warmth, as if by life-preserver-clinging onto him, he might be persuading him to stay. He might be making him realise that without him, Olli would surely drown. Harris kissed his neck, nibbling gently there, perhaps leaving a mark that would remind him for at least a few days following their parting that what they had shared was really there – had once been within reach. Then with his breath, he traced a path down Olli's clavicle to his nipple. There he took this tender part in the pincher tip of his teeth, with a sharpness that stimulated it and with a tinge of pain that told Olli, revolutionarily, that his caption was starting to conceive of sex in an entirely different way. That he wanted him to know, on their last night together, with a great unknown stretched out before them both that, while

Olli was technically his *second*, as far as Harris was concerned, he was, in rare sea-stack-bird kind of way, first and one-of-a-kind for him.

He succumbed wholly to Harris's navigation of him, slackening all tension in his body so that he became entirely reliant on his captain to steer all functions, other than breath – though even that slowed to a near still-life state. Muscles and joints at complete, trusted repose, his body dangled over the supports of his captain, who stepped up to the crease with competence, exploring the more masculine crevices of Olli with a first-time curiosity. It was like, though Harris was himself male – and in a textbook sense –, there was a mystery still to be found in the folds of another man. Especially one who was complementarily, contrastingly, smaller and un-similar enough to render him an enigma. Harris rose to the gift of having a man – different-from-himself – at his complete disposal. It was a novelty... in truth: for them both. For a man as big, as strong, as Harris: to have a body that he would use *thoroughly*, the only person in his history to take him *fully*, but also to have to navigate that alone, must have been, if only appeared, as a challenge. Harris would need to plan and prepare the point of entry. Once he had Olli stripped, pulling him into himself and his taut expanse, at integral intervals, for warmth against the wintry night and occasional seaspray, he then lowered him again to the blanket-covered deck and, returned, to his cinnamon scroll. Then he worked out its knots, loosening it to take his length further, right to the base, and this time, without the benefit of pre-lubricant other than the wet from his mouth.

He committed to the transfer of himself ultimately. Watching Harris, taking his use *of* him, in. But never tensing, never instructing, never telling him to take him in some way, otherwise. His own manhood was the only part of him that was drawn, directing encouragement to his lover that what he was doing was working. Loose and nimble, on his back, Harris rose Olli's knees to rest either side of his ears as he set about the completing of his hole for receiving. Harris was thorough in his preparations. Careful in the work out of knots via the tool of his tongue. Learning the difference in the anatomy of sex with Olli, showing him through his loosening-up efforts that he saw this as something special, something only they shared. Something sacred. As orchestrator of their last night aboard *Queen Elizabeth*, Harris had chosen to orient Olli differently. Typically they had lain with their feet toward the bow. However, Harris had decided to have Olli with his feet toward the railing that their makeshift bed had them hard up against. With his arse reaching for the moon, and now especially well-worked, widened and watered by Harris's tongue, this meant that, as Harris slid inside him – standing, like the drilling of a pier's mooring – Olli had a view of the sea.

So well-administered was Harris's tendering of him that he was able to slide in full and fast, all the way to tap the depth that only Olli had allowed him so far. All the way to his base, Harris relishing the sensation of being stopped by the start of his rod. As was satisfying for Olli to see. Staying loose and his captain keeping control, Harris held Olli up, his spine straight up – in place for piling by one hand, fingers spread in grip of his lower back, and with the other, a rope held. The rope-end was drawn from a pile that in part provided their privacy screening. Harris used it as lateral leverage and means to deliver his trademark stroke. But from a position that was new to him. *Elizabeth*'s roll grew with the rhythm of Harris as if the force of his member was enough to sway her.

Against waves, Olli saw his captain as he did that first day on deck at sea. His god against a vast canvas. Only this time, he had him to himself, all of him, in himself, and with a backdrop more dramatic by far. With the sway of the sea, his captain's scenery changed. Stars to churning sea, churning sea to stars. In synch with his stroke. Olli felt his own release growing within him as the size of the force entering him rubbed off all inside him. Indescribable satisfaction, like the scrapping of a lifetime's sea-voyage-barnacles off the hull... more satisfying by far.

But this was his captain's play; he would not finish first, not until Harris. This clashed with the gentry of his captain, for Harris wanted him to finish. In fact, the sooner he did, the more appreciative he would be, given that Olli did not even touch himself. But any finish brought them both closer to the end of their last night together, perhaps forever, and so they would, them both, starve this off.

At the edge, Olli swayed full. One eye on Harris, one eye on his backdrop –

of sky-to-sea sway, in movement with inward stroke; Olli started counting the waves as if these were sheep, starving off completion, calculating their rotations to prolong their final communion. So well had Harris prepared him through speech-by-tongue that he was ready well ahead of schedule. But as he started focusing more on the backdrop – as much as possible while being piled by the most formidable penis he had ever encountered –; and as he did, as he focused away to starve the finish, he started to notice a pattern. Between sky-appears, which equated to a single wave, the sixth wave was the largest, and he could see it coming, peaking above the rest, stretching into the horizon. The waves were not always easy to make out in the night, like bobbing oil, but honing in on the horizon was a good measure of size of the waves, which as they grew closer, would rise up and blackout a panel of stars. It was hypnotic. Two, four and then a big sixth: the six-wave rule. Counting them helped him gain his composure and allow his captain to catch up. As Harris's heaves in and out of Olli's port quickened, jolting in that characteristic signal of his impending arrival, swelling in threat of breaching the harbour, Olli could focus on Harris again, swallow him in, and allow himself to approach arrival, as well. As Harris's breathing became hoarser, as the course to being complete neared arrival, Olli was himself slipping into his captain's swing. Though, the waves behind Harris kept him from succumbing – slotting unease into their humming. Two, four, then the big six. Two, four, big-six. His eyes adjusted to the night, and came to pick out the telltale crests of the sixth waves, stretched out before him; that swayed the *Queen* each time they hit, spreading along her broadside. And the panel of stars that they wiped out as it neared their turn to strike.

In abject horror, in dismal disbelief, coming at them, in the distance, was a sixth that defied all the laws, towering several sixth-waves above the rest, even from a horizon away. It struck *Mary* first, tilting her to her tipping point, and have-to-be beyond, like a toy tug boat, capsized by the sudden submersion of a consequences-be-damned dirt-faced boy during bath time.

A rogue wave, he thought.

He recalled the drunken accounts in the seamen's bars of the great mariner legend. *Mary* was gone, destroyed; he was sure of it, forget her. And they would be next. As Olli tightened up all over, each muscle taut with terror, this had the opposite effect on his lover, oblivious to the oblivion headed their way. The grip of Olli's ring around Harris-into-him pushed his gently captain past the point of pulling out and springing into action to save them both.

"Harris!"

But it was misunderstood. Harris reared up, dug in, bucked deeper as his release rose in him.

"Olli!" He shouted back, "I love you."

There was no time to explain or even get Harris off of him; he was too strong, too deeply embedded in him and in the throes of unloading. They had seconds only, as the wave careened for the side of the *Queen* while she headed at speed. The wave – as if fuelled by the felling of lesser waves in front of it and the ill-fortune of the *Queen*'s sister ship it had just toppled – gained speed, swallowing up more waves ahead of it, gaining momentum, rushing toward them with an almighty roar.

Save him, he thought.

His only instinct.

The wall of water rose up and over them. It blocked out the moon as well as stars and plunged the entire deck of the *Queen* into darkness. But Harris was still elsewhere, eyes closed, torso convulsing with the pumping of his load into Olli's closing up bulkhead. Running on pure, unadulterated, captain-saving adrenaline, Olli – still with a shuddering, splashing Harris inside him – vaulted upright from his back to topple Harris over and land on top in one swift crisis-summoned-strength manoeuvre. Then, just as the wave grabbed hold of *Elizabeth*'s hull, starting a roll she was never designed to correct from, he hooked one arm through the railing, holding his captain under the arms with the hook of his other, and Harris's waist with the grip of his legs. It happened too fast for Harris, still delivering, to process, the wave hitting with a speed and force that the *Queen* could not counter.

"I've git ye," he shouted, locking his joints around his captain.

Tipped off-guard, Harris, like putty, fell out of Olli, the ribbons of his offload falling vertically, down the length of the foredeck and to the stirred-up sea below. Harris was heavy-mass of man, and in a still-climaxing state, was sweat-slicked and slack weight. He did slip slightly, down toward a certain-to-be-swallowed-by-the-sea death. But Olli would not let that happen.

"I've git ye," he repeated, seizing up past hurting; determined, even if this was the end, that he would go down holding his man.

Harris, now-spending-into-the-sea, switched over. The military man Olli had only suspected so far came on deck; he climbed up Olli – whose arm's were reaching their limits – to grip the railing himself and scoop up Olli into his much more capable arms.

It happened fast.

Yet, hanging from that railing, the sea a free fall distance below them, time seemed to stand still: pausing there, them alone on the tipping point of the *Queen*.

"I love ye," Olli blurted out as Pacific cold washed down their naked bodies like bodily entrance of an electric eel.

Harris, strong. *Stronger than any monster wave*, Olli would have thought, had he the time to think. Pulled Olli into him and kissed him deep.

Against all reason – as if Harris really was Poseidon and had chastised a legend of the seas for encroaching on his final night of love-making – the *Queen* righted herself, the freak wall of water passed to cause havoc on horizons elsewhere.

They landed as a lump back on the deck, washed clean of blankets and any clothes – but safe. In the distance, *Mary*, miraculously also, had righted herself, too. And was lit up, engines stopped, assessing her damage. As well, the all-engines stop command was given on *Elizabeth*. Meaning their nakedness was illuminated on the deck for all to see. But he did not let the threat of exposure devalue the victory. He had succeeded with Harris, where he had failed Robert.

I saved him.

Irrationally, like American teenagers at the back of the bleachers lacking any care for the wrath of authority, they kissed passionately in the full, Fresnel lens of the *Queen*, peacetime lights illuminating them like captain's table newly-weds on a maiden voyage. Limbs entwined, they folded further into each other, partly for warmth against the chill of wet bodies in a mid-ocean night but more out of savouring each other. The peril was still present and it was still as if this embrace was their only preservation from a watery grave. Had they not had a near-death experience, he might have paced himself – saved himself from upset, given the end of their romance was so apocalyptically in sight. But *Elizabeth*'s uncertain state kept any chance of pacing away. In shock, all that mattered was savouring each salt-soaked second with his captain. Near-disaster was distraction from the thought of losing him at first light; eroded him, above even the threat of discovery, disgrace and incarceration.

"Sweep the deck!" An officer voice shouted from the bridge. "Check for damage. We're sitting ducks."

U-boats, after all, were under the influence of the waves, however rogue.

Harris pulled away from their embrace. He was even more magnificent in the *Queen*'s spotlight. Every sweep of muscle, every glisten of wet was perfect, of a prime male line. He looked Harris in the eyes, blue and bottomless, whirling him in, holding him. But also showing uncertainty, hesitance of discovery. Fear, for the first time.

"Ah chose this place carefully," he said, touching Harris's lips with a kiss, being in some small measure dominant for a change. "You're safe wi' me."

And he pulled Harris into an embrace, mixing his *love* for him into the love he had had for Robert.

"Ah wid ne'er let anythin' happen tae ye. Ye kin trust me."

And sure enough, search of the deck and the damage – surprisingly, minor – was assessed by a team of on- and off-duty officers without discovery. The place he had chosen shielded them from view, and when given the once over, the lights were off again and *Elizabeth* back on course for her port-ward troop delivery.

"I've never had anyone look out for me before," Harris said, as they dried in the rush of night air of their *Queen* picking up speed.

"There's nothing ah wouldn't dae fur you," he said, matter-of-factly, in a serious calm.

Harris, still stronger, bulkier, the man, and wholly the more encompassing of the two, actually succumbed to sleep first this time, Olli kissing the small in the crest of his neck as he reached rest.

"Ah'll miss ye," he whispered to his captain, this time with his head capped under his chin. "Ah wish ah could convince ye to stay," soon succumbing to sleep himself.

They woke late, deep in the Gulf of Aden. Dangerously on show. Naked, entwined, the morning Pacific sun on their skin, the sound of sailors on the foredeck, readying *Elizabeth* for docking in the Suez.

"I have ta go, Olli," Harris said, tracing his lips, drawing out his thoughts once more.

You said that already.

"But I'll *never leave* ya."

"Aye."

He meant for it to mean insincere, sarcastic, in the that's-what-they-all-say vein. But sadness sucked any intended cleverness, nonchalance from his response. Leaving only a pathetic plead: *Don't leave me, please.*

"How–" kiss, "do–" kiss, "we–" kiss, "leave" kiss.

Harris was being playful, his form huge and muscular, and even more Adonis-like in the sun of a Pacific morning, he thought *in* mourning.

"Don't worry, ah'll git ye awa' safely."

He delivered it flat-pan. And followed it up with a retreat; stark naked to his secret stash just inside the hatch – of seamen attire for those serving scenarios that sometimes warranted a change of clothes afterwards.

Harris was the picture of a slutty sailor in them.

"Aye, it becomes ye," he said.

He took him in with his eyes, resisting the urge to take his captain in via his openings as well – in plain sight, punishments be damned. The seamen's stash of clothes were medium, the right size for your average able seaman.

But there was nothing average-sized about Harris, whose height and muscle-bulk bulged out of the disguise from every seam, most notably down the length of his inside leg. Already filled by thick thighs, the cotton crotch of the sailor pants stretched in a manner the manufacturer had never dreamed on the design page: so pronounced that each vein of his manhood was traceable.

"It's a smidge snug," Harris agreed, his confidence returned – and warranted, and actually enjoying the masquerade.

The ship was in lockdown and the deck off-limits to all but the crew while damage was assessed. Yet all this while the *Queens* maintained their current bearing and evasive manoeuvring. How briefly they had remained at all-engines stop after a titan wave almost winded the world's two largest liners and sent them and two troop divisions funnel-first to the bottom of the Pacific.

They had stopped longer for Robert; why?

He let the thought pass and plotted out for his captain how best to get to the nearest laundry, where he could source more appropriate attire. It was along the lines of the storage-room-duck-ins between passing personnel that he had used many times before to navigate the decks between his service of different departments. But his caption was built to stand out, to catch the eye. And so he provided him cover; in his deck whites, making a point of helping out with the clearing of water caught in the crevasses across the foredeck, while Harris slipped back the way he had come the night before, into the hatch: for the last time.

Suez as a seaside city had nothing of the California coast about it, or even the Scottish shore-cities – that were cold, with waters uninviting, yet still safe and homely. It was a war stage. The tides were in the enemy's favour, and as much as the Med' was being touted by London-command-central as a 'soft underbelly', Hitler's Europe was, no mistake, an iron fortress. Olli was on deck when they docked. Entrance to the grand Suez Canal, and the memories enfolded in its steep, manmade banks, side of mind; the imminent departure of *this* man occupying the main channel through him. As she clung with last breath to the pride of her Empire, Britain had historically regarded Suez and her canal as lifeblood. A vital artery from India back to London docks. But for Olli it was a barren place. Of now-painful loss, soon to have one more.

He had asked Harris to stay.

Harris had refused him.

He'll be alright, he told himself, lacking conviction. *Others will rise to his protection.*

The second thought was more plausible.

He is too beautiful to be lost.

Others would rise out of the grips of warfare to comfort him. Yes, there would be others now, after he. There would be other *instincts* that would incite desire. His old self would want this for him. Harris deserved to be happy, especially with the North Africa campaign horrors that awaited him. But selfishly, he would have preferred to have kept him to himself. Off-boarding commenced even as her engines were still slowing. There was no orientation time, no chance to remain on board. Troops were ushered off so the carriers could be turned over for their return trip; to take on the wounded – those fortunate enough to return – and the prisoners of war – fortunate perhaps, also. Deterrent desertion policies were in full swing, with the troops herded off both *Queens* with new efficiency, a renewed urgency for the men to restock the frontlines, with little chance for second-guessing and attempts to remain on board. That made it all *too fast*, *too public*, for a proper goodbye.

He waited for him on the spot along the *Queen*'s deck where Harris had called on him during their first morning after. Now, it was a short way down from where the troops of Harris's part of the hull were disembarking.

"Harris," he called when he caught sight of him, again surrounded by admiring mates.

"Go ahead, fellas," he said.

Harris joined him at the railing.

He searched his face like he was panning for gold, trying to capture him, commit him to memory – already disheartened by a deadening knowing that this was not truly possible and that any memory, like those of Robert, would fade with time.

"Tak' care o' yeself," he said, failing to keep the emotion from his voice, and the welling from his eyes. "Don't be a hero."

Harris just smiled, handed back his usual, confident grin. He liked to think this was because he was the one from their pairing going into real danger, and therefore did not have the same fears about someone he cared for. But an unkind part of himself countered that the more likely explanation was that Harris, perhaps, did not feel the same.

"This ain't goodbye, Olli," he said, with the same calm confidence. "We'll meet again."

"Sure," he said. "O' coorse," smiling, though preferring that Harris had just returned the perfunctory pleasant goodbye and left it there.

Perhaps he thinks he is kind, leaving it open.

"Can I write ya?"

"Aye," he said, extending his hand.

Harris took it and pulled him into a hug as well. Buried in the centre of Harris's chest, all efforts to be strong slipped away as he wrapped – only part-way around – his own arms around the bulk of a man he loved. Stifled sobs slipped out as Harris's scent transported him back, like the cruel false pretence of a troop carrier, to their first night together, and his mind went to the loneliness, emptiness and isolation of time between the bookends of Robert and Harris. Not wanting to let go and emerge alone and *aware* of the lonesome life that awaited him.

"I love ya, Olli," Harris whispered into the small of his neck, burying a kiss there, then leaving to return to the rest for a war adventure away from America, away from the *Queen* and away from Olli.

VI

AQUITANIA

He watched Harris as long as he could, disappearing into the beige of Suez city until he was nothing more than a mirage on the heat of the city horizon. He stayed there, his gaze transfixed on the place where his captain once was. However long, he could not be sure, but until *Elizabeth* was empty of troops at least. As soon as he broke visual contact with the last sighting of Harris, the tears came, shuddering through him in a desperate outpouring of grief. For Harris, for Robert, for a life at sea again, without them both.

But then he saw *her*.

Out of the corner of his plain of vision, she steamed, sailing toward Suez as if for him alone. With her unmistakable, out-of-time, four-funnel design. He would recognise her anywhere, even through a tear-soaked squint through the Suez sun.

"*Aquitania*," he said to both no one and *someone* in particular. "Aye, richt then."

It was a sign, a chance at redemption. He would harness some small piece of Harris's bravery. Meeting the captain had been a nice distraction, an absorbing interlude. But he owed it to Robert to find out the truth, and besides, he could not stay on his *Queen*. She was for the two men he had only ever loved.

I will not sail on her alone.

Aquitania was a workhorse, living up to her war pedigree. Destined for the scrapyard on delivery of *Elizabeth*, how wrong she had proved Cunard; as a carrier of troops, she had held her own with the younger, larger ships and done it in style. The last vestige of a by-gone age: not strictly an Edwardian liner, though still possessing all the finesse along with the mettle of, too, being an almost born-into-war ship. He resolved to join *Aquitania* in a more formal, able-seaman capacity. He would not pursue sex as a matter-of-fact, as had been his objective in the start – and after Robert. As pleasurable as the sight of washing troop-dick was. As much as he would miss – and probably slip below on occasion to witness – this, if he was to learn the truth of Robert's death, and avenge his memory with justice of some small kind, then he would need to get back into the ranks, somehow and of his own volition. Not with his supply-arsehole. No, with aptitude of seamanship skills, all that Robert had trained him in during their time at sea together.

The Cunard White Star liners were, it should be noted, the linchpin of the entire Allied troop carrier operation. The Americans – new to war – had not the fierceness of competition, not the iron constitution, to produce liners approaching this class. Competition. That which had driven France and Great Britain into a Herculean struggle over national status, to build the biggest and fastest of transatlantic liners, in pursuit of the coveted Blue Riband. Among the Axis powers, Germany and Italy had their own contenders. But these were stuck in port. As the battle raged on through mainland Europe. The French line had some valiant vessels, but with her flagship, *Normandie*, still toiling in New York – in the throes of war service conversion, yet to carry a single troop to the frontlines – Britain, and Cunard, ruled the troop-carrying waves.

Though strictly under command from the Admiralty, smooth operation still called on Cunard for administrative control, and the company had makeshift offices in most strategic ports for such undertakings. The Cunard Suez office was makeshift enough, but then again, so was the whole of the

Suez operation. Suez had been a *gateway* since the opening of its canal during the height of Victoria's reign, and it was a transient place still. Dust-swept, swarming with the comings and goings of troops. At the humdrum, it was a dry heat, but the mass congregation of men made the air damp and ripe with their scent – being among it, breathing it hard-deep, of which did lift his spirits somewhat. Cunard had set up shop in the port authority offices on the waterfront. Staff sat behind a booth running the length of the bureaucracy benches, the sound of the turning of fans throughout requiring him to shout to be heard.

"Yes, can I help you?"

"Aye, I'd lik' a transfer please, fae TS *Queen Elizabeth* tae TS *Aquitania*."

"You're Cunard crew?"

"Aye."

The man serving him was middle-aged and bloated. The red of his cheeks and the beads of sweat on his brow suggested he was a heavy drinker, struggling with the local climate. He looked around him, the office readied by staff free to serve.

"It's not always possible, you understand," he said, "but if you'd like to come into the office, I'll see what I can do."

The office was quieter and as uncomfortable, though his attendant seemed to relish the chance to get off his feet. Him sitting with heavy relief at the desk in the centre of the room.

"Hot as hell, it is," he said, mopping his brow with a crusty handkerchief. "What was the name?"

"Turner. Oliver Turner."

"Right," he said, reluctantly pushing himself away from the desk, travelling across the room on his swivel chair. At the filing cabinet, he stood up. "Turner, you say," commencing his search through files in the top draw of the three-tied cabinet, "of *Elizabeth*."

"Actually," he spoke up, remembering the last-minute articles White had secured for him. "Ah *have* come fae *Elizabeth*, bit mah lest articles wur wi' *Mary*."

"*Right*," he said, making his frustration known with the slam of the cabinet draw. "That would be within draw three then, under 'M'," sitting back down for the search. "That's odd," he said, after two file-flicks through, "there is no record of you. You will have to stay where you are, I am afraid."

I can't go back, he thought.

"Sorry, lad," he said, "I cannot transfer you without current articles."

"Can't ye juist create freish articles fur me?"

"Certainly not," he said, indignant. "We have policies for a reason, young man. We're at war, you know. Why do you want to go to *Aquitania* anyway? She's a much older ship."

"Aye, ah owe it tae him, don't ah," he said softly.

"Pardon?" He asked, absently, back at the top draw, irritation more pronounced. "Maybe under *Elizabeth*," he muttered as he thumbed through.

"Ta for ye time."

Olli got up to leave.

"Hold up," he said, pulling out a file, "found you. Turner. Oliver Turner, an officer formerly of *Queen Elizabeth.*" His tone changed as 'officer' left his lips. "Sorry that took so long; your file, rightly, was under 'A'. Your transferred articles are all in order, yes, for the RMS *Aquitania*. For your position as Second Officer-in-training."

The Cunard man returned to the backroom desk and opened up the file.

"Says here that your articles were transferred to *Aquitania* some time ago, not sure why you weren't informed. If you allow me a few minutes, I'll write up a copy of your current articles for your records, then you will be good to sail, sir."

Astonished, confused.

"Wha is responsible fur th' transfer?" He asked.

"It is signed by a Captain Bell," he said. "Ah, and see here, that is unusual."

"Aye," Olli asked, only furtherly confused now and in shock from a spectre of a lover lost at sea.

"In all my time with Cunard, I have never seen that."

"Aye."

"Your position, it's secured for life."

He remained silent, unknowing of the significance, as the Cunard clerk handed him a notarised document.

"Mah mail," he thought aloud. "Shuid he write."

"Yes, all mail will be forwarded to *Aquitania*. We run a tight ship here at Cunard, Officer Turner. At least we try to, circumstances considered."

She's as beautiful as Robert described, he thought as he boarded her.

She was a grand dame of a ship, even painted drab grey and swarmed with the bodies of 4,500 men. But after her refit, with her fine furnishings removed and her veneers boarded over, her strength and resilience showed too. *Aquitania* was a workhorse, living up to her war pedigree. As a harbinger of troops across two wars, she held her own alongside the younger, larger ships. And did so in style. Her turnaround was less urgent than his *Elizabeth*'s, which gave him time to collect his possessions – that numbered very few. She had travelled up from Australia, yet, he quickly learnt, her deep draft had made her hazardous to navigate through Australian and intermediate Pacific Island ports. So, she would now take over a new role: for the third and fourth months of 1942, she would transport troops from America's west coast to Hawaii. There was irony in her being tasked with tending to Honolulu. It poked at parts of himself he was trying to heal over. Oddly, however, the symbolism of the voyages that lay ahead was welcome in some compartments of himself.

The time had come to step up, he told himself, *to learn the truth, in justice to Robert.*

The start was idyllic, had a meant-to-be feeling to it. On arrival, his presence was swiftly received and announced to the senior officers. The captain, an Isambard J. Smith, even showed him to his quarters.

"This was Robert's cabin when he first started on *Aquitania*, all those years ago," Smith said. "Robert was one of the finest officers I have had the fortune to serve with. His memory is held in the highest esteem throughout this ship. Before he–*departed*–he made clear to me personally his wish that you,

Oliver, should have every opportunity afforded to you. And I intend to honour Robert's wishes."

The captain put a hand on his shoulder.

"At the time of Robert's passing I was Captain of the *Mauretania*. Months later, when I took up this post on *Aquitania*, a letter from Robert was waiting for me. Those damned censors had stripped out much of it, but I got enough from what was left to understand the request. Somehow Robert knew I'd end up back here. Makes sense, I suppose; it was always my wish. Anyhow...it's taken a while for you to take up this position, Oliver, but I would have held it for you as long as I was in command of this vessel. Robert felt strongly for you and this ship for him. I hope you find what you are looking for here."

"Aye, sur, and ah."

The captain turned to leave him, as the significance of the *Mauretania* at the time of Robert's death hit him:

"Captain."

"Yes."

"Is Mr Arnold still aboard? He transferred here during the US3 troop convoy."

Blood rose in him just at the utterance of *a* name that he had banished from his thoughts for more than a year now, let alone his lips... Saying *that* name sent it all rushing in. The deception, the blackmail, the bastardly behaviour that drove Robert to abandon it all. To give up all hope, to turn his back on love, to see no possible way out, to take his own life. In the Robert void, Arnold rushed in. The sight of him, his despicable boyhood, small and jagged, in Robert's room. Hooked, as if machine-made, to ensure and induce formulaic harm. He had made introductions to Robert's father to gain access to Robert himself, a noble, competent officer, but in the realm of sex: fragile, breakable. The blackmail that had no doubt pushed Robert over the end, the salacious film, that he had held over Robert like a hangman's noose until he could not take any more. Until *ending-it* became the only option that he could see. And learning now, the lengths Robert had gone to, the planning involved securing a future for him. It made him feel the ballast of *guilt* for having waited for this long to investigate. Shame for indulging in another love before setting himself to solving the wrongdoing of his first. With the utterance of a single name, his heart broke all over again.

Closing the space between the door and Olli, perhaps sensing a seriousness, gravity to the enquiry. The captain replied, up close.

"Arnold?"

"Aye, Kenneth Arnold. He joined *Aquitania* soon efter Robert, soon efter his *death*. During a sea halt."

"Sorry, Oliver. In more than twenty years on this ship, I have never known any member of crew by that name or any Arnold in fact."

He used a different name, then?

"And," the captain added, "since Robert's–*passing*–there have been no new additions to this crew. Except now, except for you."

Captain Smith left Olli utterly at a loose end, coming to question some of the truths he thought he knew. His quest for answers was likely to be more challenging than first thought.

The cabin was spacious and all his own. After his brief stint on *Mary* and his return to his *Queen* in basic, shared accommodation that he spent hardly any time in, being here reminded him entirely of Robert. The cabin had clearly lay dormant, being dust-covered and stale-smelling. Unoccupied, as a captain held it in trust for a friend's prodigy's possible arrival. Being here was emotional enough, but learning that the joining of *Aquitania* was something preordained by his lost lover, made the situation harder to bear. Like Robert was still here, looking out for him, while he had been off on trysts trying to forget. And the guilt was set to rise with the discovery of an envelope on the coffee table. It was addressed to him in a familiar hand, dust-coated too.

Officer Oliver Turner, Aquitania

The envelope had been opened and resealed with wax from the censorship office. Inside, the letter was painfully short, and the last, shortest line stolen by way of censor:

Olli,

I won't pretend that I am not disappointed about how things turned out. But I hope you find what you are looking for and that, in some small way, *Aquitania* can help you, as she has me, for so many years before we met.

Yours always,

Robert

The sight of his hand, marked on the page, like an apparition captured on camera, brought the dark roll of cruel memory back again. That it had been read by a third party cheapened it, violated his final sacred words. Not only did he need to share this last piece of Robert in the living world, but strangers had got to it first. It was not his alone, it had been torn open, and its contents searched, taken from him, like Robert, too.

Out to sea, the coast of Suez long lost from the horizon, night already several hours in by this time; it was then when he had finished his duties for the night and was now faced with the prospect of retiring that restless retched him. The pressure to live up to Robert's memory by proving himself able in an officer capacity weighed heavy on him, convulsing the diaphragm. But he would not confine himself to his cabin and that cryptic note, either, even simply for the sake of sleep. And so, instead, he would take advantage of his returned authority and acquaint himself with the ship Robert had loved. He would do this by embarking on a tour of its interior and the men he shared it with.

Return voyages were different affairs entirely during war. Especially this particular one, when even the fantasy for peace felt a distant dream. Such voyages, therefore, were solemn occasions. Those being transported, unlike the freshmen headed for the fronts, were damaged or corrupt in some way. These were the injured and the imprisoned. This leant the ship a sombre sway, which matched his mood that first night on board. But even on sombre ships, sex could be found if one knew where to look. Not looking to serve himself – the feeling of too-soon after Harris, and too-soon after joining

Robert's ship, strong – Olli turned to voyeurism, instead. Watching as a high-impact recreational activity was his game. His ship tour was punctuated with the pleasures of seeing men, and his officer status allowed him to move freely without raising any suspect rebuttals. He focused his attentions on the prison portions of the ship for that first night, which were generally more conducive to spectatorial pleasures. And it was a fruitful, spirit-raising excursion that he re-exercised over the nights that followed.

Senior Axis captures – the intelligence wells – were kept off-limits, even to his as-officer station. And that was fine; they were too implicated, in his view, to be looked at and enjoyed, anyway. It was the innocent infantrymen that *Aquitania* had captured in her iron flytrap to return to America for the duration of the war that captivated him, keeping him coming back. These men were held below the waterline in spaces of the ship traditionally used as storage for motorcars or passenger cargo, and quickly his visits took on meaning leagues from *just to look*. Murmurs in the officers' mess from those who spoke German told him that the Axis officers captured, thinking they were in confidence, sometimes boosted of atrocities occurring in the North African campaign and Hitler's Europe proper. And whenever one of these enemy officers would be overheard gloating about killing any Allied man in a particularly malicious manner, it would be met with Allied counter-offensive. His officers would often act first, boasting later in the smoky confines of their mess in the evenings, of roughing up these men, bringing them down a notch. But the attitude to the young infantrymen captured was different among the crew of *Aquitania*. Compassionate, even. Provisions were made, wherever possible, to make their journey to America as comfortable as possible, and he found himself conducting surprise inspections of these areas of the ship on occasion, as was within his purview, to make sure that such treatment stayed this way. He'd readily admit that, in part, his tours were recreational, to enjoy the sight of them, as well.

Most were young German men, little older than himself, skinnier and bruised with the beat-down of war, but still stunning specimens of the fitter sex and symbols of everything right with the world. They were no different – he came to see – from the brave American, Canadian, British, Australian and

New Zealand men. Not, in fact, removed from those he had chiefly had the pleasure of accompanying and servicing on outward journeys since the start of the war. He would call on them to watch the glisten in their communal showers, their bodies stone, their manhoods wet and enticing, but above this, he would head below to make sure they were well treated, fed and respected. The way he would want for Harris to be handled, should it come to it through German captive.

As the days at sea rolled on and he settled into duties on board, surprise inspections of these men increased. As this did, their welfare became more vivid in his mind. These visits, he came to realise, gave him hope. A purpose. He, in a small way, was ensuring that they were indeed out of harm's way and would be kept from harm's way all the while that the egos of old, vapid men raged on. Such men were using the young, disposing of their Biblical beauty bodies with the callous regard of careless players leaving tin toy soldiers to corrode in the winter. By the halfway point of his voyage, he found himself making the descent into the hull more often. It veered in meaning to a mission which meant he even hoped Harris would too be captured by a compassionate crew like his, who would respect him, preserve him and, yes, take him, too, away from the pointlessness of this war's theatres.

"You are making excellent progress, Oliver, quite excellent," Captain Smith said in his cabin over an after-lunch whiskey. "I wanted you to know that. I cannot fault your commitment to your post and have heard no shortage of praise from the other officers. High praise indeed about your aptitude to your studies and the carrying out of your duties."

"Ta, captain."

"It gives me great pleasure to say this, dear boy. Robert was right to believe in you so strongly, and I was right to keep this post for you."

Smith's captain's cabin beneath the wheel deck was one of the few spaces on board the ship that fully retained its interwar character, from its crystal chandeliers and drinks cabinet through its heavy drapes and Edwardian furniture. Captain Smith was at home there, among the stiff swede and burgundy-browns of his surrounds. Fat and big-bearded from a good number of years in comfortable command.

"I hear that you've taken especial interest in the prisoner decks and the checking of inmate welfare," he said, swirling the whisky in his glass, watching it, as if the distilling process was still underway, aided by his steady hand.

"Aye, sur."

"Commendable," he said, biting on his cigar, puffing, "commendable, and particularly for a young lad. It can be too swiftly forgotten that for prisoners of war, the fighting is over, and our duty to set a civil example is that line in the sand. It separates us from the enemy," he said, raising his tone to effect with the last line, as he suspected the captain was accustomed to doing among parties of more than two – when entertaining or discussing politics of British politeness back in London. "But," Smith said, raising his cigar hand toward his guest, "if I might put one suggestion to you."

"Aye, sur."

"If you are looking to show compassion, dear boy, you need not look so far from home. This ship is full of our *own* boys, their bodies and wills broken... returning home with the guilt of leaving the war early and their lads on the field, both those still fighting and those not so fortunate. There is another man you remind me of, Dr David Holding, working in our infirmary. A bit quiet, reserved, but showing the greatest compassion in taking on the care of the most vulnerable of our lads. These are the young lads, you see, that sadly our Lord should really have relieved on the battlefield. Men who return home to lives where little quality awaits them. Without livelihoods. You might, and this is only a suggestion, my dear boy, but I suggest you consider visiting him and the men in his care. Our boys need your compassion, too, Oliver, now, more than ever."

Aquitania's infirmary department expanded and contracted like an iron lung, meeting the depends on her particular passages and the sick in her hold. On outbound journeys, it spanned only slightly larger than peacetime; even, on occasion, a few of its sick bays would be turned over to crew accommodation. However, for the return trip – when it split in two: part hospital ship, part prison transfer – these facilities spread considerably across multiple ship sections to meet the demands and accommodate the needs of additional doctors. As had been the case in Suez, when Dr Holding joined them. Not being the resident doctor, Holding's treatment rooms were in one of the repurposed sections of the ship, two rooms in particular which, during peacetime, would function as a men's barber and women's hairdressers. Fresh from his whisky with the captain, he decided to visit the dear doctor, bracing himself for much more confronting young flesh to see.

The halls around Holding's practice were surprisingly quiet, like he had found a corner of the ship about which others had forgotten. This was deliberate. They kept the most severely afflicted separate from the rest, close to the sea doors for easier burial and in away from the men with lesser injuries so as not to heighten their distress. It was in these sections of the ship that sadness slept. Sometimes eternally, slipping into the sea in small services each morning. As he had gleaned from the captain, Dr Holding was the only physician to tend to these men. He had a role, this doctor, turned to management of their decline. His task: to make them as comfortable as possible. Tending to those at the end while the others got on with ones that, perhaps, would fight again. When he arrived, he found that one of the rooms was empty, while from the other, light poured out, the door ajar. Not thinking to knock, he entered.

On the table, his penis pointed, erect and lubricated, swinging in rotation like a zoetrope, slapping off the young man's raised thighs. At first, the sexual sight relieved his own fear of encountering terminal suffering. But when his presence in the room drew only the attention of the doctor and without any reaction, he realised that what he witnessed was itself a therapy. Dr Holding was working an able-aged man's legs with a vigour that had sprung his penis into action. As erotic as it appeared, this young chap was undergoing treatment. The doctor was younger than he had anticipated and much more handsome. He bore a striking resemblance to Robert, in fact. Though... in truth... that likeness faded as his eyes settled, and he realised in sobering admittance that this was his own lonesomeness stirred by *Aquitania* talking, rather than an actual similarity. The doctor was, he would estimate, late-thirties, tall, slender and distinguished-looking, albeit bookish. Dr Holding acknowledged his presence with a glance, but without disruption of his working of his patient.

And I need *for you to come*, he thought, out of place.

"Officer Turner, I presume," the doctor said.

He nodded.

"To what do we owe the pleasure?"

The doctor spoke as much to his patient as to his visitor. Olli was staring; he knew it. But he could not help it, either. The man Dr Holding was working over was as beautiful as any of the prisoners he had taken it upon himself to watch over, now that he could gaze upon treatment-in-action. Young, could not be more than twenty, blonde with blue eyes and a jaw with all of the sharp-edged refinement of a cutting stone. His body, fully naked, mounted before him.

How can I not look?

He traced the lines of the patient's torso, defined, prime, bruised from battle, and came to rest again on the sight of his penis. One leg lay flat, while the other: Dr Holding had that draped over his shoulder. His hands, oil-covered, rubbing the thick thigh of his treat-ee with such devotion that his dick swung in that circular motion.

"You will forgive me if I do not disrupt my treatment," Dr Holding said, digging deeper his oiled-fingers, themselves brushing by the spin of the young man's member and sack, increasing the rate and firmness of its rotation.

"At least something still works, aye doc," the young man said, unmoving.

And he realised, catching sight of a tear-bead in the corner of the patient's eye, his otherwise motionlessness.

"This is Mr Stephens," the doctor said as-statement-of-fact, "he is paralysed from the neck down following severe spinal trauma. This means that his muscles need to be worked manually. Muscular dystrophy is inevitable, of course, but with some care, there is much that can be done to prolong the process of decline."

The sight of the young Mr Stephens' penis being so spritely still drew his eye.

"Entirely natural," the doctor said, joining him in his gaze. "And, in fact, a positive sign."

The doctor set down Stephens's leg, and the spinning stopped, but just for a moment. As he reclined the second leg and got to work on the muscles, it sprung into rotation once more, around the opposite direction.

"You're...very–*dedicated*–doctor," he said, trying to sound clinical about it but running on in an unmeasured manner.

"Is that why you came here, Officer Turner. To assess my...dedication?"

"Juist tae observe," he said, straightening up, asserting some authority.

The doctor eyed him up a moment, staring silently, the sound of oil massaging muscle and the slap of a penis on rotation all to come between them.

"Yes, I have heard that you have been paying regular *observations* to the prisoners on board. I am pleased that you have seen fit to devote at least some of your time to the plight of those on *our* side of this struggle."

"Aye," he said, keeping his gaze, feeling his appreciation for the doctor's work growing with each word.

"You are rather young to occupy such a position," the doctor said, focusing his workings to the underside of his patient's legs, in his glutes region.

An odd finger or two, straying to the warm fold between leg and manhood muscle.

"If you do not mind me saying so."

"Aye, 'suppose ah am."

He sensed the doctor was using intimidation tactics on him, focusing on muscle groups closer and closer to his patient's penis and arsehole areas, perhaps an effort to unsettle him. It had the opposite effect.

"Sae doctor, is thare a specific area o' medicine ye specialise in, or urr ye in general practice?"

"Psychiatry," he said, lengthening his muscle strokes, "originally. Though before the war, I moved into more *physical* therapies."

"In whit sense?"

"Athletes mostly," he said, gripping Mr Stephens by both ankles and pushing his knees to his chest.

Stephens's erect penis slid lubricated through his thighs to rest heavy and full just above the clutch of his opening. He was an amphitheatre champion, though entirely reliant.

"College varsity, for the last ten years. Young men in their prime, turning their bodies to competitive sport. Not, in fact, dissimilar to my role now. Take Mr Stephens here," he said, putting his weight on the folded legs of his patient, that swung his penis again, and with each right turn, opened his entrance – inviting inward-look. "He is a pro-athlete, yet unlike the men I tended to at Harvard and Yale and Brown, and wherever else they sent me, he has been on the field without any care for the toll this would take."

He did not say a word himself, too busy being enticed by the sight of Mr Stephens, folded and inviting like that.

"It is no different," he went on, "and we often use sports metaphors to describe war and send our youngest, brightest and fittest in to bat for us, but when it comes to the muscles, to the body trauma, there is no care. Fellows like Mr Stephens here are expected to play at their peak for months on end, years even, without any attention to the toll it takes on the body, less still, on the mind. And when they find themselves with an injury, as he has, it is not enough just to stitch up the wound and send him home. Because it is then where the trauma comes true; there are other areas needing attending to, if he is to recover."

"Ta, doctor, n' ye tae, Mr Stephens, fur allowing mah visit. Ah wid lik' tae learn mair aboot yer wirk 'ere. A'm needin' tae git back tae mah duties noo, however. Ah finish at 2300 hours, wid ya be free fur a tour o' yer facilities then?"

"Yes," he said, "I have a treatment with Mr Stephens booked in for 2200 hours and will come to the bridge after that so we can discuss further."

The doctor's technique and philosophy stuck with him. In fact, he was most distracted for the rest of the day's duties, thinking about what he had said and how our young athletes could be better attended to in the game of war. And, in particular, the *technique* of his therapies focused on the rapid movement and massage of muscle.

In fact, he thought, as 2200 approached, *I should like to see that particular technique again.*

The thought of it was too distracting on his duties anyway, and so he finished up early and headed down to the doctor's treatment rooms, just before Mr Stephens's allocated time.

I will ask the doctor if he would not mind me sitting in.

This time the door to the treatment room he had found the doctor in before was closed, however light from the door's bottom gap told him it was in use. This, together with the familiar rub and slapping sounds from before, said to him that treatment was underway. Perhaps he had another patient or had started early with Mr Stephens's appointment. So distracted by his own eagerness to sit in, the thought of knocking did not even occur. Inside, on the treatment table, lay Mr Stephens. At first, as his eyes adjusted to the light, it looked as if the technique was the same. Same, except with the doctor on top, his hands working on the muscles of his patient's upper chest. But then, as his eyes focused, the full extent of the doctor's service came into field.

They're fucking, he realised.

More specifically, the doctor was *facilitating* Mr Stephens fucking him. Straddled on top of him, their bodies both naked and oiled. The doctor massaged the muscles of Mr Stephens's upper torso while, from below, he worked the length of Mr Stephens's one responsive muscle. Its total length was worked. In and out of himself. With the same vigour and attention to rhythm as the doctor had applied to his top half. Stimulating the muscles. The patient was more verbally responsive than he had been in his earlier treatment, which, together with the slap of skin-on-oiled-skin, had meant that Olli's entrance came without notice. As had been the case with the decorum-of-door-knocking only moments earlier, the notion of retreating and leaving them to it did not cross his mind, it being too enticing a view of union. Fucking was nothing foreign to him; it was procedural, process- and outcome-driven. He respected that. Dr Holding's practice, it appeared, was similar to his own, though backed by prescription. But as much as he had practised it himself within his more modest, fleshy profession – too routine to be called *amateur* –, this marked the first time that he had peer reviewed fucking. Observed it as a partial practitioner, and in this respect, it was a fruitful fuck.

For himself – having both fucked and been fucked for functional purposes in the past – the act's performance that he was now privy to offered entirely new aspects of the action. Firstly, the *perspective* was different, fucked and being fucked; never before had he the chance to observe the mechanics from the back. The jubilance with which the doctor's anus swallowed the patient's phallus and the jellying of anal-jowl-area as it made contact with thigh and complete consumption of the penis. The doctor, as much as he tried to separate him out as a colleague for experimental purposes, was looking more and more like Robert with every bounce and swallow. He was becoming Robert with every shake and jiggle, as if the dear doctor had gifted him a view of his anal-hungry lover, using himself as a surrogate. From this vantage, he saw his jellyfish man of war, his hungry cunjevoi.

Mr Stephens, too – who had registered his presence – made his appreciation for the treatment known, his body limp, but his eyes acute, locked on to Olli's with a plea of *don't stop this*, followed by words of encouragement to the doctor, *ride me, doc*, among them. A consummate professional. The doctor, arse-jowl-deep in his treatment delivery, must have registered something amiss, turning. The response was unmistakable, an affront of jigs-up terror. His usually pompous exterior stripped away by the exposure, his posterior slumped on his patient's penis, a look of defeat – for them both – followed. Slouched and still, sitting low on Mr Stephens's shaft, the doctor's hands sunk, too, upon Mr Stephens's chest. But just for a beat. Like Mr Stephens had inflated him through the insertion, the doctor soon straightened up.

"Yes, I will," he said, resuming his rhythm of full-bodied muscle therapy.

He took this as his cue that this session was private and returned to his cabin. The loss of Robert and now Harris... The spectacle of selfless treatment that he had just witnessed... Together with his own resolve to only watch and not take part himself in any activity – at least while the memory of them both was still fresh – led him to a resolution he never thought he would need resort: self-pleasure.

"Consent was given," Holding said, bursting into his cabin just as he finished over the underside of his desk.

Holding was flustered-ly flung together – his shirt half-buttoned and back-to-front. In his anxious state, he did not seem to notice the scrunched expression of Olli-relief, timed precisely with his entry.

"Dr Holding, claise th' door, wid ye," he said, pulling himself further under his desk to conceal that he was exposed from the waist down.

"And it was *informed*, too," Holding added, catching his breath. "The consent. I made sure of it."

He gestured to the chair across from him.

"Not that *that* matters, I suppose," Holding said, slumping into the seat offered. "But leave Mr Stephens out of this, I implore you."

"I'm nae sure ah ken ye meaning, doctor."

"With the prosecution. For buggery and violation of codes of conduct. As his physician, the responsibility is mine and mine alone to bear for the... incident. Mr Stephens is not to blame; he has enough to contend with. I am asking you. I am *begging* you, have compassion, man."

"Howfur aboot ye tell me whit happened?"

He gave a resigned sigh, his shoulders sinking further.

"Very well," he said and set out the evidence.

Holding explained that on joining *Aquitania* in Suez, he was assigned to manage the suffering of two categories of men. The first was the easier of the two to treat. They were those men whose injuries were so advanced that it was not likely they would survive the journey home. For them, he was charged with palliative care and easing of suffering through to the end. The second category of patient in his care was of the much more complicated sort. Those with psychological trauma, the men who had been discharged from service after failing to cope.

"In my field, we refer to this as 'shell shock' – a widely understudied and misunderstood ailment. These are the men we would sooner forget. But Mr Stephens is a unique case. He suffers from acute physical trauma, a severed spinal cord that had rendered his body mute from the shoulders down, who now, unsurprisingly, is plagued by problems of the mind as well. Men like Mr Stephens are the inconvenient truths of war," Holding said, retrieving an envelope from his breast pocket and sliding it across the desk.

A storm was brewing outside, and he only registered the roar of waves and rain against his porthole on seeing the marks of the censorship office. The familiar signs of opening and resealing that he had come to recognise in his duties as an officer – dispensing mail among the sailors. It was addressed to Mr Stephens. Inside, the letter carried the censor's blackout, scratching over key phrases, but only on the first page.

"To save you the read, it is from Mr Stephens's fiancee, who, after hearing of his injuries, is writing, with regret, to call off their engagement. It was held by our censor office and deemed to pose an unacceptable risk to morale. But, it was still processed and sent to *Aquitania* as a matter of protocol. I only gained access to it via special request to the captain, on medical grounds, to glean better insight into Mr Stephens's state of mind and to aid me in my psychological assessment."

Holding elaborated that Mr Stephens had come under his care a week before the arrival of *Aquitania* while he was working at Suez City Hospital.

"Intent on preparing Mr Stephens for his arrival in New York, and his discharge from my care, I decided to share the contents of the letter with him. To prepare him – case history had taught me – for what was already going to be a shock on his return home. Mr Stephens had by this stage expressed suicidal thoughts to me in our sessions, chiefly relating to his perception of himself as *lacking* in a masculine capacity and his ability to provide for his fiancee on his return through gainful employment and childbearing. He took the news of his broken engagement poorly. Profoundly so, turning all his efforts within our sessions over to a campaign of compassionate euthanasia. With only days to treat him and having had come to care for him – admittedly, in more than a professional capacity, but still with his wellbeing as my chief concern – I embarked on a treatment regime of sexual stimulation followed by psychological therapy. Unconventional, I grant you. Unethical, many of my esteemed colleagues would testify. And on that, of course, illegal, given our sexes. But I stand by my course of action, all of which was led by Mr

Stephens, not myself."

Holding looked drained, defeated, deflated. Like what he had intended to be a justification for his treatment methods was, invariably, coming across as a confession. His position, so radical, his proposition, so blatantly preposterous. He had doomed himself to be diagnosed with a perverted psyche. Through sharing the story with the authority that had uncovered his crime, the catharsis that he was perhaps courting had failed to present itself. As if, when it came to it, he lacked the conviction to face inevitable disgrace with a strength of conviction.

"Men like Mr Stephens," Holding said in the tone of a summation, subdued but somehow statesman-like, "they fall in battle, fighting gallantly, much braver than I would have, and yet are not immortalised as heroes through death. Imprisoned, in fact. Returning as shells of their former selves in *in-able* vessels to a society that both does not know how to treat them, and more tragically than that, would prefer that they had not returned at all. I took a Hippocratic Oath, Officer Turner, and I have tried to live my professional life by a philosophy to do no harm. And while the gatekeepers of my profession, and the overlords of our judicial system, too, will no doubt rule that I have harmed Mr Stephens through my conduct, this was, in fact, the opposite of what I was working to achieve."

He went to stand, though the touch of himself against the wet wood of his desk reminded him of his state of undress. So he sat back down instead.

Holding hung his head, awaiting arrest.

"Doctor," he said, not wishing to prolong the prognosis, save a clear of the throat. "Ta fur explaining yer treatment regime tae me. It's nae mah intention tae tak' action against ye. Oan th' contrar, ah tae feel a duty of care tae Mr Stephens 'n', wi' ye, also subscribe tae the benefits of sexual services."

"I don't understand," Holding said, raising his eyes, though keeping his head at its present incline.

"Ah am not a medical perfaissional, bit ah believe in yer principles, 'n' know that the field of psychological medicine still holds mony unknowns, 'n' requires pioneering treatments sic as yers, which ur clearly underpinned by compassion 'n' a commitment tae betterin health. Ah dae nae intend tae halt ye, doctor, oan th' contrar, ah wish tae hulp."

Through consultation with the doctor and by bending the sympathetic ear of their captain, he used what spare time he had outside of his officer duties to help set up a treatment facility on *Aquitania* that would advance Mr Stephens's care. This included provision on board for innovative hydro- and sweat-therapies through restoring the ship's pools and Turkish baths. All of Dr Holding's patients were able to benefit from these new facilities. While the ship's chief surgeon did not subscribe to the benefits of alternative therapies, he gave his assent on the proviso that Dr Holding confined himself to palliative and psychologically impaired patients. For his part, he ensured that the doctor received complete privacy for the provision of his treatments. This included baring himself from observing as much as he had wanted to sit in. Holding showed his appreciation by joining him each evening for a cognac, neat, over which he would share his progress. Sexual services only formed a small part of Holding's prescribed treatments. Primarily, trauma patients underwent hydrotherapies as an extension of more conventional, couch-based regression therapies. And his palliative care patients benefited also. Using bunks refashioned as aqua-gurneys, Holding relieved pain and tension on the joints and ligaments of most damaged men, even holding out hope of their survival to reach port, where they would have access to additional facilities that could further life. He even started talking about paths to physiotherapy and eventual recovery for patients whose prospects had been decidedly death-directed before the set up of his bespoke facilities. Occasionally the captain would join them for these spirited meetings to hear about the program's accomplishments – not all of its particulars, of course.

It was the small, yet profoundly meaningful, sexual branches of his practice that excited the doctor most and that he spoke about at length over their evening drinks. Naturally, this was the subject that Olli was most keenly interested in too. Something that he assumed the doctor, with his psychological training, was aware of, though did not raise at any point. The autonomy and security of practice had also given the doctor scope for experimentation; one program he spoke of was the repurposing of the saunas by soldiers who had been dishonourably discharged after accusations of 'corrupt morality' – being caught in acts of sodomy.

"Curiously," Holding said, upright with the excitement of new discovery, "these men are returning to America to face trial and likely prison terms. Yet still, they seek out opportunities for fellatio and anal intercourse. And, following such encounters, appear more relaxed, and even optimistic, in our sessions. This challenges the medical community's received wisdom on sexual deviancy; rather than rejecting their sexual impulses, these men find meaning, place-hood and comfort in each other, even as we transport them to face judgement. If only I could publish what I have observed. And be a harbinger for change."

The doctor's enthusiasm had all the infectious tug of a tropical disease, and he sensed in the doctor's speech a reminder of how he had saved him from a similar fate. It seemed to be an expression of his gratitude; the doctor would dedicate the most detail in his debriefs to an update on the progress of Mr Stephens, who had become somewhat of an obsession for the doctor.

"It's remarkable," he said at conclusion of their final night before arrival in New York, "the transformation in Mr Stephens's mental state in such a short time."

Over many evenings, the doctor had chronicled each of his treatments and their effects on his preferred patient. The regain of control that the weightlessness of water brought him; the clarity of focus of sweat treatments, which he had based on anthropological records he had read of the 'sweat lodge' spiritual transformations of native American tribespeople; in each case, it was the inclusion of a range of sexual therapies that Holding had employed which held the purest promise.

"In all my experience in psychiatric medicine," he said. "In all the case files I have read, in every corner of every library and each page of the literature – and believe me, I've looked –, nowhere have I found an iota of anything resembling the progress I have seen in Mr Stephens, in such a short space of time. Certainly, never before have such novel approaches been possible. With your help," raising his glass, "a real difference has been made in the quality of Mr Stephens's life. Yes, experimental, personal and invasive methods have been part of my profession's past. Many of these dark, if murmurs of my field hospital patients are to be believed, and more borne out of this particular conflict, yes. But my experimental methods are intimacy-based and, I believe, more effective for it. I've observed it myself among the other men and in my own experiences during formative public school rites of passage. Put men together exclusively for extended periods and introduce an external, unified threat – danger most preferably, from a common enemy – and these men galvanise their bonds. The Australians have a term for it on which their entire identity is built, 'mateship': brothers-in-arms, homosocial intimacy. And what I have done with Mr Stephens, through *embodied* care of his wounded sexual self, with respect and driven by the tenets of no-harm and with the agency of the patient as the primary concern, with this, I cannot help but feel, all modesty aside, that what *we* have done on this great ship is to pioneer restorative psychological treatments. Treatments that will, maybe not in my lifetime, but *will*, eventually, be acceptable as part of a more grounded, inclusive, and patient-oriented medical future."

What the doctor had to say made much sense to him, as someone who had lived his life through subscription to the advantages of masculine sexual servitude. As welcome a distraction as helping the doctor with his practice had been for him, the more invested he had become in the doctor's progress and findings, the harder it ultimately proved for him not to draw parallels with his own experience. He rose his glass, consciously pushing the thought from his mind:

"Tae yer research, doctor, 'n' tae th' advancement o' yer profession."

It was as the sun was setting over the familiar New York docks and as *Aquitania* came in to moor alongside the modern *Normandie*, deep in the throes of conversion, that *I'm leaving* came as the voice of the doctor from the doorway. It pulled him away from his marvelling of the magnificent French liner that he had only had the pleasure of visiting briefly, those years ago.

"Mr Stephens has asked me to stay with him, to continue his treatment, and I have agreed."

He knew enough of Mr Stephens's station to realise the man was in no position to bring the doctor into any kind of employ for administering his care. This decision was ruled by the doctor's heart.

"I'll be sorry tae see ye gang," he said.

"I am at a loss for how to thank you."

"Juist tak' care o' yeself," he said, "that be cheers enough fur me."

The doctor closed the door.

"I have feelings for him, Oliver. Unprofessional feelings. I should not be confessing this to you when I have not even had the strength to admit it to myself yet."

"Aye, ah understand."

"And he says he has feelings for me, too."

The doctor paused as if expecting a response, and when none was received, answered himself.

"I know he is confused. I know this is case-study-transference, and I remember my oath. But still, Oliver, all this considered: I want to stay with him, to continue his treatment, and maybe, when he is ready, let him go."

Then, after another pause, he said in the tenor of truth:

"I would give up everything for him."

His speech was that of a man resigned to his fate, afraid yet anchored on a path.

"Ye kin write me," he said.

"What we talked about can never be committed to the page," he said, with a grip of his arm. "No, my friend, I'm afraid this is goodbye. I will never forget what you have done for me. You are a brave man, and Mr Stephens and I are lucky to have met you."

"And ah ye, doctor," he said. "Ah wish ye 'n' Mr Stephens success. Ah hawp that ye fin' a wey tae publish yer research," though even he knew that the doctor's ideas and practices would remain unpublishable, and probably punishable, for at least their lifetimes, and perhaps the sum of these. "Ah wish ye happiness," he revised more sincerely. "Please be canny, doctor."

Holding did not reply. Was he perhaps also wishing to remain authentic rather than pretend all would be fine in front of the one person he had been able to discuss his situation with openly? In place of a response, he embraced

Olli for a length, like it was the threshold before he embarked on a dangerous and uncertain research expedition, not wanting to pull away. When he finally found the courage to let go and turned to leave, he paused at the door one last time.

"Oh yes, one final request. The letter, may I have it?"

"Letter?"

"From Mr Stephens's fiancee, may I have it?"

He had forgotten about it wholly. He searched the paperwork on his desk. Between his dual commitment to competence in his duties and provision of the doctor's privacy of practice, its surface had become overgrown.

"'ere it is," he said, retrieving it from the base of his desk's pile, examining it as he handed it over.

Its familiar double opening from the censor's office, and other markers, that he now saw, as if for the first time:

Dr Alfred Archibald, Chief Surgeon
RMS Aquitania
NOT FOR DISTRIBUTION

And in the space of passing it over, all the pieces fell into place. As the picture of what *may* have actually happened started to clear from the haze of hearsay:

"We run a tight ship–"

There was no envelop and no censor scratchings; Robert's 'suicide' letter would never have gotten through uncensored; it must have been hand-delivered.

And most startling of all:

"All mail will be forwarded–"

How did he know to send the letter to the Mary, *only he knew of the last minute boarding...and White.*

He ran from the cabin leaving the doctor and his post, only one imperative on his mind, and another terrifying *I should have known*:

"I have never known any member of crew by that name."

He looked out over to *Normandie* and, inexplicably, locked eyes with White on a lower deck of the ship. On being sighted, White grinned with sinister recognition of the deduction and retreated back into the liner. He raced from the cabin, knocking a Cunard representative on a mail round as he went, headed out and onto the docks.

Robert. He's alive!

VII

ÎLE DE FRANCE

He moved with a sole-minded purpose along the dock he had got to know well in the dark on his last visit. Then up and onto *Normandie*. He ran by the same gangway, too, with which he had gained illicit access last time. He entered as workers were exiting for the night. Without stealth in his stride, he knocked by several refitters as he went, arousing attentions of the American men who guarded her.

"Oi," one shouted as he brushed by him at the top of the gangway, "where do ya think ya going?"

He ignored him, too busy trying to recall in his mind how far down the 1,000-foot superliner he had travelled relative to his own cabin and White's last known position. Having to now also contend with the chase of Americans trained for this, hot on his heels. Once around a bend in one of her passageways, he slipped into one corridor after another attempting to shake them. Though he did not realise it at first, muscle memory was leading him deep into the bowels of *Normandie* along a route that he had travelled previously. Clearly, the brute intrusion of his monster Frenchman had injected in him an ingrained impression of the ship and passages known only to her countrymen who, following the fall of France, were no longer trusted to tend to her. The extent to which his brutal enter, earlier encounter had shaped aptitude at adopting the same path that his invited attacker had employed to take him on his previous passage through the ship was evidenced by the state of change he now encountered. On first frequent, *Normandie* was still wholly un-war-functional. She was the luxury, Blue Riband-holding symbol of state that, though *Mary* would have the last victory of prompt passage, remained, indisputably, a work of French form over English function. Amid her refit, however, she was unrecognisable under the tutorage of American army men instead of craftsmen. A vast jumble of scaffolding and cladding in once-grand communal areas. Detritus of paint tins and workmen odds-and-ends in her no-longer-stately accommodations abounded. Her conversion was hasty, irrational, and without regard for conservation of art interiors that, should victory be achieved, would be reinstated as a matter of post-war prosperity necessity.

Lightless. He leapt over painters' planks, electricians' exposed wires and bunk installers' half-assembled frames to wholly throw off his unfamiliar-with-her-intimacy-interiors pursuers. Only once he had reached the engine room did he stop for breath and to reassess his objectives. The muscles that had guided him by memory to the final leg of what would lead to the forgotten engineer's office in the very base of the ship where he had been beaten and violently fucked...willingly, by a brutal hulk of a Frenchman...needed to be overridden. He was not there to hide but to *find*. After losing those, probably now several, Americans who had followed him into *Normandie*, pursuing him as a threat, he was freed to scout out himself. To hunt down White, and finally, to learn the truth.

But, he thought, panting – adrenaline still pulsing after his flesh-memory-driven flight through the ship that had led him into the vastness of the superliner's engine area. *I wouldn't know where to begin. Her superstructure, most likely, is also where the Americans are conducting their sweeps.*

It seemed too great a task for one man. To both outsmart the pincer movements of trained, though less bodily familiar – perhaps – men, while also hunting down a man who, first, had advance knowledge of his arrival, and second, had successfully outmanoeuvred him already. He leaned against the wall at the central hub of the engine room control area, his breath refusing to steady. Resigned that it was an impossible endeavour; the only outcome he could hope for being to hole up in the office his Frenchman had hiddenly fucked him in last time, then try and slip out through the night, without detection. He felt defeated and deflated, sinking like he was mine-stricken, listing against the bulkhead and succumbing to the floor. The original quest that had propelled him from *Aquitania*, *his* new ship, and onto this one in search of answers and even a possible location had left him with only a cowardice failure in its wake.

How long he stayed there, slumped on the floor of an engine room on a ship that had not seen service – like the manhole that pressed against it – for longer than her design had ever intended, could not be said soundly. It was for a length that had led the moon high into the night. Probably plenty of time, too, to have roped in a much greater force in the search-and-neutralise efforts of a guarding consignment craving such an opportunity for resistance. Finally, he resolved to follow the safe path of retreat to the office of hard fucks. Wait it out until he could formulate a plan of retreat. Perhaps re-attack from a different angle at a more opportune time. Just as this decision had been made. After he had slid back to his feet, poised to push away from the bulkhead for that office path return. Just then, the panel beside him beeped into life and mobilised him, too, as if with a hypodermic needle to the heart.

Fire!

One light after another on the panel beside him, followed by a spine-shaking siren throughout the ship.

"White!" He cursed.

Officer life 101, he recalled, Robert's voice ringing inside him, *forget the U-boats, forget the mines. Fire – that is what we fear most at sea.*

A crack of hope within him had let Robert's voice inside again, and, like a jolt of life-giving charge, he sprung back into action. Red lights flashing, sirens sounding. The ship's state-of-the-art fire systems retaliating, purpose returned. White was destructive, the ultimate threat, who had just thrown a catch-him clue; the lights across the grid of the ship's compartments, coming to life in sequence like pins on a map, as White sparked a trail of destruction through the ship. The minutes between lights seemed to clock up an aeon. He watched them, timing their turn on to predict a trajectory of interception. The trail led through C Deck, in the centre of the ship, along all of her grandest rooms: tinderboxes of paint tins and timber scaffolds. White had already ignited an uncontrollable chain reaction, he thought, as he was drenched in water from the ship's sprinkler system. She was designed to withstand fire. All the technology available had been incorporated to keep her safe at sea. Though not from arson without a crew of her countrymen to protect her. All the fire-safe automated systems in every sea city along the Atlantic could not compete with a madman running through her with an open flame and haystack supply of ignition points. But he would not give up, as he had so hastily, so stupidly, before, with Robert.

I will stop you, he thought, counting down to the last light on the panel like a starting pistol that would head him back up to the superstructure: on the hunt.

It was a barren haul. He knew it. He'd surveyed fuel sources through her like a chief engineer of breachings of watertight compartments too many. The cruel flashing lights on her panel told him hopelessness even before his pursuit had him panting through her passageways. Yet, he persisted. Amid the chaos of fire and smoke – the joining of New York's finest firefighters still some time away –, he continued in his quest to locate White, which even with the aid of the panel lights in his mind proved difficult. He raced the outer decks that were furthest from dockside access to avoid further detection from onlookers – her interiors having become too smoke-filled for him to enter. As the minutes passed further and *Normandie*'s future grew more grim, the New York skyline succumbed herself to smoke, and he started to worry for his own chances of retreat. After some time, too long to turn the tide, fire crews arrived. In a desperate attempt to stem the spread of fire through her, and unable to gain access to her inferno hull, these men resorted to flooding her decks. They filled her with torrents from their hoses. It was a mistake that would chime the death knell for the once-proud liner. Jetting water into her from just one side – as her frame swelled and screamed under the intense temperatures of chemical-fuelled fire – listed her dangerously toward the Hudson and away from the dock. This meant that his only means of logical escape was now cut off to him. The realisation came as White emerged from the smoke of one of the corridors leading from her stern. Moving toward him, ready to strike.

"Ye led me tae think he wis deid, how come?" He shouted across the short stretch of decking between them, close as he dared go to the man who had deceived him, making him only just able to make himself heard above the death cry of the elegant monster liner.

"To hurt you both," White returned, "the way you had hurt me."

Normandie's length and their placement on her stern – at the side that was at a slow incline, sloping into the Hudson; this meant they remained beyond sight of authorities – out of hope for rescue, too.

"Ah don't understand, whit did ah dae?"

"You're not the only one to have loved an officer, Oliver Turner. I was in love with *him* first, ever since he arrived. But I clearly don't possess your particular...charms. And that was OK, I was willing to accept that, be happy for you, even. Especially when love found me. When I met Kenneth. But you couldn't let me be happy, could you?"

There was a wrongness to White. A wickedness in him. And, it was there from the start. White was a Mary...and the worst kind.

Normandie was nearing her end now, laden over with water yet still burning out of control. Explosions sounded from deep within her as her final shrill reached a level where conversing was no longer possible, and her incline, an angle where both needed to grip hold of a fixed portion of her deck to stop from keeling over and into the river. But words were not necessary. He could see that white rage had gripped his newly uncovered adversary. It was like by setting fires throughout this great ship, White had ignited the final combustible cylinders of civility within himself. White lunged at him, and his place beside the access points into *Normandie*'s burning belly. They collided, struggled just as she was reaching the end of her own stranglehold on sky. But he managed to break free of White's grip just as she passed her personal tipping point. White was thrown off footing and into the passageway and down some stairs to be consumed by flames. His screams rung out just as Olli, facing certain death himself, ran down the now-near-vertical slope of her stern as it rolled toward the river. Diving off her edge into the shocking cold of the Hudson. He swam back toward Robert's ship with every fibre of adrenaline left in him: a tidal wave of *Normandie*'s struggle finally coming to an end with a capsize on her side, which sent him at speed into *Aquitania*'s side, where darkness flooded over him, too.

Death came as sublime release;
from pain, from loneliness;
Robert was there;
in a phantom ship in the sky;
more perfect and handsome than ever.

It took a time for his eyes to adjust as he slipped in and out of sleep. A time for Robert to take complete definition from the smudge of light and circles of colour before him. But once he had fully focused, blinked twice as that extra measure, he reached up and kissed him. Full and hard, pulling him down to join him on the cloud of his heavenly plane. Robert did not resist, but neither did he reciprocate. And once he broke their lips for air, his Robert even pulled away.

"Ahem," Robert said, in the guise of clearing his throat, "it must be the drugs, doctor," speaking to a presence off-field, out of Olli's range. "He's confused."

"Indeed, not surprising given the head trauma," a second, familiar-though-unable-for-him-to-place voice said, also with a clearing of the throat. "I must be getting on; I have conversed with the ship's surgeon about his condition."

"This young man owes you a great debt, doctor," Robert said.

"No, captain," said the doctor, pieces of the surroundings finding their fit. "The debt remains mine. Goodbye, Oliver," the doctor said from further away, "and take care."

He wanted to turn and thank the familiar doctor's voice. For what exactly, he was not yet sure. But the directive he gave himself to move did not correspond with the expected action, and before he could transfer limb to speech, the sound of the door closing could be heard, and the sight of Robert, his beloved, swiftly consumed all other concerns once more. He pawed at Robert again, managing to grip him this time – though only weakly – and to pull him into a bear hug. On this take, lips moved across lips of both parties, though Robert draw away again when Olli found himself once more out of breath.

"Olli, stop it," Robert said, with a sternness he had never received from him. "You must rest. And you made your choice."

The exertions made his view foggy again, as pain and confusion crept over him, like a mist across once familiar waters, making them strange.

"Are you in pain," Robert said.

His Robert, sounding compassionate, like himself once again.

"I can fetch the ship's doctor..."

He grabbed for him in giddy panic, pain shooting through, but he did not care. He held tight through it to Robert's arm.

"Please, darlin'. Don't lea me. Nae again."

And darkness returned to visit.

It was a calmer sleep this time.

When he woke, Robert was at his side again. His clammy, knuckles-swollen hand rested in the home of his officer's larger, fatherly one. He had never thought of him like that, until then, when weak and worried – that he would disappear again, die again, and that, as before, he would have no say in the matter. Clarity was faster coming this time and with it a less encompassing numbing of pain – just a dull hum. Night had come, and the cabin, large and ornate, was candle-lit, the flames of wicks swaying with the roll of a sea-bound passage. Less drugged-up this time, he was better able to *read* Robert. To know that he had tracked his second waking; sufficiently for reaction-readiness and with head bow and lack of looking at him; all signs that there was gravity to come.

"What did you mean 'not again'?"

Confused, dazed, he reached for him, but Robert pulled away.

"You said: 'Don't leave me. Not again.' What did you mean?"

He must have become weak, he thought. Because, like he had on the first night with Harris, then again on their farewell; there, on his first night back with Robert, emotion rose up inside him like an awful, unwelcome winter storm, thundering him into ugly upset. Tears came in a shuddering, painful mess. It broke through Robert, cut to the part of him that he knew: loving, devoted, eager to please.

"Tell me," he said, softer, leaned over him, eyes darting across his tear-streaks for meaning, like he would one of his charts.

"Ah thought ye wur deid. He tellt me ye hud murdurred yersel', 'n' losing ye a'maist destroyed me. Ah couldn't bare tae gang thro' that again."

His violent storm sobs found themselves smothered by the comfort of Robert's body on top of him, and he held on tight, watertight.

"I'm not going anywhere; you're my world, Oliver Turner," he said, warm as a glowing hearth in his ear.

And he buried himself into the scratch of that stubble and the softness of those lips – until a more lasting sleep came.

When he woke again it was to be alone in the captain's cabin, the sun some company.

Waking into the panelled wood place was like falling back into a comfortable sleep, principally because its tonic was like salts, smelling sweetly of Robert – putting paid to his first-wake fears, of it-had-been just a dream. In his absence, Robert had settled, set up a captain's cabin with more and varied personal effects. His photos were back; these were among the first aspects of the room he noted, as were some books and artefacts, presumably picked up along his travels, that had now been set up to homely up the place. Railwayana, he suspected, was the term: relics and clippings from the Victorian age of steam, in specimen cases and across shelves throughout Robert's den. In his absence, Robert had come into his own, become comfortable. More assertive. He had, by all appearances, thrived. Without him: his officer had become a captain.

On the mantel, in *his* captain's study, standing folded in front of a wall-hung cabinet of curiosities – with rusty sleeper nails and old ship rivets and a pinned menu from *Lusitania* – was a card with "Oliver" on the front. Seeing that hand again, made freshly with ink, against the backdrop of fallen engineering marvels, prolonged the haze of suspicion that it was all a dream, too good to be true. Inside the card were two life-saving lines:

> When you're ready, come find me on the bridge.
>
> I love you.

The final line was some way down the card and written at a different slant. Like it was added with haste and after ponderment. The captain's cabin was in the bridge portion of the ship, so reaching Robert was only a matter of climbing one flight of steps. At the landing, to the wing of the wheelhouse, he paused a moment, watching Robert, in all his full seafaring captain regalia. He looked taller, calmer there.

He's thrived without me, he thought.

Half proud, half disappointed.

"Officer Turner," Robert said on sighting him, "good to see you up and about, shall we take some air? Hendricks, take over, would you?"

"Whit ship is this?" He asked once they were alone and out of sight, tucked into a corner of one of the bridge wings.

"*Île de France*, of the French line."

Robert said it distractingly, eye on the open sea horizon, past the scatter of ships of the convoy, in the immediate field of view ahead.

"Ships are like islands, Olli," he said to the flatline, where deep blue met white. "They pass each other in the night. Sometimes their paths even cross, and in the worst of cases, collide. But they always remain separate, even in collision. That is how I had to come to accept your decision, not to join me here. *But*," after some pause and sea-spray, "since the good doctor and I pulled you from the Hudson yesterday, and based on what you have said to me briefly, this has stirred inside a dangerous hope that I had thought was now buried."

Robert turned to him. Like he was the only thing in focus between the bridge and the horizon. Like he was land newly spotted after months at sea – unsure himself, it seemed, about whether to trust his own eyes.

"I had given up hope on us, Olli."

He searched himself for the words to explain, but none came to him.

"I'm sorry, darlin'," he said. "Ah wis led tae think ye wur deid. Edward said–"

"Edward? Edward White?"

"Aye, mah darlin'. He betrayed us baith, he tellt me ye wur deid, worse, that ye hud murdurred yersel', 'n' convinced me tae flee, said that Kenneth wis comin' fur me, 'n' that yer lest wish wis fur me tae be safe."

His speech was truncated, detached, without time to be structured for coherence.

"Sae ah left," he said as summation.

"And you believed him? That I would leave you. Us. That I would just throw all we had away."

"Bit yer letter–"

"What letter?"

He fished it out of his pocket. By miracle, it had survived the Hudson and the laundering of his clothes. Torn and smudged, but still intact, and he handed it to Robert.

"Where's the rest of it? The part where I explain what happened, the plan, our escape–," he stopped himself, as all apparently dawned on him: exactly *how* the deceit had managed to play out. "This is all he gave you."

He nodded. Understanding, now, himself too.

"'n' 'twas ainlie by chance that ah learnt th' truth, whin ah decided ah wid seek answers 'n', somehow, jyne *Aquitania*. That's whin ah fun oot whit ye hud dane fae me; bit aye, yer death remained a mystery."

Comprehension spread across Robert's expression like sun breaking through after the passing of storm.

"Because *they* thought I was dead, too. My plan for us was just for us, though White had knowledge of it."

"Aye," he said, stepping closer, understanding fully as well, and placing one hand upon the railing, the other in the small of Robert's back; it fizzed to his touch like a chemical reaction of volatile substances.

"'n' 'twas ainlie thro' anither letter fae th' guid doctor, wha ye'v noo met," he added, "'n' a missing envelope 'n' th' haun o' a censor, that ah realised, na, dared hawp, mah loue, that ye leed. 'n' sae ah pursued it, tracked doon Edward. Confronted him, 'n' that story kin wait 'til anither time," he said, sliding his hand beneath the belt of Robert's pants to rest atop the crest of his cheeks.

"There is more to the story, Olli," Robert said, breathless; now himself, his old Robert, once more. "More you do not know, potential danger ahead for us. Edward fooled me, too, and besides him and dangers, there are other things... *Indiscretions.*"

He said the last word like his mouth had sucked in lemon in the formation of its syllables; it was hard for him to say, clearly, coming from his body in shudders.

"I was hurting," he added, sheepishly, in keeping with the man Olli knew.

It was a relief, to have located his officer after such a time, and to find him, after some probing, more or less, as he had left him. News of indiscretions was welcome, too, he viewed, as it would help with his own conversation of hurting and the taking of another captain who, it would be difficult to reveal, meant just as much, but in entirely different ways. Like two brilliant liners in convoy, both beloved but belonging to entirely different eras, sporting different fine lines, serving entirely different, yet equally vital, seafarer needs. He slid his hand into his new captain's pants, between his plump cheeks. It was a homecoming.

"Olli, we need to–"

"–efter," he said, taking Robert's hand from the railing to hush his lips while he toyed with his captain's porthole.

"I've missed ye," he breathed into his captain's mouth, speaking both to him and to his *below*.

Robert's lower lips pulsed at his touch, tight after unuse – but eager.

"I kept it fresh for you," Robert said, "just like you taught me."

My sea squirt, he thought, *how I've missed you.*

He dropped to his knees and brought down Robert's pants with him, spinning him to the sea. His arse was fuller than he remembered, likely because he could never really bring himself to look at an arse since his. He planted his palms, one on each cheek, pressing, kneading him like an artisan a fine dough. Getting him ready. Robert arched his back, hands planted and spread wide on the railing, just at the sensation of touch – down there. He savoured the reveal. Kneading his captain's doughy centre, pressing together until the thumbs of each hand touched, and then bringing them out again. In circular movements, increasing with the pace of his captain's breath, until, as an out-of-time jerk, he pulled cheeks apart to reveal the into-mouth of his lover. The lips only he got to *see.* He had planned to watch a while, to take in the sight of Robert's opening against the backdrop of convoy open sea formation, but the pull was too great, and as swiftly as his squirt was squinting in the midnight sun, it was hidden again, sucking in Olli's tongue. He had not lied. Robert had not reneged on his ready-to-receive rituals and, for someone who had recently embarked on his own patterns of keeping himself ever-ready for someone he cared for – tasty to the tongue –, it was appreciated.

Rosemary, dill, and a hint of mint.

He was like a fine Sunday lamb, scrumptious and willing. Almost too precious to touch with anything other than an organ with taste buds. But as he burrowed further and further into him, new-captain cheeks spread so far that their soft tops touched the lobes of his ears, he came to know that a deep filling was what they both needed. And so he pulled back, Robert's softened, moistened, urchin opening puckering in readiness – having been held in trust for him.

"Urr ye hungry," he said, again to them both, but below first.

Without waiting for an answer, he was upright and inside his Robert again. Fully, trench-ly, the nerve ends of his penis alive for the first time in years, reaching into the spongy softness of his officer, who absorbed him in, sucking out a speedy load from them both in long-overdue expressing of a love that they had thought lost at sea. Robert hung over the railing, sure to tumble into the sea to never resurface had it not been for the pull on his hipbones of Olli. But Olli, who would never let go again, not ever, gripping only tighter at the moment of into-load, which was when Robert spilt forth, too, through the bars of the wing deck and into the sea, mainly. Some of it ventured onto the edge of the promenade deck below. On-ship and within vicinity, of soldiers on their voyage to war. Some looked up to see their captain, clothed as far as they could tell – but thrashing about in the greatest of agitations, like a wayward life raft caught in a tropical cyclone. But they thought nothing much of it, for he thrashed with purpose. Authority. Dogged commitment to his undertaking. And knowledge that, whatever happened, anything could be overcome. However much he flaunted the forbidden, as long as he had *his one* inside him, his was a double iron hull.

He repacked his captain and sent him back to work on the bridge with a full belly. *Île de France* could not spare a cabin for him to stay in, which was for the best, as it saved the pretence of having to sneak in to see Robert each eve. He resolved never to leave his backside again. The office of captain, well, it came with distinct deckhand lover advantages. A cot had been set up for him in front of the mantlepiece, provision to rest in on first joining the ship. That went unused, of course, their close quarters, unquestioned, as was the privilege of taking the captain as a lover and of being two men who, by all outward mannerism, were below buggery suspicion.

With several hours still to pass before supper, and another feeding of his captain, followed by a shared captain's private table meal, he unpacked his possessions that the good doctor had arranged to be sent over, under secrecy, just before *France* set sail. It was prudent he felt, and Robert agreed, that his true identity be kept secret in the wake of the demise of *Normandie*, *France*'s former flagship.

France was crewed almost entirely by Americans – as a safeguard against any potential occupier-sympathising Frenchmen –, and investigations into *Normandie*'s destruction – a significant blow to the Allies' troop movement ambitions – were already in full swing. Descriptions of the young officer seen running into her in her final hours circulated like leaflets dropped from enemy airspace – from the officers down to the engine room workers. The risks of White's sabotage efforts being pinned on him seemed high. Even Robert was taking little chance when it came to his shielding, the look he gave on his arrival on the bridge earlier – it expressed regret at having summoned him. For the rest of the voyage, to where he was still not sure, all his movements would be within the confines of the captain's cabin.

Among the rationed items he possessed and now unpacked was a parcel wrapped in brown paper. Inside were letters, a dozen or so bound in twine. Atop the pile was a note signed by Dr Holding:

> Dear Oliver,
>
> These arrived for you just as you left.
>
> I have asked the captain to forward all your future mail to my New York address, and I will then forward your letters into the care of Captain Bell.
>
> Take care, my friend.

All the letters were in the same round, wildly confident hand. Each had initially been addressed to him care of *Elizabeth* and forwarded to *Aquitania* by Cunard's office. Now, they came to a cabin on *France*. They all had already been opened and resealed, bearing the mark of the censor. It was with some emotion that he opened up the earliest of the letters. It was dated the day he had left *Elizabeth*.

He kept his word, he thought, curling up in the window recess, the sight of soldiers playing ball on the deck outside, with convoys-in-sea as scenery, proving the perfect Harris reading platform.

> Olli,
>
> I told you I would write you. I always keep my word. And this

> first letter comes just hours after I last saw you. When we parted, I was pleased to see that, apparently, our friendship has meant as much to you as it has me in the short time we have known each other.
>
> We are on █████████████ headed █████ towards █████████████████ I think. This is the first chance I have had to sit down and write you. I do not know how long it will take for these letters to reach you, or how much will be taken out of them before they do. But I promise to write you everyday, my friend.
>
> I expect my next letter will come when ██████████ Until then, remember me. And know, deep inside you, that I look forward to visiting your home again, and spending the night as a guest.
>
> With warm affection, your friend, Harris.

As much as he hated the censors for taking precious words from him, he delighted in the code Harris employed: underlying key phrases to signal their illicit history and intentions toward each other. As he progressed through the pile, the coding became more ham-fisted, as did the censor's black marker. Resentment for this invisible third party and their growing blockades between he and Harris grew through the pile, and he found himself wishing Harris would stop wasting his letter space with details of his troop's movements and particulars of the fighting he faced. Until that is, over the course of a number of letters, he realised that this was code, too. Just as *your home* meant hole and *deep inside* referred to how he wished to make love to him again, the slip-slide streaks of black across the sun-weathered letters of his lover came to signify something within themselves.

In a particularly lengthy letter in the latter portion of the pile, Harris wrote:

> I've been writing Alice, too.
>
> I have been since the day I left her. Every day, except the night we met, my friend.

And I write her still now, every day. About the weather, the food, and with questions for her about the ranch and the goings-on back home. But never. Never, my friend, about what I am actually feeling, about this experience.

What I am trying to say is:

I tell you, more, Olli.

More than I tell Alice.

That line, one blissful, uncensored, Harris-coded, personal line between just them two meant everything to him. And it stuck with him, in thought, up to the time when he was due to feed Robert:

Do I? He thought, *do I...*tell *Harris more?*

A post-feeding sit-down with Robert was something new. The setting, in his new captain's dining quarters...it was civilised, silver-trimmed. He did not mind it. He liked seeing Robert in a successful situation. But in terms of *their friendship*, the domestic dimension was novel.

"Tell me, mah darlin'," he said, "aboot *Mauretania*."

Robert put down his cutlery, finished his wine, and set out the story.

"I had decided on the night before we returned to Sydney...when you suggested that we not go back, that I would find a way for us to be together, away from my family, away from it all."

"'n' Kenneth?"

"Convenient, I thought. The shove I needed to realise that my life with you was what I wanted."

"'n' yer existing lee? Whit o' that?"

"A sham. A sham marriage, a son I never got to see, a father who despised me."

"How come didn't ye let me in oan th' plan ?"

"I had intended to, but I made a mistake, Olli, in trusting White. Again and again on each turn. It was his idea to give you a sedative. Kenneth, *he* said, was actually harmless and just wanted a shot at officership training. And the photo negatives were merely a foolish move to secure that, or so he claimed. And I believed him, them both. And so, we drugged you, and I joined *Mauritania*, with the plan being for me to assist Kenneth, get him in the door–"

"Bit he wis awready in th' door, Robert. He hud th' favour o' yer faither, 'n' yer wife's name..."

"It was a bluff, Olli. Problem was, I didn't realise that it was a red herring, too. A double bluff at my expense. I fell for it."

"Ah don't understand, whit happened?"

"He came for me, once onboard. Tried to solicit sex, which I refused, then," and Robert's breath shortened with the retell, "and when I refused him, he turned violent. Retrieved a knife and came at me. We struggled, and...he was killed."

So he was the death.

"I didn't mean to, Olli. But he wouldn't stop, and when I refused him, he just turned."

A knock at the dining door denied him the chance of reply, which was welcome, he thought, as Robert's story had left him little sure how he should. He was impressed by how calmly Robert had handled it, indeed, though much about the story still had a feeling of distance about it.

"Sorry to disturb you, Captain," came a voice from the door, out of view. "But you asked to be informed ahead of the escort; they should be with us within the hour."

"Very well, Murphy. I will be on the bridge shortly. It's all right," Robert said when he sat back down, "we have time...for us."

"I'd ower ye finished yer meal oan th' bridge," he said, pushing his plate aside, keen to keep them both on form. "You kin arrange it, can't ye, Captain? Juist fur a brief, private tour."

Am I testing him? He wondered.

But if he was, Robert's response would have passed him.

"Of course I can," he said with hardly a pause and not a seam of hesitation. "Give me twenty minutes, then come find me in the wheelhouse. Use my stairs from near my cabin."

"Aye, there's a guid captain."

It was a relief to brace the sea air once more, just briefly, as he ascended the stairs in secret to the wheelhouse. His day in Robert's cabin with Harris's letters had left him feeling pent up like a bureau draped in a country retreat during dreary winter months. Had it just been him on board, he would not have concerned himself so much with strict confinement. By now, would have found a way to mingle among men, even those in search of a stranger. But he was thinking about the safety of two now.

Three, he thought, in correction after the afternoon's reading.

Troopship decks were tranquil domains in the dark, when all the men were below, washing and glistening, or sleeping and bunk-hopping. But he felt glad that he was en route to a prearranged penetration, for being on deck again, at night, alone, made him think of Harris, and want for him to *visit* his home once more. Robert was legs spread, body draped over the central ship wheel of the wheelhouse on his arrival – entirely stripped bare, save for his captain's cap.

The setting suits him, he thought.

He admired the way his wide, presenting gait peeled his cheeks apart all of its own – to show off his entrance, sloppy and loose. His back arched with acknowledgement of his entrant's eyes upon him, his hole winking a welcome. It was a tidy treat of a proposition. To have him there, pressed against the pedestal of a grand liner's primary propulsion-steerer, with the ocean spread out above the arch of his back, through curved glass before them. The night sky brightened the foredeck, and the bridge, too. It starlit all-manner of equipment and dials and wood-wheels at his disposal: for use in the refuelling of the ship's captain. Robert was ready, expectant. He moved in front, into the space between where his captain had draped himself and the glass. Taking Robert's chin and raising his eyes to greet.

"Kin ah steer her?"

Robert nodded.

He circled the wheel-with-presented-captain-draped, like a lion sizing up snared prey. Slowly, curiously; calculating how best to proceed with the feed, how to prolong the toying-with to make the eventual devouring taste ever the sweeter – safe atop the food chain. He touched as he carried out his assessment of best-course-of-entrance, from warm flesh to polished wood, up and over the slopes of his bent captain, up and over the ridges of the wheel he had strapped himself to; full circle. After a few rotations, he noted that while his captain's body was unflexed and ready for use, his knuckles were white, gripped to the wheel. He traced their bumps and the length of each finger, bringing their tension undone. Once both hands were off the wheel, he moved Robert adjacent to the steering. Then, he bent him over further until a right angle and lined his hole up like a pilot preparing to navigate a narrow strait into a harbour and backed his captain's hole onto the tip of the handle in the nearest line to it. It was a proportionately knobbed wheel for a large liner and was mounted on a platform of considerable height. The particular grip he chose for the captain's hole was one notch below the handle that was level with the waiting, right-angled captain. Getting the captain into line to receive it while maintaining the ship's current course, therefore, required some piloting and a further lowering of the captain toward the floor – knees bent, his torso cranked between his thighs. Eventually, it meant the folding of the ship's captain right down to his knees: the elevation of arse with the lowering of his face, right to the floor. He worked his captain in the fashion of a pumpjack in an oil field – well-greased and easy to handle, his captain responded well to his navigations, and soon he was fully aligned.

On this wheel of considerable size were handles of considerable length and girth, too, with man-hand-filling bulbous tops that sloped to a slender base. His captain whimpered as Olli, with two hands on his arse, eased the handle into him. As he stretched, the white traces from earlier feeding gathered around the rim to keep the ship's captain supple at the helm. Tears sprung as his captain arrived at the broadest point, and he held him there, at his edge, savouring the sight of his captain at his most dilated. Full of wood. Robert was now an attachment of the wheel, the captain one with his ship's steering. Only now did Olli feel ready to try his hand at steering *France.* Using his palm as a stopgap against Robert's rim, he lifted him – slowly, slowly, back to his feet. The ship responded to its captain's anal command, and he was proud to watch him in action, the power of direction over the liner's immense engines inside him. Now Robert's rim was at the top of the handle's incline. His hand beneath, taking his weight. When he removed it, Robert slid onto the wheel at speed, his ass swallowing swathes of the handle's length and relief spreading through him at having passed and taken its widest point into his depths.

Careful now, he thought, gripping Robert's cheeks to delay the last inches of descent. *Don't hurt him.*

This was the one granule of White advice he had clung to and held as sacred in his relations with Robert. Knowing full well the twists and turns of the male anal-anatomy and the critical limit for non-give objects, like wood, he looked under his captain at his rim, suck-fast to the handle and wanting more. And, once sizing it up in relation to the handle and what he knew his captain was ready to handle, he let him go, allowing him to drop fast, all the way to his stem so that he came to rest fully fixed, the ship's knob venturing several inches further into his depth than had been before attempted. How pleasing it was for him to see, his sea squirt stuck firm to the felloe, his cheeks spilling over either side to rest atop the spokes of the wheel, splayed out like compass points, one of which was stuck right up inside him. Then, Robert fully fixed, he gripped other handles of the wheel and continued the evasive wartime course; his captain careened on the wheel as he was navigated by hole in upper then lower directions.

"See that, captain. Howfur weel she responds tae th' pull o' th' wheel wi'in yer arsehole."

"Yes, si–ah," was all he could manage, labouring under the roll of the ship in a swell together with the rounding of the wheel into positions where Robert could no longer maintain a straight line of entry.

"Noo," he said, detaching his captain-attachment from the wheel once he had reached the hard edge of the pedestal.

Robert whimpered a bit as he was yanked to get back up and over the bulb of the handle. Once free, he looked into the gaping opening of his captain, on all fours, catching his breath. He watched with fascination as his captain's supper from earlier dribbled from his lower lips, over his taint, to drip and pool on the floor. Robert looked through his legs, too, saddened at the sight of Olli spilling from him.

Perhaps that's far enough for one night, he thought. *Then. Again, perhaps just a few paces further. Give him a proper stretching out. Run him through some earnest sea trials.*

To show he cared, he leaned in and gently kissed the messy, bloated arse lips of his captain.

"Let's shift up some notches 'n' stretch oot her legs wi' a chaynge o' bearing," he whispered.

Leaving Robert – still, as a heap-with-wrecked-hole on the wheelhouse floor – he donned the captain's hat and took the wheel, bringing *France* back onto a steady course. He then scooped up the cream from the floor and used it to lather the top prong of the wheel. Robert's eyes widened with a hint of horror for what might be asked of him next, him planting his palm as a plank across his loose opening, plugging it, keeping in what remained of Olli, his only lubricant against the onslaught ahead of him.

"I'll haud her steady, while ye climb up," he said.

"Yes, sir."

Robert's knees were shaky as he scaled the wheel's spokes to arrive atop it, feet planted on felloe, either side of the top spike.

"I'm afraid," Robert said, letting go of his broken hole to steady himself, allowing more of Olli to spill out before Olli himself stemmed the flow with the cup of his hand, steadying his captain, taking some of his weight.

"A've git ye," he said.

He pressed his lips to the small of Robert's back – sweaty ripe – and lowered him onto the handle pointing directly skyward: it would reach even deeper into him. Robert cried out, louder this time, as his at-its-limit hole expanded over the bulb, then brought him crashing to the base, coming to sit on the felloe. Robert cried out again on impact. Olli wrapped his arm around his waist, pressing the flank of his face to the sweat-tremor of his spine.

"A've git ye, mah loue. Noo relax 'n' trust me."

Robert continued to writhe for maybe four moments more, resisting the impaling; then did what he was told and allowed his body to go slack, hanging on the spike, with only Olli's hold to keep him upright. He then, holding Robert's waist – propped up with the handle inside him, his legs handing loose –, steered the ship on that zigzag course again, allowing Robert to roll with the ship while the wood stood firm, rubbing up the parts inside him. When Robert grew hard, and his tears turned to familiar groans of appreciation, he moved in front of him. Kissed his belly tenderly, under which Robert had a chunk of wood deeply embedded.

"Ye'v dane weel, mah loue. I'm proud o' ye."

Robert started sobbing again, with gratitude this time. Pulling Olli close, though struggling against the constraints of being propped in place by a bulbous wooden stake. Knowing it was now time for sweet reprieve and refilling, Olli himself undressed and lay a bed for them both with his clothes. Then, draping one leg of Robert's after the other over the bends in his arms, he scooped him up and over the bulb of the wheel-handle by the strength of his now-years of deckhand helping, and onto their makeshift bed. Able seamanship had made him strong, and he transferred his captain without concern. It was only when he got his captain onto his back, legs over his shoulders, to properly inspect the state of his hole did he realise the extent of the damage that had been done. The hole, *his* hole, throbbed with trauma, bent beyond what it had been trained to take. And looked now dried out. Before him, Robert's cheeks flushed red, and his chest rose like the waves of the swell outside.

"I'm sorry, Olli," he said as if he had let him down by being in no state to take further force below.

"Ye did sae weel," he said, kissing his lips in both places with such tenderness that he almost didn't taste. "I'm proud o' ye."

And he was. Earlier thoughts of whether he perhaps *told* Harris more were now settled. Harris was *more* than Robert, *more than* Robert could ever be to him. Had reached depths inside him that no one had before; mobilised affections beyond the physical that he had not thought could manifest among men. But. Equally. Robert was more than Harris, too. His rubbery commitment to please in any and every way meant everything to him. He kissed Robert's mouths tenderly again, wetting them, requisitioning their recovery.

"Ye look hungry," he said to one mouth, "a guid feed wull fix ye richt up," to another.

They were interchangeable, these mouths of Robert. Which was yet another characteristic of *this* captain that distinguished him. Harris was strong, handsome beyond any attempt to describe, and made him ache in ways no other man could; but Robert ached *for him*, and he loved him for it.

"Let's git ye fed 'n' intae bed," he said, to *his* captain's lower and most in-need lips, singularly this time.

And without further intrusion, with a solely selfless delivery of nourishment, he expressed a meal for his captain, throbbing from the trauma of ship-steering that Olli had put him through. And his love for him, his need to give him the reward that would help with the healing led him to express it in only minutes. Elevating Robert gently, with a palm at this lower back, he delivered the meal to the waiting, chapped lips. His seed pooled in the upward-facing recess of his entrance, his hole taking it in in desperate gasps, coating the swollen pits of himself. Like a desert-dehydrated soldier being delivered life-saving droplets from a hip flask of a passing journeyman, Robert sucked it in, every drop, until the recess of his cheeks was dry, but his lips moist again.

"Thank you," he said on completion of the last drip, going limp, ready for sleep.

He dressed his Robert and himself and wiped clean the wheelhouse. He then lifted his Robert to his feet.

"Juist one mair instruction fur ye, the lest, ah promise. Summon some men tae guide up 'ere. Tell thaim that some correction o' coorse be necessary, for unexpected swells. Dae this as ye gang aboot yer day, then come back tae th' cabin 'n' climb intae bed, 'n' ah wull hae a further feed fur yer rest."

Robert nodded.

"Guid laddie," he said, reaching between his arse cheeks, feeling, even through Robert's briefs and the cotton of his pants, the pout of his below-mouth; better, but still hungry. "A loue ye," he added, kissing his neck and returning to the cabin the way he had come.

As instructed, Robert was back within the hour. Olli had his uniform off again and his arse tucked into bed as soon as he was in the door. It was red and swollen and dry again. He expressed another feed to coat his lips.

“Thank you,” he said again, “I needed that.”

He wrapped him tight in his arms and, after feeding, returned himself inside to rest there. There was plenty of room after Robert’s wheeling, but still, he was impressed with the suction of his sea squirt, which held him there. He resolved to stay inside him for the night.

“You deserve this, mah darling,” he said, “now sleep.”

Previously, instinctually, he would have withheld this as something sacred, something only of the man now taken from him. Only something Harris and he shared, just in roles-reversed. But this was wrong, ill-factual; he reflected while holding Robert, who descended into sleep quickly following his ordeal. What he had experienced was not, should not, be his and his alone. Robert had given himself to him, placed his welfare and the rear-ment of his anus in his hands. And he owed it to him, *loved* him sufficiently, to ensure that what was *his* was, at least in knowledge gained, something to be shared between them. Robert’s hole was not easily sated and took every advantage of having a source of nourishment throughout the night. He surprised himself at how he could sleep still, just waking at intervals with a fresh offloading. After dawn, they both awoke with the into-Robert delivery of a morning meal.

“Mornin’, darlin’.”

He was going to ask how Robert was, how he was feeling. Though the sight of him in the morning sun stopped this question. His cheeks were full with colour, his eyes a brighter blue than he had seen them since first-clap on *Elizabeth* and, most suggestive of all, his arsehole was strong again. Without swelling and back to its pretty pinkness, made supple from its nightly supply, yet had also bounced back with its elasticity – like he had been given the elixir by rectum administer. Elasticity made itself clear to him as he withdrew, struggled to. Once disconnected, Robert rolled over to rest on his chest. It was like their Australian retreat, the comfort and carefree love of a southern land.

The sound of aircraft overhead soon brought them solemnly back to the sea and out of their indulgent interlude.

Then, Robert sprung from the bed with a dimension of play Olli had not seen from him before. Admiring his hole in the mirror before dressing.

"Into port today, Olli, I probably won't be able to see you again until we dock, but we have a few days layover this time. So we will get to spend time together."

The declaration made him realise, as was the absurdity of troop transfer life, that he still did not know where they were headed.

"Whit's oor destination?"

"Port Elizabeth, South Africa."

Word direct from the British Admiralty – who now had complete control of *France* since her namesake's occupation – was that she should vacate all crew on arrival. For further refit, her captain included. It was welcome news coming with accommodation in the city.

The morning after arrival in port, he returned to their room in the King Edward Hotel. He had given Robert instructions to flush himself out in preparation for some further treatments, returning to find him in just his briefs. He found him kneeling in the bumped-out window seat of one of Edward's stately rooms, watching intently the parade of Royal Air Force men below. It was hard to think of him there, in his briefs ready for tending to, as a father and a married mariner. Having just come from the markets along Military Road, that snaked through the streets to pass right below their Edwardian hotel, he was more than familiar with the finery on view: many square jaws and round buttocks in tight trousers with protrusions at the front to entice the viewer. He tossed the brown paper bag with his assortment of topical ointments and oils onto the seat beside Robert and slid down his briefs to conduct his inspection. Just as all the airmen Robert watched so intently would have been inspected before receiving their flying orders. Though, he was probably more thorough than most air force inspectors, spreading Robert's cheeks to assess the health of his lips – that looked fully recovered, though perhaps a little dry – and then even peeling back the pout of them, to test deeper, by means of tongue.

"Good boy," he said, satisfied by the cleanliness of his captain.

Retrieving his jar of honey and cinnamon paste, he set to work on the restoration project. Condiments were applied into Robert's hole like a putty, pushed in at least as far as his longest fingers could reach. Then, with the remaining honey from the jar stroked along his shaft, he began grinding the treatment home. Robert stayed transfixed on the men below, bobbing with the beat of having the anal remedy worked into him. This was not pleasure nor play; this was platonic detailing – like, in a perfect realm, mates would do to each other as a matter of mutual manicuring.

"Oan th' lookout fur a'body in particular," he asked as Robert started panting with the pulse of prolonged entrance into him; as pleasure came into play, and Robert began to mist-up the morning glass, pressing his cheek to it as his entry reps increased.

"No one else has had me," Robert said in fogged speech against the glass, "not in the way that you have *had* me," them both getting close now.

"Bit..." he said, teasingly, pulling back, keeping them both at the edge of the end.

"*But*," Robert said, the pull of his head back.

"Aye," with clasp of his captain's hair and a yank of the head in this direction, then that, then around, eventually to allow their mouths to touch. "Tell me," he said, gathering speed in his stroke again.

"He was an airman, and he is based here."

"Aye."

"And I *took* him."

"Whaur."

"In my," and in the elation of completion, "mouth!"

And the shudder of Robert's body, his tightening around him, even full of honey and cinnamon, led to the adding of cream to the mix.

"Weel, that shuid keep ye at bay fur a while," he said, swabbing what had escaped from Robert's lower lips and transporting it in a few swipes to Robert's upper mouth, which licked his fingers clean. "Bit ah think, we shuid pay a visit tae yer airman, 'n' arrange a proper feed fur this end," he said, kissing his face.

"I love you," Robert said, falling into his arms, relief at – chronically tame, charmingly so – confession complete.

He cleaned Robert with his tongue, then packed him into pants and a shirt.

"Leid th' wey, captain."

The hotel that played their host began life at the start of the century, as 'King Edward Mansions' and as long-stay apartments, and had retained this feeling of the luxury long stay throughout its contemporary public areas. Robert used the telephone at reception to confirm with his airman that a visit was convenient, including that it would encompass the presence of a guest. And also booked a car for them with the attendant.

"Irvine is based at the airport, which was only opened last decade, and has been specially extended to the south for the accommodation of the R.A.F. School," Robert explained on the short drive to his airman's lodgings.

A fellow Scotsman? He wondered.

Robert's familiarity with the location was unveiled as he directed their driver away from the main entrance of the school. Directing instead along the road running parallel to the airstrip, to low-set barracks that lined the space and where light aircraft were stored. Robert did all the talking with their driver. The driver, fair-skinned and familiar, he thought, from what he could see of him in the rear-view mirror. Though this being his first time in South Africa, much of the place seemed familiar, even now when notions of Empire felt old-fashioned. There was much, for example, that spoke to Victoria and his parent's generation, feeding the feel of the place.

"*Île de France* has made the crossing without convoy on a number of occasions over the past few months," Robert explained, as if in answer to a question with the way he looked at him.

He spoke in a lowered voice, the loose-lips-sink-ships mantra clearly strongest learnt for him, captain of a prominent merchant liner, yet not large and important enough to secure constant military cover. And also *not* of the speed of the *Queens*, who could effortlessly outrun any other amphibious threat.

"As the Imperial Japanese started to push further into the Indian Ocean, local air force boys came to offer escort for critical approaches, which is how

I met Irvine."

The area was a mix and mismatch of arid and sand in parts, and lush vegetation and inviting seas in the same general areas. Among this setting, the airport was objective-driven for the transportation of mail to Cape Town. And the British air force wing was, even more so. Formless and functional, she was a war bride squatting in the flattened stretch on the city's outskirts. The airmen accommodations were dark and disarrayed and carried an ambience of come-and-go about them. The block of accommodations Robert led him to was like a motel on a middle America interstate highway; uncared for, though recently built, and suggestive as only being frequented for a brief encounter. Something that seemed to suit their arrangement well. *It's like a navvy camp*, he thought, as they approached one of the rooms.

Its curtains drawn, but door ajar, Robert led a path up and in. Inside was roomier than expected, with several bunks and a separate kitchen and seating area.

"Afternoon, Flying Officer Ward," Robert said on entry, awkward uncertainty plain.

"Afternoon, Captain," his airman replied, comfortably, formally, *Englishman*-ly. On one of the bunks.

Irvine was reading by desk lamp from a stack of British newspapers.

"Allow me to introduce Officer Turner," Robert said, discomfort-ability plain, still.

Irvine left his paper and took his hand firm. He wore his flight jacket despite the heat of the area, but beneath it had on only a singlet and cotton draws.

"A drink, gents," Irvine said. "Captain, you know where the good stuff is kept, fancy fixing us something?"

"How ur we faring?" He asked while Robert busied himself in the adjoining room.

"Have them on the ropes," he said, tapping the pile with curled fingers, "but on policy, I never believe everything I read. Good o' Churchy's V-day is still a while off yet, and many of our lads won't get to see it."

Irvine was public-schoolboy-handsome, with features that were unmistakably English breeding. Clean-cut, wholesome, righteous, but with a mischievous look to the eyes and a playful half-grin that seemed permanently in place. He was beautiful, he agreed. He was very young, too young to know his own mortality. But then again, by this stage in the war, most were. He was a good match for Robert, he thought.

"A' th' mair reason tae mak' th' maist o' whit we hae, ah suppose," he said, landing a hand on Robert's airman's shoulder.

"Right you are," he said, "and speaking of. Cap, how you getting on with those drinks?"

"Ready," Robert called.

In the adjoining room, Robert had served up spirits for them both in cut crystal glasses. In addition to its kitchenette, the accommodations had a small table stacked unusable with papers. Resourceful, amenable, Robert had brought his own. Naked on hands and knees and with his back as flat as a plank, one glass on a shoulder blade, the other on his opposing buttock.

"Efter ye," he said, pleased by his captain's initiative in breaking the ice.

Irvine's grin extended the rest of the length of his lips at the display.

"I've never been invited to drink at a captain's table before," he said, taking up a place on his knees at Robert's head; Olli was all too pleased with *his* seat, at the arse.

Irvine traced Robert's chin with care.

"It's good to see you, mate," he said, clinking his glass with Olli's, "and to meet you, too. To new mates."

They took a sip.

"It's a crakin' drap," he said, having heard other Scots say that, though not knowing his whiskey himself.

"We Scotsmen have good whiskey," he said, "though, I confess, I'm more Englishman in my blood by rearing, though the Scots are the grander sort. Me old man sent me these single malts, along with these glasses as a care package in my first month. Mark of a man, he had said in the note. And I only drink it when Robert comes by."

"How did ye twa meet?"

Conversation volleyed between Robert's airman and himself, Robert making his contributions non-verbally. Both made use of their Robert-table-ends, like he was an antique dresser carved of the finest, rarest wood, with a grain that was smooth and a feel that warmed to an appreciative touch. Robert was eager to make his presence felt, nudging and rubbing the crotches of the men that bookended him, warming them, too.

"Ah," Irvine said, "now that is something of a wartime adventure within itself, that–" finishing his glass and topping them both up from the bottle to the side of their breathing table, "–is probably best told through *illustration*."

Irvine left and returned with a marker in hand. His manhood bounced in motion of his movements beneath the cotton of his undershorts as he moved, as evidence of the attentions of Robert's face against it.

"May I?" He asked Robert, who in turn looked to Olli for assent.

As a military man himself, Irvine seemed to appreciate the poetry in their arrangement. He nodded, and Irvine proceeded to sketch out in thick marker the landmasses along the four sides of Robert's table as a start to their story. Having been well-trained in mapping by Robert, he recognised it immediately as the Indian Ocean. Sketched with surprising aptitude on the curvature of Robert's back, and oriented for his benefit, with the west coast of Australia at Robert's lower right arch, the east coast of Africa to his upper left.

"This was our theatre," Irvine said. "At the start of the war, I was flying with the boys around Italy and the Med', but as the Pacific started heating up and our navy lads were needed in the north, the importance of the Indian Ocean merchant lanes expanded, too. I was stationed in Perth in Oz," he said, positioning a cross on the line above Robert's right buttock, "and our focus was on providing air cover for the troop transports on this route to Egypt, *here*," adding a dotted line to the left, "and *this one* down from Singapore," marked with a firm line.

Robert wriggled in apparent agreement to being marked by his airman. Agreeable to be used, not just as a stimulating table, but as a canvas for the get-to-knowing of two men of importance to him as well. Irvine's cotton undershorts had a buttoned front, and with the nudging of Robert against it, he was starting to poke through. Without the need for words this time, Irvine looked down at Robert and then at he. As a gesture of approval, he removed and lay himself out on his captain's table, swelled and close to hard, nuzzled in the meeting of Robert's two cheeks, his knob extending like a volcanic island grouping into the ocean mapped on Robert's back. In a one-handed action, Irvine pulled the elastic of his shorts over and under his manhood and guided his rod into Robert's waiting mouth. The pace of Robert's airman's story picked up as Robert worked him, and soon he had joined him *in the fruits of* the captain's table. As Irvine explained, a transport escort would often receive his flight orders only at the last minute – allowing, that was, for several hours of flying time, which was sometimes needed to locate convoys travelling under radio silence. In this case, he had set out expecting to find *Aquitania* but spotted a stricken and on-fire light cruiser instead – HMAS *Sydney*.

"I recognised *Sydney* immediately," he said, pumping both into either end of their connecting companion. "She was a familiar sight in these waters, and I had had plenty of opportunities to distinguish her in the past, when she was in formation with large troop transports, such as the two *Queens* around Bass Strait at Oz's south-east, somewhere here," he explained, rubbing Robert's underbelly, in an off-the-map illustration that took the opportunity to also brush by his under-bush and growth. "When I reported what I had seen, I was ordered to return to base, which made no sense to me because I knew *Aquitania* was expected in these waters too, and with *Sydney* out of action, I wasn't about to leave all those boys without air support." He cradled Robert's chin as he said it, running his fingers down to his throat, which was fattened by the length of him.

He's trained him well, he thought.

Robert took him effortlessly, right down to the stem, and Irvine was the kind of airman who would strut proudly among a mass of men in military communal showers. Irvine, too, equally, seemed to admire how well Robert had been trained in the rear-ending department. He took a break from his story to focus on his stroke and to enjoy the sight of effortless swallowing of dual meats at opposing ends. There was an air of mateship about the arrangement and an intimacy that was as much a bonding as it was a working up to a deposit. This time he was the one who topped up their glasses. Though it was mid-afternoon, and the sun was still some hours off setting, the room was darkened enough to warrant the overhead light to illuminate for each other the sight of either-ended service. The curtains, yellowish from airmen smoke, did not quite meet at the middle, sending in a slice of outside sun across the plank of the captain's tabletop, with his inserted bedposts at either end. Cleanly done, like a skilled carpenter would a dovetail joint. Shadows cast across them on occasion as airmen returned to their accommodations. At one point, one shadow seemed to linger for a length that warranted him to turn to inspect, though the glare kept him from seeing whether it was an onlooker or simply a passing cloud.

"Not to worry," Irvine said, tension rising within him to break the casualness of his speech. "The boys of *this* room won't be back for another two days, at least. I always make sure, when the, *our*, captain makes the trouble to visit, that we will not be disturbed. I'm normally based near Cape Town just so you know, but transferred over for this visit. Us flyboys look out for each other. If ever you need anything, anything at all, you just tell my boys, those R.A.F. lads based up north 'specially, that I asked, and they'll help you. Most of those boys already owe me a favour or three."

He felt their table tightening as the first sign of Robert's neediness to receive; Irvine got back on track with his tale and told the rest of their military meet-cute with factual efficiency.

"Soon enough, I found the source of *Sydney*'s woes – what we now know was the German auxiliary cruiser *Kormoran*, masquerading, most unsportsmanlike, as a Dutch merchant ship. She had, presumably, been laying in wait for *Aquitania* but encountered *Sydney* instead. *I*–," a moan of closeness disrupting, "en*gaged* her. And she," another, "returned *fire*. She got me, and I had to parachute out. But I got her too. She went down. To the lads' credit, they picked me up in one of their life rafts, and I stayed with them until *Aquitania* came along and rescued us. Turns out," the bodies of them both bucking as Robert's entry points clamped in unison for a double-ended deposit finish, "our captain here," gripping his neck for an extra deep thrust, a move he met with a double slap of arse cheeks, "also put the lives of men over bullshit orders, and stopped to rescue us. We were both disciplined for it, and our sweet-mouthed captain here lost his ship. I've never forgotten it, though, and whenever I can, I provide escort for him into safe harbour, making sure he– *I'm coming!*"

"Me too," he said. "Hold it." Their faces clenched. "*Now!*"

And together they flooded into Robert, and he swallowed each ounce with appreciation until they were dry and their table was legless on the floor; they arrived both on top of him, their mouths, as new mates, touching, just briefly, sealing their friendship.

"Ye lost yer captainship o' *Aquitania* fur him," he said, hand on Robert's thigh, on their ride back to their hotel suite.

"I assessed the risk," Robert said, sounding again like the Chief Officer he had met in a corridor on his first voyage, "and decided that we were close enough to friendly shores for a rescue. And I would do it again."

"Whit happened tae *Sydney*?"

"We don't know. She was never seen again. Lost with more than 600 souls, almost certain. Irvine blames himself for not staying with her, thinks it was a fool's errand to go in search of her attacker. A hero's guilt."

He wanted to ask more: about the circumstances surrounding Robert's arrival back in port, about the loss of his captainship, about how he ended up on *France*. But, he could also see that the subject was robbing Robert, already, of his both-ended-feeding glow and so ceased with his questions.

"Say, Captain," he said, lighter in tone, "ow aboot a visit o' yer ship's progress. 'n' mibbie a night-stay. You're th' captain, efter a'."

It was the tonic of an idea he had hoped, with the redirection of the driver to Charl Malan Quay, timed just so, with the dawning of dusk and the lighting up of the city. But the attempt at affirmation of Robert's continued command turned to a nightmare as they approached the quay to find *France* being stripped. Her chandeliers, woven carpets, furniture; all evidence of her luxurious interiors, being ripped out and piled on the quayside. Whereas other troop transport conversions were done with care for the withins and with thought for postwar prosperity, she was getting *gutted* like a magnificent mammal on a whaling vessel, her miles of panelling torn out rather than bordered over. Robert went red and riled all over, to the point that he needed to hold him back from storming starboard side and putting a stop to it.

"Olli, let go," he said.

"Na, Robert. Something's wrong 'ere."

The manner of execution, the cloak-n-dagger of the nighttime conversion. All pointed to something sinister. Something that reminded him of the downfall of *Normandie* not long ago. He held him in his arms, ensuring they were out of sight, taking back his wish to puff up his partner's captain credentials. Unwilling to put him into harm's way, even if there was only the sliver of possibility that his conspiracies were plausible.

"I know what this is," Robert said, writhing, "it isn't a troopship refit. It's a prison ship gut. And I won't let them."

He hated to do it, but he pulled rank. Gripping his captain's arse cheek, his tips touching the doughy, filled softness of his entrance.

"I'm in command 'ere, Bell," he said. "And wur goin."

Robert shot him a look of initial hurt. Of seeing cruelness in he for turning his advantage in this way. He hated it and began slow rotations of the hole he loved to soften the order.

"Trust me, darlin'. Please."

"Yes, sir," he said.

And he kissed him deep.

"Guid laddie."

He had kept his captain from storming his own ship, purely based on an inkling that it was unsafe. But now that he had Robert's attention, fresh off the telling of tales of true bravery in the face of authenticated combat scenarios: he did not know what to do.

"Th' order tae vacate *France*, wis that unusual?" He inquired.

"Unheard of," Robert said, resentment still strong as they crouched inactive, out-of-sight, while his ship was stripped. "But I didn't challenge it because I was thinking of *you*. I was thinking of *us*."

He gave him a pass for the tone, which would normally have been met with disciplining – longer wait times for feeding, for example.

"'n' oor hotel, 'twas booked fur us?"

"Yes, by the Admiralty."

"Is that typical?"

"*No*," his tone softening, "but we *are* in uncertain times, Olli. The screw-up of the Americans with *Normandie* has probably refocused our crew on the handling of former French assets."

Robert's shoulders sank, a mix of helplessness with the destruction of his ship together with the reminder of his loss of *Aquitania*'s command, he guessed.

"Suddenly, *France* is no longer the lesser asset she once was," Robert said in apparent realisation.

This last part was an almost undertone, uttered as a murmur – like it was directed more to self-pity. An internal memo to the Robert Bell hall of disappointments of authority, drawn more from the minutes of their earlier meeting with his airman than it was a serious contender for their reasoned conversation. He ignored it.

There's no time for this, he thought, as the instinct of danger took on waters within him.

"Wur nae staying thare th' nicht."

Decided, he would power ahead with his command. Yet when the directive was spoken, it lacked the commonsense he had hoped for.

Why not? He asked himself.

But he could not answer. He was unsure. Almost positive, in fact, that he was *probably* overreacting, yet indecisive enough not to take a risk so soon after being reunited with Robert. He felt like he was failing on all fronts of command himself. Hurting his captain and uneasy within, so soon after assuming *meaningful* command. It was beyond the domain of a captain's arsehole. He changed tactics. Standing up, in partial view of the ship-stripping crew, he slipped a hand under the band of Robert's pants – to touch the wet cream of his well-broken-in arsehole.

"Shall we tak' Flying Officer Ward up oan his offer o' hospitality? Hae some guid food 'n' approach this situation wi' ye in command 'n' wi' fresh eyes 'n' full," inserting some fingers, "bellies, come mornin'?"

Robert mellowed to custard and returned to his trusting, grateful self.

"That sounds nice," he said.

And so he, hand in arse, ushered his submissive captain into a city-hauled cab and away from the quay before they could be seen. He had Robert sit on his hand at his side in the back of the cab for the journey, alternating finger combinations inside him like they were pacifiers of a teething infant. It was a tactic at trying to keep Robert calm, he told himself. Still, mostly, truthfully, such fiddling was to disguise his own discomfort at a feeling of impending danger, even as they left the city and headed for the now-darkened airfield for the second time that day.

He had the driver drop them at the airport, so they could walk the length to Robert's airmen's accommodation. A few of the accommodation blocks were lit up by this stage, including Irvine's, each section at a different level, like steps against a backdrop of dark and barren excess in the distance. As they approached, he noticed that Irvine's door was ajar.

He's left it open for us, he thought, relaxing, squeezing Robert's rump with relief that they had a place to hide away for the night – until he could settle the indecisions about how best to proceed.

Inside, the cut crystal glasses were on the floor together with the turned over, drop-less bottle of Talisker to the side – the rectangle of where Robert had set up table still pinpointable by the diagonal glass positions. The adjoining bunks-room was in darkness, but still, once his eyes adjusted, he could make out, only just, an outline. Unmoving.

"Wait ootdoors," he said, fear flooding in.

He closed the door and Robert outside it.

"Irvine?" He called to the unmoving figure.

No answer.

"It's Oliver, urr ye sleeping?"

Chillingly, *sleeping*, he knew as soon as he said it, was innocuous, a euphemism, a misnomer. Confirmed; when he felt his way to the figure on one of the bunks to touch his stone-cold leg. But he still could not *see.* Feeling by the bunk, he found a switch. Even with the flood of light, it took time to take in what was before him: the horror of *him* laying there. It was Irvine, that was certain, the figure, he was naked, and his member was impressive and fresh enough in his memory for him to make an immediate identification. Its limpness made him sad, however, in the initial confusion of recognition. But still, in that low light, under the canopy of another bunk above, his face was obscured. Even so, even in the barest outline of shadow, he could see, poor Robert's airman had died horridly. Morbid, horrible, needing-to-know fascination drew him in...and in, under the canopy to the dark, to see. At first, he thought he had a hammer in there with him, resting against his face. That he had been beaten to bed with it would have been preferable to the trauma he had, in fact, endured.

Throatfucked with a knife, he thought in terror.

Like the much smaller, under-gunned merchant cruiser that deceived a purpose-built fighter with false flags, Irvine's horror corpse lured him in. His death; so grotesque that it was only when up-close and too late to erase the visceral-age, the vice-ful-age, vengeful dying did he realise what it meant. That Irvine's attacker had replicated their sex act but in reverse. As Robert had taken Irvine's penis, the pube-length of his throat, so profoundly that his girth had impressed itself and inflated the ripples of his neck. Now, Irvine had the same...except the protrusion was sharp-edged, cutting a channel inside and causing death. Without the appropriate training of a carnival sword swallower, the virgin intrusion had taken his life. It had caused the most unpleasant of performances for those who would later witness it.

The shadow across the gap, he reeled back in realisation, *was watching.*

And just as his thoughts turned to Robert alone outside, and understanding that *this* was, in fact, the further front from a safe harbour...the shadow returned, across the light from the frame, blackening the room, as a piercing scream blocked out all hope.

VIII

PRESIDENT COOLIDGE

Olli,

I am sorry that I couldn't keep my promise to you, to write every day.

I got hurt

It was a tank accident.

I should feel lucky, I suppose. But it's hard for me to stay upbeat right now.

I'm in the military hospital in New York.

I know this is a lot to ask, but, will you visit me?

I really want to see you.

Alice will come, of course.

Yours, Harris.

He folded the last letter from the Harris pile he had picked up in Port Elizabeth, over and over in his hands on the ride to the hospital. He had not slept, not properly, in weeks. Robert was at their hotel. He made him stay to rest. In fleeing Port Elizabeth they had headed by bus to Cape Town, then boarded *his Queen* while she picked up more G.I.s en route to Suez and then back to New York. They had fled without possessions, with only the money from Irvine's room. Though he would never say as much, Robert hated him for having taken it, but he was more pragmatic about the necessity of having at least a coach fare for them both. And he promised his captain that he would, somehow, find a way to avenge his airman. *Elizabeth*, as magnificent as she was, laboured through the humid conditions around the south of Africa. Through heat and with passenger capacities that she was never designed to weather. There was a feeling of fatigue within her and among the men she carried. Even though they were arriving fresh to war fronts. The war, especially through the Pacific, was felt more heavily among the mostly Americans that now crammed her hull. And as much as the men tried themselves to keep morale high, the cramped conditions were not conducive to upbeat outlooks, and, as much as losses were attempted to be kept separate from the men, news, as is its nature, often reached them.

One such loss event that was a keen topic of discussion during he and Robert's stowaway stay concerned the loss of *Empress of Canada*. She faulted along a route similar to what they were travelling, only weeks before. *Canada* was sunk at midnight by an Italian sub. She was mainly carrying refugees. The irony is that the majority of those taken to a watery grave were, in fact, Italians. It highlighted for the men the indiscriminate pointlessness of the conflict, calling into question exactly what it was they were dying for. Robert absorbed this melancholy of men off to a meaningless war the most. He stayed in Olli's old service rooms, not venturing out, even during the day when these spaces clambered unbearably with the inner workings of the *Queen*. In fact, that was when he slept, claiming that only such commotion could clear his head enough for sleep to claim him.

City Hospital on Roosevelt Island was an imposing proposition, with functional lines and a central tower stretched with two wings without ornamentation. Having a history that included serving as a penitentiary up and into the previous decade, as soon as Olli was let off outside, only one object held him: to help Harris out of this place and back to someplace more homely. Inside was busy, bustling. Courtesy of the challenges the Americans were facing in the Pacific, the U.S. Philippines, particularly. Harris had marked him down as family, and the maindesk clerk directed him up to his ward in a private room at the far end of the main corridor of the west wing. Men in this section of the hospital were in recovery. Yet many of them, it was clear, were still suffering. Some, it seemed, had been wheeled there not because all they needed now was rest, but because there was nothing more the doctors could do for them – as new waves of the wounded came their way. One man, burnt all over, shielded his face as he approached; in shame, it seemed. The scarred man sat stranded in his wheeled chair at the end of the corridor. He was near the number matching the room Olli was looking for and an orderly in conversation with a woman outside it.

"I cannot let you in to see him ma'am, you're not on the list. I'm sorry."

"Oliver," she said, breaking from conversation with the orderly. "I understand," she said back to him, kindly, as he returned to his station watching guard of the rooms of this section. "Oliver Turner?"

He recognised her from the photograph he had seen. Probably when Harris had passed it among his West Point mates on the deck of *Elizabeth*. He recognised her. Certainly, undoubtedly. She was the woman of the photograph, yet she was different from what he had expected in the flesh. Older.

This war will do that to you, he thought.

"Alice," he said, shaking her hand.

"I have heard so much about you, Oliver. Harris will be so happy to see you."

"How is he?"

"I don't know; he won't see me. He's asking for *you*."

Did he go red? He was not sure – whether he cared, either.

"I'm sure he doesn't mea–"

"It's fine. Just," taking his hand, "I would really like to see him, Oliver."

She looked at him, searchingly, probingly.

How much does she know? He wondered. *How much has he* told *her?*

"O' coorse," he said, then entered – after identifying himself with the orderly.

"They've given me my own room," Harris said, facing the window and without turning.

"Hullo, Harris."

"I knew you would come," he said, still with back turned. "That's probably up there among the most pompous thoughts I've ever had. And it's probably no place of mine to expect it from you. Or to enjoy having any kind of pull over you, but there it is – I've been expecting you."

He did not mind. It was the truth.

"I'm sorry it's taken me sae long," he said, slowly closing the gap between them, "I've hud tae come a– lang way– tae git 'ere."

"Stop," Harris said.

He froze, still half a room from his beautiful, full back.

"How come," he asked, a slice of flirtation in his tone.

Harris hunched over a little.

"Because," he said, turning the wheelchair to face Olli, "I'm not sure if I want to see you after all."

His face dropped when he heard it. Like Harris had slapped him, drawn him there just to hurt him.

"See," Harris said, "the way you look at me."

It took him a few moments to piece together his meaning. Harris was paler, sure. Thinner, understandably. Bruised and bandaged. But he was also more beguiling than his memory, as a coping mechanism, had allowed him to be formed in his mind. Then he saw it, the reason for the chair, for the distance. Harris had a bandage on his left forearm, but that was superficial, a graze, hardly worthy of segregation in a private room of a military hospital wing, away from the only superficially wounded. The *real* bandage works were below the knees. Midway down towards where his feet should be.

"I lost my feet," he said. "I was in the tank division, and the blasted thing came down clear on top of them. While all my mates were killed."

He smiled. Wholly inappropriately, but as an impulse in response to Harris's downturn not being him-related.

Who was selfish now, he thought.

At first, Harris emoted something he had not seen before. A look of having taken offence that segued to confusion and then irritation at Olli's lack of disgust or in any way being put off by the sight of him.

"I've missed ye, terribly," Olli said, continuing on a path to close the floor span between them. "I'm glad you're hame."

"This changes things, Olli," he said, looking to the folded-down pedals of the wheelchair, where his feet should have rested.

"Nae fur me, it doesn't."

"Well, it does for me."

He reached him. Could smell him again. It was more than he ever had hoped possible. Leaning down, he kissed him gently on his lips.

"A loue ye," he said.

Harris did not respond, rolling himself past him and to the side of the bed.

"Urr ye in pain?"

"Yes. You should go," Harris said. "I'm sorry, Olli. You can come back later if you want. But now I need the orderly."

He looked to the door.

"Ye don't need him," he said, sweetly, "you hae me."

Harris stared him down as if in threat of holding him to the offer.

But he stood firm, staring back, smiling still.

"Fine," he said, grabbing the blanket folded over his lap and tossing it onto the bed. "Want to see the reason I wanted you to leave, Olli? Want to see how fucked up my life is? Fine, pass me that bedpan because I need to piss, and I can't even manage that on my own anymore."

He took in each syllable of Harris's agitation like it was fine verse, like the *threat* of an invite to help was, in fact, a most longed-for proposal from his handsome suitor. He got on all fours. From this position, he could see clear through the wide spread of his captain's seating. His bare knees, as was the custom for men of his masculine stature, were parted as far as his mobile seat would allow, the lower portions of his thighs pressed to the wood of the chair arms. But still, at this absolute distance, from his seat-levelled view, he could see that Harris's manhood was of such a mass that it still touched and rose up the sides of its crotch enclosure. In the minds of men-who-court-the-company-of-men, memory of another's manly parts is often inflated by recollection of the heat of the encounter. Yet, in Harris's case, even lustful, sublime recollection falls short. He smiled at the mass of Harris-meat before him. It was the second reunion, and that these parts of Harris had survived the war unscathed, to emerge fuller and more fragrant – more so as he crawled closer – than before flushed his cheeks with an indefatigable rush of need.

"Sex couldn't be further from my mind, Oliver. What *is it* with you and sex?"

Yet he persisted, crawled closer.

"If you want to *help* me, get me the bedpan, so I can relieve myself, otherwise leave and fetch the orderly."

He arrived, on knees and palms, shoulders touching the insides of Harris's remaining stretch of limbs. Face-to-head with Harris's member, which peaked out of the seam of his hospital gown to rest at the chair edge.

"Ye don't *need* th' bedpan," he whispered to Harris's member head, kissing its salty tip, "ye *hae* me noo."

He brought tongue- and dick-tip to touch, inciting Harris to begin his release. Lowering his head to angle below the line of the chair in easy projection of Harris's hose.

"Ye hae me," he said to his member once more. "Ready whin yer, captain," to his face this time.

"Stop this," Harris said, embarrassed, uncertain, but softer.

"Let me hulp ye," he said, another teasing-tongue-touch-to-the-tip. "Relieve yersel'."

He kept fixed on Harris, their eye-line unbroken – a pact of commitment to the task, of sorts. Harris stared him down a while. Minutes passed. But he did not let up, did not *give* up the offer to assist. To *help* him in a fashion that was more personal, more embodied, more loving than an orderly or porcelain piss pan could. He would not even allow himself a blink, letting his eyes dry as a tiny mark of solidarity to his cause. After a time, minutes close to ten, surely, Harris accepted the offering.

"OK, Olli," he said, gliding the tops of a softly clutched hand across his crimson cheek, "if you insist."

And then the flow began.

Golden and warm and bitter salt into his mouth, with the force and head of a hot-day lager. There were instincts at play with the receipt of experiences as new as this, and Olli, eyes on his captain, felt uncertainty himself as his mouth, as wide and hollow as he could make it, started to fill to the rim. Instinct told him to stop. To drop away, to exhume. But stronger than these instincts was his will to not let Harris go, to not let him out of sight, to perform even the basest of functions in a manner that would show him that he cared. And so, pushing against these instincts, as the foam of Harris's hydration reached the brim of his mouth, he swallowed. In one long, deep gulp, he took Harris into him. Years of cock servicing had taught him the talent of circular breathing – used to such musical effect by the indigenous Australians – and he drew on every ouch of this talent this time to reboot his breathing – the need for air, of which, had become critical by the second gulp. But he remained determined.

Don't waste a drop.

It was all that he could think.

Of course, he should have expected such a cascade of a stream from Harris. He was a man's man, the image of the masculine ideal. The man of myth, the demi-god that fearful mortals would offer as sacrifice to forces they did not understand. But only if they could catch him first. Liquid gold, the essence of Harris, it filled him in a larger sense than the *other* form of release and as a more routine kind of offloading. It was the everyday conveniences that Harris now found himself struggling with, but Olli felt gratitude in taking into him. The stream went on, and he continued his commitment to not spilling a drop. Moreso, to sail toward savouring it, as adjustment took shape. The need to adapt to the new scenario of manly servitude had shown itself in usual ways. Puffy eyes, tear ducts activated. It transported him to the Clydebank slipway and his first encounters there, on his knees, barnacles breaking skin, cold slime of seaweed adding a sting as he attempted to take a riveter for his full length for the first throes. Pushing against the tight recess of his throat made it a struggle, then. But he tamed that; in time. Older and better-versed now, he gave himself only the time of this first few mouth-fills experience to evolve. Though a few droplets of tears escaped, he maintained servitude eye contact and a commitment to measured drinking and intake of breath for the duration of his service, without a loss of any of Harris.

However, Harris, as was the case in all instances, was best of credit. His initial, stubborn, almost vengeful releasing into Olli subsided with each passing swallow. He caressed Olli's swollen, piss-downing cheeks and then, eventually, allowed himself to *enjoy* the release. Reclining his head and breaking the stare-down himself, *letting* Olli serve him. And perhaps a full minute later – as a highlight of the *need* for release that his Harris must have felt – the proud, golden, salty stream started to slow from a torrent to a stream and then to a trickle. But he would not rest on his responsibilities. In fact, he heightened his efforts, closing his lips over the expanse of Harris's hand, impressive enough to fill him itself. And returned to teasing with his tongue, inviting a release of the final droplets that would allow him to be fully comfortable again. And when he thought that Harris's hose was entirely extinguished, and therefore, that his standing-in for orderly and bedpan had been carried out. He reminded himself of his oath to *help* and thus that he was serving a function for the man he loved – even if this function had opened him up to a new, more *belly-filling* realm of pleasure. He forced himself to stop, the near-impossible-*to-stop*, circular tongue tasting of Harris's tip. To instead tuck his captain's member away and respect his not-feeling-sex mood; until, by a firm hand on the cusp of his neck, he received confirmation that, through service, the desire for sex had arrived. Harris had accepted against his own stubbornness that Olli had been serious in his statement of love; a solitary tear had escaped Harris's duct, too, as he reclined his head and settled in, in trust, to the provision of Olli to his needs.

"I love you, too," he said, his manhood now full, the salty tinge of pre-seed touching Olli's tongue already. "More than *anyone*."

Olli, already fuller with Harris than he had ever before been, this time let his hero lead the way, helping only to bring his gown up and over his head so they could be skin-on-skin. Like he had with Robert onto the captain's wheel, Harris guided his Olli back on to *his* wheel. Harris delivered direction, having confidence back in himself. Instructing him in how to navigate the severed parts of himself to still make love, without pain. And in fact, due to the acrobatics needed to straddle a wheel-chaired war hero without touch or strain to his lower tender limbs, this resulted in deeper penetration of Olli's inners, a right reaching up into him. And, because he had refused any such adventure since they parted. He felt pain, too. And this made him happy. As if Harris had passed his pain onto him, to follow it with a soothing balm of his own making.

"Mair than anythin'," he echoed, as Harris finished in him, his legs draped either side of the chair-arms, his arse angled at the most profound possible inclination, his lower body in a bat-skeletal configuration. "I'm ne'er letting ye go again."

He redressed his first captain and cleaned him, too, with a cloth and hot water. Harris let him, their lips touching after completion of each section of him.

"Will you stay with me, Olli?"

"Aye," he said as he dressed his own self, lingering a moment with a touch of his cream-filled opening as he pulled on his briefs. "Aye, always."

Harris smiled. He wondered how long it was since he last had.

"I love Alice," he said, still smiling but with a calm seriousness, "but not in the same way that I love you. I love you *more*, Olli. But I've made a commitment to Alice, and I need to tell her the truth. It's time I let her in."

Harris's eyes searched him in a way that said: *Will you still stay?*

"Aye, ah understand," he said, kissing the recess along his neck, just under his chin. "Ah wull be back tae see ye this efternoon."

Outside, Alice was waiting.

"Will he see me, Oliver?" She asked.

Her respect for the significance of him in Harris's world impressed. Though, he was still nervous about the prospect of Harris disclosing their particulars.

There are laws against it, after all, he thought.

But still, he nodded. Ushering the orderly to attend.

"He was quite clear that he did not want anyone allowed in, other than you, Mr Turner."

"Aye, ah know," he said. "Bit he haes hud a chaynge o' hert."

He turned to the door to reenter and get more explicit permission, but Alice put a hand to his arm and stopped him.

"Oliver, it is quite alright," she said. "This young man is only doing his job and can accompany me in."

The orderly nodded in agreement of the terms of entry.

"Aye," he said. "Ah wull be back to-nicht. 'twas a pleasure meetin ye at lest, Alice."

"And you, Oliver," she said. "And *thank you*, I could not have done this without you, truly," pausing with her hand on his arm, "know that. You have meant so much to my husband–"

Future husband–

"–that I want you to know that it did not go unnoticed."

She leaned in and kissed him on the cheek. What to make of it, he did not know. Her lips were scarlet and sharp, purposeful, he thought.

"Thare is hee haw ah wid nae dae fur him, he's mah *best friend*," Olli said, in their code.

"I *know*," she said, in a way that confirmed for him that she, in fact, did.

And Alice entered Harris's room, the orderly in tow.

Something does not fit, he could not help but think on the ride home to Robert and their hotel room. *Certain things were wrong.*

Photo.

Husband.

I know.

And it hit him with all the force of a surprise torpedo.

He pulled Harris's final letter from his pocket and scrutinised it further. The censor strikes. They were consistent in all places except one, the final line:

> Alice will come, of course.

He held the folded paper with the scribe of the last line up to the light of the vehicle window. Yet already knew, before the truth led the way, what the deception had been.

> Alice will come, of course. ~~But I won't tell her, I won't ask her, until I've seen you.~~

It was not that *photo.*

Not the one passed among West Point recruits on the promenade decks of *Elizabeth*, but instead, belonged to a different, stuffier, more subterranean time. Not Harris, but his first love. Not a fiancee, but a wife.

Robert, he thought in anxious realisation, as the fade of sun against the haphazard scribblings of an unofficial hand revealed the final line.

Slowly, painfully, stupidly for his duty to protect the ones he loved:

> But I won't tell her,
> I won't ask her,
> until I've seen you.

Panic swept through him like a tropical fever. And was followed by further waves of decisions needed-to-be-made. If *she* was here, *who* was at greatest peril, and, more pertinently, who would he *deem* worth saving first?

"Driver!" He shouted, "turn around, take me back."

Maybe it should have troubled him that it was not a harder-to decision. That there was no hesitation in putting the welfare of his broken Harris over that of his at-rest Robert. But there it was, he had decided. The adrenaline made it feel both that it took an aeon to reach his collection point on a return journey but also exactly too quick of a passage when he did arrive, not feeling that he had the know-how to remedy his mistake. He raced back through the corridors of the hospital, the way he had come. As he approached Harris's end, his heart sank when he saw that there was no one outside, not Robert's wife, not the orderly, not even the other patients.

"Harris," he called as he walked into his captain's room.

A curtain was drawn in front of Harris's bed at the far end of the room. In the light of the window, he could see a shape on the other side, on the bed.

"Harris, it's Olli, ur ye sleeping?"

When no response came, and the silhouette behind the curtain remained unmoving, panic inside started to overwhelm, as if the whole horrid chain of events had been a hallucinogenic drug he had ingested and against which his body now reeled. As if he could sense that a loss of consciousness was coming, Olli ran to the bedside in large strides, gripped the curtain and pulled it away. There was something of the uncovering of a corpse about the exercise. And even as he moved at speed, the rational part of himself was preparing for an investigation-style identification of Harris's body. But nil could have prepared him for what actually lay in wait for him behind the war hospital gauze.

It's not him.

Like the inhalation of particularly pungent smelling salts after a dizzy spell, the discovery behind the curtain revived him wholly; relief mixed in with a revulsion laced with – it disgusted him to feel it, but there it was – rogue arousal. Like a new-to-the-beat Victorian detective may have experienced in the first throes of the Whitechapel murders. It was unconscionable, a glimpse into the shared grotesque of the human sexual appetite that, on encountering a prostitute, split open and displayed, a man might feel, deep down, a perverse fascination, even liking, for the sight of genitals, also brutally brought forth. This was no doubt part of the commentary the villain was making about Oliver and his *kind* via the grisly display. The orderly, a handsome young man himself, once, now hogtied on the bed, face down with, again, an F–S fighting knife thrust up a receptacle, this time his behind. The orderly, as with Irvine before him, had taken the full seven inches of the double-edged blade. Right to the handle. There was a look of irreconcilable calm on the orderly's face, who, in death, took the object with ease.

Robert's peril could not be clearer. He felt the need to return to him as intensely as a deep-sea fisherman on the edge of a tropical storm – knowing now, seconds counted. Yet as he had in the cab, Harris held him there. He had made him a promise, and he had meant it. As the shock of the orderly's discovery subdued, the pieces of the motive behind Irvine's death started to show themselves. As he eyed up the rimmed edge of the handle that poked out of the orderly's accommodating orifice. It was the same *type* of knife, standard issue in the British and US raiding forces. There was no clue there. What was revealing was where on the bodies these particular raids had taken place. And also Robert, as the link between them.

Robert is the clue.

His thought process unfolded as follows:

In the afternoon light in the cramped quarters of an airman's accommodations *Robert* had come to know intimately, Robert had taken his airman's shaft *orally*, airman on his knees, and he *anally.* All this played out while a shadow watched through a parting in the drapes of the airman's room. Irvine, the recipient of oral service, was later killed by a military dagger down the throat, getting penetrated like Robert had been before – this resulted in another link: the orderly. The unneeded help, who received a deadly thrust in the manner that Robert had received Olli with as regularly as a nurse-man's rounds, up his posterior. But why this orderly and not he? And where did Harris factor in? The orderly was markedly bent; he had thought so on first meeting. *Male nursing* was often a profession to attract men of a certain nature.

Was that it? Deaths fuelled by a hatred of bendy men?

As he pondered the ill-fitting pieces of the mystery, a fleck of white caught his eye. It was only just visible, at the base of the handle that disappeared between the cheeks of the deceased.

Paper.

Wrapping each hand with left-over bandages from the table beside the bed, like a boxer ahead of a match, he peeled apart the orderly's buttocks to take a deeper look. Through the bandages, he could feel that the body was still warm, and at the point where the handle turned to blade, there found a letter skewered. The thrust was neatly done, with only minor slits to the young hole and a single trail of blood from entrance to scrotum, suggesting that the orderly had objected, seemingly impossibly mildly, to the object's insertion. *Drugged, perhaps.* He teased the edges of the paper with his fingers that poked from his bandaged hands. But to no avail.

I'll have to pull it out; I'll have to unfuck him.

The removal caused lightheadedness. The manner in which the skin caught and stretched against the retreating blade, the way it *grew* out of him like seedling from soil. And when out, root and all, the way the wound stayed. Lifeless, the arse not springing back with the resilience that he was used to witnessing. And the sight of failed muscles and torn interiors. It was selfish relief to push the knife back in after retrieval of the papers, enabling a part of him – shrinking the longer he stayed with the corpse – to focus on the calm of the orderly's repose. He turned, too, to the clean-ness of the re-intrusion – cheeks and overhang of the handle covering over the point of piercing –, like the white sheet returned over the body on the slab once the identification procedure was complete.

Oliver,

It was a pleasure meeting you, and I hope that you have enjoyed our game as much as I have. So far. It is far from over. Here, in the entry point of this young man – a part of men that you are so familiar – you will find options. Articles for two different vessels. But it is not as simple as choosing between two ships. You must choose between men, too.

You have been greedy, Oliver. Not only have you pursued a man who was spoken for, but you were not content with just him. But we can't all win, Oliver. And you can't keep them both to yourself.

I have arranged for Harris to be transported to San Francisco: to board the SS *President Coolidge*, a U.S. vessel. There is a car out front: if you choose to join him, this will take you.

But beware: if you go for Harris, Robert's safety can no longer be assured. He has had my protection for too long and is now your responsibility. And so, if you decide to take on this responsibility further, there are articles for you both for another ship, his own SS *Île de France*, now in New York, where you and Robert can live out your life together.

Next move, well, it's yours, but I would not delay if I were you.

The pieces in this game are changing all the time.

He stood there in snuffed unknowingness, reading soiled papers a second time and watching the bound bundle of orderly on the bed in the hazy background, with a handle out of his behind like he was a magnetic mine, dagger drawn into him, bound to cause damage to his hull. Time was ticking. Each second he stayed was a second closer to discovery with the body. And certain arrest. As it was, there were witnesses to place him there: the clerk at reception who had directed him to the room, the burnt patient who had watched him enter. He had to leave, but he was frozen by indecision, clutching the articles, already defeated.

Whichever ship I choose, I lose one of them.

"No," he said, to the room where Harris had been little over an hour before. "*I* choose the ship."

He waited with Robert for Harris on an island in the South Pacific. Well, more pointedly, he waited for the ship that he hoped carried Harris to him: SS *President Coolidge.* She was due in that hour into Espiritu Santo in the New Hebrides. It had taken almost two weeks for them to get there. Since he had left Harris's hospital room, at that time an orderly's tomb, and exited the building by a back way, hailing a New York cab well away from sight of the hospital, to return to Robert. Through the pooling of skills and contacts, and stowaway competencies of them both, plus considerable call on the trust and compassion of Robert to aid him in the long-shot journey to return to a new lover he had known nothing about, they found themselves awaiting the ship's docking.

Stood on the largest island in the archipelago, Robert, an expert chartsman, had chosen their watching location carefully. It offered clear sightlines out of the main channel – the Scorff Passage – as well as the path that *Coolidge* would travel in on. She was approaching from the south on the inward side of Tutuba Island, a long land-limb that curved over the Santo harbour, offering shelter but obscuring their view out to sea and preventing sightlines of much of the ship's inward bearing. As the mid-point of the 1940s drew near, the Pacific had become for the Yanks a major theatre of war. Espiritu Santo in the New Hebrides – of joint British–French management – had established itself as a launchpad for the Americans. And the need to protect it had never been greater, the island chain sitting, as it did at that time, on the precipice of Japanese occupation to the north. Resultant of this proximity was the stalking of these waters by Japanese subs. These had led the Allies to implement a range of defensive measures to protect their Pacific fleet and their militarised harbour units.

"That's the most logical entry point into the harbour," Robert said, from behind his binoculars from their viewing position at Million Dollar Point, his arm out to sea along a line of the Scorff Passage. "And so we have these minefields set up," tracing rows in the water in front of them. "Our ship will approach from the south, along a path that will bring her *between* the minefields. But we won't see her until she enters because her orders are to only commence her entry course from a point *out there*," and he directed to the island dead ahead, but really, to a position behind it. "The patrols will guide her in," and he handed the binoculars to him and pointed out one such patrol that waited at the mouth of the southward passage, where *Coolidge* was scheduled to soon appear.

Through the binoculars, at two circles on the path ahead, he watched. The patrol disappearing from view.

"That's standard procedure," Robert said, "could be approaching the *President* now for the journey in."

Anxiety rose as he watched the two circles, wishing for a ship to enter them. But also, not wishing it, because once she did arrive, he would then be faced with whether Harris was *actually* aboard, and if aboard, whether he was alive. It seemed like a slight hope. Why, after all, would his aggressor tell the truth. What incentive did she have to offer an adversary a fighting chance? Was it all an elaborate misdirection, or worse, a trap? A means of luring Robert out into the open? These questions made him feel especially exposed and further guilty for having asked this adventure of Robert. He rested a hand in the space in the small of Robert's back, about to say thank you when–

"No," Robert said, with shock that struck him like a collision, "what's she *doing*?"

Still watching through magnified circles, he swung to the other access point to the harbour to find, to his horror, a ship steaming at speed into the channel. She filled both of his circles, and behind her came the flashing lights of a patrol ship. Sending a frantic warning that, even he knew, would be too late to heed, even if it were seen. It was a worst-case-scenario situation, like being atop an iceberg in the Atlantic, seeing a magnificent liner in full lights coming for an immovable object. Watching and screaming for it to be seen in time, yet knowing that it would not; that these cries went up into the frigid night never to find the ears they needed to.

The mines were indiscriminate, claimed her with two blasts in close succession: one near her engines, the other her stern. Stricken, she swung toward them. At this distance, he stood as witness to her captain's steering of her stride – the turn from triumph-at-safe-harbour to the terror of recognition that she would falter.

"He's beaching her," Robert shouted, "come on."

Like a whale casting itself ashore in a desperate, primal instinct, the grind of iron upon reef rung through the cove as *Coolidge* attempted, with what propulsion remained in her, to leave the depths and mount onto land. He and Robert ran to meet her as she shuddered from the water and skidded across sandbank and reef, with an almighty cry of the shredding of her iron underbelly – a final death cry.

Evacuation of her started promptly, with soldiers headed for shore passing Robert and he before reaching her base. It was an orderly, unpanicked affair. He even overheard some soldiers saying that savage teams would collect their belongings once all were accounted for. But this calm did little to dampen the vibration of dread inside him.

What had happened? Why had she gone against her safe entry orders? And what about Harris? How would he get off? If he was even on board.

By the time they reached her position on the reef, some thirty minutes had passed since the blasts. She was upright but listing to port. There was no sight of Harris, or indeed any wounded soldiers. Up close, she looked even more like a slain whale, with ropes about her hull, along which soldiers were descending, some with souvenir components of the ship, like ancient whalers striping a carcass.

"Where's th' infirmary?" He asked one man as he left one of the ropes and waded through the shallows.

"Just fore of midship," he said, continuing away from the wreck.

"What's th' best wey o' getting thare," he said, following him, "please," taking his arm.

"See that hatch," he said, pointing to an opening along the side of the ship.

"Aye."

"That will take you to C deck and the first-class vestibule, head fore from there, past the dining salon, and you'll find signs to it."

"Ta."

"But you shouldn't go, fella," he called after him, diverting his point to the coral on which the beached liner was resting, "she's slipping. It's not safe."

He ignored him and headed for the rope that led to the hull door at the base of the barnacle-covered *Coolidge*. It dawned on him that he might not have the strength to scale the way inside.

"Stay 'ere," he said to Robert, "and keep weel clear."

"Not a chance," Robert said, his hands at Olli's waist, "here, I'll give you a boost. Getting over the curve of her hull will be the most difficult part."

And he was not wrong. Given her list, the first leg of the climb was an overhanging challenge in the slipperiest of barnacle-bellied conditions.

"Fine, gimme a boost. Bit then ye lea me."

"How are you going to get him out by yourself, Olli?" He said it sternly. "You need me," cupping his hands, "here, put your foot in."

It was a slimy struggle, and with each failed attempt, he felt himself getting more flustered and his upper body more depleted. But eventually, he made it up and over onto the side of the stricken liner. This part was much more accessible. A relief, he could almost walk it. But, then, the reason why dawned on him – her list was becoming much worse, and in quickening intervals –, it urged him on and into her hull. To his surprise, Robert had managed to wrangle the assistance of a fleeing soldier and was now almost over the first hurdle of her hull himself.

"Go ahead," Robert shouted up to him, "I don't know how long she'll hold."

Being inside her, navigating her slanted corridors, edged him back to *Normandie*. On his last visit to New York, the sight of the grandest French liner still keeled over and frozen in the Hudson, it had stuck with him with as much intensity as the sight of Irvine and that orderly in stillest sleep. He followed the signs to the infirmary and found, to his dismay, that these rooms numbered more than one. Of course, he should have known this from his own experiences, but it made the search, now, much more difficult. On his way, he came across another man, also searching. They conversed only briefly, enough for him to know which rooms had been searched. He noted that there was one room toward the far end that appeared to be locked. He knew it, *felt* it: this was where Harris was. And like he had at the hospital those several weeks ago, he headed for it, deeper into the hull as she continued on her sand-ward list.

"Harris," he called as he pounded the door. "Harris, it's Olli, are you–"

And the door opened onto an infirmary chamber smaller by far than Harris's hospital room, but still into Harris's room, for sure.

He's alive.

On the far side of the room, in that same wheelchair that he had been when they parted, he sat. Thinner and paler and more defeated-looking than when he had left him, but alive. Against the wall, wedged in the corner in line with the ship's incline.

"You should not have come, Olli," Harris said as he raced in, and the door crept closed behind him, like by the hand of a ghost.

"Hullo, Oliver," came a man's voice from behind him.

A familiar voice.

He spun and found, standing there, a crucial, fitting piece of the mystery. A man, burnt terribly, the one from the hospital who had shielded his face. But the voice was unchanged, that same pompous, London-proper accent.

"Hullo, Edward," he said. "Ah thought ye wur deid."

"Damn nearly was, my boy. Damn nearly, when you let me fall into that inferno and leapt to save yourself."

Edward stood guard of the door, that same standard-issue knife in hand that had killed Irvine and Harris's orderly after. He ran the dagger across the scars of his face. The point in and out of the heat craters that had settled there.

"But here I am. And there you are, as youthful and *pretty* as ever."

His burns were substantial and had rendered him free from instant recognition. But it was his eyes that were most changed. One was blood-flooded and lidless and surely without sight. The other was changed, too, darker, madder than memory.

"You certainly have good taste in men," Edward said smiling, pointing the knife to Harris. "Even broken, he is quite the specimen."

"Lea him oot o' this," he said, moving for him.

"Ah ah," Edward said, pointing the knife toward him.

"Whit dae ye hae against me?"

"Everything," he said, smile gone. "You took everything from me, Oliver; the least I can do is take something from you in return."

"You're crazy, mate," he said as the *President* slipped beneath them.

"Maybe, but you could at least thank me."

"*Thank* you? Fur killing Irvine 'n' then comin' efter Harris, tae?"

"Yes, for *not* killing him. Or you, for that matter. I went against *her* on that one for you, Oliver. Thought this *test* might be a bit more fun."

"Ah don't understand, Edward. Whit ony o' this means. Ah hae na idea whit's gaun oan, ah ainlie met ye, 'n' Robert fur that maiter, by chance."

"Aha!" He said, lunging forward, then pacing back. "Now, you can't be stupid enough to believe that, surely?"

"Believe whit?" He asked, hope fading in him at the chance of continuing on a path of rational conversation.

"Why in chance, of course. We're at war, my dear boy. The most global and cunning of wars the world has ever known – and you, my fresh-faced, sex-opportunistic friend, have been at the centre of it from the start."

"Whit start?"

"Since Gourock, when you 'smuggled' yourself on board. I knew, of course, right from your climb up that ladder. Chief Stewards, we are senior members of the crew, technically, though we never get the respect of our other line managers. But if there is one thing we know, it is the comings and goings. I knew as soon as you arrived, and I followed you. How quickly you wormed your way into Robert's bed, and how quick Robert was, too, to take you in. Unsurprising, of course, given the role of your father in all this."

"Mah faither?"

Renewed interest and a scary suggestion that there might be something more than madness to this story swept through him; as the *President* slid and listed further still, and, in one daring move, the tables turned.

"Yes, he's part–" Edward was interrupted. Shot down. Sent to the sloped ground on the opening of the infirmary room door by force much more of this world.

"Olli," Robert shouted as he entered, with the requisite force to knock Edward to the floor and to strike his head on the way down.

"Whit aboot mah faither?" He shouted, in vain, to Edward in pooling blood.

It ran from his temple in grotesque chunks from where he had struck the edge of an infirmary slab, which also bore chunks from Edward's burnt head.

"Olli," Robert said at his side, hands on his shoulders. "We have to get out, *now.*"

"Ah need tae know," he returned, rolling Edward out of the pool of his own internals-makings.

There was a glimpse of consciousness there. His dark eye phasing in and out of focus.

"Whit aboot mah faither? Whit aboot Gourock? Why ur ye, why ur *she*, efter me?"

Edward smiled, a grin of graveyard-tender-elation.

"Fuck you, Oliver Turner."

And as he faded, he turned to Robert, took him in.

"I'm glad it was you," he said, a glimmer of the genuine Edward he had once thought was there. "Get out, Robert, leave them. I love you."

And he was gone. Dead. This time he felt for a pulse, to be sure. But their torment was not through. As soon as Edward's one lid covered over his deep-black eye, the ship slid further still, and worse, in one almighty slam, fell over completely on her port side. The whale was dead, and the sea, as ever, sought to claim its own. Now the sliding was continuing, and the grinding sound that he had heard when the ship beached herself run fullest through the internal cavities, like a last-ditch, 'get out' siren.

"Olli!" Robert shouted. "There's no time!"

Harris!

It hit him that his reason for being there was in reach, though now overturned too, and in pain, having landed on the bandaged bundles of his stumps that, in the tropical heat, had a hint of green to their ends that he knew meant only further trouble and probably cuttings, or worse. He went to him, on the wall that was now a floor, and he kissed him. It would have hurt Robert to see it, he knew, but nothing else mattered to him now than Harris and being with him.

"He's mah Alice," he whispered after a kiss that was not returned. "Forgive me."

Harris grabbed his face. Firmer than his frail frame looked like he could have.

"Oliver, listen to me." He spoke with the intonation of a captain to his men. "You have to leave me. You have to listen to your *friend*."

He knew by the infliction of *friend* that Harris understood the nature of the situation, however impacted he was by the fever of tropical infection. Whether he *forgave him* for it, he could not tell.

"There's no time," Harris concluded, weaker, losing the backing behind his grip.

He gripped him back. Held his jaw at each side in the cup of his hands.

"Wur 'ere fur ye, Harris. Baith o' us, wur getting oot th'gither."

And he turned to Robert, desperate.

"Darlin', hulp me. Please."

And Robert did, joining him at the other side of Harris.

"Ready," he said, as Robert joined him in a scoop position, an arm under his knees, another at his back. "Hurl."

It was hard going, and the groans of *Coolidge* sliding off the shore and back to the depths of the sea made it feel – as they carried Harris through her and back to the door they had entered – that, with her movements, they were not moving at all. But they were, and they made it, to the opening.

"We hae tae jump," he shouted, out of breath and strength.

She was picking up speed, steaming down the slope of the shore and toward the channel.

The waterline was seconds away from flooding through the access point through which they had entered.

"There will be a suction as she goes under," Robert said. "As soon as we are out: paddle like hell."

"Aye," he said, the Santos shelf speeding toward them. "Oan three."

"Right," Robert said.

"Yin."

"Olli," Harris said.

"Twa."

"Let me go," Harris said, pulling against the arms that cradled him.

"Three!"

And they leapt from the *President*.

The water was tropical, warm, but it churned with danger. From the mid-point to the bow, the ship was swallowed at speed, more rapidly than even she had travelled toward the minefield that would mark her end. They sank at first, then the suction began. Harris worked valiantly to free himself, to unburden the men that had come in to save him. But he refused to let him go. Either of them. With Harris in one hand and Robert in the other, he kicked and thrust in the direction of the tropical sun. In the frenzy, he found a moment of calm. Belief in a noble act. If he died, that did not matter, just as long as he did not let go. The pull continued, and at one point, they were deep enough along the shelf that his ears started to hurt and his lungs to burn. But he kept kicking, and his grip only tightened with the feeling of being close to spent. Then, as quick as it had come, the *President* was gone, and her pull on them lifted. Now. With his and Robert's legs kicking, they started back to the surface and then burst into breathable area, all three still connected. With what energy he had left, he dragged Harris and Robert up onto the sand at the edge of the shelf, coming to rest, his grip still strong, and the blue sky with circling aircraft still above head.

"Ne'er," he said, pulling them onto his chest. "I'll ne'er let gang. A loue ye baith."

IX

ROMSEY

She lay heavy in the Tail o' the Bank. Heavier and lower in the water than when he had first joined her almost four years before. She was still painted in her war greys, though the streaks of sea-going staining now adorned her, like the marks of a tree, showing her labour and the toll of intense service she may have been designed for, but was never expected to undertake. They were together, the three of them. He did not even suggest to either Robert or Harris that they should stay behind. Because he would not have let them. He would not have *left* them. Not ever, ever again. *His* Queen, *Elizabeth*, had gotten them there. It was a homecoming, the natural choice of ferrying him and close to 10,000 soldiers back to Britain. The cradle of his love for them both. The voyage arrangements took some wrangling. The fallout from the *President*'s downfall had been considerable. Omitted information from her sailing orders was the official explanation for her steering into the head of a 'friendly' minefield. But, of course, there was more to the story. And he was implicated. As was the Robert and the Bell name, and of course, so was Harris now, too. Edward, at his end, had guided him there, back to the beginning, to his father. And it was well time now that he got to the truth of the conspiracy, of Irvine's death and Harris's enslavement.

Harris did not like to speak of his experience on board *Coolidge*. Of Edward and how he ended up alone and locked down with him. He was proud, Olli knew from first-solid-man-bump on the New York docks. It was a male, military man thing. He loved this about Harris. But, after the trauma of having his lower legs taken from him, this pride had augmented into armour. Harris had never been a burden to anyone. And not only needing to be rescued but to be *carried* over the coral sands to the Santos U.S. hospital was, he could see, coming about on more than he could manage. But Harris did manage. Each of them did, amid war and the limitations of vessel-hopping that relied, in each of their cases, on the influence and assistance of others. Robert proved his mettle especially, leaning on the contacts he had made in both the merchant navy and the air force, to get them back to New York and then, in time, a placement on *Elizabeth* to be ferried, with record troop numbers, to Gourock.

Gaining passage on one of the *Queens* back to Scotland proved perhaps the easiest of all arrangements by that time in the war's progression. New York, being a city of big buildings that bustled with beautiful young men ready to serve throughout much of the war, was brought to a boil during their time there. Harris, whose neglectful tenure upon *Coolidge*, together with the petri dish, humid conditions of the Pacific, was left with wounds in a state of putridity that threatened not only to encroach and take from him more of his limbs but to take his life as well.

As soon as Harris was well enough to travel from Santos, Robert had arranged for their passage to New York while Olli paved the way for, on arrival, Harris to come into the private care of the good doctor. Still savouring the support of his soldier companion, the doctor had set up his own practice. By day, he treated the wounds of the returning injured – physical and otherwise –, and by night, he opened up the subterranean portions of his practice to provide his more unorthodox healings. And under his tutorage, Olli was taught how to treat Harris holistically, including how to nurture his severed pride and enliven their sexual life, both during healing and into the time beyond, when his wounds would have fully healed into stumps that were solid. In these rooms of spas and plunge-pools and steam, Harris started growing back the parts of himself that he could; his muscle, his bulk, his desire to *be* with Olli again. To *take* him, even as a man without feet. The addition of Robert to their relationship had proven positive, too. Robert and Harris became *friends* in the un-underlined sense. They, clearly, came to care for each other as both quite similar men. There was no sex, and this was not discussed. Though they did know enough about their liaisons with Olli for these sexual dimensions of their own lives to not conflict. Robert took Olli inside him, Harris gave himself inside of Olli; there was a symmetry to it from which more selfless mateship was sowed; a bond based on male-to-male appreciation.

On Olli's insistence, Robert was under treatment too, for psychological traumas that, unlike the visibility of a soldier without feet, carried a certain taboo, even for the twentieth century. It was the stigma of diseases of the mind. Through the good doctor's and Olli's encouragement, Robert and Harris became agents of each other's recovery. Robert would tend to the maintenance of Harris's legs with all the receptiveness and attention to service that he prided himself on providing in the bedroom with Olli. Harris, himself coping with disablements of a more inner nature, took an interest in Robert's recess spaces and especially his life beyond the walls of the doctor's secret gentlemen's health spa. They found common ground and built upon that together. There was much to bond and sort through with each other on topic-planes that Olli knew little about. It meant they harmonised, in meaningful ways, at another register.

For example, both were men with women; one destructively married-to, the other at-a-crossroads engaged-to. Strategies for paths to possible resolutions was one topic the men could proceed down together, uniquely, given the common thread of the illegal intimacy with Olli that they both shared. Another conversation was children, Robert who had one – a son – that he missed terribly, and Harris who wanted one, just as terribly.

On arrival in New York, he had feared he might lose Harris to conservatism and duty to Alice. Robert, it would seem, proved pivotal in persuading Harris toward a different view: if he stayed with Olli, perhaps he could have it both ways. A ranch and children and a male companion, too.

The buzz of adventure about the place in and around New York docks was a player, too, especially with the sad sight of *Normandie*, still in her berth but stripped down to her hull. The story of her demise and connection with Edward, of which he had now relaid. It was an energising time to redraw battle lines.

Mussolini was dead, and Italy had surrendered as the Allies pushed up through the underbelly of Europe and the Germans were in full retreat in the East. And for Harris, affectingly affirming had been the end of the North African campaign favouring the Allies. It was electric, and there were many murmurings of Britain amassing troops for the liberation of France from the sea. It was into this mass formation of men that Harris decided he would follow Olli. To see the adventure, and likely the war, to its end at his side. With again the aid of his *Aquitania* captain, Robert had arranged for crew-leave papers for himself and Olli under aliases. At the same time, the good doctor, many of whom's clients came from one of the two *Queens*, wrote a referral for Harris to a specialist in London.

He was on deck with them both as they entered the Clyde and passed the shipyards where he had lent a hand – and a mouth and an arsehole – to the men who built *she* who returned him there. The area had been heavily shelled by the Luftwaffe in the intervening years since he lived there, leaving the outline of the tenement skyline much more jagged on his return sail-by. While being back on the *Queen* felt right, there was not much of a feeling of home about the passing. Places of interest to his rearing were a perfunctory pointing out to Robert and Harris. He could not see and did not even much care whether his childhood lodgings had survived the bombings – pushing down any thought as to what that might say about him. There was, of course, a significance between himself and Robert and the Clyde banks, and how far from secrecy to comfortable commitment they had come together; from their start, he had been relieved not to be with Robert when they passed the dockyards, so he would not need to connect that place he knew so well and from his knees with a new, outward journeying adventure. Now that he passed this place with Robert it came with a realisation that the slipway was never home. Anchorage at the Tail o' the Bank in this moment brought only anxiety, for his decision to keep the men he loved with him, to take them into conflict again, now only left him with questions.

What would he learn on this return to the place where his adventure had begun? What pieces remained to be found? What further secrets were there to be uncovered? What, actually, *did he know about any of it?*

"Let's stairt wi' whit we know," he said over a pint at a table in the corner of the pub overlooking *their* Queen.

"This one's missus is a murderous bitch," Harris said with a clap on Robert's back.

They laughed. Harris was the last man any would expect to hear in disparaging speech about a woman, being the consummate red-blooded Yankie gent.

"Sorry, Robbie, but it's true," squeezing his arm and taking a deep sip of his brew.

There was a romanticism to the three of them, he thought; in a quiet corner of the pub – the fire casting warming, a-Highlands-glow across their faces. Harris looked almost like his old self, across from him, over a pint, smiling at Robert.

"No," Robert said, "don't be. You're right. She's a right old cunt!"

And again, they laughed to clang of pint-glass. There was a locker room familiarity between the three of them. Between Harris and Robert, especially, he thought. They were unburdened by the need for pretence around their attraction – strike that, *sex* – with a man. But also, they kept the simplicity of not having seen each other naked to simmer. There was a mystery between them. It was better than he could have wished for.

"There is *that*," he said, bringing them back to topic – though *not really* wishing to, wanting to keep *this*, the banter, the bonding.

His Harris was back. Of course, they were seated, so the wheelchair was conveniently concealed – perhaps even to a mostly-healed Harris, several pints in it was possible that even he could forget. And his Harris had filled out again, too, in his face, in his arms and shoulders. He was, once more, even in a wheelchair, *the* finest specimen of a man. The kind that caused the turn of heads of pub-visiting-men and females akin. And clearly, this being his first visit to the United Kingdom, there was a sense of excitement of a traveller abounding him – the potential danger, perhaps even, 'amping' (as he had often heard the troopship Aussies say) that excitement up a little.

"But what else do we know," he said, reluctantly, again, drawing them resolutely back.

"That I'm a traitor," Robert volunteered, putting onto the table Edward's final breath, final effort to divide them.

"Aren't we all, Robbie," Harris said, again with a raise and emptying of his glass and a hand, softer this time, on his mate's shoulder.

He gestured to the barman to bring them another round.

"Well, clearly a wasted attempt," he said when the drinks were once again before them. "But there is *something* in the connection between your wife and my father."

Maybe now wasn't the time, he thought.

Watching them, at ease, on land. Clearly, they were not in wanting to venture into this now. He resolved to let it pass, to commit them to one night of drinking and light banter. Of mateship, to draw on the Australians once more. To-morrow they could revisit wh–

"Captain Bell," came the interruption of a fourth party, who joined them at their table with his own drink in hand. "You know, I had a suspicion I might run into you this week."

"Officer Adams," Robert said, the joy sapped from his address.

Adams was a ginger male, freckled and full-faced, in the throes of late thirties. Attractive enough, but a weasel-way about the eyes and his overall manner, and allover awkward way of an 'A' Christian name that he could not remember.

"You say you suspected I might be here?" Robert asked after he had done the introductions.

"Just with your wife's presence at the Navy Convoy Conference to-morrow," he said, curious suspicion crossing his eyes that sat round under brows of no colour.

"Of course," Robert said, toeing the line. "I'll be sitting this one out. Edith has it covered. What time was the start of the conference again?"

"10 am, in the Navy Control Office."

"Yes, of course. Well, it was good seeing you again, Officer Adams. But if you'll excuse us, we better be getting back to the ship."

"Quite, on *Elizabeth*, are you?"

"Yes," he said, and they left.

The town was awash with seamen ashore from *Elizabeth* and other lesser vessels of merchant and military assignment. There was no shortage of places for the men to drink, and they stopped at a few before arriving at the top of the hill to overlook the bank and *Elizabeth* and settled on an old mariners' pub with rooms. There they sat together in one of the window alcoves and amended their plans. Visiting the offices of his father the next day was now succeeded by staking out Edith's appearance at the Convoy Conference. The conference had been known to them; however, it now had a lineup of speakers suggesting something of the conspiracy that lured them there. The original lodging intention for that night also required a rethink. It seemed unwise, in light of all that had happened and the care taken to get them there *undetected*, to return to *Elizabeth*, inebriated and with it probable that Edith was in the vicinity. The pleasantness of this particular pub, aptly called *Captain's Rest*, with its heavy, smoky, wooden interiors and warming ales that went down with ease at their table with lantern light presented itself as a perfect option for the night.

"Ah hae yin room, if ye lads don't mynd bunking doon th'gither," the thick-Scotch-publican said from behind the bar.

Though it was now the forties, and women in war settings were becoming more visible, these women were still mostly confined to the ranks of nurses and armament factory work. War was still the purview of men. Men who slept together, bathed together and generally *lived* together in all manner of intimacy and without any insinuation of indecency about the prospect. That was the publican's perspective, anyhow. The view of he, Robert and Harris, of course, was much different. Though the fact of this, together with the actual logistics of how this 'bunking' down might look in practice, did not dawn until after carrying Harris up the stairs and onto the one double bed. Only when the door of their room was shut, and with it, the pub, for the night. They were all three of them, pickled by the night's drinking. It was a novel event for them to be together as a *group*, in a social setting that came with drink and where Harris presented as the least lucid among them, slumped on the bed, focused on the stitched fold in his pants where his feet should have been. The amputation would, the good doctor had warned him, lower his tolerance for alcohol, with the readjustment of body mass being a long process. It was a caution, it would seem, that he had forgotten.

"Olli," Robert said, searching him with a look of genuine wanting-to-know, "what happens now?"

"Let's git Harris intae bed," he said, but Robert's expression remained unchanged. His question, unanswered. "Why don't ye hulp me?"

Robert knew the routine. Harris had healed beautifully, compared to some of the amputations he had seen in helping the doctor as an attendant in his practice; compared with other men, Harris – in all respects – was by far the best. Minimal scarring and a good amount of skin covering the end of the bone – that stopped just shy of his ankle –, meant that the termini of his legs had symmetry and even a nice, soft curve to them. But pain was still present, and before bed, Harris slept best with a gentle massage and the application of petroleum jelly to the flesh seam – to help with scar healing and relieve dryness and itching through the night. He lifted Harris's chin so their eyes would meet.

One of the reasons men drink is to forget traumas and to numb pains. However, there is always a point where reality rushes back. Harris was there, remembering the loss of his feet. 'Phantom limb', the doctor called it, a vivid sensation of his feet still being there, of which had probably helped in the forgetting. This, together with the amputation making it harder for Harris to carry his liquor, left him in a lump of defeat on the bed. He kissed his lips. "Wur going tae git ye ready fur bed."

He hooked Harris by the armpits and lifted him, as Robert, carefully, slid his pants down his legs and off the ends, caring not to touch Harris's lower tips as he did. Harris's mood declined further as his stumps were exposed there, for he and Robert and himself to see. He recognised the attitude as akin to their reunion in the New York hospital when the wounds were still fresh and bulkily bandaged. But he was not going to let Harris pity himself, not when, he believed, there was no reason for it. Robert, too, whose fondness for Harris was plain, looked upon him emoting the entirely opposite. He admired how well Harris had healed and, with proper feeding and physiotherapy, how he had grown back into what he could only guess, himself. In his shared drunkenness, Robert took the opportunity to admire the package of his mate, resting fat and full there, between the thickness of his legs. It was queerly out of character for Robert – and, he thought, a sign of psychological progress from his sessions with the good doctor. And the signs of psychological development continued during their bedtime treatment. Instead of *asking* permission, Robert set about tending to his friend's nightly therapy of his own initiative. With a wad of jelly scooped from the travelling care-kit the doctor had packed them, Robert lathered the substance onto his palms as he sat, crossed-legged on the floorboards, the stump nearest to him in his lap, just shy of his own expanding crotch.

He watched Robert with pride as he set to work massaging the lower extremity of his mate, taking away itchiness and dryness of his broken limbs and spreading stimulating, pleasing sensations out of each of his lubricated fingers swirls. Harris settled into the service. Watching his friend work on him, settled into himself once more as well, finding the pride in his appearance that both Olli and Robert were hero-worshipping. Harris reclined on her elbows on the bed, even arching his head with a swing of swagger. He watched the two of them, *bonding* through the joining of opposing limbs. Harris revelled there, on the bed, enjoying Robert's self-less servitude to the care and wellness of his ample limb ends.

Was a love forming? He asked himself. *Should I feel jealous? Threatened?*

But he did not. Not either. Felt nothing akin to these. They were men, and men were intended to be shared. This was their point of difference. Their chance, as the *harder* sex, to *do* sex differently. Less possessively. More inclusively. And they both surrendered themselves to this philosophy. And that they did it in the presence of him, and without apparent concern or even consciousness to his being there, made him sure that he had made the right choices, in keeping them both and in bringing them together. Harris watched with a cocky, detached, only vague-acknowledgement of all Robert was doing to serve him. In turn, Robert's rubbing reaching high up his limb and plying more plentiful ply-ment of ointment prescribed to ease, but which was now pleasing to him, too. Harris fell into the treatment, the attention to him. Seeing himself through Robert's attentiveness, how Olli had always seen him: as a heroic hulk of a man.

Robert was his treatment now, he realised. *His Robbie.*

Yet still, with realisation, jealousy evaded him. In fact, he edged himself back into the further recesses of the room, away from where the bedside light could reach him. So he could watch them. So as to not intrude on the only two men he had ever loved, in the learning stages of a love for each other. Naturally, they would be the optimum fit. There was an inevitability to what he was witnessing. He had brought them together, as a thread, as a link between two men of vastly different sexual persuasions. And he, oscillating as he always had, enjoyed and loved them both. *But*, he only now realised, there was something uniquely theirs that was forming. Something that bound them profoundly. Harris with his upstanding, principled, apple-pie, all-American symbol of the new world; and Robert, also principled, but in servitude to duty and others in a very British sense that Olli himself had *had* to bypass to court the men he had. And Harris, drunkenness and all, was starting to see this in his Robbie, too. Robbie never would, of course, recognise this particular worth of his own, as was his nature. His selfless, self-deprecating nature made him so loveable. And – and again, this came without jealously – he realised that the innocence in Robbie was closer to Alice, to the life Harris did *want* to lead, beyond the war, beyond what men needed to do, in order to get through. And watching it was like watching the birth of spring across Europe that allowed the Allies to resume their assault on tyranny that – he had heard through the newsreels – was undyingly underway.

Robbie, performing hero-worship-working of Harris's limbs, bouncing between them on the broad boards like they were fairground attractions as if to lather them was, within itself, the highest honour. But also, finding boldness there. Again, he was pleased to see this, a step-up in his officer's confidence. Robbie made furtive glances toward Harris's growing manhood as he worked his stumps; Olli could see that, to Robbie, the mystery bulge between his mate's legs teased him as being *as* brash and tantalising for treatment as the ends of the limbs he was working on. But Robbie, as was his way, did this shyly still. Even under the influence and with all the advancements that the good doctor had made with him on his character; each time, Harris would catch Robbie's timid crotch-ward gaze. Catch him in the act of looking with his masculine, deep-blue eyes. Robbie, in return, would dart his eyes away, having been caught in the act. *Harris*'s hare-in-headlights older seaman was admiring him. Each time, Robbie would flick back his focus to the working of Harris's ends after the bashful fleet away. Olli knew why, and, he believed, so did Harris. For Robbie, returning to the sight of Harris's limb-ends, bringing his attention back there, was not in any way a disappointed departure, nor a concession on what Robbie would rather be doing or looking upon. No, it was a move that said – and he knew enough to know that this was what he also *meant* – that working Harris's ends was a privilege for him, a labour of love, and that, intensely, Robbie needed his new friend to realise this. But – *And this was new*, he thought – there was boundary-crossing building there, too.

He's fluffing him up, he realised, watching Harris's chest puff up to his touch like prime poultry getting prepped in a prize pen.

Robbie gave Harris a recovery potential that Olli perhaps could not. And also brought Harris on to a path of pride that he *deserved* more than any man Olli had *had.* Harris transformed before his eyes under the treatment of Robbie. *Transformed.* Like Harris had never lost his feet. He appeared as feetful, baroque and bulky as the day Olli had met him. He would have had no hope of building this up in Harris, he believed. This was a unique characteristic of Robbie, and he was immensely pleasured to be witness to it. Pleasured as he knew, with Robbie, Harris would stay. Harris was smiling. No, not quite. He was firm-jawed, the corners of his mouth engaged. Knowing that eyes were on him, that *he* was dominant. Alpha. Supreme male. And those at his phantom feet – one massaging his before-ankles with relish, the other watching, desiring from the darker gradients of the room – were there for his use, for any use he might desire, or *require*.

"I need to piss," he said to the shadows, spreading his hand across the bulge in his briefs, tugging at it. "Are you able to help me with that, Oliver?"

Robbie shot him a glance of un-surety. Robbie had lost himself in the service. Another point on which he approved. He sprung into action, moving across the cracked and age-fissured floor on palms and knees to take up position below bed level, in catchment traject-ion of Harris's to-be stream, just as he had before.

"Aye, Captain," he said.

Robbie rubbed with renewed focus. Like a racehorse resolved not to need his blinders. But blinders were required to keep him from peeping when the rustle of fold-down of brief and slap against thigh of a dick-released was there; there and too enticing a glance-treat for Robbie to resist. Olli then noticed in his periphery that the rubbing had ceased, remembering his own first sighting; he even struggled himself to keep his gaze locked on Harris's face, with his member a hazy lump of largeness in the visor of his view. The stream was ale-flavoured this time and even more palpable. Still bitter, but retaining highlights of a hops and barley of Harris's homebrew. Best served warm, direct from the tap. This time, Olli – also benefiting from the boldness of a bounty of beer inside his belly – took a more skilled approach to recycling Harris's tap release. Allowing the brew to froth to the rim before drinking it down, for head to form, in a smoother draining than last time, and then repeating the receipt of beer from Harris's filter. There was relief – and he would stake, pleasure, too – in sharing the brew; and as that relief rolled out of Harris and into a receptive, appreciative, receptacle, Olli folded into it, striking up a rhythm, using the occasion as an opportunity to develop his palate and demonstrate that, from the position of his lover, at his phantom feet, having a utility for the provision of relieving functions, was a benefit, to him, of the situation they had found themselves in.

Harris was a big man, and in him, held a supply of beer that even someone as thirsty for it as he was would soon find himself full up with. Most astonishing to him was that, while maintaining a steady stream, Harris's tap also found the stamina to start to rise. Beam-ward, like a stern out of the sea after an aft iceberg strike to the bow, expanding along the length of his thighs, like an inflatable fairground hammer for a high striker, proving him as victor of the strength test through the expansion-while-streaming alone. He remained committed, moving up on the incline with him, without spillage or break to eye contact. Then the stream stopped. It did not taper out, nor slow, even. But stopped, as if cut off by the steady hand of a skilled barman after a perfect pint. Timed just as the head in his mouth was at its frothiest. He held it there as a grateful glass, Harris's beer bubbles bursting across his lips, salty and tangy and consistent with the rest of the batch he had enjoyed. Harris winked, and he took this as he cue for last drinks, taking his final serving of Harris brew in drawn-out, considered, *savoured* swallows.

"Good work, sailor," Harris said as the final pool of his brew disappeared down Olli's throat. "Time for your reward," and he gripped his dick.

It was already hard and upward facing, but by Harris's steadying hand, shot up even prouder, his mushroom head engorged.

"Climb on," Harris said.

And he did. Feet planted either side of Harris's thighs, he lowered onto his captain until their faces met. Harris filled him, stretched him, more than usual. As if the absence of feet meant the blood available to flow and pool in other extremities was now disproportionate, expanding Harris's appendage too, as it stretched out Olli and found new recesses in him in which to grow. Harris kissed him and winked at his Robbie as he did.

"You're part of this, too, sailor," Harris said, "get up here and kiss me."

Robbie bounced from his cross-legged position and onto the bed with all the bolster of a good boy on Christmas morning. But, then paused there: a breath's distance from Harris's lips. With one hand on the crest of Olli's arse as he rode him, Harris gripped the scruff of Robbie's neck with the other and pulled him fast – but pausing too, just a hair's width from the touching of lips, then pulled him the final sliver of space so that their lips touched in a first kiss.

He let them have their moment while he focused on getting a rhythm going with the polishing of Harris's pole. Harris, ever the gent, sought his lover's consent before progressing beyond a kiss.

"Olli," he said at the crest of a bounce. "I am yours, all of me. Are you prepared to share?"

He turned to Robert, whose eyes told him that the same question burned in him too.

"What's mines," he said to Harris, still bouncing, "is yers," he said, turned to Robert.

And with that, he commenced the changing of the guard – with a swiftness of execution that assured him of his power to still surprise the men in his life, both. It was over to Robert now, for the removal of pants and then navigation of his arse up and on to Harris. The grimace of Robert in his struggle to lower on to the captain was a compliment. Harris was a grander prospect than he, but Harris was also *his* to share, and therefore it was a treat to provide Robert with a phallus much more fat. And long. And unbridled to handle. Like a wild stallion that only he had the experience to wrangle, thus far.

Conversely, and again, this was not a case with jealousy-causing consequences. As Robert struggled to millimetre his descent of Harris's member, Harris's eyes rolled back with the pleasure of a receptacle tighter and only-one-previous-careful-though-testing-owner at his disposal. And Harris and Robert continued to kiss throughout as their interconnection reached its most intimate. He felt an accomplishment in there, with the new acquisition: the joining of his two favourite assets – Harris's centre, un-amputated limb and Robert's lower, sea squirt receptacle – into a tie-breaking display of each other's fine qualities. He chose to recede back to the shadows to watch, to enjoy their bonding further. And it was a sit-down occasion, as Harris held his Robbie in a way unique to *them*, as they worked out the contours of their love-making. And this took time. Good, intense, love-and-liking-for-the-other sex is like that: it progresses slowly, like an eager explorer charting previously un-navigated shores.

"Perhaps," Harris said to the shadows, Robbie's waist gripped in a pincer movement that, firmly, permitted Harris to rise and return him onto his staff, "there is room in Robbie for us both?"

Robbie shot a look to the shadows, too, uncertain as to his own sucky hole's capabilities. Relying on he to decide for him. And he did; in a once-more swift manoeuvre, he was in Robbie within only a few crests of the captain's making.

At first, Robert refused him, denied expansion any further. But it was not a request he was making, and with a trace of the dilated mouth already full with Harris, he *instructed* those muscles he knew well to loosen and let him in. He covered Robert's mouth for good measure, stifling a whimper that, if allowed out, would only tighten him further.

"Let me in," he said into Robert's ear. "Lik' ah trained ye fur."

And, on cue, Robert did. He was allowed in. To slide in and up alongside Harris. He was like a tender nudging up against a much larger liner, finding room in water while also performing a vital function: ensuring the liner reached its moorings, wherefrom its cargo could be unloaded. But, as tenders have the power to do, he held back from driving the liner he was rubbing up against to its completion of the voyage – not yet.

"Yer nook is ready," he whispered to Robert as he and Harris expanded further inside him, "tae *serve* in a mair, *expansive* manner."

"Thank– you,– sir," Robert said in broken breaths as he relaxed deeper onto the double member expansion. "I want to– to *serve*."

"Guid lad," he said, again at a tenor that could not be heard by Harris, who, caught up in the sensation of Robbie on three sides and Olli on the fourth, seemed perfectly content to persist on the current course to completion. "Ye commitit' tae preparing Harris fur bed, 'n' ye don't wish tae let him doon, dae ye?"

"Never," Robert said, forcefully, the first declaration of clear intent that evening.

A soft whimper escaped after he said it, as Harris's and he's swords crossed in a furthering exploratory, expanding endeavour. Harris hardly stirred at the committed outcry, himself committed to the navigation of touching and working with his intimate member, the two men who meant much to him.

"Guid lad, here's whit a'm waantin' ye tae do..."

What he set out for him in his into-the-ear instructions was about trust and navigation of limits, each of his mens' of which he was aware. There was risk involved: damage, was possible, *probable*, the good doctor would likely have ruled – *inadvisable*, would have been his academic advice, if asked. But these were war conditions. *That* mask, behind which many a man would hide before; then when war ceased, and a return to families happened...they then came to find that one of the men that found comfort in the posterior from them, would come looking for them, in the hope of something more. These would be familiar tales. But, he was now convinced, as standard and trite in these twentieth-century times as such tales might come to be, that these did not apply to *this* particular war epic. The significance of this sex, here and now, would outstay the ceasefire. In fact, he would ensure that the specific risqué enterprise onto which his two men were about to embark would be both pleasurable and done within the confines of his protective promise to them both: extreme pleasure that averted any damage to either mate. It was through this ethos that he instructed Robert to grease up his slipway with petroleum jelly and back it onto Harris's stumps, one by one, in an anal-passage-massaging rotary motion. The handover was handled by he with the same swiftness of movement that had been employed throughout the night so far. Robert was lifted off the double anal offer, the two dicks splaying out at the point of release. Then, before Harris could complain *too* much, he had sat, himself, on Harris's member and employed a more vigorous wave-riding rhythm to make up for the looser offering now available to the room's ruling alpha male.

"Noo, Robert," he said to him as Robert descended from the bed to the floor, "mind whit ah taught ye. Tae yer limit bit na further."

Robert nodded. He had his instructions and set to work in their execution. Turning his Captain Bell onto a ship's wheel attachment, it turned out, was good preparation for Robert taking his *other* captain's bulbous, bigger handle. It was not about a fetish for the object at his behind: the stump. He knew this. Were it, he would not have commissioned the treatment – he would not have allowed for the progression to sex of Harris with Robert. Such a fetish would have implied that the amputation had *changed* Harris, removed two parts and added a further phantom appendage in the vein of *thingification*.

Any fetish would have been a pleasurable debasement, but one driven by a baseless, objectifying lust-for-lack of his feet-less limbs. This was absurd by Robbie's reckoning, as he knew by observation of their burgeoning romance. He had come to learn this via ethnographic means, through the science of observation, and first-hand knowledge of the sex-drive principle. A fist and forearm could have been refashioned for a similar purpose, were brutal penetration beyond the penis the mission of this assignment. But that was not *it* at all; not what Robbie felt for Harris, and not what he would allow Robert to perform in the service of Harris. *Taking* his stumps was more *personal* than that. As sex between wartime sailors often is.

For those *less* than the finest cut of beef that is Harris, sex is insecurity; for Robert, that was the case, at least – he had too much experience in the field to credibly claim this himself. But with Harris, it seemed, there was a reflection of self in the affliction, something of the common humanity that *lesser* perceptively-oriented men – like Robbie – could cling to. He, of course, did not see his Robert as in any way inferior, knowing, though, that Robert felt himself so. And in sex, *felt things* have a tendency to surface with military precision.

Like depth charges surfacing enemy U-boats, sex brings everything to the surface. And latching on to Harris's stumps and their penetrative power was profound to Robbie, in the haze of a night out and ample ale, granted. But such profoundness was why he prescribed it as the climax to their first extra-to-he male encounter. In a pinch, instead of being about *making use of* – to his own bodily limits – the phallic extensions available to him, Harris's stumps declared themselves as active agents in the seeking out of further massage: this time through the encasing of Robbie's inner orifice.

The limit of two, now-highly sensitised parts of two damaged men, new-as-lovers, meant that the acts undertaken that were new to them both, too, resulted in: pain and close-to-retreat, *at first*, but morphing, with patience, a letting go, and with time: pleasure and an intimacy without inhibition. All while he worked to orchestrate the erotic feasibility of the pageant: vigorous working of Harris's length with his anus in unison with Robert's backing on to Harris's stumps with his own. The gratification of the sensation across all three of Harris's lower limbs spoke to his appreciation and the end of – he hoped – any more feelings of spent-ness in his appeal and ability. And with Robert, he kept mindful of the importance of drawing that imaginary line along Harris's limb, of the extreme beyond which his arse – as well prepared as it was – could not pass. There were pleasures to be plundered for himself, too, atop Harris's ship's wheel, steering the course for Robert's inward taking of Harris's other and also-sensitive stumps.

"Need tae go again?" He said, at a crest of riding him, doubling as a drawing of Harris's attention away from Robbie's changing of stumps.

"Sorta," Harris said with a flush of colour.

"Dae it, fill me up."

He could see it was a struggle to go while engorged. But eventually, it came, flooding into him. And he kissed Harris as his warmth filled him.

"Ta," he said, "a loue ye."

The finale, when it came, came for them both – his two men, that is – in a joyous outpouring. Robert across the dusty floorboards of their dorm, and Harris deep into the recesses of he. And when Harris did come, pouring forth with an intensity of release that he felt across his inner walls, Harris – and this, he appreciated most – took him by the neck, strong and purposeful, and said:

"Thank you, I love you."

And after, the three of them spent and gathered together under cover of a Queen bed quilt. They were one inter-wrapped mass, retired to rest for the few hours of dark that remained, with a view down the rooftops running in steps to the Clyde. Steps that, at their landing, met the lights of the *Queen* proper, on which they had arrived.

Harris was holding Robert come morning. Harris on his back, with Robbie cosied into his armpit, like a cub into a bear in the wild. He left them to sleep, to carry on their bonding into the day – making arrangements with the publican for them to stay another night as insurance against any possible disturbance.

They had been through enough, he thought, as he made his way to the control office on foot.

There was a feeling of final confrontation to the conference he would observe from afar. But also, of a *going back to the start* about it. Before he had boarded *Romsey* on that motionless Clyde morning back in 1940, he had called into these offices in the tow of his father. As his father had on the deck of the tender, last visit, instruction was to wait in the wings of the action, which was what he would be doing once more. Admittedly, with little more known about what exactly the action that he and his lovers had found themselves caught up in could be, and what – if any – resemblance it might bear to the action his father was implicated in. Paternal connection doubts were dashed when, after noon, from his concealment in the scenery to the side of the office entrance, he witnessed his father emerge. The fatherly exit came after that of some conference delegates in a mix of military and civilian gear. Incrimination inserted itself in the place of beneficial doubt as he witnessed a woman he knew emerging with the man of his blood. Edith was smiling. It was, he suspected, what any who knew her would describe as her stereotypically smug demeanour, while his father was the opposite, caved into himself like a death-row inmate on his way to the gallows. His father was paler and frailer than his memory held him to be, less assured, too. Was it the war that had taken this toll on him, he wondered, or a more personal plight borne of something deeper within? He watched him as he walked the recline down toward the Clyde, debating whether to run after him for a confrontation or to keep an eye on Edith, who, he only now realised, was nowhere to–

"Hullo again, Oliver," came *her* voice behind him. "Why don't you come inside."

He darted about him, uncertain whether to run or to follow her.

"Or...if you prefer..." putting a hand on his shoulder and pointing in the direction of a group of men from the conference, still in conversation in the garden grounds, "I could call out to those gentlemen there and have you arrested for trespass."

He selected the first option, following Edith up the stairs and into an office off the main corridor. The corridor where he had waited for his father years before. The room was in the spirit of a study, with floor to ceiling leather-bound books and charts over small reading bureaus lit with banker lights. Framed on the walls were two oils of famous British ocean liners of the past, Cunard's *Lusitania* and White Star's *Britannic*.

"Magnificent, aren't they," she said, when he was only just in and past the close of the door behind him, "those four-funnelled liners. We've only *Aquitania* left today, the last of her kind, a real one-off. But I suppose you've come to learn that, haven't you, Oliver?"

"Ah've sailed in her, aye," he said flatly.

"And how did that come about?"

He did not answer.

"I know, of course. It was by *fucking* my husband."

"Then why ask th' quaistion?"

"Because I wanted to see if you would say it. And if not, what effect *my* saying it would have on you."

"'n'?"

"Nothing. No reaction. Just as I suspected."

"Meaning?"

"Meaning, Oliver, that your dalliance with my husband was as calculated, as planned, as my own. Carried out to an end with experience and cunning."

"A conspiracy," he said, raising his eyes to heavens.

"No, no, no," she said in short, sharp blurts. "Give me some credit for having *read* you. No grand conspiracy, just survival and a personal competency of controlling men. Which I admire. In fact, it is why I have tolerated you and allowed my husband to be *turned* by you, Mr Wood."

"Ye hae me a' figured oot," he said, following the calling of his real name, "kin ah go then?"

She laughed. It was a dry, empty sound, like the hull of a ship just launched, without its fittings, hollow.

"*Tolerated*, Mr Wood, past tense. You see, unfortunately for you, I lied.

You, if anyone, should admire that. There *is* a conspiracy here. And it is one that you *will* play a key part in. And lucky for you, my respect for your turning of my husband – however distasteful I find the ends – means I am going to share with you the important position you will play in this whole saga, right now."

She strode to take up position between the oils into place in front of the mantel.

"What do these two great dames have in common, Mr Wood?"

"Thay sunk," he said, begrudged to volley with her, but too intrigued not to...the promise of all pieces of the story to be revealed, too tantalising a proposition.

"They *were* sunk," she corrected, a finger lifted like a pedantic governess. "During the previous war, by the Germans, this one by mine," pointing to *Britannic*. "This one by submarine," to *Lusitania*. "And what were the strategic advantages of these sinkings?" She asked, clasping her hands with a presentation style more suited to the lectern of an auditorium.

He shrugged.

"Uncanny! Yes, nil," she said. "In fact, counter-to-the-cause," performed with a clear relish in the recount. "Only thirty were killed on *Britannic*, which was working as a hospital ship at the time, and so had little strategic advantage anyway. Yet, she was the largest liner to be lost in the war, and as reparation, Germany was stripped of *Bismarck*, renamed *Majestic*; she became the White Star flagship and remained the largest ship in the world until *Normandie*."

She took a satisfied breath, letting her words stay adrift in the air like a compelling exhibit at trial.

"The sinking of *Lusitania*," she continued her presentation of the facts, "was even less of a benefit to the Germans; her high civilian death count, in fact, was far more effective in the service of a *British* victory than a German advance, dragging the Americans into the war. And, I can tell you, this British triumph was no accident."

She walked to the centre of the room. Where, on a small mahogany games table was a chess match mid-game. Picking up one of the dark bishops and inspecting it in the crater of her bony, sickly transparent hand, rolling it back and forth with the unfolding of her story...

"I spent an illuminated evening with Robert's father last year. Now he, being as he is, a man, like his son, but broader, just as prone to impression. On the drink, and slight of feminine hand, he divulged to me the whole sordid affair, stretching to upper government echelons that involved deliberately sending her into dangerous waters to court the Americans into conflict. And, sure enough, this sinking was a *factor* in the Americans declaring war. However," she said, returning the bishop to his place in the game, "this declaration came almost two years later!"

It was a court drama played out within her self, Edith rebutting herself.

"And so, even for the British, these sinkings had no *immediate* benefit to the war effort."

The narrative did not relay as complete, having dropped off dramatically without the necessary sloping intonation of oral storytelling.

She set about resetting the chessboard pieces into their start-game posts.

"We have a son, you know," she said as she did.

"Aye."

"I suppose he told you that I *keep* him from him?"

He did not answer.

And she smiled that same thin grin that she had seen-off his father with.

"Chess was the first game I taught him, as my father taught me. A *real man*'s game," she said in a manner that, he knew, was intended as a strike against Robert's fitness as a father. "Teaches men strategy, patience. Forcing them to think steps ahead, to anticipate the opponent's next move, next, several moves. And that the path to winning, among competent players, is seldom the most obvious offensive position. It is the *luring* of the opponent to *believe* they are following a path to victory, to allow them to believe in it, when in fact, that this opponent is playing to the smarter man's own plan."

"Git tae yer meaning, wid ye?"

"Very well," she said, the match now set.

With the knife side of her hands, in swipes of four pieces swept by each hand at a time, Edith brought the two rows of pawns to meet in the middle of the board.

"*This*," she said to the pieces ready for battle before her, "was the war into which the ships depicted in the oils adorning these walls were lost. A war of trenches and inch-by-inch infantry in-fighting for the most part. Toward the end, though, the tanks came and with them the potential to break through the lines. But never quite did the theatres of war shrink the globe. But *this* war," returning her foot soldiers to their starting positions with surgical backward knife-hand swipes. "This is a war with scope, with seas to cover. And for all the talk of miracle weapons and one-punch solutions, *ships* mean more now. And *sinking* ships means more now, too. And therefore, those looking to make capital from the conditions of war, and who are tenacious enough to position themselves within this playing field," rubbing the checked space between the facing rows of pieces, "it is here that players—"

"Players lik' ye 'n' yer faither, yer mean?"

"Exactly," she said with a single clap in a scissoring swipe and a smile more genuine, the satisfaction that he was following her story.

"Sae ye sink ships, bit why, 'n' how?"

"Come now, you must have figured *some* of this out for yourself."

He looked about the room, filled with charts and maps, and thought of Robert, of his training, of Robert's father's station at the Admiralty.

"Ye hae access tae thair sailing orders, 'n' know thair coordinates at ony given time," he said.

"Yes, and sell that information," she said, "the posters had a point; loose lips *do* sink ships but also fill the pockets of rampant capitalists."

"Bit thare is mair tae it." He said, giving her credit, waiting to learn more, but also growing warier.

"Yes..."

"Sabotage, tae. Th' *Normandie*, th' *President Coolidge*."

"Yes, quite. Plus many more besides, on both sides of the Atlantic. You see, our expertise, like all industrious pursuits with a solid methodology, was borne out of trial and error. As is all good experiments, our *business* has had all the twists of the most interesting of laboratory glassware."

She picked up another piece from the set, a knight this time.

"We started out with some key successes," she said, admiring its curves, "adopting a traditional calvary, scout-and-attack approach. The big win for our client–"

Client, the use of this term to describe her treachery stuck in his side like a spear.

"Cunard's one-funnelled *Lancastria* in 1940, sunk while evacuating troops from the Battle of France, with a loss of life that, this very office informs me, could be as much as 6,000 souls, a fatalities number well beyond her *capacity* of 1,300. It's a sinking top men mostly managed to keep hush-hush, but, of course, we have enough documentation to return an accurate target status report. She stands as the largest single-ship loss of life in British maritime history–"

Ill-feeling rose in him like sea-sickness on a first stint as a seaman. That *she*, as instigator of the ghastly, for-cash, grab of life, even had the lost men's own authorities as her personal archives to chart the success of her *campaign* to her *client*. Worse, and now gloated as having a national-best that was no doubt used to commission further kills.

"But!" She said, returning the knight, broadside, to the table surface alongside the playing board – as one would when a piece was defeated and out-of-play for the rest of the game. "This was a rarity – a fluke, I confess to you, Mr Wood. We got lucky. Using the coordinates we provided our liaison in Berlin, one of their ace bombers managed to deliver his payload directly down her funnel! A feat of aim, as a sodomite, I am sure you will appreciate, Mr Wood."

Her derogatory tongue did not engage him; he was preoccupied with the plight of the men of *Lancastria*. The picture she painted, broken necks due to life jackets after jumps from the sinking hull. Or, choking in fuel oil, or those who died in the capsizing – unable to clamber onto her upside-down hull – or, worst of all, he thought, those subjected to strafing by the Germans when they were in the water, still hopeful for salvation.

"It was a success," she said smugly. "But as we soon learned, one that was hard to *replicate*; and one that came at the greatest personal sacrifice to the resources of our clients. Not to mention our in-house overheads in orchestrating these open ocean assaults–"

The sickening continued.

"No. There was a simpler solution of benefit to both our client and our bottom line. Think of that, you must! And– and you will be interested in this– we found our winning formula with *Bremen* the next year. Burnt out of action as a barracks ship in the safety of her own country by the exertions of just one man. It served as a trial run for our more, let's say, logistically difficult crippling of *Normandie* less than a year later, that you, I understand, had a backstage pass to..."

"Git tae th' point, whaur dae ah come intae a' this?"

"Now that is the truly intriguing plot point, isn't it, Mr Wood? How did a *loose* Clydebank boy find himself in the middle of all this?"

Loose. It cut through him. This woman had managed to see into him more than any before, including her husband. Managed to *see* him for what he truly was. Normally, he would not mind, he would embrace it, even, but he minded now.

"Patience, Mr Wood. We are almost there. These lone-wolf missions, you see, proved much more effective, much easier to accomplish. And will mean, come the end of Germany in this war, the continuation of *my* services for the next power. And so we arrive at the beauty of this business: it does not depend on any particular outcome. It does not *end* with a ceasefire. If this war was one based on technology, the next, believe me, will be one of *intelligence* and *subterfuge.* Akin the chess match, and the business opportunities for us, these will only increase. In fact, our biggest clients of late – I don't mind telling you – have been the Soviets, it was for them that we finished *Bremen* and *Normandie*; they are, you see, playing both sides – in this respect, we have a, shall I say, aligned *modus operandi.*"

"How come ye don't mynd telling me a' this?"

"Finally! A perceptive question... Because, Mr Wood, you are a player, too. You always have been."

Edith plucked the two queens from the safety of their shielded back rows. Then, placed these queens, exposed, at the centre of the board.

"Two queens stand before us. The king is God, the endgame, but the two queens, they are game-*changers*. And you've sailed in them both."

She circled the board, keeping the two-queen pieces in sight. To arrive at an opposing position.

"I've followed your story with much interest, Oliver Turner, *née Wood*. The late Mr White – you made sure of that – reported your – shall we say, *swift* – entanglements with my husband at the dawn of your own cunning slip aboard *Elizabeth*. White was convinced that you were a competitor in the running of our course. But he, a sodomite too, would have believed anything that might incite your removal from my husband's side."

"And whit o' yer husband, ye bitch," he said, at his edge, "you think he's a sodomite, tae? Conveniently, fur ye. A distraction fae th' fact that he simply cuid nae *staun* you."

Converse to his intention, Edith seemed to thrive through the suggestion. Carrying on with further fuel.

"I have little sympathy for faggots, myself," Edith said, strangling the two queens in her cold-en-ing fingered clasp, "further, Mr White was so pitiful that I could not help but relish the delivery of him to suffering. And he gave me ample justification: he fucked up the convoy halt – said that there was no way of holding the ships there any longer and sent through coordinates that were *off*. But I knew it was sentimentality toward the new boy that had got the better of him. Keith, was it?"

"Kenneth," he spoke up, another puzzle part revealing itself.

"That's it! An equally horrid name, mind you. But useful. A patriot to his Nazi cause, and willing to kill, and to martyr himself to it. Young men like him make for efficient agents in our business and can often be sourced from the client directly – allowing us to wash our hands of them if they don't turn out quite straight. But even these players are not without their risks. Had that halt been successful, it would have been a king-hit, perhaps a tide-changer, but with such missions," pressing the pads of two fingers on the points of the queens, "the windows are brief, too brief in that case. The coordinates not quite right, the evasive movements after that, well, much too effective for our intel to pay off. And little did White know that his failure with the halt was when Kenneth was already dead. Hope you can appreciate the scale of achievement in that halt; in the same year that White made up for messing up the US3 convoy halt with *Normandie*'s fire – a sort of *supplementary* olive branch for our *other* client – we tried again to halt one of the Queens for long enough to get a king-hit, sending the *Curacoa* C-class light cruiser into her path via some other inside men – the *Curacoa* was on escort duty, you see. It went to plan, *Queen Mary* sliced clean through her...but did she stop? No, she carried on, leaving more than 330 of those poor bastards, of her own countrymen, to their fates; not something that's likely to make the newsreels. But back to Kenneth and that *successful* halt that failed to yield...when the lad turned up dead without the downing of a single Allied ship to his sacrifice, I paid attention. Realised that there was *something* to it, beyond the grieving of an aged, infatuated nancy steward. And so I took a greater interest in Robert's love affairs, both with you and then that airman."

"Irvine," he said, though he had intended it to be internally vocalised only. He felt some sympathy swell in him for Edward, though the memory of the *President* calamity kept this feeling from ebbing much above pity.

"Yes, a sweet, misguided boy. He actually propositioned me, so, silver lining there: not all our air lads are, shall we say, exclusively *anally* inclined."

"Sae why murdurr him," he blurted out.

The outburst coming with remembrance for the shock of discovering Irvine, in his bed, exposed, dagger down the throat, and the broken aftermath that was Robert.

She smiled, that of-the-gutter, lifeless grin, "why to hurt *him*, of course," she said. "And to toy with you, his keeper. It was a game. It was...*fun*."

He wanted to lunge at her, to strike, to take her to the floor in a fist-swinging fit. A fit that would not let up until all trace of that smug grin was submerged in her blood.

"And I gave you ample clues to know he was in danger, to formulate a counteroffensive. Your driver," she said, "he was the pilot who took you from my husband during the convoy all-stop. I am surprised you did not recognise him."

And now that she said it, he did.

"An advantageous errand man he has turned out to be. But," she said, interrupting herself and his intentions for harm, circling the games table, like a grey nurse shark on circumnavigation of a cage too-flimsy. "I have not answered your question. Why is it that I don't mind telling you all this? Because, dear fag, you *should* know what you are about to take the fall for."

She was silent for a whole rotation of the board. It let the silt of the reveal settle.

"Let's return to our *game*, shall we? My husband never had the fortitude for it; this game. But, I have a suspicion that strategy is more in your wheelhouse. Imagine, if you will, that this board – just one tile in the larger games table of this war –, imagine that it represents the merchant navy. In this case, in *this* war, instead of pawns as symbols of the merchant vessels. Instead, the vessels of our game, *this* game, are larger, more significant – meaningful enough in the fate of the tides of war to signify that vessels can pose, even, as *this*," holding up one of the queens, "the most powerful piece on the board. Able to move any which direction, outflanking any offensive threat from both sky and sea, while also shrinking the conflict by delivering ground troops to wherever they might be needed most, all the way around the moat of Europe. The king is God, but he needs protection. He is vulnerable. Odds are stacked against him. The queens, however, move with impunity. As *grey ghosts* across the seas. You, Mr Wood, are going to sink one of them."

"Ne'er," he said.

"Not personally, you fool. Not personally, of course. In fact, you won't need to lift a finger. All you need to do is take the credit. *Normandie* actually qualifies you for the job, with your description already atop the pile of suspects for her arson. You see, you've tied it all up neat and nicely for me. Solving two problems with a single channel out of a burning harbour. Blame will be accredited to you, be certain of that. Those turbines are already in rotation. The contract has already been signed for the job, a hefty sum, I don't mind saying, that will safeguard the future of our business. Well, sorry, my business, now."

"Wha fae."

He made note of a glimmer of uncertainly in her composure.

"Why not?" She said to herself, but also aloud. "It couldn't hurt. The Soviets," the story unfolded, "now that the tides are turning to to-morrow for them, they are looking to the *next* war, one where intelligence and strategy and lone-wolf attacks are more effective. And we will be there to help them, and the Western powers, too, of course. We do not discriminate."

"Why me?"

"I'd like to say it isn't personal, but the best deals always are. Despite my husband's affections and, no doubt, advancements of your own sense of your manhood. You are, still, but a silly, easily led to moral disease, boy."

She talked in a cryptic rhythm, like what he imagined was akin to the rhyme of a Sunday paper's crossword creator after filing a week's work, but also with perverse piety. The murders, their manner, he now understood. Her ritualistic, brutal, fucked-up morality. That was the final puzzle piece.

A clock in the room chimed on the hour. 1 pm.

"Ah, showtime!" Edith said. "You see the real reason why I told you all this was as a stalling tactic. The classic, bait 'n' switch. The 'castle move' in chess. Right about now, your father will be en route to *Elizabeth*, the *Queen* that will sink. It is too late for you to save him. Also, about now, your fellow deplorables – my husband among them – are being detained. It is probably too late to save them, too. But I will cut you a deal. Get onto the *Queen* and take the fall, and I will think about sparing them. But you'll have to hurry."

He raced from the room and toward the harbour. As he left, he saw Edith carry one of the queens from the board to lie flat alongside the knight from before.

She was claiming her as already lost.

Edith had timed her final tango to the tee. Even with hightailing it down the hill to the quay, knowing that all he cared about in the world was at stake, together with his own blood, she knew that on arrival at the quay, he would still have a choice to make. A choice, that is, only if he managed to get there with enough time to choose any of them at all. Two tenders prepared to pull away before him, unfastening their ropes from the cleats in unison, no doubt by design, to make his choice harder.

Of course, by instruction, he thought, straining through a stitch in his side, determined to keep his momentum up to the pier.

As he neared the two tenders, he could see his father aboard the one nearest him, *Romsey* – from which the whole adventure had begun. How peculiar it was to see him on board, the only passenger, from what he could make out, on the very vessel from which he had set out at the start. Even from a distance, he could see that his father had aged beyond the number of intermediate years since last at his side.

Perhaps, he thought, *missing me?*

But the sight of his father did not dissuade him. In fact, it was a break in the case, steering him toward the tender of his choice, steadfast in his selection, sure that the only way to avert personal disaster was to choose the *other* tender. Seeing his father had helped him. It was the clue that located the lovers-two, who must be carried in the belly. And out of sight, of the second tender. He felt a sense of one-upmanship as he clamoured on to the *other* one: *Calshot*. It was roughly the same size as *Romsey*, yet its large single-funnel lent it a more stately appearance, more befitting a tender to an ocean liner like *Elizabeth*. Edith was astute, had proved this. But on this particular ultimatum, she had come up all pawns. She, no doubt, had thought she had presented him with a quay quandary that would divide him, perhaps to the point of choosing neither.

The choice is clear, he thought, doubled over, catching his breath. *Always has been, before even meeting these men.*

To show-work: he had chosen to *leave* his father long before his adventure had begun, and through its course, had come upon two men worth dying for. The path ahead was plain. *Romsey* departed as he was still catching his breath and as she did, he locked sights with his father, who on seeing his son – who he had perhaps already reported missing, and now suspected, dead – rose slowing from his seat, forlong in the look he had of him. There was sadness in that look, he thought. By the time he had caught his breath and his own tender was underway, *Romsey* had a head start of several tender-lengths. He made his way into the cabin to commence his search.

It was empty.

And the *Queen* they were headed for had only a skeleton crew, undergoing maintenance ahead of another troop run – the perfect conditions for Edith's arson ambitions. *Calshot*'s cabin interiors, though long since turned to the transfer of six hundred servicemen at a time, had been returned to their pre-war configuration. Fine tables were covered in white linen, and the boards removed from the wall veneers, revealing the rich reds of her wood panelling. One table, at the end of the cabin, had a single meal setting in place, complete with silver cloche. Under the lid, binoculars and a dagger were plated up for him. The dagger. It was the same as before, standard-issue, as had been used as a deadly phallic weapon on Irvine and, lesser to him, the orderly. Also present was a menu card with *Elizabeth*'s letterhead. In place of edible items, embossed in gold lettering were two lines:

Your move.

Q. E.

"You like to watch, don't you?" He said as if Edith were seated opposite the settings that had been laid out for him.

Sliding the dagger under the waistband of his trousers and hanging the binoculars from his neck, he headed back out onto the deck of the tender as an adventurer in hostile waters, to the spit of the icy water swept up on deck. Through the binoculars, he saw Edith at the shore, also watching him through binoculars of her own.

"It's the game," he said, understanding the initials.

Q. E.

He was between two queens, *Elizabeth* and Edith, the most powerful pieces in play. And he needed a strategy. With magnified eyes, he saw. *Recognised.* His tender pilot – Officer Adams, from introductions the night before. They had been right not to trust him, though, clearly, he had done his damage anyway. Then, he turned his sights to *Romsey*, just in time to see his father take a back-of-head strike and disappear from view. And with a cold rush, like the assault of an unsuspected wave across the bow at sea, realised that he would not find Harris or Robert on *Calshot*. Edith had outmanoeuvred him. She was, as she had been since the start, working several moves ahead. Anticipating his decisions. She had known he would choose his men. This was the punishment: she would take them all from him.

Her next move came without waiting, *Romsey* turning off course of *Elizabeth*. At first, he thought they might double back, return to the dock to have his lovers and father taken away so that he would be forced to watch them pass. But this was not the direction that *Romsey* was headed, and the coldness of first *Calshot*-realisation stayed inside him, reckoning that what Edith had in store for them would be much worse. A blazing finale, no doubt.

He needed to start playing, he resolved. Rather than fleeing, as had been his strategy so far.

He needed to strike back.

Tail o' the Bank was now a chessboard, and if he had any chance of winning, he needed to go on the offensive. Edith, as powerful as she was, was not a *piece* in this portion of the game. She *controlled* the pieces, *Romsey* and *Calshot*, and would use them to come after *Queen Elizabeth*, now wide open for attack...but she was not *on* the water herself.

Come on, Olli, he thought, feeling the limit of the time he had in which to decide slip away. *You need a piece in the game.*

He resolved to go after Adams. Bracing the weather – now turned grim –, he scaled his way up to the wheelhouse to overpower him. And he did, with the bud of his knife.

Did I hit him too hard? He wondered, as he pulled the limp body off the wheel and laid it onto the deck, the point of impact reddened and bleeding.

He pushed the thought away, locked himself in the wheelhouse and charted a course in pursuit of *Romsey*. Too abruptly at first. Having learnt all he had by observing Robert, this craft was more responsive to handling. He steadied her and aligned into *Romsey*'s wake, upping his speed. The chase was on. As long and above-waterline towering as she was, the *Queen* blocked much of the Clyde service lines from view, including other traffic. No sooner had *Romsey* cleared the back of her was she struck by a liner. The colossal cracking of iron clammer of the collision skipped across the choppy Clyde like a foghorn's final warning.

"*Fuck*!"

He pushed his tender to its limit in an attempt to reach her. The liner, *Lairdsburn*, had given her all-stop order – he had experienced it frequently enough to recognise it. But *Romsey* was already on her side and taking on water. She would be under before the liner had any time to react. *Calshot* reached her within minutes. By when her bow was already only his height from the water's churning surface. *Lairdsburn* had come to a stop downriver, past the *Queen*, and was lowering a lifeboat. He knew this would come too late to make a difference. *Romsey*, too, carried lifeboats – two. One had been lowered and was now gone, en route to the liner she had been struck by. His magnified view told him that none of the men on board this lifeline were *his*. These Edith pawns would, unequivocally, inform any rescuers that there were none else on the vessel.

And so he found himself back on *Romsey* as she started to slip below the Scotch-stretch waves. The second lifeboat was useless to him; its bottom buckled. Though there had been no sign of men other than Adams when he had stormed the bridge, now he could make out shapes about the piloting deck. However, *Calshot* stayed without engines, drifting toward the *Queen*, clearly having no intention of offering assistance. *Romsey* groaned as the water rushed in, weighting her down like stones in the nightgown of a midnight swimmer. She was growing tired and would not keep her head above water for much longer. Inside the cabin was his father, unconscious and bound with rope. His decision was made to sting surer with the sight of him up close; he reached for the dagger to free him, only to stop himself.

Find them *first.*

His search took him into her hull, now almost flooded. And there he *found* them. Also bound with rope. Also– he checked for breath– *breathing.* He tried to revive them, but it was no use. And the situation down below was becoming critical. He managed to get them both up into the cabin alongside his father, just as the surface of the water had swallowed the whole of the lower compartment in which he had found them. The *Lairdsburn* lifeboats were still too long away to lend assistance; in fact, it was now stalled by

Romsey's craft, no doubt informing them that there were no other souls on board. He freed his lovers and then father with the dagger and propped them against the cabin wall. He had spent enough time in seamen's messes to know that he had only seconds now, that the final moments – once the heavy hull was brimmed and only the superstructure remained – of the sinking would be rapid. In the cabin were two life-preservers, just two. The rest had, from what he could see, been stripped out. He had been *given* binoculars and a dagger by his opponent but had not thought to take at least one lifejacket from *Calshot* and now cursed himself for it. Even in the adrenaline-fuelled final seconds, as water flooded into the cabin, he knew this failure to calculate ahead based on *Calshot*'s resources would haunt him if he managed to survive the game. He fastened the two jackets to his *choices* – it seemed less straightforward now, as the icy Clyde rose to just below his father's chin.

"I'm sorry, dad." He said, weeping already for him. "Forgive ye," with a kiss on the cheek.

And he left him, getting Robert and Harris out and away from the tender just as she slipped below the surface of the Clyde to take his father with her.

—

Breath burned;
Breast of life jacket under each arm;
Battling, paddling for shore, on his back, willing himself to not slip below;
To ensure the sleeping men he loved stayed the right way above the waves all the way.

Soon after *Romsey* took her dive, smoke started rising from the deck of *Queen Elizabeth*. *His Queen*, as she was once known, but who now felt removed from him, at water level with her.

Her story, for him, was now over. He would not attempt to save her; all effort was on getting to the sand and warming the men between his hands – or by his body, or whatever he could fashion to keep them from slipping away as well. There was faint thanks for the cover of her burning, which allowed him to slip ashore. Even if she sank, this no longer mattered, as long as his two Kings were protected. They were, after all, the aim of his game.

There would be no memory of the final length, or even the first grasp of silty shore.

Panic got him there, in a fog of primal need to save them.

Memory recommenced with him laid on the beach, Robert and Harris clutched underarms like the prizest chests off a dashed armada. They collapsed into him, their frantic breath the only warmth on offer.

He stripped them.

With the urgency of a battlefield surgeon.

Down to their navy- and army-regulation long johns, bunched and made translucent with wet. These would need to go, too. He rolled them off hairy limbs like pretzel dough, near-ready for a bend. He rolled off their under-cotton intimates until their bodies were bare; their meat river-bloated and – he touched to make sure – their warmest parts, in no danger of damage, and then, he pulled them into him again. Rolled them onto him like the fold-in knots of well-kneaded dough, bringing the coarse-sanded bodies of them up and over, onto him.

Harris was limb-ended from below the knee. Stubbed, but still...as with all of him, perfect. Even in amputation, his lines were fine. And that warm meat, moist and musky with the exertion of the to-shore swim. On john-removal, he had brushed, but now he grasped by the root. A meat bunch so mighty that his fingertips fell far from meeting. But enough grip to pull Harris up and over-onto him more. Had he grabbed hold of Harris's flanking, hairy flesh appendages instead, the tip distance would have been much and much. Such was the volume of Harris.

But this anchor point was supremely more supple. Brash, but not really used, other than on him and, recently, Robert too. A top shaft, the strength, the woven sea-rope, gave the graft to pull, but what flopped like a sack over a shoulder, on the webbed space of his hand – the source of the musk – was the supple, scented section of him: all that carried his essence.

Both were precious and engorged, the fullest part of him, impressive, above par on any seen-perfect man. But more so with war-shortened limbs. Harris groaned as he was towed by groan up and into a hypothermia starving embrace. That always-about-sex qualm of his.

Robert was next. First love and the slender-er. Also, the softer – not body-soft, his body was lean and taut, but supple, too. Harris had lost his legs below the knee and was wounded mentally. But Robert's wound had been with him longer, stretching back to the dominance of a disapproving father and the degrading demeanour of a wretched wife. Robert was the demure one, and to scoop him up, he swept below, brushed by his manhood and commandeered his meant-for-entry point.

My sea-squirt, my salty cunjevoi.

Sometimes skin-tough with a bait-goo interior. Not Robert, his sucky point; it was as squashy pink out as it felt to probe in. And that's where he gripped and tugged on up and to him. His sucky point could take it, welcomed the masculine – albeit fingered – pull-in.

Left hold on the root of Harris, right – the less dominant, the bent logic that was his – knuckle deep in the meaty rump-folds of Robert, pulling them both to him. Loved equally, but imbalanced, too, in the ways that Harris was more, but Robert *turned* more between them. All for that moment, of shivering, breath-visible, sand-coarse into and over male active and passive appendages.

It was more to take in. Intimacy. Further than the broad wood-floored fuck of the sloped tenements to the Clyde.

"We need to get her," Robert breathed through trembling, sand-glittered lips. "Avenge your father."

Was it part of Edith's setpiece – that his Kings, two of them, also knew of her plan prior to mate-move?

The gravelly words grated deeper than his hearing. He hadn't given his father thought since hitting the water with his two men. Not since then, and his desperate attempt at a beaching.

"He's right, Olli," Harris came in his opposite hearing orifice. "We need to get the *bitch*."

And so there they were; left-adrift sailors in propellor's churn that lapped to their waists. White pro-pulsed foam, on the beach – a generous descriptor for the silt of the Clydebank – where the sight of *Elizabeth* fleeing captivated him.

Heaviest in the water he'd seen her, with a troop-laden cargo, leaving him and his, ablaze and under attack; taking her chances with a desperate adventure into the high seas like before, a daring dash into a war that, he felt, may not be quite over.

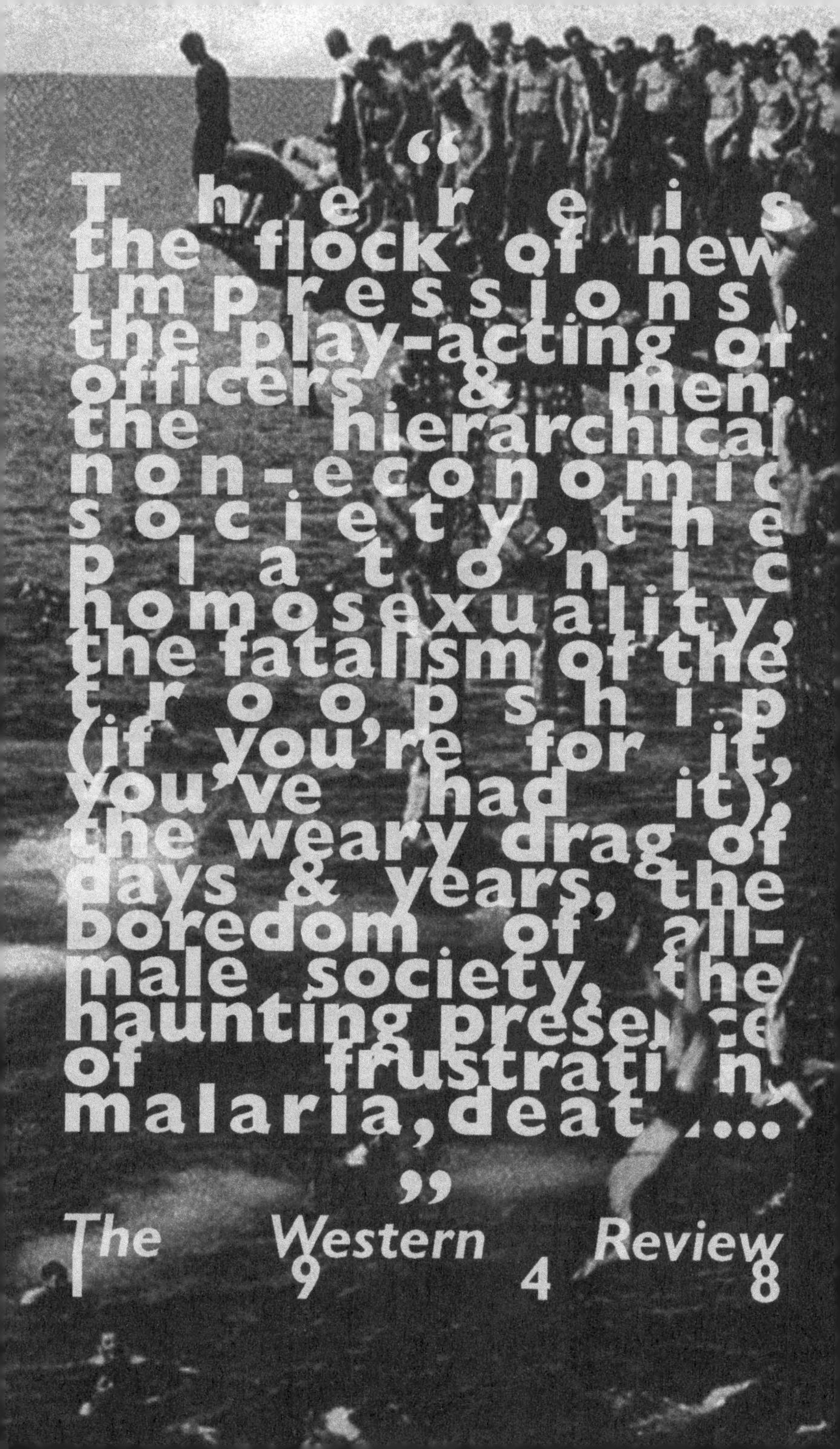

"There is the flock of new impressions, the play-acting of officers & men, the hierarchical non-economic society, the platonic homosexuality, the fatalism of the troopship (if you're for it, you've had it), the weary drag of days & years, the boredom of all-male society, the haunting presence of frustration, malaria, death..."

The Western Review 1948

LOO
S E

Joseph
Brennan

LIPS